CROSSFIRE

NOVELS BY DAVID HAGBERG

Twister
The Capsule
Last Come the Children
Heartland
Heroes
Without Honor
Countdown
Crossfire

WRITING AS SEAN FLANNERY

The Kremlin Conspiracy
Eagles Fly
The Trinity Factor
The Hollow Men
Broken Idols
False Prophets
Gulag
The Zebra Network
Crossed Swords
Counterstrike

CROSSFIRE

DAVID HAGBERG

A Tom Doherty Associates Book
New York

CROSSFIRE

Copyright © 1991 by David Hagberg

A Tor Book
Published by Tom Doherty Associates, Inc.
49 West 24th Street
New York, N.Y. 10010

Library of Congress Cataloging-in-Publication Data

Hagberg, David.
    Crossfire / David Hagberg.
        p.   cm.
    "A Tom Doherty Associates book."
    ISBN 0-312-85162-6
    I. Title.
PS3558.A3327C76   1991
813'.54—dc20

90-27405
CIP

First edition: June 1991

Printed in the United States of America

0 9 8 7 6 5 4 3 2 1

This book is for my mother, Katherine Sampson, who has always sung my praises, and for Laurie, who has always been my praise.

——— PROLOGUE ———

MARCH 6, 1945
GOLFO SAN MATÍAS, ARGENTINA

THE SUBMARINE WAS NEARLY SILENT and mostly in darkness because her batteries were low. A short, wiry man, dressed in black leather trousers and a heavy white turtleneck sweater, stepped through an oval hatchway into an after storage compartment between the diesels and rear torpedo room. He stopped and held his breath to listen. He was certain he had heard something. Metal against metal, a scraping noise somewhere below. Between the deck and the tanks.

For several long seconds he remained where he was, listening, but the sounds did not come again. His imagination? They were all tired, strung out, nervous. It was the end now, and everyone on the crew understood what that meant. It was finally getting to them.

Captain Ernst Reiker continued through the compartment, his soft-soled boots making no sound on the grillwork of the deck. The torpedo room hatch was partially closed. He pushed it open on its well-oiled hinges and looked inside. The compartment was barely lit by a single dim red bulb over one of the torpedo tubes. The air stank of unwashed bodies and machine oil, laced with the alcohol used as propellant for the torpedoes.

The four men housed back there were all asleep in their hammocks, suspended over the stored torpedoes. One of them snored softly. They were good men—boys, actually. Several of them, in his shorthanded crew of thirty-nine men and officers, had hardly begun to shave. It was a shame, because none of them would see the fatherland again. The war was over. Germany had lost. Once they ditched the boat and went ashore, they would have to remain on Argentine soil. There wouldn't be many other places in the world where, as Nazis, they would be accepted.

More's the pity, he thought; in the short time they'd been together as a crew, he'd come to admire them for their naïve trust in him and for their tenacity under difficult conditions.

He took one last look, then turned and retraced his steps through the engineering spaces. It was very late, time to get some sleep himself now that his daily inspection tour was completed. Yet he doubted that he would be able to shut down his brain as easily as had his teenaged crewmen.

Reiker, at forty-four, was old for the German submarine service. Most of his peers had either died in the war or had been promoted to command fleets or battle groups from desks in Berlin or Bremerhaven. But he'd been turned down for such promotions because of something in his past, in his background. It was something he'd always denied, but it was no use. He'd gone as far as he could possibly go. Much farther than he should have.

All along he had known, of course, that there would be no honor for him at the end, though, ironically, his last orders to bring the submarine across a hostile sea had been loaded with words such as devotion to the fatherland, honor, heroism. But this time there would be no medals to be had. No marching bands. No cheering crowds at the docks. And he'd known it.

But he was a German officer, bound by his oath to the Führer to continue even though the war was over. There were no more battles on the North Atlantic to be fought, nor was there anywhere for him to take his boat and crew. No home port.

So many buts, he thought as he stepped through the hatch into the red-lit control room. So many ifs. So many questions . . . with no answers.

"Captain on the conn," his second officer, Lieutenant (jg) Lötti Zigler announced. The sonarman, helmsman, and diving officer all came briefly to attention.

"At ease," Reiker said tiredly. "Anything yet?"

"No, sir," Zigler said.

"Where's Dieter?"

"At the periscope."

Reiker crossed to the ladder and peered up into the attack center. His first officer, Lieutenant Dieter Schey, his cap on backward, was hunched over the handles of the periscope.

"See anything, Dieter?" Reiker called. He was too tired to climb up and look for himself.

Schey, who was only a few years younger than Reiker but looked about twenty-five, turned away from the eyepiece and shook his head. The hair on his head was blond, but his beard had come out medium brown. "Nothing. No lights, no movement . . . in the bay or ashore. We might as well be parked at a desert island."

Reiker looked over at the nav station where a stool had been set up for their one passenger, RSHA Major Walther Roebling, who had come aboard with their cargo. He had brought with him a letter signed by the high command, giving him and the Reichssicherheitshauptamt—the Reich Central Security Office —complete authority over the submarine and her crew. The secret service officer had spent nearly all of his waking hours perched on the stool, watching the control room crew at work, and tracking their position across the North Atlantic and then south across the equator. He wasn't in his customary position now.

"Where is he?" Reiker asked Zigler.

"He hasn't been here all night, Captain. Not since dinner."

"Ernst, let's put up the snorkel and run the diesels," Schey called from above. "No one will hear us, and we need the electrical power."

"Just a moment," Reiker said. Something was nagging at him. Something was wrong. He could feel it. Something about the major.

"Call his quarters," Reiker told his second officer.

Zigler picked up the interphone and punched the proper number. After a half minute he looked around and shook his head. "He doesn't answer. Shall I go check?"

Reiker reached up and hit the comms button. "Major Roebling to the control center. Major Roebling to the conn, please."

He turned again to Zigler. "If he isn't here within sixty seconds, I want the boat searched for him."

"Aye, aye, sir."

Reiker climbed up into the cramped attack center and took Schey's place at the periscope. At first he couldn't make out much of anything. But gradually he began to distinguish between the dark shoreline and the even darker water. There was no moon tonight, and the sky was partially covered with clouds. He was able to see an occasional white line of surf breaking on the narrow, rocky beach, but nothing else. His first officer was correct. There were no lights, no signs of any human activity whatsoever, toward land or out to sea.

"What's with our little spy?" Schey asked softly at Reiker's elbow.

"This is our supposed rendezvous point, Dieter," Reiker said, making a second 360-degree sweep. "For twenty-four hours we have remained at periscope depth, waiting for someone to show up. Still nothing."

"Maybe they were delayed."

Reiker looked away from the eyepiece.

"No one thought it would end so soon," Schey said. He shrugged. "So badly, for us, that is."

"Why isn't he up here, Dieter? Why hasn't he ordered a party ashore to find out what has happened?"

"His orders . . ."

"His real plan, perhaps," Reiker murmured. Most of the mysterious cargo they'd taken on at Bremen was stored beneath the deck plates in the after storage compartments where he thought he'd heard the noise.

"You think the little bastard is up to something?" Schey asked.

"I think I would like to ask him that. Tonight."

Schey nodded grimly. "In such a fashion that he will not lie to us."

"Yes."

"What is all the commotion?" Major Roebling called irritably from below.

Reiker looked down into the control room. "Come up here, Major. I think you'll want to take a look at this."

Roebling, who was a slightly built man with the pasty complexion of one who'd spent too much time underground in bunkers, narrowed his eyes. "What is it, Captain?"

"I think it may be our contact at last."

"Impossible . . ." Roebling said quickly, then cut himself off.

"Nevertheless, you should come have a look for yourself, Major."

Roebling started up the ladder and Reiker and Schey exchanged glances. Schey lifted his sweater slightly, exposing the butt of his Luger.

"Now, what is this you are seeing?" Roebling barked angrily. "I am in no mood for your silly little games tonight."

Reiker nodded toward the periscope. "See for yourself."

Roebling studied the captain's eyes for a moment, then bent over the periscope and looked through the eyepiece. Schey took out his pistol.

"I don't see a thing," Roebling snapped, then he looked up into the barrel of Schey's pistol. His eyes widened. "Are you mad, Schey? Put down your pistol. Now. Immediately."

"First we would like to have a little talk, Major," Reiker said.

"You're a dead man," Roebling growled.

"But you are not the one holding the pistol at this moment," Reiker said. "Zigler," he called below.

"Aye, aye, sir."

"From which direction did Major Roebling come just now?"

"Aft."

"Your quarters are forward," Reiker noted.

"I was in the crew's galley. We were out of coffee forward," Roebling said.

"Zigler," Reiker called again.

"Aye, aye, sir."

"Send someone forward to check out the major's compartment. Search it, and let me know what you find."

Roebling was glaring at Reiker, the raw energy of his hate strong enough to be a nearly palpable force in the cramped quarters.

"Yes, sir."

"And then send a party to the after diesel storage compartments. Break into the cargo we took on at Bremen."

Roebling tried to push forward, but Schey jammed the barrel of the gun into the major's face, and he stopped.

"Sir?" Zigler called up, evidently confused.

"Break into the cargo. Open some of the boxes. I want to know what it is. Now. On the double!"

"Do you understand what you are doing?" Roebling asked through clenched teeth.

"The war is over, Major," Reiker said. "Or very nearly so. We all know this. Which means there is nowhere for me to go, nowhere for me to take my crew. I would like to know if there is anything in the cargo you brought aboard that would be useful for us."

"It is for the Reich. You have your orders."

"There is no longer any Reich. So whatever you brought aboard at Bremen is now for you. I would like to know what it is. I would also like to know what you were doing back there a little while ago. It was you I heard below decks."

"You son of a bitch, you have your orders—"

Schey roughly shoved the major up against the escape trunk hatch, and jammed the pistol barrel so hard into his forehead that the front sight broke skin and a thin trickle of blood ran down between the man's eyes.

"It is my captain you are talking to, Major. With respect now, please, or I will splatter your brains all over the bulkhead behind you." Schey was grinning. He'd been waiting for such a moment ever since they'd left Bremen.

For the first time Roebling appeared to doubt his own safety. He looked from Schey and Reiker to the open hatch leading down to the control room.

"What has happened to your rendezvous?" Reiker asked.

"I don't know. He was delayed. Maybe he is dead. I don't know."

"What are your orders in such an event?"

"I am to hold the boat here for a full forty-eight hours."

"And then?"

Roebling said nothing.

"We're waiting," Schey warned.

"Captain," Zigler called from below.

Reiker looked down into the control room. Zigler was holding a small rucksack open.

"He has an Argentine passport under a different name," Zigler said. He sounded excited. "There is money here, American dollars, I think, and some civilian clothes. A notebook."

"Going someplace?" Schey asked casually.

Roebling's eyes had grown wide, and he was swallowing repeatedly, his Adam's apple bobbing.

"Captain, his bag was stuffed in a message buoy."

"Waterproof," Reiker said. "You were planning on abandoning the boat. Here? Tonight?"

Roebling held his silence.

"Answer the captain," Schey demanded.

Roebling seemed almost to be holding his breath now, as if he were waiting for something. Reiker tried to see into the man's eyes, tried to probe what was in his brain. Something was happening, or was about to. He had been getting ready to abandon ship. And he had been in the cargo spaces. . . .

Reiker's gut suddenly tightened. He hit the comms button and screamed into the microphone. "Get out of the cargo spaces! Now! This is the captain! Get out of there!"

Three explosions, one after the other, rocked the boat, sending Reiker sprawling off balance and nearly through the open hatch.

Schey was stunned for just a moment, but it was enough for Roebling to snatch the pistol out of his hand and shove him back.

Sirens were sounding all over the boat.

"Emergency stations, emergency stations!" Reiker was shouting into the comms.

"Have Zigler toss my bag up here," Roebling ordered. "Now!"

"Flooding aft of the main battery compartments," a crewman radioed desperately. "We can't handle it back here!"

"Seal the boat!" Reiker shouted. "Blow all tanks and prepare for emergency surface procedures!"

"My bag!" Roebling demanded, keeping the pistol trained on Schey.

Zigler tossed it through the hatch, and Roebling snatched it. He opened the escape trunk hatch, grinned as he stepped inside, and then slammed it shut, dogging it down. Immediately the hiss of water filling the trunk became audible.

"Captain, all after tanks have lost integrity. The explosions must have damaged them," Zigler shouted.

There was pandemonium below in the control room. Everyone knew that the boat was going to the bottom, that there was no saving her. But at least the crew forward of the battery compartments would be safe in watertight spaces. Some of them would have access to escape trunks once they reached the bottom, some two hundred fifty feet below the surface.

Schey stepped across to the escape trunk hatch and dogged it down so that Roebling would not be able to get back into the submarine. Then he reached up and shut off the master valves, cutting off the escape trunk's water supply. With the trunk only half filled, the major would be stuck inside until they let him out, or until he suffocated for lack of oxygen.

Someone was screaming something on the ship's comms, and water was pouring into the control room as Reiker and Schey scrambled down from the attack center. Already the boat was listing nearly twenty degrees to starboard, and she was definitely down at the stern.

"Shut that hatch!" Reiker screamed.

Zigler, shaking his head in fear and disbelief, was bracing himself against the list. "We can't!" he cried. "All the hatches have been sabotaged! We're going down for sure!"

Reiker and Schey immediately slogged their way to the after hatch and put their shoulders to it, but it wouldn't budge. The hinges were frozen.

The water in the lower half of the control room was already chest deep, and as the boat continued to roll to starboard, sparks flew from a control panel and the lights suddenly went out, plunging them into darkness.

All through the forward compartments of the boat Reiker could hear his men screaming, crying out in blind panic. But it was over. In a few short moments they would be dead.

He looked up toward where the attack center hatch would be, though he could not see it in the total darkness, and felt at least a small measure of satisfaction. Roebling would die too, the precious Reich's cargo, the cargo that was to have saved the war effort, the cargo he'd been honor bound by his oath to deliver to this shore, going down with him.

The water was cold as it came up over Reiker's head, and his main regret was that he would never see his wife and child again.

BOOK ONE

1

PARIS

THE CROWDS, both pedestrian and vehicular, were thick at the Concorde end of the Champs-Élysées, slowed by the weather that had turned particularly nasty on this late afternoon. The temperature hovered around the freezing point, and a gusty wind drove frigid rain that sometimes turned to spits of snow in long plumes and swirls down the broad avenue. It was rush hour, and it seemed as if the entire city was tangled in one, large, snarled mess.

Nevertheless, a few Parisians were strolling hand in hand through the Tuilêries gardens, mindless of the weather, though none of the restaurants or vendors had their tables out.

The tall, well-dressed man with the briefcase left the gardens, crossed the street, and made his way up the broad walk to an old, ornately designed four-story building, the roof of which bristled not only with chimneys, but also with aerials and a variety of satellite communications dishes. A brass plaque announced: EMBASSY OF THE UNITED STATES OF AMERICA.

"Good afternoon," the man said to the Marine guards just inside the main hall. He handed his briefcase to one of them and his American passport to the other. "I'd like to see a consular officer."

"Mr. McGarvey?" the one Marine, whose name tag identified him as Selkirk, said, studying the passport.

"Yes, that's right. Kirk McGarvey. I live here in Paris," the man said, smiling pleasantly. He was well built and almost handsome in a rugged, outdoorsy way. His eyes were a startling green, and were wide and very direct. His accent sounded definitely East Coast, possibly Boston.

"You know that your passport has expired, sir?" Selkirk jotted down the number.

The tall man nodded. "That's why I'm here. Silly of me, actually, that I didn't notice. I've been to Brussels on business for the past few days, and the border crossing people outside Valenciennes pointed it out. Thought I'd better come in and get it renewed or something."

The other Marine, Danberg, had put the briefcase through the scanner, then handed it back. "You can see someone who'll fix you up just down the corridor to the right, sir," he said. He glanced up at the clock above the door. "But you'd better hurry. It's nearly six, and most of them are probably gone or on their way out by now."

"I see," the imposter said, smiling. "But I suppose you boys will be here all night."

Danberg shook his head. "No, sir. We get off in a couple of minutes ourselves."

"Well, you'd better bundle up good. It's not very nice out there now."

"Yes, sir."

The man turned and walked across the big hall, his shoes making no sound on the marble floor. No one was around. The building seemed deserted. Halfway down the long corridor on the right, he passed a flight of stairs, exactly where he knew it would be from the blueprints he'd studied. At the end of the corridor, he knocked once at the door with a frosted glass window, and went in.

A counter ran the width of the room. Behind it was a large office with a half dozen desks, all but one of which were empty. An attractive woman in a red knit dress, a white scarf around her neck, her plastic security badge clipped beneath it, was speaking on the telephone. She looked up, did a double take, and then put a hand over the mouthpiece.

"Yes, sir, may I help you with something?" she asked. There was no one else in the office. Her red coat and her purse were lying on a chair in front of her desk.

"It's my passport," the imposter said carefully. Something was wrong here, but it was a calculated risk he'd had to take. "It's going to have to be renewed."

"Is it urgent?"

"Not yet," the man said. "I could come back tomorrow if it would be better."

"It would."

"First thing?"

"Nineish."

"Very good," the man said. "See you then." He turned and left the office. No one was around to see him hurry to the stairs and go up. He pulled off his gloves and overcoat, and before he reached the first-floor landing, he had clipped a security badge just like the woman's in the consular office to the lapel of his brown jacket. The badge identified him as a special assistant to the ambassador.

The title and his name, of course, were not real. And had the woman known who he actually was, she would have run for her life.

Inside the consular office, Carley Webb put down the telephone, and gathered her coat and purse. Before she went out she scrawled a note about the man with the passport problem and left it on Cedric Evans's desk.

There had been something oddly familiar about the man's face that had startled her for just a moment. So much so that she'd forgotten to get his name, but he'd be returning in the morning, so it didn't matter. In any event, it wasn't her job. Her work in the consular section was merely a cover for her assignment with the Central Intelligence Agency's Paris station, a position she had fought hard to get, and one she relished.

There were many women on the staff, but no others were full-fledged case officers. Most of them worked as secretaries, or cipher clerks, or in a few instances as translators. The Paris station was the Company's largest operation in Europe, even bigger than Bonn, because this was the central clearinghouse for all information funneling back to Langley. She was resented by some of the women because of what she did, and partly because of her looks. At thirty-three she had lost her innocent little-girlishness and had developed into a sophisticated, even beautiful woman. In the right light she could have been mistaken for a young Audrey Hepburn, with her long delicate neck, small angular face, wide dark eyes, and slender frame.

Just now she was finishing the developmental stages of new network that had been code-named SPARKLE. Contact had been made and was firmly established with two high-ranking officers in the Soviet embassy, one of them the third assistant to the KGB's Paris *rezident*, and the other the second assistant to the Soviet's military attaché. Both of them were men, both of them had a crush on her, which of course she encouraged, but neither of them knew about the other. Each man thought he was working alone with her. The value of this particular network, aside from the obvious benefits of having such assets in the Soviet embassy, was that by working them both, she had a continual check on the veracity of the information they were providing her.

"The day will come, Carley, when they will want to make love to you," Thomas Lord, chief of station, had warned her.

It hadn't happened yet, but with Vladimir Rudichev, the KGB officer, the moment was fast approaching.

"I'll deal with it when the time comes," she'd told Lord.

"Perhaps we should begin weaning you out. Stewart can gradually begin to take over."

"Not yet, Tom. Please. Just give me a little longer."

Lord had been like a brother, or even a father, to her from the moment she'd been transferred from Langley. He smiled. "Just be careful, kid. Will you at least do that much for me?"

"Sure," she'd promised. It was pride, of course. She'd come this far on her own; she didn't want to drop out just as the gold seam of information was beginning to produce results.

Besides, she told herself, pulling on her coat as she headed down the corridor, Rudichev and Guryanov were not her only problem. She was going to have to make another decision, and in some respects an even larger one, very soon. Maybe even tonight.

Nearly everyone had left early that afternoon because of the weather, though she supposed Lord would still be upstairs in his office. The afternoon summaries went out via encrypted burst transmission at seven, and he almost always stuck around to make last-minute additions or deletions. Fine tuning, he called it.

She crossed the main hall and turned in her security badge to the Marines.

"Good night, Miss Webb," they said.

" 'Night," she replied, starting for the door, but then she changed her mind and came back. "There was a tall, good-looking man in to see me about renewing his passport a few minutes ago. Did you get his name?" Because of terrorist attacks, U.S. embassies worldwide logged in visitors, carefully scrutinizing their parcels and papers.

"We just came on duty ourselves, ma'am," one of the Marines said. "Must have missed him."

The other Marine had turned the registration book around so that he could read the last entries. "Here he is, last one in. Name is Kirk McGarvey."

"Kirk, here?" she said. "I didn't see him."

The young man shrugged. "That's what it says, Miss Webb. Logged in for the Consular Section at 1758 hours, briefcase checked."

"That was only a few minutes ago," Carley said, her mind going to a dozen different possibilities but rejecting them all. "Who else came in, just before McGarvey?"

"Henri Perigord, also for the Consular Section. But that was much earlier, ma'am, 1527 hours."

Carley remembered him. "No one else in between?"

"No, ma'am. Is something wrong?"

"I don't know," Carley said. "But the man who logged in at six wasn't the Kirk McGarvey I know."

"Someone impersonating him?"

"Possibly," she said, glancing toward the elevators. "He said he'd be back in the morning. I'll check it out myself."

"Anything else we can do in the meantime?"

Carley had glanced at the registration book. Beside Mc-Garvey's name, the Marine had written his passport number. It was something. She looked up. "If he returns tonight, give me a call. I'll be on my beeper."

"Will do," the Marine said, and Carley turned and left the embassy. It was possible that the Marine who had logged the man in had made a mistake about his name. But she couldn't see how.

It nagged at her as she hurried, head bent low against the wind, to catch a cab on the avenue Gabriel. But the man was gone. There was nothing to be done about it until morning.

The embassy's second-floor corridor was empty, but the imposter could hear the high-pitched whining sounds of a computer printer coming from somewhere above. He held up for a second or two just within the landing.

Most of the diplomats and other embassy personnel would be gone already. But the CIA's communications center on the third floor would be fully manned, and some of the Agency's high-ranking officers would probably still be there, getting their seven o'clock summaries ready for transmission to the States.

It was a bit of insider information that not many people knew; not secret, just not publicly known.

"What we need, Arkasha, is a diversion," the general had told him at their last meeting in Tripoli. "You are to be my chosen one for this work. I'm putting your skills to use again. Just like the old days. Only this time no one will know that it is you. It's rich—they all believe you to be dead."

General Didenko was a tall bear of a Russian, with thick black hair, Brezhnev-like eyebrows, a broad Siberian forehead, and a swarthy complexion. He continued, "Paris, I should think, would be a good start. Then Rome, perhaps Bonn. Lisbon, then Brussels." The general smiled, but not in friendship. "But I will leave the exact details up to you. As and when you need information, your contact will be standing by in each city. Paris to begin with."

They were walking along a beach east of the city, Didenko's bodyguards trailing out of earshot behind them. The breeze off the Mediterranean was cool but not unpleasant.

"Are you up to this assignment?" the general asked. There

was a rumor that his position in Moscow was in serious trouble. If it was, however, the trouble was not reflected in his face or in his manner, which was confident.

"A diversion for what?" the man who was posing as McGarvey asked, his voice soft, even gentle.

"Are you capable of this?" the general demanded, ignoring the question for the moment.

The imposter nodded. "Yes, I am capable, but first you will tell me what your real plans are, Comrade General. You are no Baranov."

"No," Didenko said. "Nor are you his tool any longer. Now you belong to me." He smiled again and took the man's arm. "But come, Arkasha, and I will tell you everything you wish to know. Simply everything. Then you will see why I have picked you."

The imposter stepped out of the stairwell, hurried across the corridor, and let himself into one of the offices, closing and locking the door behind him.

CIA operations were, for the most part, conducted one floor above, where security, both electronic and physical, was tight. There would be Agency people in the corridor at the stairwell doors and elevator. Armed. In the early planning stages it had been a bothersome detail. It would do him no good to simply shoot his way onto the floor. Even if he successfully penetrated the station, he'd probably not get out of the building alive, and certainly not without being spotted and followed.

Laying his coat and gloves on the desk in the tiny office, he took off his suit jacket and tie, putting them aside as well. Next he took his pistol, a Walther PPK, out of his shoulder holster, screwed the silencer tube on the end of the barrel, set it on the desk, and then took off the holster and began unbuttoning his shirt.

The communications center was directly above this office. At this moment there would be at least a dozen technicians and operators up there, perhaps more, as well as a few million dollars' worth of sensitive communications and cryptographic equipment.

On the far side of the building, but still one floor above, were the secure briefing rooms and the offices of Chief of Station Thomas Lord and Assistant Chief of Station Bob Graves. Both were highly capable men, absolutely vital to the Paris operation.

Without them, CIA operations would suffer in all of Europe for a long time to come.

Someone was at the door, trying the knob. The imposter snatched his pistol and switched the safety off as he stepped into the deep shadows in the corner. The only light in the room came from outside.

Moments later a key grated in the lock, and the door opened. An old man, stoop-shouldered with a heavy paunch and white hair, came in and flipped on the light. He was alone.

For a moment the old man didn't understand what he was seeing: the clothing on the desk, the man in the corner. But then he started to step back, his left hand coming up as if to ward off a blow, and the Russian shot him in the face, the bullet destroying his left eye, flinging him backward, half out into the corridor.

No one was supposed to come down here. The man had had no business being on the second floor at this hour.

The imposter rushed to the doorway and looked out into the corridor. No one was there. Apparently no one had heard a thing. No alarms were sounding.

Hurriedly he dragged the man's body back into the office. Using his handkerchief, he wiped up the blood and cranial fluid that had leaked from the wound in case someone else came this way in the next minute or two.

He closed and relocked the door, flipped off the light, and took a deep breath to ease the tension in his chest.

It had been a stupid mistake, one that might well cost him the mission. Now someone would come looking for the man. It was time to hurry.

The Russian smiled grimly to himself as he took off his shirt and peeled the tape away from the eleven pounds of C4 plastique around his chest and flanks.

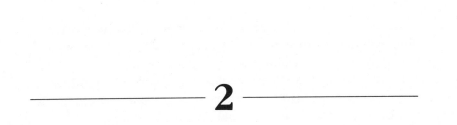

2

THE BAR AT THE Hotel Inter-Continental, near the Place de la Concorde, was full, but it was still early, so there weren't many tables occupied in the adjacent grillroom. Three men sat at one table in the corner, sharing a bottle of wine as they waited for their dinner. The waiter hovered at a respectful distance.

Horst Höehner, at sixty-eight, was by far the oldest of the three men. He had flown up from Vienna on the weekend and had spent the past two days exchanging information about Mueller Leitner, a Nazi concentration camp guard believed by Simon Wiesenthal's people to be living in retirement in Paris.

Höehner was completely hairless over his entire body. This condition had to do with chemical experiments he had been subjected to from 1941 until 1943 at Dachau. Since he had no hair in his nostrils, he always had cotton stuffed in his nose to filter out dust. And since he had no eyelashes, he was constantly blinking his eyes to keep them clean. His lack of eyebrows and his obvious wig lent him a bizarre appearance.

But his mind was sharp, and his experience at the hands of the Nazis had not made him bitter as it had so many others. He had become instead an extremely determined man.

"We must move with care this time, Horst," his French host, Maurice Gavalet, cautioned. It had been the same since yesterday.

"It does not matter to me that Leitner—or Mann, as he has called himself since the war—may have become important to France. His good deeds cannot erase the crimes against humanity he committed at Auschwitz and elsewhere. Crimes, I think I have proved to your satisfaction, that were in some cases committed against Frenchmen. And they were not necessarily Jews. Some of them were members of the Resistance."

Gavalet was with the Deuxieme Bureau, and had been handed the assignment of dealing with the Wiesenthal group whenever the Nazi hunters' efforts brought them onto French soil. He'd worked with Höehner on several other occasions, some of which had not turned out so well for the French government. But he respected the Austrian not only for his tenacity, but for his obvious high intelligence and old-world charm.

"It's not that, my old friend. It is, as I have said from the beginning, a matter of firm identification."

"Mann is Leitner," Höehner declared.

"I'm not so sure," Gavalet replied gently.

The third man at the table, younger than the other two, was Carleton Reid, an American from the embassy, whose official title was chief of security. But Gavalet and Höehner both understood that in reality he worked for the Central Intelligence Agency. He had been asked to help because the man Höehner believed to be Leitner had worked in the United States from 1946 until sometime in the early sixties, when he had emmigrated to France. By then he was a multimillionaire real estate developer who had begun to share his wealth with hospitals and universities.

"There's no way of telling for certain merely from studying old records," Reid said. He had been a college football standout. He still maintained the build and the somewhat boyish competitive attitude. "They could have been altered. Would you want to put that kind of a brand on an innocent man?"

Höehner liked Americans for the same reasons most Europeans found them difficult to take: it was their brashness and, he supposed, their naïveté. They thought they could fix everything, and often did. In some ways he'd been like that as a child ... before the world caught on fire. But this time he felt a certain resentment toward Reid. "There were many innocent men and women and children in the camps," he said slowly.

"There is a way to make sure," Reid continued. "As you say, Leitner fathered at least a dozen children with women in the camps."

"Those records are confidential—"

"Just listen to him, Horst," Gavalet interrupted. "Please."

"Some of those children must have survived, and we think that your people might know where they are now."

"To what point, Mr. Reid? Do you expect them to step forward and somehow identify their father?"

"Yes, as a matter of fact I do."

Höehner was startled. "What in God's name do you mean to say?"

"All we need is a blood sample from any of them. Just one of Leitner's offspring."

"You mean to match blood samples with Mann's to see if he is really Leitner? It will prove nothing."

"Not blood types," Reid explained. "But DNA matches from the blood. No mistakes. One hundred percent certain."

Höehner said nothing. It was the new science. Perhaps his wife was correct. Perhaps it was time to forget, or at least retire. He managed a thin smile.

"We want to cooperate with you, Horst," Gavalet said. "Believe me when I tell you that this is the new way, the only way to make absolutely certain that we would not be sending a good and innocent man to prison."

And there she was again. At the door. Höehner could hardly believe his eyes. He groaned and shook his head.

"What is it, Horst?" Gavalet asked, alarmed. "Are you ill? What's wrong?"

"It's her," Höehner said. "Evidently she's followed me from Vienna."

Gavalet and Reid turned in the direction he was staring in time to see an intense-looking woman dressed in a raincoat, a white sweater tucked into a long dark skirt, and tall black boots start across the dining room toward them.

"Who is she?" Reid asked.

"Maria Schimmer, an Argentinian treasure hunter, if you can believe that," Höehner said.

"What?" Gavalet asked, amused. "Schimmer. Is she of German extraction?"

"Her grandfather supposedly was an Abwehr general. Went to Argentina with his wife and his son, a navy lieutenant."

"Were you after them?"

"No. They were merely soldiers, no better or no worse than most."

"What does she want with you?" Reid asked.

"Wait for just a moment, and unless I can drive her away, she will tell you. Believe me, she will tell you."

"*Guten Abend, Herr Höehner,*" the woman said, her voice deep, almost masculine, her accent definitely South American.

"In English, please," Höehner said. "It is the common language at this table. What do you want of me, Miss Schimmer?"

The woman glanced at Gavalet and Reid. "Your help, sir. The same as before. I thought perhaps that once you were away from your stuffy offices in Vienna you might change your mind."

"I have not. There is nothing I can or should do for you ..."

"I don't give up so easily, you know," she said, a faint smile at the corners of her sensuous mouth. She had taken off her scarf. Her dark hair, a brown so deep it was almost black, was very long and pinned into a knot at the nape of her neck. Her cheekbones were high and well defined as were her eyebrows, giving her an aristocratic look. But it was obvious that she had spent a lot of time in the warm sun recently. Her color was high, and becoming.

"I'm sure you don't," Höehner said. "But you are wasting your time ... and mine."

"Then help me, and I will be out of your hair—" She caught herself too late. "Sorry."

"Help with what, exactly, Ms. Schimmer?" Reid asked.

She looked at him. "I'm trying to find a submarine."

Reid's mouth opened but nothing came out.

"Allow me to introduce my companions," Höehner said graciously. "Miss Maria Schimmer. Carleton Reid, chief of security at the American embassy here in Paris. And Maurice Gavalet, a French police officer whom I have known for some years."

Both Reid and Gavalet rose and shook her hand.

"I'm intrigued, mademoiselle," Gavalet said. "Won't you join us?"

"Yes, do," Reid said. He was obviously curious about her.

She glanced at Höehner, who nodded wryly. "Perhaps I can offer you no help, young lady, but we won't send you away hungry."

"*Gracias*," she said, smiling warmly as Reid took her coat and Gavalet summoned the waiter to take it, and to bring her a wineglass and a place setting.

When they were settled, Höehner poured her a glass of wine. "Miss Schimmer wishes to find a German submarine which she claims was captained by her grandfather when it disappeared on a secret mission to Argentina at the war's end. She believes that my influence in certain circles might help in her search."

"I have reason to believe that he made it across the Atlantic and was sunk in Argentinian waters either by an American patrol or perhaps by a mine," Maria said. "I would like to find his boat and . . . his body."

"All those records would be on microfilm at the National Archives in Washington," Reid said.

Höehner held back a slight smile. "Miss Schimmer is not a scholar. And that pile of microfilm is daunting to say the least."

"The information might not be in those records anyway," Maria said. "But they'll be down in Freiburg in interviews with naval staff."

"I thought Nazi records were stored at the Berlin Documents Center," Gavalet said.

"Not the naval documents," Maria said. "They are stored at Freiburg."

"You have been to see them?" Höehner asked.

"It was worth a try," she admitted. "But those records are open only to scholars. To a man such as yourself. So, you see, you are my last hope now."

"I have been to Freiburg," Höehner said. "Just after you left Vienna. Your grandfather, as it turns out, was in reality Abwehr General Hermann Schimmer. He escaped to Argentina with his son, your father, Naval Lieutenant Joachim Schimmer, in the spring of 1945. Neither of them were in the German submarine service."

Maria looked at the wineglass cradled in her hands. "You checked in Berlin as well."

"Yes."

"I lied to you," she said after a long hesitation.

"So it would seem," Höehner said, not unkindly.

She looked up, defiance in her eyes. "Joachim was my step-father. He adopted me in Buenos Aires six months after my real father was killed in an auto accident."

"What was your real father's name?" Reid asked.

"Rolph Reiker. He came with my grandmother to Argentina after the war was over. They were supposed to meet my grand-father there."

"The submarine captain?" Höehner asked.

She nodded. "Ernst Reiker. But he never showed up. My grand-mother died of influenza two years after that, and my father married an Argentinian woman who died giving birth to me."

"And your father died when?" Reid asked.

"In 1970. I was sixteen years old."

Höehner was staring at her, an odd expression on his face. "Why did you not tell me this at our first meeting?"

Maria closed her eyes for a long moment, and when she opened them, they were glistening. "Because you would have thrown me out of your office."

"Why is this?" Höehner asked softly.

"My grandfather, I was told, was a good man. But my father was not. He was a murderer. A paid killer."

"For whom?" Höehner asked, his voice barely a whisper now.

"Ex-Nazis."

"Who did he kill for these . . . monsters?"

"Jews," Maria said.

Höehner looked away. "He was a very bad man, your father. I knew the name, but it took me a moment to realize that it could be the same man."

"So you see why I need your help."

"No, I do not," Höehner whispered, turning back to her, his eyes blinking furiously. "Leave sleeping monsters lie, Miss Schimmer . . . and you are Schimmer, not Reiker. Remember that. It may save your life one day. Now, go."

3

THE MAN WHO HAD identified himself as McGarvey had divided the plastique explosive into two large masses. He set one aside, and then pulled the small metal desk into the corner next to the single window and climbed up on it.

Working quickly but precisely, he molded the plastique tightly against the ceiling and the corner where the outer wall of the building met an inner wall. The puttylike material was very pliable because it had had several hours to absorb heat from his body. The blueprints he'd studied had revealed that this was one of the spots where a major structural column ran up from the basement all the way to the roof. It was one of the main supports for the floors above, including the communications center. The explosion would not only blast a huge hole in the floor, but would also cut the main column, causing much of the rear face of the building to collapse into the courtyard. The floors above would likely come down as well, sandwiching everything and everybody between them.

It was the same principle that had brought down the Marine barracks in Beirut. He'd been there. The operation had been crude, but it had been extremely effective.

The destruction of the communications center and the deaths of the CIA's chief of station and his assistant would give him a certain amount of pleasure, as would the operations he'd planned against Rome and Bonn and Lisbon. And General Didenko's plan was as brilliant and audacious as it was necessary. He'd seen very clearly why a diversion was needed to keep all Western eyes pointed this way.

But he had developed another, even more satisfying aspect to this mission. One that he'd naturally not revealed to Didenko, but one that no force on earth could stop him from carrying out.

It was owed to him.

McGarvey. The name had crystallized so rigidly in him that it had finally etched a very deep canyon in his mind.

The man would die. But the method of his execution, the date and place of it, and the finger or fingers that would pull the trigger would provide the final solution to a problem that Arkady Aleksandrovich Kurshin had lived with for nearly sixteen months.

The irony, he had decided, would be lost on no one. In the very end he would make certain of it.

When the plastique was in place, he took the camera from his briefcase and in two practiced moves removed two parts that had been designed to look like ordinary batteries. In fact they were batteries, but they also served as miniature radio receivers and detonating devices.

He embedded one of the detonators into the plastique, then hurriedly got dressed, stuffing the second lump of plastique into his briefcase and pocketing the second detonator.

Ignoring the body on the floor, he eased the door open and peeked out into the corridor. No one had come to find out what had happened to the old man. But they would be coming soon.

Kurshin looked at his wristwatch. He'd been in the building

less than ten minutes. He'd given himself twelve minutes to finish and get clear.

A bit more than two minutes remained.

Closing the office door behind him, he hurried to the far end of the corridor on the east side of the building. He had to pick the lock of the much larger office here. This one belonged to the chief of the embassy's Commercial Section, and was divided into a secretary's area and an inner room.

He went into the inner office, pulled the desk into the corner, and, as in the first office, molded the plastique into the corner between the outer and inner walls, up against the ceiling. The main corner column rose at this point from the basement. So did the gas main for heating and for the kitchen on the fourth floor. Directly above was the chief of station's office. Next door was his assistant's.

Inserting the radio-controlled detonator into the explosive, he got down off the desk and again checked his watch. Less than a minute had passed.

Reaching around to the back of his head with both hands, he dug his fingernails into the skin at the nape of his neck and ripped open a large, bloodless gash. The latex mask pulled away from his skin with a sucking noise, and when it was off he tossed it aside.

Next, he took a small square of tissue paper from his pocket and gently opened it on the desk. From inside he withdrew a small vial and unstoppered it. It was filled with a few drops of blood, unfrozen. He dribbled the blood over his right hand and three fingertips, then touched the desk, the wall next to the light switch, and finally the doorknob.

Before he left, he glanced back up at the plastique in the corner, and grinned.

The corridor was still empty. He pulled on his overcoat and gloves, and, briefcase in hand, hurried to the stairs and down to the ground floor. He paused for a second or two on the landing, then went the rest of the way down into the basement, where the service areas for the embassy's general population were located.

The kitchen was lit but deserted, as he knew it would be. Meals were rarely served from this kitchen unless there was a major reception going on.

He went back to the service and loading elevator on the

east side of the building, where he picked the old lock. With a few seconds to spare, he found himself outside on a side street, and he walked off into the dark, rainy evening, his head bent into the icy wind, merely another pedestrian on his way home.

4

ALLAN BERRINGER, SECOND ASSISTANT to the Paris station's chief analyst, Sam Vaughan, rang the buzzer at the steel security door that led into the third-floor communications center. He was a younger man, still in his late twenties, fresh out of a four-year stint in the air force after college, and he had yet to learn any patience.

He rang the buzzer a second and then a third time. "Come on," he said, half under his breath. He was carrying a thin file folder marked TOP SECRET.

The light behind the eye-level peephole was blanked out, and a moment later the electric latch clicked. Entry to the center was by personal recognition only.

"You're going to be an old man before you're thirty, Allan," Susan Steiner told him with a smile. One of the cipher clerks, she was exactly one year older than he was, and had her two children with her in Paris. Her divorce had become final eight months earlier, and she had a slight thing for Berringer.

"I'm already old," he said, handing her the file. "Bob sent this over. It has to be included."

"Hold on and I'll give you a time stamp," she said. It was a receipt for the classified documents he had delivered to her accountability.

Berringer stepped out of the entry alcove and on tiptoe looked over the opaque glass partition into the operations room.

"Here you go," Susan said.

He turned back to her and took the receipt. "Where's Sam? I thought he was here."

She glanced up at the big clock on the back wall. "He left a few minutes ago. Said he'd be right back."

"That's odd. Did he say where he was going?"

"Downstairs to his office, I think. Said he needed something."

"Have him call Hizzoner as soon as he gets back," Berringer said. It was the chief of station's nickname.

"Maybe you'd better go down and fetch him. You know how he gets sometimes."

"He should have retired ten years ago," Berringer said, shaking his head.

"Except he's smarter than the rest of us put together."

"Ain't that the truth."

Berringer left the communications center and started back to the briefing room but then thought better of it. "What the hell," he muttered, and he turned and went back to the stairs.

Sam Vaughan's age was a secret to everyone on the embassy staff except for Personnel, and they refused to talk. The current best bet was that the "old man," as he was called, had to be pushing seventy. Berringer guessed seventy-five was more like it.

It was said that Vaughan had been one of the old cronies of Allen Dulles, the headmaster of the World War II OSS and king-pin of the early Agency days, and had, along with the legendary Wallace Mahoney, helped create the CIA's Analytical Section that eventually was renamed Intelligence.

"Look for the anomalies, kid," Vaughan was fond of saying, "the glitches in the fabric of what you perceive to be the real world around you, and you'll be well on your way to bagging the bad guys."

Easier said than done, Berringer had learned on his first day out. On paper it was easy to pick out the odd lot in the series: apples, oranges, hammers, pears, bananas. But in reality it was much more difficult to pick out the one improper motivation for one of your madmen who was making waves that would peg him as the plant, the double, the agent, or the source gone bad.

Bonn and Berlin stations were having a hell of a time keeping track of the action in the new Germany. No one knew which side was up. It was a situation that would likely last for years.

Here in Paris things were no easier. "We're the final arbiters," Vaughan had once told him. "The European buck stops here on its way to Langley."

But in the months that Berringer had been in Paris, two things had begun to happen to him. The first was that he was beginning to see some sanity in his work after all. The proverbial light at the end of the tunnel. And secondly, he had developed a deep respect and an abiding fondness for the "old man."

There was no light showing beneath Vaughan's door, but it was unlocked, so Berringer went in and flipped on the light.

"Sam . . . ?" he started to say, but the name died in his throat.

Vaughan lay on his back just within the doorway, a puddle of blood and cranial fluid under his left ear.

"Oh, Christ, oh, Christ Almighty," Berringer whispered, suddenly too much spit in his mouth and throat.

It was hard to think straight. He wasn't a field officer. Those Joes called his type the "eggheads." Well, eggheads bleed just like everybody else, he wanted to scream, but he was having a rough time talking or moving or doing anything else. It was impossible to believe. Yet this was one of the realities that Sam had always talked about.

"Don't just stand there, kid," he would have said. "Get the lead out of your ass."

Gingerly, Berringer leaned over Vaughan's body and felt for a pulse at the side of his neck, knowing full well he wouldn't find one. He didn't.

Careful not to step in the blood, he picked up the telephone, realizing that he might be destroying evidence by touching anything, but it was already too late. And the desk seemed to be out of place.

He got through to the chief of station upstairs in the briefing room at the same moment he saw the plastique high in the corner.

"Christ," he breathed. "Sir, I'm downstairs in Sam's office. Sam is dead, and there's a bomb stuck to the ceiling. At least I think it's plastique ..."

Before he could hear what Lord was shouting to him, he dropped the phone and climbed up on the desk.

Up close he could see the detonating device jutting out of the amorphous mass of plastique.

He reached up for it, his hands shaking, and he hesitated a moment longer. The thing could be on a timer, or it could be on a contact switch.

"Christ," he swore again, and he yanked the detonator free, bringing with it an ounce of the explosive.

Kurshin stood in the darkness just off the rue du Faubourg Saint Honoré less than a block from the embassy, understanding full well the significance of what he was seeing.

He could just make out the side and back corner of the embassy. The office window just below the communications center was lit. Someone had already discovered the body, and no doubt the explosive.

The rain had changed to snow, and although the winters here were much milder than in his native Yakutsk, his cheeks still stung with the cold. Traffic had not slowed down, despite the weather. And even more people were out on foot.

It was all meaningless to him now. He had miscalculated. His timing had been off, and he was seething inside. He set the tiny transmitter in his pocket to the number one position and switched on the arming circuit.

An instant later he pressed the fire button, but nothing happened. His eyes narrowed. He pushed the fire button again. But there was no explosion, no thunderclap and rush of flames and debris from the rear of the building. Only the traffic sounds, muffled by the falling snow, penetrated the fog that seemed to be enveloping him. He could feel his rage and frustration mounting.

"Push the button and let's get the hell out of here, Colonel,"

Stepan Bokarev said, coming up from behind him. He was the KGB's number four man out of the Russian embassy, and Kurshin's contact. He'd been handpicked by General Didenko. He was not as bad as some KGB officers Kurshin had worked with in the past, but he still lacked imagination.

Kurshin held his rage in check by sheer force of will. "I have already fired the first one."

"What ...? But there was no explosion," Bokarev said in disbelief.

"Somebody has evidently discovered my handiwork in the first office. Look for yourself—the light is on."

Bokarev peered through the blowing snow at the back of the embassy. "Shit," he muttered once he had picked it out. "Blow the other one. Look, that light isn't on."

"Not yet," Kurshin said softly, another idea forming in his head. By now the CIA chief of station and his assistant would have been told and they would no longer be in their offices. The communications center would be deserted as well, although he didn't think they would evacuate the entire building. They had already found and disarmed the bomb.

The question would be whether someone would suspect that there might be other bombs planted in the building. If so, they might look for them. They might go office to office. But quietly.

"What are you waiting for, Colonel?" Bokarev asked. "If they have indeed disarmed your bomb, they must know that the detonator is radio controlled. They will come looking for us."

"They are too busy right now getting their people away from the communications center to come looking for me. That will come later. We still have plenty of time."

"Fuck your mother, for what?" the KGB officer demanded, his voice rising.

Kurshin turned to him, and the man visibly blanched. "We will wait, Stepan Ivanovich. And I will not fail, do you understand this?"

"I'm just ... suggesting, comrade, that we retreat for the moment in order to survive so that we can fight another day."

"I'll pass along your sentiments to the general."

"I ... I'm sorry, Colonel. I guess I'm just not used to these kinds of assignments."

"Go back to the car, start it, and prepare to get us out of here. But do not turn on the headlights."

Bokarev glanced toward the embassy again, then nodded. "Whatever you say, Colonel," he said, and he turned and started toward their car, which was parked fifty yards away.

Now we wait until they turn on the light in the chief of the Commercial Section's office and discover the bomb there, Kurshin told himself. The waiting here in the snow was like the waiting at home when, as a young man, he had hunted sable and arctic fox for their pelts. The quarry knew the hunter was there, waiting for the kill. But in the end it made no difference. Kurshin felt the same bloodlust now.

He set the transmitter to the number two position, his fingertips brushing the firing button but not pressing it.

Someone would die tonight; he was going to make sure of it. The general wanted a distraction. He would get one.

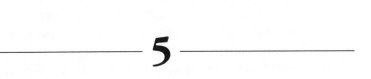

5

THREE TRAINS HAD ARRIVED within a few minutes of each other, and the Gare du Nord was a madhouse. Kirk Cullough McGarvey pushed his way through the crowds in the main hall and made his way to the rue du Maubeuge exits, where he pulled up short beneath the broad overhang.

It looked as if it were snowing much harder in Paris than it had been out in the countryside. And every Parisian, it seemed, had lined up for the three or four available taxis, the line snaking back and forth through the barriers, policemen directing the human tide.

He swore under his breath as he put down his overnight bag and briefcase and pulled on his brown overcoat.

His apartment was just off the rue La Fayette, barely a half-dozen blocks away, and normally he would have enjoyed the walk. But not tonight. Tonight he was tired and irascible. He wanted nothing more than to get home, take a very long, very hot shower, and relax with a violin concerto on the stereo and a drink or two. Above all he wanted no hassles.

Hunching up his coat collar against the biting wind, and hefting his bags, he started resolutely away from the station, his thoughts naturally going back again to the business he had conducted in Brussels over the past two days.

"You have two choices, monsieur," the investments adviser at the Banque de Bruxelles had told him. "Because of the sharp decrease in the prime rates on the international market, your investments are no longer earning so much. You must either modify your standard of living, or you must begin delving into your capital . . . a course of action the bank would strongly advise against, of course."

"Of course," McGarvey had replied. He was not a wealthy man by any standards, but the money he'd invested provided him with a decent income.

There was a third option, but it was one McGarvey had not discussed with the man. He could move his account elsewhere. Perhaps back to Switzerland where he'd once lived, what seemed like a century ago. Perhaps back to the States, or even to the island of Jersey, whose banking laws favored the investor at the expense of the British government.

The broad rue La Fayette was snarled with traffic, but he managed to get across with the lights in a surge of pedestrians, all of them apparently in the same black mood as he.

He was a businessman only by necessity, he kept telling himself. He had to oversee his investments personally because he had never met a banker or investment counselor yet who knew his ass from a hole in the ground. Why else, he asked himself, did a serious discussion with six of them, on six different occasions, produce six completely and wildly differing answers?

But his mood this evening was dark from something more complex than simple money worries. Even if he halved his expenses, he would still live well. It wasn't that. It was the other thing Hoden had said to him at the bank.

"You must understand, monsieur, that you are no longer a young man. In a few short years you will turn fifty." He shrugged, the Gallic gesture galling just then.

"Still a few years to go," McGarvey had replied, smiling. "I don't think there's any need to worry on that score just yet."

But the fact of the matter was that he was no longer the wunderkind he'd been in the old Agency days. As someone had once said at Langley about the old sage Wallace Mahoney who'd just passed sixty-five: "A good man, but he's already living in his future."

It was a cold wind that blew without the promise of summer to come.

Premature, perhaps, and yet the role he'd been playing as expatriate American first in Switzerland, then in Greece, and finally here in Paris, was wearing thin. He'd been at it for a long time, more years than he cared to remember; ever since the Carter days, when he'd been dumped from the CIA for not following orders.

They were bad times then, with more bad times to come. He'd been sent to Santiago to assassinate an army general who'd been responsible for thousands of deaths, and who would, if left to his own devices, kill thousands more.

Someone in the Carter administration had intervened and a recall order had been issued. But it had been too late. Hardly a night went by that McGarvey didn't remember the face of the general, the look of surprise and hurt as he stumbled and fell to his knees and then onto his side in a growing pool of blood. "It wasn't supposed to happen this way," he seemed to be saying in McGarvey's dreams.

Overexuberance, they said. Taking matters into his own hands. Operating outside his sanctions. Failure to keep a grasp on the world political climate.

Then why had they come back to him in Switzerland with their problems? And again here in Paris two years ago? Why hadn't they left him alone?

A dozen places, a hundred faces flickered through his mind at the speed of light as they often did. He never forgot a face. Never. Not one of the madmen who had worked for him, not one of the men, and in two instances women, he had killed . . . especially not them. Not one of the friends who had betrayed him in the end.

Christ, it all still hurt, even now so long after the fact. Sometimes he could hardly stand it. It hurt even worse, he supposed, because of his maudlin worries of late.

He had become lonely again, bored, anxious. Another stage of his life was about to end and he wanted to hang on to the old and familiar even though he knew that was impossible.

Whenever change came for him, it always seemed to involve the woman in his life at that moment. And each time it went just as badly, perhaps even worse, for her as it did for him ... in the States a million years ago with his wife Kathleen; in Switzerland with Marta Fredricks; and finally with Lorraine Abbott fifteen months ago. He'd driven her back to California to save her sanity as well as his, but it still hurt.

Just as his next move would hurt.

Trouble was, he told himself as he turned onto the rue d'Hauteville, he had no idea where he would go. He only knew that his leave-taking was imminent.

Out of habit he slowed his pace slightly so that he could scan the street: the pedestrians, the traffic, the windows and doorways facing his apartment, the two narrow alleys that led back into courtyards. But nothing seemed out of place this evening.

There was no one coming for him, friend or foe. Trotter was dead, and so was Baranov. None of the rest really mattered.

Halfway down the block he mounted the three steps to his apartment building, let himself in with his key, and switched on the timed hall light. It was too late to get his mail from the concierge, and he didn't want to bother with it anyway, so he started up the stairs to his third-floor apartment, more tired and weary and, he supposed, frightened than he had been in a very long time.

At the top he put his overnight bag down, unlocked the door, and pushed it open with his toe. As he bent down to pick up his bag he smelled the perfume, and he closed his eyes for just a moment. He didn't need this now, especially not now.

"What are you doing here, Carley?" he asked, straightening up and entering his apartment.

"Waiting for you."

McGarvey closed the door and flipped on the light. Carley Webb sat in the armchair by the window, her coat lying over the edge of the couch, her legs crossed. By the way she squinted her eyes at the light, he figured she had been there in the dark for some time.

"I thought you were busy all this week," he said.

"And I thought you'd gone to Brussels."

He held up his overnight bag and briefcase, then put them down by the couch. He took off his coat and gloves and went into the bedroom where he tossed them on the bed. When he came back out into the living room Carley had gotten to her feet and was gazing out the window down at the street.

"Anybody?" he asked.

She turned back. "Were you expecting someone?"

McGarvey managed a tight little smile. "Once a spook always a spook, is that the game? Still want to move in with me?"

Her nostrils flared as they always did when she wanted to make a retort but was holding herself back. It was one of her little habits that he'd always found particularly annoying.

Why me, he'd wanted to ask her on more than one occasion. Why did you single me out of the crowd to get involved with?

But he was afraid he knew the answer. He was afraid she would tell him that, like Marta Fredricks, who'd been his lover in Switzerland, Carley had been sent to his side to watch him. Marta was a cop with the Swiss federal police, and Carley worked for the Company. He was a former assassin. One of the unmentionables who lurked in every secret service but whose existence the Western services steadfastly denied. He had to be watched. He made people nervous.

With Marta, the relationship had lasted for five years, until Trotter had come over from Washington to bring him back into the fold. With Carley, the relationship had begun to pale almost from the moment it had begun.

She was too young, too demanding, too self-assured, too self-centered, and egocentric in some ways. She was a woman, he supposed, of the nineties, whereas he still belonged to another age.

"Do you want a drink?" he asked, loosening his tie. He took off his jacket, draped it over the back of the desk chair by the door, then took his holstered pistol from the small of his back and laid it down.

"Just wine," she said, watching him.

He went into the kitchen, opened a bottle of Chardonnay, and poured a couple of glasses. When he went back into the living room, Carley was at his jacket. She'd taken out his passport and was looking at it.

"Lousy picture," he said, handing her the glass of wine.

"It's expired," she said.

"I'll come in one of these days and have it taken care of," he said. He took it from her and tossed it on the desk. There was something wrong. He could see it now in her face. It was as if she were frightened of something. "What is it, Carley? What demon is after you this time?"

"Your eyes are green," she said softly.

"You've just noticed?" he said with a laugh. "But then there'd be a contrast. His eyes would be brown."

"What?"

"Your madman," McGarvey said crossly. "Your Joe. Your agent."

She was shaking her head.

"Come on, Carley, let's cut the bullshit. You work for the Company. I know it, and now you know that I know it. You're young, beautiful, obviously very talented. Tom Lord would use you as a handler. He'd be a fool not to."

"You don't know what you're talking about," she said, turning away.

He took her arm and pulled her back. "Christ, are you here to tell me that the son of a bitch is putting a move on you and you don't know whether or not to go to bed with him?"

"Why are you doing this?"

"What's the matter, kid, a case of the moral jitters?" He was being unnecessarily cruel, but he couldn't help himself. It was over, couldn't she see it? Hadn't she seen the signs? Couldn't she guess that he couldn't stand to be watched, his every move cataloged and then hashed out at the Monday briefings? "Lord, how the man snores." "His bathroom habits are absolutely abominable." "His lovemaking is adequate, providing he keeps his mind on what he's doing."

She tried to struggle away from him, but he held her arm tightly, knowing that he must be hurting her.

"You want to sleep with him? With your Russian madman? Go ahead, don't let me stop you. Hell, it'll do wonders for your career. Look what sleeping with me has done for it."

She stopped struggling, her eyes beginning to fill. He let go of her arm.

It was always the same. His watchdogs never fought back. It wasn't in their contract. "Treat the man nicely, Carley." "Do what the man says, Carley." "Don't upset the man, Carley, no telling what the son of a bitch might do."

"I never slept with you or any other man out of necessity," she said.

"The Company has its own special necessities, hadn't you realized that?" He smiled sadly. "I mean, look what it's done for me."

"Do you want me to get out of your life?"

"I never wanted you in it in the first place."

She looked up at him for a long time, then handed him her wineglass and went to get her coat.

He wanted to go after her, to say the words that would bring her back, undo the hurt he had inflicted on her. But he did not. The time was right for her to go. Any later and her hurt would be a million times worse. But he felt terrible.

He'd known what she was from the beginning, yet he had taken her to his bed, also knowing full well that this day would come and what it would do to her ... to both of them.

She pulled on her coat before she turned back to face him.

"Just go," he said. "I don't know why you came here in the first place."

She picked up her purse. "I wanted to warn you about something."

"Us?"

She shook her head. "It's something else. A man showed up at the embassy late this afternoon claiming he was you."

"What?"

"Same brown overcoat and gloves, green eyes, same general build. Even looked like you."

"You saw him?"

"Just for a second. Said his passport needed renewing. I checked. The number on his passport was the same as yours."

McGarvey put the wineglasses down, switched off the lights, and went to the window, where he cautiously pulled back the curtain and looked down into the street.

"What did he look like, Carley? Specifically."

"I don't know. I didn't pay *that* much attention to him, and it was only for a second or two. But he had green eyes, about the same general look as you."

"Hair?"

"Light brown."

"Accent? He spoke English?"

"Yes, of course," she said. "Educated. East Coast, maybe."

"Boston?"

"Yes," she said. "Who was he?"

As far as he could tell, no one and nothing out of the ordinary was down there. No strangers lurking in doorways, no odd car or van with too many antennae parked up on the curb.

He turned away from the window. "He showed my passport to the Marines, spoke to you briefly, and then left?"

"Yes. Who was it?"

"Someone . . ." McGarvey said half to himself.

"Out of your past?"

"Maybe."

"Who?"

"He's dead."

"Who, Kirk?" Carley demanded. "I sent him away, told him to come back in the morning."

"It's impossible," McGarvey said. "I killed the man myself." He could see it in his mind's eye as clearly as if it were happening at this moment. He could see the man go over the rail and into the water. He was dead. He had to be.

He let the curtain fall back and turned on the lights again. Carley was staring wide-eyed at him.

"Kurshin," he said. "Arkady Kurshin. But he's dead."

6

ALLAN BERRINGER SAT HUNCHED in the corner in shock, blood pumping from his mangled right hand, yellow spots dancing in front of his eyes.

He had no idea what had happened to him. One moment he had withdrawn the detonator from the plastique and had turned to climb down from the desk, and the next moment he was here on the floor, a ringing in his ears and his right hand destroyed.

The bomb had not exploded; he knew that much. But what had happened to him? It was hard to make his brain work. First Sam Vaughan, and now this.

It had to be the Russians. They were Sam's bad guys, after all.

Someone came pounding down the corridor in a big hurry,

and Berringer managed to turn his head to the doorway as Tom Lord appeared. There were others right behind him.

"Son of a bitch," the chief of station swore, squatting down beside Berringer and yanking off his tie. He began wrapping it tightly around the young man's wrist.

"I don't know what happened . . . sir," Berringer said weakly. His voice sounded muffled and far away to him. The sound was more frightening than the pain in his arm.

Graves was doing something to Sam Vaughan's body.

"He's dead, Mr. Graves. Shot in the head."

"Did you see it happen?" the assistant chief of station asked. He looked at Lord.

"No, sir."

"But you pulled the detonator, is that it, son?" Lord asked.

"I didn't know what else to do, sir. Was it the right thing?"

"You bet it was."

"Radio controlled," Graves said over Lord's shoulder. His face loomed large and white in Berringer's eyes. "Blew his fingers and half his wrist off."

"Get me a first-aid kit down here immediately," Lord ordered. "And call an ambulance. We've got to get him to the hospital before he goes into shock. Evacuate the building."

"Right," the assistant chief of station said, and he turned away, issuing orders to the others who were gathered out in the corridor. Berringer thought they were making too big a fuss over him.

The flow of blood from Berringer's hand wasn't stopping. And the throbbing pain was intensifying with each second. "Was it the Russians, sir?" he asked.

"Don't worry about it, kid," Lord said, as the fire alarm began to sound.

"There might be others," Graves shouted over the noise.

Lord glanced up at the mass of plastique on the ceiling. "They were after the comms center, that's for damned sure. Maybe that's all. I want Technical Services over here on the double. Tell them what we're dealing with. And have security start a room-by-room search. I want this out to Langley as a flash, right now."

"You got it," Graves said. "Hang in there, kid. The ambulance is on the way."

"Yes, sir," Berringer replied weakly. He looked up into Lord's face. "Why would they do this, sir? I thought they were supposed to be our friends now."

"I doubt it was the Russians."

"But Sam told me—"

"Don't worry about it. Probably terrorists. France is full of them."

"But how'd they get in here?"

"I don't know, but we're sure as hell going to find out."

"Are they gone?"

A startled expression crossed Lord's face. "Good Christ," he muttered. He turned away. "Bob!" he shouted. "Graves!"

The assistant chief of station was there a second later. "First-aid kit is here."

"Get security. I want this building sealed immediately. The kid just asked if our terrorist chums are gone."

"Of course they are. They wouldn't have hung around to pop the detonator. We've alerted the French police. They're on their way."

"Do it!" Lord barked.

"Right," Graves said, and he hurried out.

Susan Steiner shoved her way into the office, pulling up short with a little cry when she saw Sam Vaughan's body. She'd brought the big green first-aid kit from the communications center.

"Smelling salts—he's starting to drift." Lord's voice floated somewhere out ahead of Berringer.

Susan was there, over him, her mouth half open, her face contorted into a mask of fear and worry.

"Come on, Allan," Lord said close to his ear. "It's only a little wound. Come back to us."

Susan put something under his nose, and it was as if someone had shoved a needle into his head, instantly clearing away the fog, a big wave of nausea rising and then subsiding just as fast.

"Are we all right, sir?" Berringer cried. Something clutched at his chest, and his heart began to flutter.

"Where's that ambulance?" Lord yelled.

"It's on the way," someone shouted from the corridor.

A Marine appeared in the doorway, his weapon drawn, and said something that Berringer didn't hear. It was becoming dif-

ficult for him to catch his breath, which he thought was ridic-
ulous.

He was flat on his back, and Lord was on top of him now,
pushing at his chest. He wanted to tell him to stop, but he
couldn't breathe, and the lights began to fade.

7

"A RUSSIAN, THIS KURSHIN of yours?" Carley asked after a moment. "KGB?"

"Old Department Viktor, but better than the rest," McGarvey said, the bad memories tumbling one after another in his head. "He was one of Baranov's people."

"And Baranov is dead. You killed him. That report I did see."

McGarvey smiled inwardly. At least one pretense between them had been dropped. She had seen the report: ergo, she was admitting she was CIA.

"And Kurshin," he said.

"Then what are you talking about?" she asked in exasperation. She pulled up her coat collar.

"The man you described could have been him. Same eyes,

same build, same accent. The same *cojones*. He had those all right."

"But he's dead."

McGarvey nodded.

"Then it's someone else who has a grudge against you." Carley shook her head. "And from where I sit, I suspect that on a clear day I might be able to see a crowd of them. A few women among them, I'd bet."

"Weren't you warned before you started?"

"Repeatedly," she said. "But for what it's worth, Kirk, I swear to you that you were never an assignment. I was just told that you were very smart, very good at what you did—when you did it—but that you had a bad track record with women, and a very big chip on your shoulder for some reason."

"And dangerous?"

"Murphy doesn't like you, from what I'm told."

Roland Murphy, the general, was the director of the Central Intelligence Agency. He was a friend of Lorraine Abbott. He thought that McGarvey had put her to hard use. And he despised assassins. He was from the old, "honorable school," as he called it.

"I've never entered a popularity contest."

"No," Carley said, and she started for the door.

"Let me get my coat and I'll drive you. My car is in back."

"Don't bother," she said. "I'm not going home yet. Besides, you've made it perfectly clear what's become of us. I heard your great lecture about excess baggage, so I guess I've half expected this day for a long time."

"I'm sorry, Carley. It was my fault."

"Yes, you bastard, it was," she said. "You want to know the funny part?"

He said nothing.

"I could have fallen in love with you." She looked at him one last time, then turned and left the apartment.

McGarvey could not stop himself from thinking that all of his women had made their grand exits in the same way. Each of them had blamed him not only for their leave-taking, but for their falling in love with him in the first place.

At the window, he watched as she appeared below in the street and hurried toward the intersection to catch a cab. She was young and bright, and she had gotten out soon enough to avoid permanent damage. With luck she would find someone soon who would make her happy and give her babies before the job killed her femininity, her humanity. The business did it.

When she was gone, he turned his thoughts back to whoever was trying to impersonate him, and why. He'd gotten an ominous feeling about it, whereas although Carley had thought the incident odd, she seemed more curious than perturbed. It would be reported to security, of course, but unless the man actually came back tomorrow, nothing much would probably come of it.

In the kitchen, he dumped both glasses of wine into the sink, then poured a large Jack Daniel's on the rocks.

Kurshin's body had never been found. He had been seriously wounded, and he had fallen off the ship into the sea fifty miles off the Syrian coast. It was assumed that his body had eventually washed ashore and had simply not been reported by the Arabs. A man in his condition could not have survived.

An *ordinary* man could not have survived. But by all standards Kurshin had been anything but ordinary.

McGarvey set his drink down, walked back into the living room, and telephoned the embassy. Carley had not mentioned telling Lord about her encounter with the imposter, though she might have done so. The least he could do, he figured, would be to make certain they were warned of the possibility, however remote, that something was about to happen.

The operator answered on the second ring, and her voice sounded strained. There was an odd noise in the background. "Good evening, you have reached the embassy of the United States of America."

"Put me through to Tom Lord, please."

"I'm sorry, sir, all those lines are busy."

"This is a lamplighter call," McGarvey said, using the fieldman's emergency assistance code word. *Help me, I am in serious, life-threatening trouble. Connect me immediately with an agent handler. Any agent handler. But do it now!*

The embassy operator hesitated for only a moment. "I'm sorry, sir, but your call does not have priority. Please try at a later time." She hung up.

McGarvey's stomach rebounded. Impossible. He stood flat-footed, holding the phone to his ear, listening to the dial tone. Agents in distress were never, but *never* ignored.

But the operator had said his call did not have "priority." And there was the noise. An alarm?

He slammed down the receiver, grabbed his jacket and pistol from the desk, and raced out the door.

Lord sat back on his haunches, a huge weariness mingled with a deep smoldering anger coming over him. He could hear people behind him in the corridor rushing to carry out his orders. Telephones were jangling, doors were slamming, and someone was issuing instructions about the elevator, over which the fire alarm clamored.

"Sir . . . is Allan dead?" Susan Steiner asked.

He looked up at her and nodded, seeing in her eyes more than just simple horror at the sight of death. She had cared for the young man.

"I'm sorry," he said. "Truly sorry, but under the circumstances he did the correct thing. Without him everyone up in comms would probably have been killed."

"But why?" she said softly. She looked down at Vaughan's body on the floor. "Who did this, Mr. Lord?"

"I don't know, but we're sure as hell going to find out," Lord said, getting to his feet. He took her by the shoulder and led her out, handing her to one of the other women from upstairs.

Bob Graves was just rushing up the corridor toward them.

"Will one of you see to it that she gets home, please?" Lord asked.

"Yes, sir," one of the women said.

"Carrara is on the hot line from Langley," Graves told him.

Phil Carrara was the deputy director of Operations, a man who held a fair, if tight leash on his chiefs of station. "I had Smitty send out the two-line flash, and he was notified."

"He's dead," Lord said softly.

"What?" Graves asked. He looked beyond Lord into the small office. "Berringer is dead?"

"My oldest son is practically his age."

"It was just a detonator, for chrissake, Tom."

Lord looked at him. "We're going to get the bastard."

"You're goddamned right we are."

"All right, listen up, folks," a marine guard at the east end of the corridor shouted. "I want everyone off this floor right now."

A second Marine emerged from the dark office of the chief

of the Commercial Section. He held a flashlight in his left hand, the beam bouncing wildly around the corridor. "You heard the man. Get out of here now!"

Lord and Graves sprinted down the corridor as the others started for the stairs.

"What is it?" Lord demanded.

"Another plastique device, sir," the first Marine said. He was highly agitated, and he kept flipping the safety catch on his .45 pistol.

"Take it easy, son," Lord said.

"Sir, there's no telling when this one will go off, or how many others there are in the building. We have to get everyone out of here right now!"

"You're right. There's no time," Lord said. He turned back to Graves. "Get on the line to Carrara and tell him what our situation is here. I want everyone out of the building as soon as possible, and that includes you."

"What the hell are *you* going to do?" Graves snapped. "Let Technical Services handle it. They'll be here any moment. This was meant for you."

"And that thing could blow at any moment, Bob. Now *move* it."

"I'm afraid we can't let you go in there, sir," one of the Marines said.

Lord turned to him. "Nonsense," he said. "You boys get out of here and help with the evacuation."

"Sir?"

"It's all right," Lord said, and he brushed past them and entered Kevin Hewlett's office. Hewlett was chief of the embassy's Commercial Section.

"It's up against the ceiling in the inner office, sir," one of the Marines said behind him.

"Get out of here," Lord said.

"No, sir," the Marine replied.

There was no time to argue. Lord stepped past the secretary's desk and went into Hewlett's office. The Marine shined the beam of his flashlight on the plastique in the corner. The desk had been shoved over beneath it.

"Has to be five or six pounds at least," Lord said.

"Yes, sir."

It was enough plastique, he figured, to blow out the entire

wing of the embassy, collapsing half the building into the rear courtyard.

The detonator jutted out from the center of the dull gray mass.

Lord reached over and flipped on the light switch, then gingerly climbed up onto the desk, and reached out. . . .

8

MARIA SCHIMMER HEARD THE explosion as she was coming out of the Hotel Inter-Continental.

The two uniformed doormen standing beneath the overhang ducked down instinctively. Maria reared back, but then turned toward the sound in time to see an incredibly large fireball rise up over the rooftops from somewhere toward the Champs-Élysées. A second later broken glass began to fall into the street from windows facing the blast. It sounded like musical rain. The obelisk in the Place Vendôme was lit orange and red, and a dreadful hush seemed to come over Paris.

"*Mon Dieu,*" one of the doormen said, picking himself up. "Was it an oil truck?"

"Did you see the flames?" the other asked, stunned.

"That was no fuel truck," Maria said, more to herself than to them, recognizing the blast for exactly what it was. She'd spent enough time under fire to know the difference between a fuel explosion and the blast of high explosives.

Other guests were streaming out of the hotel now. "What the hell was that?" someone demanded.

"It was a bomb, I think," a woman cried.

"A big one."

Carleton Reid, the American she'd met at Höehner's table, emerged from the hotel at a dead run, skidding to a stop on the sidewalk, the distant flames reflecting vividly in his eyes. A taxi was just passing, and he rushed out into the street and hailed it, yanking open the rear door before it came to a complete stop.

Maria roused herself and sprinted after him, grabbing the door before he could close it and forcing her way into the back seat with him.

"Get the hell out of here!" he shouted.

"I can help," she said.

Reid didn't wait to consider his choices. "The American embassy, on the double," he ordered the cabbie.

Maria glanced over her shoulder as they sped away. The French cop, Gavalet, came out of the hotel, and she allowed herself a brief, little smile. She figured she would have a much better chance one-on-one with the American. She didn't know what his relationship with Höehner was, but he might have some influence with the man. It was even possible he would have some indirect influence in Freiburg. There might be a lot of possibilities with the Americans, in view of the relationship they had with the Germans.

The driver hauled the taxi around the corner onto the broad rue de Rivoli, almost losing the rear end in the slush. Some windows there had been shattered by the explosion, and a few cars and trucks had slid sideways to a halt.

"Is it your embassy?" Maria asked. The flames shooting a hundred feet into the air seemed to be coming from somewhere beyond the Automobile Club.

Reid, perched on the edge of his seat, intently stared through the windshield. "Probably," he mumbled offhandedly. Then he turned and looked at her. "What the hell do you want?"

"How do you know it's your embassy, Señor Reid?" she asked.

"I asked you a question, Ms. Schimmer," Reid said sharply, his attention now completely fixed on her. "Who are you? Exactly what is it you want?"

"Your help."

"I don't get involved in treasure hunts."

"Just a word to Höehner, or even to the Germans at the records archives in Freiburg. It's all I'm asking."

Reid glanced out the windshield again as they approached the Place de la Concorde. A large crowd was gathering and in the distance they could hear sirens, a lot of them. "In exchange for what?" he asked coldly. "What can you do for me?"

"I'm an archaeologist. I know how to dig. And I'm a pretty fair nurse."

"No, thanks," Reid said.

They came out into the broad plaza and from there they could suddenly see the embassy. The entire rear section of the building had collapsed, filling the courtyard with hundreds of tons of debris. The front of the building leaned dangerously inward, apparently on the verge of falling. A huge tower of flame shot straight up into the air from the northeast corner of the massive pile of rubble. No one in that part of the building could have survived.

"*Sacre . . .*" the driver said in awe, pulling around a big block of concrete lying in the middle of the street. He brought the cab to a halt at the police barricades that were hastily going up.

Reid tossed a couple of bills over the front seat and leaped out of the cab. Maria scrambled after him.

There was a lot of confusion. People continued to stream into the area, but from what she could see, no one had yet mounted any real attempt to rescue people who might be trapped in the burning building.

Reid was stopped at the barriers by a pair of gendarmes and had to show his identification before they would let him through. They had seen Maria get out of the cab with him, and they said nothing to her as she slipped through directly after him.

This close she could actually feel the heat from the flames. The wind had picked up and the snow was blowing into her face, yet the air was warm. A dozen or more people, most of them without coats or jackets, stood across the street. From their dazed expressions she figured they had come out of the building, possibly before the explosion, which meant they'd been warned.

Reid cut across the edge of the square and rushed down the street. Three fire trucks raced from the rue Boissy-d'Anglas and screeched to a halt in the middle of the street. The firemen leaped from the trucks and immediately began pulling hoses and connecting them to the water supply.

Reid stopped to look back. He held out his hand. "Go back," he said, out of breath, and he turned and hurried the rest of the way up the street to where the people from the embassy were standing. He took off his jacket and draped it over the shoulders of one of the women as he had a hasty conference with a couple of the others.

Maria hesitated about twenty yards away, as Reid crossed the street and entered the embassy. Then she headed after him.

She'd just reached the stairs when he came back out, half carrying, half dragging a Marine whose uniform was in smoldering tatters. Blood streamed from dozens of cuts on the boy's face and chest.

She helped Reid bring the young man down to the sidewalk, away from the building, and lay him down. Then she took off her coat and covered him.

"I told you to stay the hell away," Reid said angrily.

"There's no time for that now," she replied, stuffing her scarf inside the remnants of the young man's tunic in an effort to staunch the greatest flow of blood. "Are there others inside?"

More sirens were converging on the embassy, and hundreds of people continued to pour into the street and plaza. Already the police were having trouble keeping them back.

Reid was obviously torn between ordering her away and accepting her help.

"*Madre*," she breathed. "No bargains. You can have my help for nothing, señor. But if there are people inside, they are dying."

"All right," Reid said, getting to his feet. "But just stay the fuck off the third floor."

She looked at the building. "I don't think there's much of a third floor left," she pointed out, but Reid was already sprinting up the stairs.

One of the embassy women came over and took charge of the Marine. She had a vacant, stunned look on her face, yet she knelt down beside the Marine and gently began wiping the blood from his cheeks. She was the one to whom Reid had given his jacket.

"What happened?" Maria asked.

"It was a bomb on the second floor, I think." She looked up at the building, her eyes and mouth opening in fear. "There have to be other people up there!" she cried. "Someone has got to help them!"

"Just stay here," Maria said soothingly. "Help is on its way. I promise you, it won't be long now."

The woman nodded uncertainly. Maria rose and hurried up the walk and into the building.

There was smoke everywhere, though it wasn't as bad as she had feared it might be. Part of the ceiling on the east side of the main hall had collapsed. Desks and file cabinets from the first-floor offices lay in twisted heaps. Papers were scattered everywhere. She could see through the gaping hole all the way up to the second and third floors, and she could even see a section of night sky lit by flames.

The stairway was partially blocked by debris blown down from the upper levels. She figured Reid had gone up that way. He was worried about the third floor. Whatever secrets were contained in the embassy, she figured, were probably up there. The Americans would be particularly sensitive just now, so she would have to be careful. She didn't want to be shot to death by a trigger-happy Marine. Yet if she was going to win their respect and therefore their help, she was going to have to go where the need was greatest.

At the bottom of the rubble-choked stairs she took off her boots and broke the high stacked heels against a piece of concrete. She put them back on, hiked up her long woolen skirt, and started up, scrambling over big chunks of ceiling, hunks of twisted steel, splintered wood, and shattered bricks, and books, papers, files, and newspapers.

The stairway end of the corridor on the first floor was burning furiously, and the stairs leading to what remained of the second floor was shaky underfoot.

She had to duck beneath a big oak beam and crawl on her hands and knees the last eight or ten feet. The corridor floor slanted away sharply toward the back of the building, and the heat and smoke were intense.

She was conscious that her hands and knees were cut and bleeding. It was very hard to breathe, and she was beginning to think she had gotten in over her head, and that it might be wiser if she turned around and went back down, when Reid appeared in an office doorway halfway down the corridor.

Through the smoke and flickering flames, it looked as if he was in trouble. He was dragging a body out of the office, but he seemed to be on the verge of collapse.

"Wait!" she cried. She had just started forward, when what was left of the ceiling collapsed on her. The floor began to cant farther and farther back, the entire front of the building threatening to collapse into the burning mass of debris below in the courtyard.

Maria's legs were pushed painfully up against her chest, and she thought she might be upside down, though in the pitch-darkness she wasn't sure.

Smoke was very thick, and between it and the heavy pressure against her chest, she was becoming light-headed from lack of oxygen.

It was stupid, she realized, but she was probably going to die here. But she wasn't ready. Not yet. There was the other thing she had to finish first. Besides, she had never thought she would die without the chance of fighting back.

All her life she'd had to fight back. To stand up for herself. She just knew this wasn't the time or the place for her death.

Except for the woman outside, no one knew she was here. And Reid was the only one who'd known her name. For a second or two, panic threatened to blot out rational thought and she struggled against whatever was holding her in place. A trickle of plaster dust ran down her leg and settled grittily between her thighs.

"*Madre de Dios*," she whispered.

More dust streamed down from above her, and then pieces of brick and chunks of plaster and slivers of lath tumbled through a widening hole.

The building was settling. She was going to be buried alive.

"No!" she screamed. "Oh, God, no! *Please help me!*"

Suddenly there was a light above her and she looked up between her knees as a hand came into view. She reached up.

"Are you all right?" a man's voice filtered down to her.

"Oh, God, I don't know!" she cried. "I think so. Help me, please!"

"Any broken bones?"

"No, I don't think so."

"All right, just take it easy, and I'll get you out of there. There'll be some more dust and things falling down on you. But it'll be okay."

"All right, all right. Just hurry, please!"

The hand was withdrawn, and panic rose up in her breast. "Don't go!" she screamed.

"Easy," he said. "The name is Kirk McGarvey, and I'm not going to leave you."

She looked up and suddenly she could see his face. He was smiling, and for some reason she thought that she was going to be all right.

"What's your name?" he asked, pulling away a big chunk of plaster.

"Maria," she gasped.

"Well, Maria, after I get you out of here you're going to owe me a drink. A deal?"

"A deal," she agreed.

The opening was getting larger, and all of a sudden the pressure was off the soles of her feet and she could almost straighten her legs, and then McGarvey's wonderfully strong hands were pulling her gently up through the opening.

9

MARIA LAY AT THE EDGE of the crazily canted stairs looking up at her rescuer, his broad face illuminated by the flames. "I thought I was going to die," she said, her own voice somehow sounding far away.

Her skirt was hiked up around her waist and her panty hose were in tatters, but she felt no sense of modesty with him. His hands were gentle as he wrapped his handkerchief around her leg, and then pulled down her skirt.

"You'll need stitches, but it doesn't look so bad."

"Thank you," she mumbled, and then she suddenly remembered Reid and the man he'd been dragging out of the office. With a little cry she struggled to sit up. "They were just down the hall . . ."

But the corridor was gone, and for several seconds she had

trouble getting her bearings. She'd been standing at the head of the stairs just within the second-floor corridor when Reid and the other man came out of the office twenty or thirty feet away.

But now the office was gone. A huge pile of twisted rubble and plaster and wooden beams slanted up into the third floor, where she could see flames and other lights. The outside? She couldn't tell. Everything was different, confusing.

"Who was there?" McGarvey demanded.

"Reid and another man. They were coming from an . . . office. There." She pointed toward the pile of rubble that had collapsed from above.

"Just the two of them?"

"I think so," she replied, a wave of dizziness and nausea passing over her. Again she almost panicked; only McGarvey's strong hands holding her made her feel safe. "But they're gone. The office is gone."

"Can you get back downstairs by yourself?"

"I don't know . . ."

"Just hang on, then. I don't want you hurting yourself any more than you already are," McGarvey said, and he turned and crawled up onto the pile of debris that completely blocked the corridor. The entire section of the building shifted with his weight. He stopped short.

Maria was watching him. "Is it going to fall down?"

"I don't know," McGarvey said. Carefully he pulled himself the rest of the way up until he was lying on top of what might have been a collapsed wall. He was looking at something on the other side.

"Can you see anything?" Maria called up to him.

"A section of the corridor. Part of a doorway."

Someone came crawling up the shattered stairs and Maria turned. A Marine emerged from the narrow opening beneath the big oak beam. He carried a flashlight, and he shined the beam on her face.

"Who the hell are you?" he demanded.

"Maria Schimmer," she said.

"She's hurt. Get her downstairs," McGarvey called from his perch.

The Marine shifted the beam of his flashlight toward McGarvey, the blank look on his face changing to one of incredulous anger. "Jesus H. Christ, now who the hell are you?" he shouted. "And what the hell are you people doing up here?" It was obvious he was frightened.

"Your chief of security, Carleton Reid, and another man are buried back here. With any luck I might be able to dig them out before the rest of this floor collapses."

"I asked who you were!"

"There's no time for that," McGarvey said. "Get her out of here. She needs medical attention."

"Get down from there . . ."

"Listen, you stupid bastard, there are people dying back here."

The Marine started to reach for his pistol, but McGarvey pulled his Walther out first, pointed it at the Marine, and cocked the hammer.

"It's your choice, kid. There's not much time to screw around."

The Marine looked from McGarvey to Maria and back again. "I can't let you go up there, sir," he said uncertainly.

"There's only one way out. Get the woman outside, and then guard the stairway if you want. But have your medical people standing by. I may be needing some help."

Still the Marine was uncertain.

The floor shifted a few inches under his feet, and they could hear the sounds of falling rubble somewhere below them.

"Will do," the Marine said.

"Where can I reach you when this is over?" McGarvey asked Maria.

She could hardly believe it. "The Hotel Roblin on the Chau-veau-Legarde," she told him. "It's not too far from here."

"I'll find it," he said. He holstered his gun and a second later he disappeared over the top, the floor shifting again and more debris rumbling below.

Bob Graves was extremely cold. He was wedged in place beneath Carleton Reid's body. They'd been halfway out the door when the ceiling had collapsed on top of them. Behind him the outer wall and most of the ceiling of the office was gone, and the wind blew snow around his head and shoulders. In addition, a great deal of water from somewhere was running along the steeply sloped floor, soaking his battered legs and back.

For a long time he thought he was hearing sirens, but then he wasn't certain, although intellectually he understood that by now there must be dozens of fire and police units around the embassy, and probably a thousand or more onlookers.

Reid had shown up a few minutes after the explosion, and had started to drag him out of the office where the bodies of Berringer and Vaughan lay, when the ceiling had given way. Reid was dead; there was absolutely no doubt of it. The heavy lintel above the door had fallen on top of him, snapping his back and crushing his skull.

Tom Lord and the Marine with him would be dead as well, their bodies undoubtedly disintegrated by the tremendous blast. They had probably been standing very close to the plastique when it went off.

That thought tightened his jaw. The son of a bitch who had done this had probably been standing outside, watching for someone to enter Kevin Hewlett's second-floor office. The light had come on and he'd hit the trigger.

He closed his eyes against the grisly sight on top of him. The rescuers would have to come very soon, he thought, or he would not make it. Either the building would collapse on top of him —it had shifted a couple of times in the last few minutes—or he would die of exposure.

Either way he would not get his revenge. And more than anything on this earth at this moment, he wanted his turn with the monster who had done this to them.

The second-floor corridor was impossibly blocked. Each time McGarvey pulled debris out of the jumbled wreckage, the floor shifted ominously beneath his feet. There was no telling how deep the debris was piled.

The firefighters were pouring water into the east side of the building, where the flames were the most intense. But the water was adding a tremendous amount of weight to the already weakened structure, and it was coming closer to collapse every second.

In the darkness and dense smoke it was difficult to maintain his bearings. The woman said she'd seen Reid and another man coming out of one of the offices somewhere farther down this corridor. It was certain he would not be able to dig his way back, but it might be possible to get up onto the third floor, cross beyond the collapsed section, and somehow make his way back down onto the second floor, *behind* the rubble pile.

Moving with extreme caution he picked his way over a steeply slanting section of wall, then up onto what remained of the third floor, over a thick wooden beam, and across a jumble of lead pipe and electrical wires into the corridor. For just an instant the thought that he might be electrocuted crossed his mind, but he figured that by now the authorities would have made certain that the electric and gas mains supplying the building were shut off.

Sixty or seventy feet ahead, the building abruptly came to an end. Tom Lord's office had been back there, but it was gone, as was everything above and beneath it. The explosion had most likely been centered there, or possibly just below Lord's office.

Whoever had been back there hadn't had a chance. He shivered.

The water being sprayed by the firefighters fell in huge sheets, backlit in pinks and reds and blues from the fire and the spotlights below and the city lights on the Place de la Concorde and beyond.

McGarvey hesitated only a moment before carefully working his way straight back to where the corridor opened into what remained of the communications center. The walls and most of the floor had fallen down into the courtyard. There was no way down.

He was turning away when he thought he heard a movement in the debris below. He held his breath and cocked his head to listen, but the sound was not repeated.

Water poured along this floor, cascading over the far edge like a waterfall. From outside he could hear sirens still converging from all over the city, mingled with the sounds of the portable generators supplying electricity to the searchlights, and the more significant noises of the continually shifting building.

He eased a little nearer to the unstable edge and yelled, "Is there somebody down there?"

Something scraped below, but there was no answer.

"Can you hear me?"

"Yes," a weak voice filtered up from below.

"Is it Reid?"

"No, Reid is dead. I'm Bob Graves."

"Can you move, Bob? Can you come to the edge? I'm on the third floor just above you."

"I can't move. My legs are pinned in what's left of the doorway."

"All right, I'm coming down to you."

"No—wait!" Graves called urgently. "I think the ceiling is about ready to come down."

"The whole building is ready to fall," McGarvey said. "Is there any water down there?"

"A lot of it," Graves said.

McGarvey had figured as much. It would be running down that corridor as well, and probably pooling up behind piles of rubble, dramatically increasing the weight on that floor.

"There's no one else up here, and there's no time to get anyone. If you're willing to chance it, so am I."

"Who are you?" Graves called.

"McGarvey."

There was a moment of silence below.

"Bob?" McGarvey called.

"What the hell are you doing here?" Graves answered. Former CIA agents, especially those dismissed from the Company for supposed cause, made everyone nervous.

"Looking for a job," McGarvey said. "Now hang on, Bob, I'm going to try to get down to you."

"I'm not going anywhere," Graves said.

The first problem would be getting down to the assistant chief of station. The second would be dislodging Graves from the rubble. But even more difficult would be getting him back up to this floor and across to where they could drop back down to the second-floor corridor near where Maria had been trapped. The stairs, if they were still open, would lead them to safety. At this point he figured it was their only way out of the building, and he was going to have to make it happen right now.

But the floor was too unstable, and the water cascading over the edge would make it difficult if not impossible to come back the same way.

He went back toward the corridor to where a section of ceiling had collapsed. In the flickering light from the fire behind him, he could see his path back down onto the second floor, but just to his right there was a dark opening beneath a thick wooden beam. A way down?

For a breathless second or two he remained motionless, trying to penetrate the total darkness in that black opening. When he was a kid in Kansas he and a few friends had gone down into a cave where they had gotten lost. They'd spent hours in the utter blackness until they had finally stumbled into the main chamber and found their way out.

He had vowed never again to be so foolish. This was worse than that cave. Much worse.

He closed his eyes for a moment. This was Arkady Kurshin's work. It had the same feel as before. The man was alive. But there was no reason for this. Although the Russians weren't exactly friends and allies, at least they were no longer enemies. This attack made no sense.

It was a safe bet, however, that this strike on the embassy, if Kurshin had been responsible for it, was nothing more than the tip of some iceberg. A diversion. A sleight of hand to hide whatever the real goal was.

Girding himself, he opened his eyes and lowered himself into the hole. "Graves?" he shouted, his voice muffled in the close confines.

"Here," Graves's answering cry came faintly from below, and McGarvey crawled deeper into the hole that immediately slanted sharply downward for about twenty feet until he could see light from outside, and hear running water below and to the right.

"Graves?" he yelled again.

"Here," Graves called again, his voice still muffled but very near.

Five feet farther, the passageway twisted sharply to the right, and McGarvey came face-to-face with a young man whose right hand appeared to be badly damaged, and he recoiled instinctively.

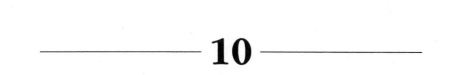

10

"CHRIST," MCGARVEY SWORE. He was in the remains of an office, the outside wall of which was gone. The emergency spotlights playing on the building from outside cast a pink glow, exaggerating the crazy angles of the jumbled walls and what remained of the ceiling. Across the room was another body, its legs jutting out from beneath an overturned desk.

He pulled himself a little closer. The young man's mouth was half open as if he were trying to say something. But his eyes were closed, as if he had fallen asleep in the middle of a speech.

McGarvey felt for a pulse at the side of the neck, but the moment he touched the skin he knew that the young man was dead.

"He's dead," Graves said from the shadows at the back of the room.

McGarvey pulled himself the rest of the way out of the tunnel through the debris into the shattered office, the icy water at least two inches deep flowing across the floor and over the edge.

"Who was he?"

"Berringer. Vaughan's dead too."

"Under the desk?"

"Right."

McGarvey crawled over to where Graves lay pinned. For just a moment it seemed to him as if the man had too many arms and at least one extra shoulder. There was blood everywhere. Suddenly he realized that he was looking at Carleton Reid's crushed body.

Graves grabbed his wrist. "Get me the hell out of here, McGarvey."

"That's what I'm here for. Any feeling in your legs or feet?"

The beam that had crushed Reid to death had missed Graves's torso by an inch or two. As far as McGarvey could determine, he was held in place by a pile of debris, most of it plaster and lath from the ceiling.

"I don't know," Graves said weakly, laying his head back in the water. "They didn't have a chance. He was here. The bastard penetrated us."

McGarvey pulled a big slab of plaster off Graves's legs as more of it tumbled down from above. Before long the pile of debris blocking the corridor would cave in on them. "Did anyone see him?"

"Vaughan did," Graves replied bitterly. "And he got shot for it. In the face, at point-blank range."

"What?" McGarvey asked sharply. Someone had just walked over his grave.

"Vaughan didn't have a chance. The bastard was in here setting his explosives when Vaughan walked in on him."

"Was it a big-caliber weapon? Could you tell? Did you see the wound?"

Graves's eyes narrowed. "What is it, McGarvey? Do you know something?"

"What about the wound?"

"Christ, I don't know. But he was shot in the face."

Old-school KGB, it went almost as far back as the Cheka days. McGarvey didn't have to close his eyes to see. It was called *mokrie dela*, the spilling of blood, a wet affair. The victim was shot in the face at very close range as a sign of discouragement to others. But hardly anyone had thought it necessary to use those methods in years. Ever since the cold war ended. And especially not in the past year or two.

It had been Kurshin's style to the end.

But the man was dead. There could be little doubt of it. What was happening here and now was the work of a madman, no doubt. Someone influenced, perhaps, by men of Kurshin's ilk. But such monsters were an anachronism in this day and age. They would not last. They could not last.

A little voice inside McGarvey's head was insisting that he not become involved.

"Do you know who did this?" Graves was asking him.

McGarvey shook his head as he continued digging Graves out.

"Goddamnit, McGarvey, if you know something, or even suspect something, you have to tell me. A lot of good people have died here."

"I don't know a thing," McGarvey said sharply. He had cleared the door lintel, which was a heavy wooden beam four or five feet long. It was pressing down on Graves's legs.

"Then what the hell are you doing here?"

"Saving your life. I'm going to try to lift this beam. As soon as the pressure is off, pull your legs out. Are you ready?"

Graves nodded, and McGarvey put his shoulder to the heavy beam. It wouldn't budge, and he had to dig more rubble away from it. Graves's legs were oozing blood, and it was obvious that they were badly broken. He had to be in considerable pain, but he didn't cry out.

"Try again," he said through clenched teeth.

McGarvey had to straddle Reid's horribly mangled body so that he could push back and up using his legs for leverage. At first nothing happened, but then something crashed behind the wall of rubble, and the beam began to shift.

"Now!" he shouted, putting every last ounce of his strength into it, and Graves heaved himself backward, pulling his legs out. Suddenly he was free.

"I'm out! I'm out!"

McGarvey let go, at the same time rolling left, out of the way, and the lintel came crashing down, the entire building shuddering under the impact, plaster dust, wood, bricks, and sections of ceiling tumbling down all around them.

"Can you crawl?" McGarvey shouted.

"I'll try," Graves yelled back over the din. This entire section of the building was collapsing.

"I'll pull you out," McGarvey said. He dragged Graves across the office and over Berringer's body, then plunged headfirst into the narrow passageway.

He could feel Graves's grip on his ankles and he waited until the man had pulled himself up behind him, and then he crawled another couple of feet and stopped. Again Graves pulled himself up.

Smoke and plaster dust were very thick in the narrow tunnel, and as he negotiated the sharp turn to the left, he had visions of being buried alive. He shuddered and stopped.

"What is it?" Graves shouted weakly. "What's wrong, man?"

"Nothing. We've got another twenty feet to go. Are you ready?"

"Yes! Let's get the hell out of here!"

Twice more he stopped in an effort to catch his breath, but he was becoming light-headed from the smoke and lack of oxygen. He wouldn't be able to go on like this much longer. Yet he could not simply stop and wait to die. He wasn't built that way.

Minutes or hours later—time had become a blur for him— he was back in the third-floor corridor, the cold wind and snow mixed with spray from the fire hoses clearing his head.

Disengaging himself from the nearly unconscious assistant chief of station, he turned around and pulled the man the rest of the way into the corridor.

"Where are we?" Graves groaned a second or two later.

"Third-floor corridor," McGarvey said. "There's a way down to the second floor from here, and then the stairs are open the rest of the way. Or at least they were."

Something crashed below them and the passageway they'd just emerged from suddenly collapsed in a huge cloud of smoke and dust, the floor beneath their feet starting to slide away from the center of the building.

McGarvey grabbed Graves under the arms and rolled him up onto his left shoulder. Struggling away from the edge, he scrambled back the way he'd first come up, working his way across the pipes and electrical wires, and then past the beam and down the steeply sloping wall into the second-floor corridor, more and more of the building collapsing behind them.

Graves was drifting. The tremendous pain that had throbbed in his legs as he'd pulled himself through the tunnel after McGarvey was mostly gone, and he was having difficulty taking a deep breath. He felt confused and frightened. He'd come this far; he did not want to die like Berringer or Vaughan or Tom Lord.

Someone was shouting something. It sounded as if it were coming from below.

He opened his eyes suddenly and tried to rear back. Somehow they'd been trapped by the fire and were about to be burned to death, though he could feel no heat yet.

"Christ, don't drop him," someone said nearby.

Graves raised his head in time to see a Marine sergeant, one of the security people, reaching up for him. He knew the kid. "Kunze?" he croaked.

"That's right, Mr. Graves," the Marine said. "You just take it easy now, hear? You're going to be okay."

"Get me out of here. The building is on fire."

"We're almost there. Take it easy, now."

There were other hands on him, and he was lowered onto a stretcher. For an instant it felt as if he were falling, and he flinched.

"Watch his legs," McGarvey said overhead.

"You McGarvey?" Sergeant Kunze asked.

"That's right," McGarvey replied. His voice swam in and out of focus above Graves.

"You're going to have to come with me, sir. There are some questions we need to ask you."

Graves suddenly panicked. He grabbed Kunze's sleeve. He had to make them understand. "You have to watch out," he cried.

"Yes, sir . . ."

"Kunze, watch out. He knows about Berringer and Vaughan. He was up there."

"I understand, sir," Kunze said, a new harsh edge to his voice. The two medics who'd brought the stretcher into the building lifted it and hurried across the lobby.

*   *   *

Carley Webb stood just across the street trying to make some sense out of what had happened. She'd been paged on her beeper and had arrived a couple of minutes earlier. Marine Lieutenant Donald Horvak, chief of the embassy's physical security detail, had filled her in with what he knew.

So far there had been little or no word about anyone on the second or third floor, though eight bodies had already been pulled out, and apparently McGarvey had shown up and rescued a woman who had been carrying an Argentinian passport.

No one had been able to tell her yet what the woman had been doing in the embassy, but someone thought he might have seen her entering the building with Carleton Reid a few minutes after the explosion.

Nor did anyone seem to know how or why McGarvey had shown up, but it was making a lot of people nervous, among them Lieutenant Horvak.

"The son of a bitch signed in a couple of minutes before six and never left," he said. "Begging your pardon, Ms. Webb, but it was his passport number on the ledger."

"It wasn't him," Carley said. "I stopped by his apartment tonight. He was there."

"Then it was a goddamned imposter, and five will get you ten that McGarvey knows something about it."

The ambulance attendants emerged from the embassy with Graves. Sergeant Kunze and McGarvey came out behind them. Kunze didn't seem happy.

"There they are," Horvak said, and he and Carley hurried across the street.

Graves was barely conscious, and McGarvey looked terrible. His clothing was torn and dirty, his left cheek was cut, and his hands were bloody.

"Berringer and Vaughan," Graves said weakly.

"What happened, Bob?" Carley asked. "Where's Tom Lord?"

"Dead," Graves mumbled. "They're all dead."

Carley could hardly believe it. "What about Carleton? Did you see him?"

"He's dead too. They're all dead, the entire crew." Graves grabbed Carley's coat sleeve. "He knows, Carley," he whispered, looking wildly toward McGarvey. "He knows about

Vaughan ... even the caliber of the weapon. They're dead ... all ... dead ..." Graves slumped back, unconscious.

"You'd better let them take him to the hospital," McGarvey said. "His legs are badly broken. I think he's lost a lot of blood."

Carley nodded and the stretcher bearers loaded the assistant chief of station into one of the waiting ambulances.

"What was he talking about, Kirk? Caliber of what weapon?" Carley asked.

"Later," he said. "Has Langley been notified?"

"Just hold on for a goddamned minute," Horvak snapped. "What the hell were you doing inside?"

McGarvey glanced at the Marine as if he were seeing him for the first time. "I tried to call Tom Lord to warn him about something Ms. Webb told me about this evening." He turned back to her. "Did you?"

Carley's stomach flopped over. "Christ," she said, half to herself, and she slowly shook her head. "No. I left a note ... I didn't think ..."

It was nearly ten o'clock by the time Chargé d'Affaires James Griffins and the embassy's general legal counsel, William Lisch, showed up.

Emergency embassy operations had been shifted to the American consulate on the rue St.-Florentin, and McGarvey had been detained to answer questions, among them questions about the Argentinian woman who had disappeared from the hospital thirty minutes after she'd been admitted.

Carley had returned from talking with Bob Graves a half hour earlier, and had been on the phone to Langley for most of that time. Until a team could be flown out from the States, she was de facto chief of Paris station and therefore chief of European operations.

They met in the consulate's second-floor conference room, McGarvey seated alone at the opposite end of the table from Carley and the two men. A Marine guard was posted at the door.

"How long had you known this Argentinian woman?" William Lisch asked. The lawyer glanced at his notes. "Maria Schimmer."

"The first time I ever laid eyes on her was this evening when I dug her out of the rubble on the second floor."

"So you admit you were up there?" Lisch asked.

"Did she tell you what she was doing in the embassy, Kirk?" Carley asked.

McGarvey was tired, and he wanted to be anywhere but there. "She told me that Reid had been helping another man and was buried. She asked me to help them. Has she been picked up yet?"

"No," Carley said. "Her passport was returned to her. We didn't think she'd be going anywhere."

McGarvey felt a little sorry for Carley. She was a good agent handler, or at least he supposed she was, but she was no station administrator. She was in way over her head here. "Has Technical Services secured the building?"

She nodded. "Phil is sending over a team. Should be here in a few hours. We've just got to hold on until then."

Lisch had followed their exchange. Again he consulted his notes. "What about this man you identified as the possible terrorist? Arkady Kurshin—"

Carley interrupted him crossly. "Mr. Lisch, that remains an Agency issue. One that I'm sure the director will address in the morning. Until we receive a clear indication from Langley and from the State Department, that subject is closed."

Lisch bridled, but the chargé held him off. "Ms. Webb is correct, of course, Bill." He turned back to McGarvey. "An investigatory commission will be assembled. May we expect your complete cooperation, Mr. McGarvey?"

McGarvey nodded. "As long as the Agency is involved, yes. But I can tell you now that I was mistaken. Arkady Kurshin is dead."

"How do you know?" Lisch asked before Carley could stop him.

"I killed him," McGarvey said.

11

"HE SAID HE KILLED the Russian."

Philip Carrara, deputy director of Operations for the Central Intelligence Agency, felt he was treading on thin ice. It had been a judgment call on his part two weeks ago, withholding information from the seventh floor. The decision was coming back to haunt him now. It was possible, he thought glumly, that his career was over.

He sat facing the director of the Agency, Roland Murphy, the assistant director, Lawrence Danielle, and the Agency's general counsel, Howard Ryan, in the DCI's spacious office.

The late afternoon outside the big plate glass windows was overcast and gloomy. The sun had not broken through the clouds all day, and it had been snowing in earnest for the past two hours.

"That was two years ago, Phil," Danielle said, his voice soft, almost effeminately gentle. Shortly after the previous DCI, Donald Suthland Powers, had died, he'd briefly taken over as DCI, until Murphy's appointment. He'd been with the Company for a lot of years and was nobody's fool, yet he remained something of an enigma. "And still no body."

"No," Carrara said. "Which is not conclusive."

"Of course by now, if the body were still in the sea, it would have completely disintegrated, isn't that correct?" Ryan asked. He was a methodically precise man.

"My experts say that's so, which is why even in the beginning we concentrated most of our efforts landward."

"Nothing from our Syrian resources after all this time?" Danielle asked.

"Nothing," Carrara said. "Though there have been a few rumors that Kurshin may have been seen alive in the region."

"In the Middle East?" Danielle asked.

"He's apparently been seen there, but the rumors came out of Moscow. Impossible to trace. Our best estimate was that they were just that: rumors."

The DCI interrupted. "What's your latest best estimate? Is it possible that Arkady Kurshin may still be alive and behind the bombing as McGarvey thought?" Murphy was a bull of a man, ramrod straight, with thick, beefy arms and a massive neck. His face was square, his eyes dark and extremely intense beneath bushy eyebrows.

"It's possible, General, but not likely," Carrara said. "McGarvey himself backed away from that possibility. There would have been stronger indications, in any event, had he survived. Something either in Syria or in Moscow. With Baranov dead—and remember that Valentin Baranov was his only control—Kurshin would have had to surface somewhere. He'd need operational funds at the very least. New identities. Even a new charter to operate."

"Didenko could have done it," Murphy said. "The son of a bitch has been consolidating his power since the KGB shakeup after Baranov's death."

"He's been watched, General."

"And?" Murphy asked impatiently. Baranov, the former director of the KGB, had almost single-handedly brought Powers down, nearly emasculating the CIA for a time, and had almost caused a major shooting war in the Middle East that could have gone nuclear.

"He's not been an easy man to follow. There have been and continue to be very large gaps in our daily summaries of his movements. Nothing we can do about it." Carrara shrugged. "What I'm trying to say is that if a resource such as Kurshin is still operative, he would have been put to use by now."

"Perhaps this was his coming out," Danielle suggested softly.

"It would have happened before this," Carrara said. "God only knows there have been plenty of opportunities ... and, from their standpoint, needs."

"Which brings us back to McGarvey," Ryan said. He and McGarvey had had a difference of opinion several years earlier that had ended in Ryan looking like a fool. The general counsel was not a man to forget a grudge.

"An imposter," Carrara said.

"I agree," Danielle supported him. "This sort of thing is just not McGarvey's style. Bombing, killing indiscriminately."

"Nor would he have returned to rescue people had he planted the bomb. He pulled Graves out of there at considerable risk to his own life."

"Ah, now *that*, however, is the man's style," Danielle said. "Take from him what you will, gentlemen, he's done a good job for us twice before. Yet each time he's gotten nothing for his efforts except our enmity, and on both occasions he's nearly lost his life."

"All the more reason for him to strike back at what he perceives is his enemy," Ryan argued. "The Marines say he signed in. They recorded his passport number."

"Carley Webb says she was with him at his apartment when the detonator blew. It couldn't have been him," Carrara said.

Ryan curled his lip. "You said yourself that Tom Lord suspected she was in love with the man. She worked as his watchdog as long as he was in Paris. They spent a lot of time together. Slept together, I'm sure."

"She wouldn't lie for him. Not against an overt action of that magnitude. Twelve people are dead, and five others are still missing."

Murphy, who had retired from the army as a major general

to take over the Agency, narrowed his eyes. He was an intellectual, but a man of action. He'd been called the "thinking man's soldier."

"What are we doing about interim operations?" he asked.

"Mike Wood is on his way over with the team. They should be arriving at de Gaulle in a couple of hours."

"Chief of station Bonn?" Danielle asked.

"Yes. He happened to be here in the city on stateside leave. I've put him in charge for now. Lou Anders, his assistant COS, will take over for us in Bonn."

"What about the long run?" Danielle asked.

"That'll depend in a large measure, I suppose, on the French. Depends on what sort of embassy building we'll end up with."

"What about McGarvey?" Ryan asked the DCI. "We're not simply going to take him at his word and let him wander off, are we?"

"We have no evidence on which to hold him," Carrara replied impatiently, holding his temper in check.

"We're taking the word of a young woman? His lover?"

Murphy sat back in his seat. "If it were Kurshin, McGarvey would be the man to go after him."

"He wouldn't take the job, General," Danielle said.

"I think I could persuade him."

Ryan got up and poured himself a cup of coffee from the silver urn on the sideboard. "You say that the man who signed in as McGarvey was an imposter?"

"That's right," Carrara answered.

Ryan turned back, a slight smile on his lips. "Then two questions come immediately to mind. First, why pose as McGarvey, of all people? Why not someone off the street? An American with a passport problem. From what you've said, he only needed to get past lobby security so that he could reach the stairs to the third floor. Almost any identity would have done."

"Unknown," Carrara had to admit. "But in this business the reason could be almost anything. Something as prosaic as a happenstance meeting between the terrorist and McGarvey."

Ryan was grinning broadly now. "Come on, Phil, you can't tell us you actually believe that. The coincidence is staggering."

"On the surface it seems farfetched, I'll admit, but . . ."

"And then there's this mysterious Argentinian woman. Young,

beautiful from all accounts, and in the building just after the explosion."

"She apparently had something to do with Carleton Reid. We're working on it."

"She's still missing?"

Carrara nodded, knowing full well where Ryan was taking it.

"Reid is among those dead, isn't he?"

Again Carrara nodded.

"The first person McGarvey rescued, at great risk to his life, was this woman. Curious, wouldn't you agree?"

"It doesn't mean a thing."

"For chrissake, she's got accomplice written all over her," Ryan snapped. "She and McGarvey were coconspirators, with Ms. Webb as their unwitting foil."

"What Howard says makes sense," Murphy rumbled.

"McGarvey sets the explosives and then goes home to wait for Carley Webb to show up, thus providing him with an alibi. Next, his Argentinian assistant pushes the button, and bang, all hell breaks loose."

"Then why did she go into the embassy afterward? It was a very dangerous thing for her to do," Danielle said.

"I don't know, Larry. Maybe Carleton Reid knew something and she had to follow him. Maybe she killed him. In the end McGarvey returned to the embassy not only to make himself out to be the hero, but also to rescue his accomplice lest she be arrested and made to talk."

There was silence.

"Phil?" Murphy asked at last.

"I don't believe McGarvey had anything to do with it, though it's possible that the Argentinian woman did. But there's more."

"Something that would prove McGarvey is innocent?" Ryan asked.

"No," Carrara admitted.

"What then?" asked Murphy, his eyes narrowed again.

Carrara extracted a photocopy of a typewritten letter and envelope that he handed across to the DCI. The envelope was addressed to Thomas Lord, Special Assistant to the Ambassador, at the U.S. embassy on the avenue Gabriel, and postmarked in Paris on January 2.

The general quickly read the single-page letter, his lips pursing. When he looked up there was a half angry, half mystified expression on his face. "This is a death threat," he said. "Aimed at Tom Lord, for"—he glanced again at the letter with obvious distaste—"for crimes against humanity as the Agency's Paris chief of station."

Murphy handed the letter to Danielle who quickly read it, and studied the French stamp and Paris postmark.

"Why wasn't this brought to my attention?" the DCI demanded.

Before Carrara could answer, Danielle looked up. "Roland, we get half a dozen of these a day worldwide. They've almost become routine." He turned back to Carrara. "Was this followed up?"

"Of course. The embassy received the letter on the third, and that evening Tom included it in his overnight summaries. He suggested no action other than a routine investigation by Technical Services. I agreed."

"Did they come up with anything?" Danielle asked.

"The envelope and letter were written with a Smith-Corona portable manual typewriter of the kind manufactured twenty-five years ago. The 'e' and 's' keys were slightly worn. The typist was right-handed, a man, but with a moderately light touch. The paper was ordinary cheap Xerographic bond found anywhere in the world, and it was mailed from the Central Post Office in downtown Paris."

"It's in English," Danielle prompted.

"A native speaker, and well educated," Carrara said. "It was the only unusual aspect of the letter. Most of the threats we receive are from obviously poorly educated people. Nearly illiterate, most of them."

"McGarvey's educated," Ryan said. "He's tall and strong, but I'd hazard a guess that his touch is moderately light. And he's right-handed."

"That's correct, Howard." Danielle said. "But so are you."

"I'm sorry, General," Carrara said to Murphy. "Under the circumstances I should have brought this to your attention."

Murphy was thinking. He waved Carrara off. "Larry is right. There was no way for you to have known this letter was anything other than routine." He shook his head. "But it leaves us nowhere."

"I still say McGarvey and the Argentinian woman are the keys," Ryan insisted.

"I agree," Murphy said, looking up. "Get McGarvey on the phone. I want to talk to him."

"Sir?" Carrara asked.

"His first impression was that Arkady Kurshin was alive and behind this," the DCI said. "Maybe he was right after all."

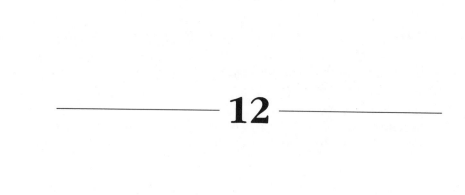

12

THE THIRD-FLOOR CORRIDOR was in darkness. It was a few minutes before midnight. Someone in one of the apartments below was playing the radio or television. Kurshin could make out the laughter from time to time. No sounds, however, came from McGarvey's apartment, or from any of the others on the floor.

He'd watched the building for a full half hour before letting himself in and climbing the stairs. As he had figured, McGarvey would be downtown answering questions. The fact that his name and passport number were on the embassy's visitors' register could not have gone unnoticed. And McGarvey's expected absence gave Kurshin the time he needed to finish what he'd begun.

Two years ago he'd stood outside on the street watching this apartment. He'd spotted McGarvey in the window. The man had made a perfect target. But Baranov had ordered Kurshin to run for his life. He had taken that advice, and still he had nearly lost his life at McGarvey's hands.

Standing in the darkness, he could almost feel and taste the salt water closing over his head. He swayed on his feet, the muscles of his body remembering the twenty-seven hours he'd spent in the sea before he'd been washed ashore half-conscious, delirious with pain and loss of blood. Only by pure blind luck had he been picked up by a three-man Syrian patrol. And it was only luck that by the time they'd been ready to report their find, he had recovered sufficiently to kill them all and make good his escape.

Memories, he told himself, his eyes blinking, his gloved hands flexing into fists. He had plenty of memories.

He set down the small leather case he'd been carrying, took a penlight from his pocket, and under its narrow beam made a quick but thorough study of the area around the door and the doorframe. He was looking for any sign that the door was alarmed, or that McGarvey had installed telltales to warn that intruders had visited while he was gone: a strand of hair, a tiny splinter of wood, a bit of dust. But there was none of that. McGarvey had become sloppy.

Turning his attention to the lock, he took out a slender, case-hardened steel pick and had the door opened in under twenty seconds.

He hesitated before stepping inside. Putting away the pick and penlight, he pulled out his gun. The only light inside the apartment came from the window overlooking the street. A cigarette odor was clear, as well as something else. Kurshin sampled the air with his nose. Perfume, perhaps. A woman's perfume. Expensive. Perhaps familiar from somewhere.

Inside, he closed and relocked the door, throwing the dead-bolt so that if McGarvey returned, his entry would be delayed long enough for Kurshin to get out. He did not want a confrontation with the man. Not yet. It would ruin his position with General Didenko.

This was the third time Kurshin had been here, and he knew the layout of the apartment by heart. At the window he checked the street, careful not to expose himself to view by anyone below. There was almost no traffic at this hour, and no sign that

McGarvey was on the way up, which gave him at least a few minutes.

From beside the writing table in the bedroom Kurshin pulled out a leather case similar to the one he carried, unzipped it, and took out a Smith-Corona portable typewriter he had put there the week before. From his case he took out McGarvey's type-writer, its twin, and put it in McGarvey's case, which he zipped closed and replaced next to the writing table. Then he put his own typewriter into the case he'd brought up.

Setting the typewriter by the door in the living room, he again checked the street. Still there was no sign of McGarvey.

In the bathroom, he pulled several hairs from the hairbrush on the shelf above the sink, placing them in one of the small plastic envelopes he'd brought.

Moving into the kitchen, he found two wineglasses and an-other glass that still contained a small amount of bourbon. He held up each of the three glasses, examining them under the beam of his penlight, fingerprints showing up clearly on all three. On one of the wineglasses, the fingerprints were narrow and delicate. A woman's. On the other wineglass and the bourbon glass the fingerprints were much larger, a man's. McGarvey's.

Peeling the leather glove off his right hand, he took a flat plastic envelope from his jacket pocket, then carefully slit the seal and removed the single thin rubber glove, much like the gloves worn by surgeons. Delicately, he pulled on the rubber glove, careful not to touch its fingertips, which had been pre-pared with a special glue.

He picked up the bourbon glass again, this time with his right hand, matching his fingertips with McGarvey's prints. The sticky surface of the glove neatly lifted McGarvey's prints off the glass.

He pulled off the rubber glove, replaced it in its plastic bag, and slipped on his leather glove.

Back in the bathroom, he stood on the toilet seat and placed a small piece of plastic in the flush tank mounted high up on the wall. The plastic had been torn from the wrapping of the plastique explosives. A simple chemical analysis would reveal what it had once contained.

He had been inside McGarvey's apartment for less than three minutes, and he was finished. Hurriedly he checked each room to make absolutely certain nothing was out of place, that he had left no outward sign that he had been there, and then listened at the door for a moment before he unlocked and opened it.

In the corridor he relocked the door, then started down the stairs. The ground-floor door opened and someone came in. He froze, holding his breath to listen.

He could hear footsteps. The stairwell was open all the way down, and sounds carried well.

The timed hall lights suddenly came on, and Kurshin reared back, flattening himself against the wall. The person who had come in started up the stairs.

Kurshin turned and went back up to the third floor, stopped to listen again—the person was still climbing the stairs—and hurried soundlessly to the shadowed end of the far corridor.

The door to the rear apartment was locked, and there was no time now to open it. He put down his typewriter case and pulled out his gun again, thumbing the safety catch to the off position.

The person on the stairs passed the second floor and continued up. He did not want a confrontation with McGarvey here and now, like this, but he was not going to back away from it.

He watched the opposite end of the corridor, his grip tightening on the gun, as a figure came around the corner from the stairs.

It was a woman. For an instant Kurshin was confused. He knew her, yet he couldn't imagine from where, and then he had it. She was the one from the embassy. The woman in the Consular Section. The familiar perfume.

She reached McGarvey's apartment and knocked on the door. After a beat she knocked again, a little louder. "Kirk?" she called.

Evidently she knew McGarvey. Well enough to have seen through the vague latex mask Kurshin had worn when he'd faced her?

She knocked again. "Kirk, it's me," she called. The timed corridor lights went out. "Shit," she swore softly.

Kurshin could dimly make out her figure in the scant light filtering up from downstairs. She was hesitating. After a moment, however, she turned and went back the way she had come.

He listened until she got downstairs. When the front door closed, he cautiously made his own way downstairs and out into the night.

13

MCGARVEY HAD JUST FINISHED in the shower when the telephone rang. He didn't bother to answer it. Instead he went into the kitchen, where he rinsed out his bourbon glass and poured himself another drink. Tom Lord had been a good man, one of the best, and it was hard to believe he was dead.

The telephone rang for the tenth time as he drank the whiskey and poured another. He went into the living room.

It was probably Carley calling to apologize or, worse yet, to ask for help. If he didn't talk to her now, she would almost certainly come over here again.

He picked it up on the sixteenth ring, and he immediately knew it wasn't her. He could hear the hiss and hollow pops of a long-distance connection. "Hello?"

"Kirk? Phil Carrara. I'm calling from Washington."

McGarvey sat down and closed his eyes. It was starting again, he could feel it. He supposed he had some sixth sense, almost an ESP, for these things. Each time he began to get itchy feet, something came up. In Switzerland and here in Paris, it had been John Trotter who'd come over to ask for help. Now Trotter was dead, and apparently his heir, Phil Carrara, either didn't believe in travel or was in too much of a hurry to make the trip.

"Kirk?" Carrara asked after a beat.

"This is an open line," McGarvey warned.

"The director wants to speak to you. I've been trying to reach you for the past hour."

"What does he want?"

"I'll let him tell you."

"What does he want, Phil?" McGarvey said evenly. He would listen, but he wouldn't lose his temper.

"It's Arkady Kurshin. He wants to ask you about the Russians."

Something clutched at McGarvey's heart. "Have we picked up something out of Moscow?"

"Nothing concrete," Carrara said. "But Carley said you brought up his name."

"I was mistaken."

"She's worried about you, Kirk. For good reason."

"No."

"Whoever was responsible for blowing hell out of our embassy and killing all those people used your name and your passport number. That's significant. And it's Kurshin's style."

"He's dead, Phil. I killed him."

"I agree with you," Carrara said. "But his body has never been found."

"Stop chasing ghosts."

"The director disagrees. It's why he wants to talk to you."

"I don't think so. Not this time. Tell him—"

"Tell him yourself." Roland Murphy's gruff voice came over the line. "Or have you lost your backbone in the past year?"

"What do you want, General?"

"Your cooperation. If Kurshin has come back to haunt us, you're the man to go after him for more than the obvious reason that he's got a grudge against you."

"Yes? Then why else?"

"Because you're cut out of the same material, McGarvey. I've said it before and I'll say it again: you're a killer, and you're very good. Whatever my personal opinion of you might be, you *are* good."

"Kurshin is dead."

"Are you willing to bet your life on that?"

"How's Lorraine Abbott?" McGarvey asked. The question apparently caught Murphy off-guard, because he hesitated for a moment.

"She's retired," he said finally.

"If Kurshin is back, and he's coming after me as you're apparently suggesting, then he might decide to go after her as well. She was part of his downfall. His and Baranov's."

"She's being watched," Murphy said.

"Would you be willing to bet your life he couldn't get to her if he wanted to?"

"No, which is one of the reasons I called you. We need your help, and you'll do it if there's anything decent left in you. If for no other reason than for Lorraine's sake."

"He's dead, General. I killed him. I watched his body go over the rail into the sea. The people who attacked our embassy were French terrorists."

"He could have swum to shore."

"It was too far."

"My people say that with the currents he could have been swept to shore if he remained afloat for twenty-four to thirty-six hours. Not an impossible task."

"He was wounded. He'd lost too much blood."

"But it's not impossible he survived."

McGarvey said nothing.

"With Kurshin there'd be more than one objective. He'd be after something else besides you."

"There've been no indications that he was active."

"Tom Lord received a death threat twelve days ago."

"It happens all the time."

"Yes, but the letter writers don't usually follow through on their threats. This time they did. Our Paris operation is in shambles. We're going to have to start all over again."

"The Russians are no longer our enemies—isn't that the word these days?"

"Maybe not our enemies, McGarvey, but they're certainly not our friends. Not yet. Perhaps never."

He could feel himself inexorably being drawn into it, as if he were a wood chip caught in a whirlpool. "He has no control officer. Baranov is dead. That we do know for certain."

"General Vasili Didenko," Murphy said. "Baranov's number two man."

Again McGarvey held his silence.

"He's still around. In fact he's been consolidating his power ever since Baranov's fall."

"Gorbachev won't allow it. Didenko is old guard."

"The man is too powerful to topple, from what I'm told. Gorbachev has taken an end run by cutting the KGB's above the line budget. Almost in half, down to a little more than three quarters of a billion dollars. And he's cut the Komitet's supply of foreign-currency operating funds. Didenko's been hamstrung, which suggests he might be trying to pull off something spectacular enough so that even under *perestroika* and *glasnost* he'll be given a free reign."

"The Russian threat is over."

"That's not true," Murphy said. "Nor do you believe it. The same thing was bandied about during the days of détente, remember? The threat has simply changed, that's all. The issues are still the same."

"Yes?"

"Survival, ours versus theirs."

"And mine," McGarvey said. "I'm out of the business. For good. Chase your own bogeymen, General. I'm retired."

"McGarvey—!" the DCI shouted.

McGarvey hung up, waited a couple of seconds for the connection to be broken, and then picked up the receiver and laid it on the table.

There were no bogeymen. All the monsters were dead. The only ones left were those of the imagination.

He laid his head back, cradling the drink on his lap, and tried to shut down his brain as he waited for the dawn. It was time to leave, before his own monsters rose up and blotted out his sanity. But Kurshin had been good, the very best.

It had grown much colder in the early-morning hours. Paris lay under a thin blanket of snow when McGarvey emerged from his apartment. He decided against taking his car. Traffic the night before had been snarled because of the weather, and it would be even worse this morning with everyone trying to get to work.

Like New York, Paris was better suited for delivery drivers and cabbies than for amateur drivers.

He walked up to the rue La Fayette, where he hailed a cab and ordered the driver to take him to the Hotel Roblin on the rue Chauveau-Legarde.

They'd gone barely a half-dozen blocks when McGarvey noticed that the cabbie kept glancing in the rearview mirror.

"Is someone following us?" he asked.

"I want no trouble, monsieur," the cabbie said nervously. "Is it the police?"

"I am the police," McGarvey said. "What sort of car is it?"

"A brown Peugeot, with two men inside. They made a U-turn after I picked you up, and they have been behind us ever since. Look for yourself, monsieur, if you do not believe me."

"I believe you," McGarvey said, without turning around.

"Where is it you wish to go?"

"The Hotel Roblin, of course," McGarvey said. "And if you are asked later, you may say that I did not hesitate in my choice of destination."

The cabbie shrugged.

A couple of minutes later they pulled up in front of the small but fairly expensive hotel just behind the Place de la Madeleine. McGarvey paid the driver and, without looking back, walked to the rue Tronchet, turned left, and headed toward Au Printemps, the huge department store, a few blocks away.

The brown Peugeot passed him in the next block and pulled down a side street. The plates were diplomatic, of the series used by U.S. embassy personnel. Carley had set watchdogs to keep tabs on him, probably at Carrara's suggestion. They were afraid that Kurshin had come back from the grave.

As soon as the car was out of sight, McGarvey turned and hurried back the way he had come, reaching the corner of Chauveau-Legarde just as his watchdogs came down from the boulevard Haussmann. They did not spot him, and they slowed to a crawl as they searched the doorways on either side of the rue Tronchet.

He walked the last half block to the hotel and went inside to the desk. The clerk looked up.

"I'd like to leave a message for Maria Schimmer," McGarvey said. He jotted a brief note on hotel stationery, asking that she telephone him as soon as possible, folded it, and handed it to the clerk. "See that she gets that."

"*Bien sûr, monsieur,*" the clerk said.

Hotels in Europe are reluctant to give information about their guests, especially their room numbers, preferring instead to pass along messages.

McGarvey hesitated a moment as the clerk turned and slipped the folded paper into the slot for room 315. Then he went into the tiny bar and grillroom across the lobby.

The bar wasn't open this early, though the grillroom was still serving breakfast. McGarvey lingered just within the doorway for a few minutes until the desk clerk went into his office. Then he stepped around the corner, hurried across the lobby, and took the stairs up.

Her room was at the end of the corridor, in the back. He listened at the door. The shower was running. It stopped a minute later, and he knocked.

After a few moments Maria Schimmer called "*Oui?*"

"It's Kirk McGarvey."

There was absolute silence from within the room.

"From the embassy," he said. "I'm the one who dug you out."

"What do you want?" Maria asked hesitantly.

"I came for that drink you promised me."

Again there was silence from within the room until the lock snapped and the door opened. Maria Schimmer, wearing a white terry-cloth robe, her hair wrapped in a bath towel, looked up at him, her eyes very large and very dark. He thought she was beautiful.

"You look a hell of a lot better than you did last night," McGarvey said, smiling. He looked at her bandaged hands. "How are they?"

"Sore," she replied. "Are you alone?"

"Yes, and no one sent me, if that's what you're worried about, although there are some people from the embassy who'd like to have a word with you."

"I told those people everything I know," she said, her eyes flashing.

"Reid is dead, you know."

She nodded. "I figured as much." She moved away from the door, and McGarvey stepped inside.

The room was small but well furnished. A window looked down into a courtyard. The bathroom light was on, and the television was playing, but the sound had been turned off. The woman's suitcase lay open on the bed. She was in the middle of packing.

"They want to know what connection you had with him," McGarvey said.

"There was no connection."

McGarvey's right eyebrow rose.

"He was with another man I'd come to see at the Inter-Continental."

"About what?"

"I'd rather not say."

"What were you doing at the embassy?"

"I was going to ask Mr. Reid for his help."

"With what?"

"Did you tell your friends the name of this hotel?" Maria asked.

"Not yet," McGarvey said. "But the Marine on the embassy stairs heard when you gave it to me."

Again her eyes flashed. "Thank you for saving my life, Mr. McGarvey, but I've done nothing wrong."

"Then you shouldn't mind talking with Carleton Reid's people."

"I'm leaving Paris."

McGarvey shook his head. "You don't seem to understand what's going on here, Señorita Schimmer. Someone killed a lot of people, and our embassy is destroyed. At this point you may be a suspect. At the very least they want to know what you were doing there."

"I had nothing to do with it," Maria flared. "I was at the Inter-Continental when it happened, and I have witnesses who can verify it."

"Then you should have no problem," McGarvey said. He went to the phone and picked it up. "This is Three-fifteen. Give me an outside line, please. I wish to make a local call."

"Wait," Maria said.

McGarvey just looked at her. When he had the dial tone he dialed his own number.

"I cannot be delayed here," she said. "I'll answer your questions."

The connection was made and the telephone in his apartment

began to ring. "Hello," he said. "This is McGarvey. Let me talk to the chief of security."

"I went to the hotel to see Horst Höehner. I followed him from Vienna."

"I'll hold," McGarvey said into the telephone. "Simon Wiesenthal's assistant?"

"Yes," Maria said.

"About what?"

"I'm trying to find a ... World War Two Nazi submarine."

McGarvey hung up the telephone, intrigued now. "You asked Höehner to help? It would seem that he would be the last person who'd know anything, or be willing to help."

"He has access to the records in Freiburg. No one else would listen to me."

"What did he say?"

"He also refused."

"So you went to Reid."

She nodded.

"What's your interest in this submarine?"

"My grandfather was the skipper."

"And?"

"They were on a secret mission to ... Argentina when he and his crew and the boat disappeared. I want to find the boat and ... his body."

"What was the mission?"

"I don't know."

She was lying. McGarvey could see it in her eyes. "Do you think they made it into Argentinian waters?"

"It's possible. I want to know for sure."

"What will you do now?" McGarvey asked. He watched her eyes, but there was no reaction.

"I'll go back to Freiburg and try again."

"Alone?"

She nodded.

Coincidence or plan? McGarvey tried to separate his unsettled feelings from what he was hearing now and from what had happened in the past hours. If Kurshin were indeed alive and active, would he have used this one? It was possible.

You cannot begin to understand the depths of another man's hate. It can be used like a tool. Like a finely honed surgeon's scalpel.

"Maybe that won't be necessary," he said.

"I'm not staying ..."

"Maybe I can help. If you want it, that is. I have a friend in Freiburg who would have access to the material you want."

For a moment her eyes lit up, but then the light faded and she became wary. "What do you want, Señor McGarvey?"

"Answers," he said.

"I don't have them."

McGarvey smiled. "You don't have any other options. Besides, you owe me."

BOOK TWO

14

WASHINGTON, D.C.

SNOW BLANKETED THE NATION'S capital and the surrounding
countryside, making driving extremely difficult. Katherine Ray
was late arriving at CIA headquarters, but she had spent longer
at the FBI's Fingerprint Division and then the Walter Reed Army
Medical Center than she thought she would. It was three o'clock
by the time she had logged in at the front desk, had her briefcase
checked, and had gone down to Records Section in the basement.

"Ray, Technical Services," she said. "My boss called."

A clerk checked her credentials and signed her name in the
visitors' log. "You've been here before?" he asked pleasantly.

"Once or twice."

"Then you won't need a baby-sitter."

Katherine shook her head.

"Too bad," the clerk said. He checked a register. "Terminal eighteen. Down the hall to the left. If you need a file runner, hit F-twelve and ENTER. Have you got the proper access codes?"

"Yes, thanks." Katherine went back to her assigned cubicle, took off her coat, opened her briefcase, and entered the system with the primary access word: THUNDER.

The terminal screen bloomed. "Welcome to Records Section of the Central Intelligence Agency. Do you wish to see a menu?"

Katherine, who worked for the agency's Technical Services Division downtown, had been assigned the physical evidence of the Paris embassy bombing case. The team they'd sent to Paris within hours of the blast had begun sending back evidence almost immediately, including samples of human tissue and blood and other body fluids, as well as fingerprints lifted from the debris in and around the office in which the bomb had exploded.

The FBI had identified many of the fingerprints from its government services files, although several sets were flagged as being of special interest to the Agency, and therefore in a closed file.

At Walter Reed, the laboratory technicians had reduced the tissue and fluid samples to their DNA signatures. Three separate individuals had been in the room. Tom Lord and the Marine guard who'd gone in with him were known. But the third was an unknown. A sample of his blood and two clear fingerprints had been found on the doorknob leading from the inner office.

There was no third body, so it was possible, Katherine had reasoned on her way over, that the mystery man was the killer.

The bothersome part was that the FBI had identified the blood and fingerprints as belonging to someone of interest to the Agency. Very possibly they weren't the killer's after all. Possibly Graves had been in the office for some reason, or perhaps one of the communications people who'd come down to the second floor when they'd heard something had happened to Berringer and Vaughan had gone inside for some reason.

Entering the ten-point identification profile for the unknown prints, she started the computer searching through the huge amount of data stored in personnel records for a match.

Next, she entered the DNA standard profile from the blood sample and began searching medical records.

Within ninety seconds the first match had been made between the fingerprints found on Kevin Hewlett's doorknob and personnel files. A name and a date of birth along with a photograph came up on the screen. Katherine's mouth dropped open.

Thirty seconds later the DNA trace provided a second match. The same name and photograph came up on the screen.

James Tilley, chief of the CIA's Technical Services Division, sat alone in the small briefing auditorium. Robert Hettrick and his forensics team people had finished with their afternoon reports and had left a few minutes earlier. The evidence that had been sent over from Paris was laid out on tables next to the speaker's platform. Behind them were three large blackboards covered with notes and diagrams.

The scene reminded Tilley, who held doctorates in biophysics and biochemistry, of his days as a student. He'd spent a good portion of his life in rooms like these, trying to unravel mysteries that sometimes seemed beyond his ken.

Looking more like a construction worker than an academic, Tilley ran Technical Services with a fair but iron hand. "Trouble is," his subordinates sometimes said, "when the boss is so much smarter than everyone else, it's impossible to put anything over on him."

This business had him stumped, however, and he was developing a gut feeling that when the resolution finally came, it would be to nobody's liking. In chemistry or physics there were always facts to rely on that would either support or destroy the prevailing theory. It made no difference which, because there were always new theories. Facts were what science was all about.

In this case, the prevailing theory was that an unknown French terrorist or terrorists had planted the bomb in the embassy. Relations between France and the U.S. were at an all-time low, because despite the dissolution of the Warsaw Pact the U.S. still demanded that NATO be maintained. France disagreed.

Hardly any of the facts supported this theory, and yet everyone was trying to make the facts fit, because the theory was convenient.

He got up and approached the tables. In his mind the most

damning bits of evidence were the pieces of latex face mask found at the scene.

The man who'd posed as Kirk McGarvey had evidently worn a disguise which, for some reason, he had discarded *before* he left the embassy. It wasn't something the average French or French-Algerian terrorist would do.

He picked up the plastic bag that contained the half-dozen bits of latex. There was a message here; he was sure of it. They were being told something by the killer. The man was tempting them to solve the mystery: "I left this for you. I'm telling you plainly that I wore a disguise. That once I'd planted the explosives I no longer needed the mask."

Tilley laid the plastic bag back on the table and shook his head.

"Catch me if you can," the killer was saying.

Sam Vaughan had apparently walked in on him and had been shot in the face with a pistol. Ballistics were certain the bullet had been fired from a Walther PPK, even though it had become badly distorted on impact with the skull.

Another message in the choice of weapon?

The killer had used McGarvey's name and passport number, which meant that either he had access to State Department records, or he'd had some contact with the man. Possibly there in Paris.

Still another message?

His secretary came to the rear door. "General Murphy is on the telephone for you, sir," she called down to him.

Tilley followed her back to his office and picked up the telephone. "Good afternoon, General."

"Anything new from Paris?"

"The team is still sifting, and we're still analyzing what they've already sent back."

"What about the explosives? Any handle on the material yet?"

"Standard C-four. Could have been lifted from any U.S. base in Europe, or purchased on the open market."

The general hesitated, and Tilley filled in the silence for him: "The material wasn't Semtex, the Polish plastique, but that still doesn't rule out an Eastern bloc operation."

"It's not likely they'd use C-four when their own material is so much better," Murphy said.

"Unless they were trying to tell us something," Tilley said.

"Make us believe one thing when in reality another was the truth. Throw us off. Misdirect us."

"What are you saying, Jim?" the DCI asked.

"Nothing more than a gut feeling," Tilley replied. "But our man is telling us too much, more than he should. The choice of weapon he used to defend himself. The facts that he wore a disguise and that he knows Kirk McGarvey."

"Which brings us to the Argentinian woman—Maria Schimmer—who, by the way, has disappeared. Have your people found any physical evidence of what she was doing in the embassy?"

"Nothing directly," Tilley said. "Other than eyewitness accounts, of course."

"She's important, I think, for a lot of reasons." Again Murphy hesitated.

"Something I should know about, General?" Tilley prompted.

"Not yet, except that I would like your people to concentrate at least some of their efforts on picking up her track in the building."

"I'll pass it along, but I think we've taken the lion's share of useful material out of the debris already. The weather and water damage have taken their toll. And State Department people in there digging around for sensitive documents haven't helped. But we'll do what we can."

"That's all I ask," Murphy said. "Keep the lines of communication open, Jim. I want to know the minute you learn anything . . . anything at all, do you understand?"

"Yes, sir," Tilley said.

The CIA had been the target, of course, and Murphy, who had never been known for his delicacy, would be charging full steam ahead. But there'd been something else in his manner, a tone in his voice that wasn't normally there. If Tilley hadn't known better, he would have suspected that the DCI was frightened.

His telephone rang. It was his secretary again. "Richard Shipman is on line two."

"Do I know him?" Tilley asked.

"He's chief of physical security at Langley. Says you'll want to talk to him."

"I'll take it," Tilley said. He punched the button. "Jim Tilley. What can I do for you, Mr. Shipman?"

"I thought you'd want to handle this yourself," Shipman said.

"Handle what?"

"We have one of your people here—Katherine Ray—under detention. Before we proceed any further, perhaps you would like to talk to her. We can't make any sense of it."

"Proceed with what?" Tilley demanded. "Why are you holding her?"

"Sir, she got into Agency computer records and destroyed at least ten complete files before one of the section supervisors got wind of what she was doing and stopped her. This hasn't gone upstairs yet, she asked for you first, but we're talking sabotage."

"I'll be there within the half hour," Tilley said. "Don't do anything with her until then."

"Yes, sir."

The Technical Services Division, which came under the Directorate of Operations, was in some respects the Agency's police force, or at least its investigative arm. They supplied Clandestine Services with the second-story men, the safecrackers, the telephone tappers, the gumshoes.

A good percentage of Technical Services officers came from the FBI or other police forces, and there was a rivalry, sometimes bitter, between them and mainstream intelligence officers.

Because of the snow it took Tilley nearly a full hour to make it across the river and up to Langley. Richard Shipman, a big, solidly-built man—even bigger than Tilley—was waiting in a conference room with Katherine.

"The roads still bad?" Shipman asked.

"That's why it took me so long to get here," Tilley said. "Could I have a few minutes alone with Ms. Ray?"

Shipman, who had been perched on the edge of the table, got to his feet. "Be my guest," he said. "I'll be in my office when you're ready." He glanced toward Katherine. "I hope she wasn't working under orders. Because if she was, there'll be hell to pay." He turned back to Tilley. "Know what I mean, sir?"

"We'll be along in a couple of minutes," Tilley said, and when Shipman was gone he drew up a chair next to Katherine and sat down. "What happened?"

"I'd rather not discuss it, Mr. Tilley," she said. It was clear she was very frightened, but determined, too.

"Sooner or later you'll have to, of course. Shipman said you destroyed some files before you were stopped. It'll only be a matter of time for them to be identified and pieced back together."

She said nothing.

"They'll have your hide. You know that, I suppose. As it is, Shipman is doing us a favor."

Still she held her silence.

Tilley sat back. "Well, let's see if we can put this together anyway. You were working on forensics, so I guess I can call John Wilson to find out exactly what you were working on today . . ."

"Fingerprints and DNA analyses of body fluids and tissue," she said reluctantly.

"I see," Tilley said. "Then you've obviously found a match. Someone here in Agency files. An officer who—" He stopped, sudden understanding dawning on him like a flash. The answer had been under their noses all along.

Katherine read something of that from his eyes, because she stiffened.

"It's McGarvey after all, isn't it," he said gently. Katherine had had a thing for him two years ago when he was in Washington. Although she had tried to keep it to herself, it had been obvious in her work, and word had gotten to Tilley. He had talked to her about it. "He's a dangerous man, which is what appeals to you, but I don't think you should pursue it. Won't do you or him any good." She reminded Tilley of his daughter away at college.

She had taken his advice, or at least he thought she had. But the problem was back, this time in spades.

She nodded. "He's been set up, Mr. Tilley."

"Was there a positive DNA match?"

She nodded again after a hesitation.

"Fingerprints?"

"Yes."

"He shoots a Walther PPK, if I remember correctly," Tilley said. "It was the gun used to kill Sam Vaughan."

"He wouldn't do it, sir. Not . . . him."

"Why not?" Tilley asked. Everything fit, of course. "He certainly had the means and the motive. He came unglued, that's all."

"No."

"I think so."

"No, sir, listen to me, please," Katherine pleaded. "If he would do such a thing, he wouldn't have done it this way. He's too good to leave his fingerprints, or to sign in with the Marines at the front desk. It doesn't make sense."

Tilley patted the back of her hand. "I don't agree with you," he said softly. "It's exactly the way Mr. McGarvey would have done it."

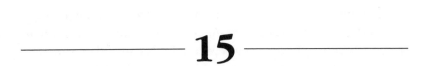

15

EVERYTHING WAS CHANGED in East Berlin. Coming into what had once been the GDR from the west, Kurshin could hardly believe his eyes. He'd not been in Germany in more than two years, and in that time, the wall had disappeared.

Passing through what had once been Checkpoint Charlie, he had to look over his shoulder to make certain he'd seen what he'd seen—or not seen. The wall, the road barriers, the glass-fronted guard hut were all gone.

He turned back and smiled wryly. The cabbie caught his expression in the rearview mirror.

"It's startling, isn't it," the man said. "I used to be an East Berliner. Now I am a German."

It was different here now, as it seemed to be different everywhere else. Unsettling. Out of focus. Even his victory in Paris seemed somehow hollow.

The cabbie left him off at the Leninplatz. He walked three blocks down to the Karl-Marx-Allee, where traffic was heavy in the early-evening hour. A black Mercedes sedan and driver were waiting for him. Without a word he got in the back seat, and they took off, heading through Friedrichshain toward Lichtenberg to the southeast.

There was even more snow here than there had been in Paris, and the roads were poorly plowed. Services had deteriorated because the economy of what had once been West Germany had been so seriously strained in the union, there was no money to give the east for roads. And still most former East Germans preferred to work in the west and live in the east.

He had read about this in the newspapers, and had watched it develop on television, but seeing the effects firsthand was startling. It gave him a sense of just how difficult General Didenko's position had become.

South of Treptow they crossed the Spree River, and skirted the Grösser Muggelsee, traffic this far out in the country nonexistent.

Kurshin held his emotions in check with an iron will as they turned down a familiar dirt road that plunged into the dark woods, the snow-laden branches of the trees nearly meeting over the narrow track. He'd been here before, under similar circumstances. But that time, however, he'd come at Baranov's bidding. He'd not been a man to be trifled with. He'd been a power in the Soviet secret intelligence services since the early fifties. An unstoppable power, an unmovable force ... until McGarvey.

To this day Kurshin could hardly believe it. Yet he had gone up against the man three times himself, and had very nearly lost his life. It rankled deeply.

They were stopped by the general's people at the gate about two miles from the main highway. The rear door was yanked open, and Kurshin got out. He was quickly and efficiently frisked by one of the guards, while the other two stood off, holding their AK-74 assault rifles trained on him. He was relieved of his pistol and his overnight bag, as well as a small penknife he carried.

One of them radioed up to the main house with a walkie-talkie, and another got in the car with Kurshin and rode the rest of the way up the hill. They pulled up in front of the big house, which in the old days had been a Nazi general's country retreat, and until two years ago had belonged to Baranov.

At least two other armed guards stood at the edge of the woods, and one appeared in an upstairs window. General Didenko had been Baranov's closest aide, and he knew how his boss had finally fallen. It had been arrogance that had killed him, and Didenko was taking no chances of his own.

Kurshin was escorted onto the porch and inside the entry hall. The guard who'd come up with him took his coat.

"Up here, Arkasha," General Didenko said from the head of the stairs. He had the same flair for the dramatic as Baranov had had.

Kurshin went up, and at the top Didenko stepped back, his dark complexion even darker in the shadows. His hair was combed back and had a sheen of oil. He was not one of the modern Russians who strove to look Western, something even Baranov had managed when the need arose. Didenko was definitely from the old school. "A Chekist," he was fond of calling himself.

This evening he wore an open-collar tunic, rough workmen's trousers, and boots that were still wet with snow.

He motioned for Kurshin to precede him down the corridor to the study at the back of the house. A fire was burning in the fireplace, giving the room a cozy, comforting atmosphere.

"I won't keep you long," Didenko said, coming in and drawing but not completely closing the door.

"It's not such a difficult trip these days."

"It no longer matters." Didenko leaned against the edge of his desk. He did not offer Kurshin a chair. "Now we have their attention, Arkasha."

"Paris was not a complete success."

"I talked with Stepan Bokarev. Under the circumstances your action was effective enough. The Paris station is in ruins. It will be years before they recover, and with a little help from our French friends, they might never completely restore their operations."

"Then we should hit Rome next. After that Bonn, Lisbon, Athens. The letters are written."

"Yes, I know," Didenko said with a cold look. "It was a nice touch on your part. Unnecessary, but nice."

"Which city?"

"Plans have changed. We are finished in Europe for the moment."

"Then you are ready to go ahead with your main objectives in Washington?"

"Not quite, Arkasha. First I have another assignment for you. One easily as important as Paris, perhaps more so." Didenko picked up an eight-by-ten photograph from his desk and handed it to Kurshin. It was a picture of a dark-haired man in a trench coat coming out of what appeared to be an office building, possibly in the States. Kurshin did not recognize him, though he looked American.

"His name is Richard Abbas," Didenko said. "Currently chief of station for CIA operations in Tehrān."

Kurshin looked up, confused, his stomach knotting.

"I want you to go to Iran and kill this man as soon as possible. Within the next thirty-six to forty-eight hours."

"What about Europe, your plans to draw off as much talent from Langley as possible, leaving them shorthanded and ripe for penetration . . . ?" Kurshin stopped abruptly, understanding suddenly that he'd been lied to from the beginning. That had never been Didenko's plan.

"You need not know everything," Didenko said. He slipped his right hand into his trouser pocket. Kurshin could see the tenseness in the man's eyes. He was expecting trouble.

Kurshin again willed himself to remain outwardly calm, though inside he was seething. "I'm not to know your final objective?"

"Not yet," Didenko said flatly. "Nor will you need the letters you wrote on Kirk McGarvey's typewriter. Nor will you need the rest of the frozen blood samples you managed to come up with from the American Hospital, or your new set of his fingerprints or his hair samples."

Kurshin very nearly lost control. A red haze seemed to rise up and blot out his vision. Again he could feel the cold water rising up over his head. He could feel McGarvey's bullets slamming into his body. The pain. The humiliation. The frustration. They were almost more than he could bear.

"You may think you have a vendetta against this man," Didenko continued, unaware of exactly how close to death he was. "That's counterproductive, Arkasha. Believe me. I want you to leave Mr. McGarvey to his own people. You have done your damage. You will get your revenge in the end. Think—what could be worse than death for a man such as McGarvey? Imprisonment, of course. For him to lose his precious freedom."

By a tremendous force of will Kurshin let his shoulders sag, as if he were a man defeated. He looked away. The general had lied to him. Tehrān had been the direction of this operation from the beginning. Paris was a diversion, but it was the *only* diversion.

"You're right, Comrade General," Kurshin mumbled.

"I understand how you feel, Arkasha. Believe me, I do," Didenko said smoothly. "I'll promise you this: if for any reason McGarvey is not killed or jailed by his own people, you may go after him once you are finished in Tehrān. We are keeping an eye on him."

McGarvey's eyes bored into Kurshin's skull. Kurshin looked up and smiled for the general. "Thank you."

Didenko returned the smile. "You fly to Baghdad tonight from Schönefeld Airport. You'll be met and your transportation across the border arranged as soon as you arrive."

"Yes."

At the door, Kurshin hesitated then turned back, willing a perfectly neutral, even humble expression to his face. "Where is he at this moment?" he asked. "Have his people picked him up yet? Is he still in Paris?"

"Why, no," Didenko said. "As a matter of fact the man is in Freiburg in the Black Forest at this very moment. With a young woman ... Argentinian, I believe. For what reason I couldn't tell you, except that they're apparently poking around old Nazi records." Didenko's eyes narrowed. "You have a flight to catch, Arkasha. It would be unfortunate if you were to forget our agreement."

"Oh, I won't, Comrade General. Believe me in this. I will not forget."

It was about power, Kurshin decided, calming down on the way back into the city. General Didenko had planned all along to tell him that McGarvey was in Germany so that he could exhibit his power over his subordinate.

But he'd learned something else: Didenko was having him followed, and meant to have him killed if he did not comply. Tehrān had to be vitally important to his plans, whatever they were.

In the darkness of the back seat of the Mercedes, Kurshin took out his gun and by feel investigated whether it had been tampered with while it was out of his possession. As far as he could tell it had not been.

They were not far from Schönefeld Airport. Kurshin could see the airport's rotating beacon in the distance, perhaps five or six miles away. But he could also see sparks, like fireflies glittering in his head. The muscles in his legs were twitching as if he were running ... or treading water.

He turned and looked out the back window. In the distance behind them was a pair of headlights. There was no other traffic.

"Slow down," he told the driver.

"What are you talking about? I am taking you to the airport," the man said.

Kurshin brought his pistol over the back of the seat and laid the muzzle against the base of the man's skull. "I want you to pull over and park."

At first the driver did not respond. Kurshin pulled the hammer back.

"Fuck your mother, I'll stop," the driver snarled, jabbing hard on the brakes.

"Easy," Kurshin warned. "Wait till I tell you." He glanced out the rear window. The headlights were much closer already.

They came to a track that led off to the right, probably toward a farm. It looked as if it had been plowed recently. "Pull in here."

The driver complied, the big car skidding slightly as they made the turn and came to a halt a few yards off the highway.

The moment the engine was off, Kurshin shot the man in the back of the head at point-blank range, the driver's body slamming forward with a violent lurch.

Kurshin got out of the car, and holding the pistol out of sight behind his right leg, he walked back up to the highway.

The other car had pulled up about ten yards away. A man stuck his head out the window on the passenger side. "What is it?" he shouted in Russian, and Kurshin smiled. He was one of Didenko's people.

"It's my driver. Something's the matter with him. I think he might have had a heart attack."

After a moment, the man in the car shouted, "That's impossible."

"Well, I don't know," Kurshin replied. "But I'll be damned if I'm just going to stand around here like this in the middle of the night. I have a plane to catch. How about a ride, comrade?"

There was another hesitation, but then the car moved closer. Kurshin stepped aside as it pulled up, idling. With the headlights no longer in his eyes, he could see that there were only two men in it.

"Now, what's this all about?" the one on the passenger side asked as he started to open his door.

Kurshin shot him in the face. Before the driver could react, he shot him in the throat and then in the forehead.

The car lurched forward a couple of yards, coming to rest in a ditch.

Holstering his weapon, Kurshin walked back to his car, pulled the driver out into the snowbank, cleaned the blood from the dashboard and windshield, and headed back into Berlin, away from the airport.

Tehrān might be important to the general, but McGarvey had somehow gotten out of Paris. He was still at large, traveling in an unexpected direction. Kurshin's original plan had been to lure McGarvey to various European capitals, killing the CIA chief of station in each the moment McGarvey had shown up.

He'd wanted to place McGarvey in a cross fire between his own people, the local authorities, and Kurshin's own gunsights. In the end McGarvey's death would be celebrated in his own home. He would end up despised.

But already things had changed, and Kurshin found he was having trouble controlling himself. Only one thing was certain in his mind now: no matter what happened, he was going to kill McGarvey. No force on earth could stop him.

16

"YOU BELIEVE I HAD something to do with Paris, don't you," Maria Schimmer said.

She and McGarvey stood across the street from Freiburg's famous Rathaus waiting for the traffic to clear so they could cross. For the past twenty-four hours McGarvey had been getting the feeling that they were being watched. This morning it had come on strong from the moment they'd left their hotel on Rotteckring.

He'd not told Maria, nor had he made any effort to mask their movements or elude whoever it was behind them.

At first he thought it might be the federal police, but they would have been more open about their approach. And so far he and Maria had done nothing wrong there, though it was possible his name and photograph had been flagged at the border crossing. Former CIA assassins tended to make people nervous, especially when they were on the move.

But he did not think it was the Germans, nor did he think it was his own people. This left either the Russians—by now he was convinced that the Russians had been behind the embassy explosion—or someone unknown following Maria for some reason.

They'd been together now for the better part of two days and two nights, and still he had no real idea who she was, or what she was all about. She was reserved without being aloof. She was quiet without being moody. And she seemed open, answering every question he put to her, but she was lying about almost everything. He could see that in her eyes, and at the corners of her mouth.

"I wouldn't be here otherwise," he said to her.

Her nostrils flared, but she held herself in check. "Is that why you keep looking at reflections in storefront windows?"

"Just a precaution," he said. The traffic light changed. He took her arm and they hurried across the street.

"Are you a spy, then?" she asked on the other side. "I thought you might be from the first. Everyone at the embassy seemed frightened of you. I've seen that look before."

"I'll bet you have."

"The third floor, that's where the CIA has its little nest of secrets. Reid was one of them too, wasn't he?"

They were to meet McGarvey's old friend from Switzerland at the Hansahaus Bierstube at noon, but McGarvey walked past the place. Maria knew enough by now not to make any outward sign that their plans had changed.

"This is serious, then," she said, lowering her voice as they continued to walk.

"Someone is back there," McGarvey said. "Anybody coming after you that you know about?"

She shook her head. "You?"

"Plenty," McGarvey said. "But whoever it is, they're damned good. Better than yesterday."

"How do you know we're being followed? For sure. Can you see them?"

"Him," McGarvey said, catching another flash of the man in

the dark homburg just rounding the corner behind them. It was the third time he'd caught a glimpse, but only a glimpse. Whoever was back there was very good.

"Is he behind us now?"

"He has been since the hotel."

"Who is it?"

"I don't know," McGarvey said, looking at her. Was she expecting Kurshin, or was he on a wild-goose chase after all, coming here with her like this? "Nobody's after you because of this submarine of yours?"

"There'd be no reason for it, unless they were Israelis still with a grudge," she said.

"Could be," he replied, knowing she was lying. He steered her across the street and down a narrow alleyway.

They came out on a broad square dominated by a tall fountain that was shut down for the winter. Dozens of quaint small shops faced the center. There were a lot of pedestrians, but apparently no cars or trucks were allowed. Across the square they spotted a taxi rank, and they hurried over to it, climbing into the first cab in the row.

"To Denzlingen, please," McGarvey told the driver. It was a separate village to the north, but barely five miles away.

McGarvey looked back as they pulled away, hoping to catch a last glimpse of the man in the homburg, but he did not appear.

"What about your friend we were supposed to meet at the Hansahaus?" Maria asked. "He may have found something for us."

"Denzlingen is his home. We'll wait there for him," McGarvey said.

They rode in silence for a few minutes. Freiburg was a pretty city with a large historic cathedral and a small but good university. But it had never been important, other than as the capital of the Black Forest region, until well after the war, when German naval records had been deposited there after they'd been microfilmed in Washington.

"I was serious back there," Maria said, breaking the silence.

"About Paris?" McGarvey asked.

She nodded. "You've not told me what you were doing in the embassy that night, or why you dropped everything to come here with me. What else am I supposed to think, except that I'm a suspect?"

"You are, and you will be until you stop lying to me," McGarvey said. "But then maybe Dr. Hesse will have found out something, and at least a part of the mystery will be cleared up."

"What mystery?" she flared. "What are you talking about?"

"What you're really after."

"I want to know about my grandfather—"

"Bullshit," McGarvey snapped. The driver glanced at him in the rearview mirror.

"Then what?"

Perhaps he was getting jumpy. His feelings about her and about the situation were confused at best. And a picture of Kurshin kept forming in his mind's eye. When the man had been directed by Baranov, he'd been nothing short of brilliant. But Kurshin was dead, and so was his puppet master.

Perhaps he was grabbing at straws. Paris had been over for him, and by his own admission he'd been looking for an excuse to leave.

But a lot of lives had been lost. CIA operations in Europe would not be the same for years.

His name and passport number had been used by the terrorist to gain entry to the embassy. That had to have been more than mere coincidence.

There were connections within connections. Plots within plots.

Something, he kept telling himself. There was something just beyond his understanding that would suddenly become very clear to him if only he continued with Maria. Somehow, she was the key.

"Then what am I after, if not that?" Maria repeated.

"I don't know," McGarvey said slowly.

For some reason that answer, or lack of answer, seemed particularly disturbing to her.

Denzlingen was a charming little village of less than one thousand people. They stopped at a *Gasthaus* on the village square and McGarvey telephoned the Hansahaus in Freiburg, leaving a message for Dr. Hesse that they had been unavoidably detained, and that they would like to meet at two that afternoon at the doctor's house. It would give Hesse time to finish his own lunch and return home.

He and Maria had lunch, then spent an hour walking around the village, looking into some of the tiny shops, and at Maria's insistence stopping for a few minutes at the church. At first he thought the gesture had been for his benefit, but she knelt and prayed, apparently sincerely.

At two in the afternoon they walked the half-dozen blocks to the doctor's stone house on the edge of the village. It was just across a narrow stream from a dark woods. An old Volkswagen was parked in front.

Dr. Hesse's aging housekeeper admitted them, showing them into the study. "I shall fetch the professor," the old woman said, and she shuffled off.

Dr. Heinrich Hesse, who claimed to be a distant cousin of the poet and novelist Hermann Hesse, had studied Swiss history in Lausanne for a number of years. He had been a frequent customer of the bookstore McGarvey had owned what seemed like two lifetimes ago, and they had developed a mutual respect for each other's scholarship.

Dr. Hesse was now professor emeritus of European history at the university, and had complete access to all sections of the Naval Records Depot. He was a tiny, wizened old man who walked with a hunch, and who seemed to have trouble breathing. He still smoked several packs of strong cigarettes each day.

The study was at the back of the house and looked out over what would be a pleasant garden in the summer. Books, maps, periodicals, and manuscripts were stacked everywhere in the cramped, musty-smelling room.

"I missed you for lunch," Dr. Hesse said behind them, shambling into the study.

McGarvey turned and they shook hands. The professor shook hands with Maria as well, a twinkle in his eyes.

"I had with me an old friend who wanted to meet you, Fräulein Schimmer. He spent some years in Buenos Aires and thinks he may have known you when you were a little girl. Horst Oestmann?"

Maria shrugged. "I'm sorry, sir, the name means nothing."

"No matter," Dr. Hesse said. "But on the other business there may be better news for you."

"You found my grandfather's submarine?" Maria asked excitedly.

Dr. Hesse held up a cautionary hand. "There seems to be a

mystery of sorts still attached to the boat. Nothing in the record is terribly clear at this point, though my intention is to continue with my research."

Maria and McGarvey exchanged glances. He could read nothing in her eyes except excitement.

"But you have found something?" McGarvey asked.

"Oh, heavens, yes," Dr. Hesse exclaimed. "The boat is there, all right, off Argentina, or at least it was there. But what it was doing that far west and at that time—the very end of the war—has been the cause of a dozen deaths."

"It was war," Maria said.

"Begging your pardon, but the most recent death connected with that boat occurred in 1978. The war was over."

17

"WHAT DEATHS?" MCGARVEY ASKED. "How do you know they were connected with the submarine?"

"That's simple," Dr. Hesse explained. "The first three men to die, and the last, had all served on a board of inquiry convened by the West German Secret Service—the BND—four years after the war, to find out what happened to U2798." He looked at Maria. "That was your grandfather's boat."

"But there were hundreds of submarines lost," Maria said. "Why a board of inquiry *after* the war to find out what happened to that particular boat?"

"It was still missing without a trace," Dr. Hesse replied. "Or at least that's part of the explanation. Remember, besides your grandfather there was a crew of nearly forty men and officers.

Good German boys who were lost. There were many parents who demanded to know their fate."

"What type of boat was she?" McGarvey asked.

"One of the last to be built. A Walther twenty-six. Not many ever saw service—they were designed and commissioned too late in the war—but apparently she was quite a technological marvel in her day."

McGarvey could hear a touch of pride in the old man's voice. "What was her normal complement?"

Dr. Hesse looked at him with approval. "She was supposed to carry a crew of fifty-seven men and officers, which meant she was terribly shorthanded when she left the yard at Bremen, or if not, then certainly when she started across the Atlantic."

"But . . . ?" McGarvey prompted. There was more. There was always more.

"She went to sea with thirty-nine men and officers . . . and one passenger," Dr. Hesse said. He went to his desk and pulled out several fat files from a bulging briefcase. "These are copies of some of the original documents. I thought you might want to study them."

"The passenger," McGarvey wanted to know.

Dr. Hesse flipped open a file folder. "Major Walther Roebling."

"Army?" Maria asked. She was shivering.

"RSHA," Dr. Hesse corrected. "The Nazi secret service. He was a close personal friend of Walther Schellenberg, who headed the foreign espionage section of the service."

"What was he doing aboard?" McGarvey asked.

"Therein lies the mystery. Presumably he was carrying either a message or some unknown cargo to Argentina. Whatever it was seemed to be of great interest to the BND."

"A lot of SS took refuge in Argentina," McGarvey said.

"Yes."

"And the BND weren't the only ones interested in whatever it was Major Roebling was up to in 1945," McGarvey said. "Interested enough to kill. Any hint of what he was carrying, or who it was intended for?"

"None, other than the obvious fact that it was of vital importance."

"The killings started when?"

"In 1949."

"Were they investigated by the BND?"

"The first few were. After that, the file was turned over to the new West German Federal Police Bureau, who were supposed to message the BND in Munich. They did so until 1978 when the investigation was abruptly closed with no explanation."

"Wait a moment," Maria interrupted. "I'm a little confused about something. The records you've been researching, Herr Professor, deal with the military during the war."

Dr. Hesse nodded.

"How did you come to learn about the BND's involvement and these murders which all occurred well *after* the war?"

Dr. Hesse smiled. "Ah, Fräulein, even old men—or perhaps *especially* old men—have friends in many high places."

Maria and McGarvey again exchanged glances. This time he knew what she was thinking.

"Then you're in danger yourself," McGarvey said.

"I don't think so. It's been nearly thirteen years since the last killing. Whoever was interested is more than likely dead and buried by now. The war was a very long time ago. What vital secrets from 1945 could be so terribly important now?"

"There's another possibility," McGarvey said.

"Yes?"

"Maybe whoever was looking for the boat and her secrets finally found them in 1978, so they no longer had to kill."

Maria sat back, closing her eyes. "Maybe the killings were a cover-up. Maybe they knew all along where the cargo was but wanted it left where it was. Maybe they were making sure that no one betrayed them."

McGarvey looked at her. "Cargo?"

She opened her eyes and blinked. "Cargo—message—whatever it was Roebling brought with him."

McGarvey continued to stare at her for a moment or two.

"If that's the case," Dr. Hesse said, "the mysterious something probably never reached Argentina. Or at least it never got ashore. If it had, there would have been no need for the killings."

"Unless they found it in 1978."

Maria shook her head. "No," she said excitedly. "I would have heard about it."

"You've evidently done your homework, Fräulein Schimmer," Dr. Hesse said.

"Argentina is a small enough country that if such a discovery were to be made—a World War Two German submarine in Argentinian waters—it would be known."

"Not necessarily," Dr. Hesse began, but McGarvey cut in.

"She's right. The government, especially in the late seventies, was very corrupt. Secrets could not be kept for long. Something would have come out, especially for someone who had the ear of a general, or a minister."

"I have friends," Maria said defiantly.

McGarvey was certain she had, but he said nothing on that subject, turning instead back to Dr. Hesse. "What did your BND friends say about the murder investigation?"

"It's a closed file. They could offer no help."

"Still?" Maria asked.

"Not so unusual, from what I'm told," Dr. Hesse said. "All governments have areas in which they are particularly sensitive. It is no different with us."

"Which could mean what in this case?" Maria persisted. "Maybe something to do with Jews?"

Dr. Hesse bridled. "I don't know." He shifted his gaze pointedly to McGarvey. "But I would like to ask why you are interested in this particular business. What has brought you out of hiding in Lausanne?"

McGarvey was stopped cold. In the several years he'd known the professor in Lausanne, never once had the subject of his past come up. There had never been a discussion of exactly what he was doing in Lausanne. Germans were too polite to ask such questions. There had been no hint that McGarvey had indeed been hiding from his past, from the legion of demons that rode like a family tree on the shoulders of every professional assassin.

"I ran into Fräulein Schimmer in Paris. She asked for my help."

"With a research project?"

"Yes," Maria said.

"One that you had unsuccessfully pursued not only here, less than ten days ago, but in Vienna as well?" he asked, turning to her.

"How did you know?" Maria asked.

"Where did you meet in Paris?" Dr. Hesse asked. "Let me guess: at the American Embassy, Tuesday night."

Maria's complexion paled.

"Are we on the Interpol wire?" McGarvey asked.

Dr. Hesse nodded. "I'm surprised you got across the border without being arrested."

"I didn't do anything," Maria said with sudden passion.

"Neither of you has been accused of anything," Dr. Hesse said. "You are merely being sought for questioning in connection with the incident." The old man shook his head. "So much violence," he said softly. "Will it ever end?"

"Not in our lifetimes," McGarvey replied seriously. "But perhaps the wholesale slaughter has stopped, at least in Eastern Europe."

"Yes," Dr. Hesse said thoughtfully. "Maybe it is less onerous to suffer the killings one at a time."

The reference to McGarvey's past was unmistakable. "Rather than thousands or millions at a time."

"What will you do now?" the professor asked, ignoring McGarvey's remark. "Return to Paris? I would think that would be for the best. Afterward, if you still wish to pursue this business ..." He let the sentence hang.

"It may have been the Russians," McGarvey said.

Dr. Hesse chuckled. "You Americans are all the same. You have Russians under every bed, in every dark closet. It was the same with us. But now we have grown up."

"French terrorists?"

Dr. Hesse nodded. "Possibly. But return to Paris, both of you. You cannot pursue an investigation of this nature as fugitives."

McGarvey glanced at the heavy file folders the professor had taken from his briefcase. "Those are not copies. They are the original documents."

Dr. Hesse's gaze followed McGarvey's. When he looked up, there was a deeply thoughtful expression on his face. "Does the terrible tragedy in Paris have anything to do with this investigation?"

McGarvey was startled.

"Have the killings begun again?" Dr. Hesse asked.

"No," Maria said forcefully. "My first contact with the Americans came only minutes before the embassy was attacked, and the meeting didn't take place there, nor was it planned."

"Where, then?" Dr. Hesse asked.

Maria looked at McGarvey. She seemed frightened, as if she were seeing her last door closing.

"At the Hotel Inter-Continental."

"Who was this American you met?"

"Carleton Reid. He was from the embassy."

"Was he alone?"

"No," Maria said. "I had followed Horst Höehner there from Vienna. He and a Frenchman, Gavalet I think was his name, were having dinner with Reid."

"Reid is dead," McGarvey said.

"You asked Mr. Reid for his assistance, perhaps with the records people here?"

"We were just coming out of the hotel when the explosion occurred. I offered to help him if he would help me. But he said no."

"What were you doing at the embassy?" Hesse asked McGarvey.

"I was having dinner nearby when I heard the explosion."

"He dug me out of the rubble. Saved my life," Maria said, but no one was listening to her.

"Why the questions, Herr Professor?" McGarvey asked.

"I received a telephone call from Maurice Gavalet in Paris. He is a policeman. He asked about Fräulein Schimmer."

"Then you know that I am telling you the truth," Maria said.

"As far as it goes, Fräulein," Dr. Hesse said sternly. "The question is, what are you really seeking? Your grandfather's grave, as you profess? Or the mysterious cargo Major Roebling was bringing to your homeland?"

"I have no interest in any cargo. I merely want to know about my grandfather."

"That is touching, Fräulein Schimmer ... or should I say Fräulein Reiker?"

"If you know that much, then you know why."

"To atone for your father's sins by proving that your grandfather was an honorable man?" Dr. Hesse shook his head. "We Germans have been trying unsuccessfully to do that since 1945. I think it is time to put away such thoughts and move forward. You carry no guilt for your father's sins."

"Will you help me, or will I have to go elsewhere?" Maria asked evenly.

"Will you return to Paris first?"

"No."

"No matter what happens here, you mean to pursue this?"

"Yes."

Dr. Hesse looked at McGarvey. "What about you? Do you see Russians under Argentinian beds as well? Will you return to Paris?"

"Eventually."

"But not just now."

"No," McGarvey said.

"I no longer need his help," Maria told the professor.

"Ah, but Fräulein, don't you see that it is because of Herr McGarvey that I agreed to talk to you, to search out the naval records," Dr. Hesse said. He shrugged. "Without him ..."

The professor was playing at some game that McGarvey couldn't yet see. The old man was dissembling for a definite purpose.

"What do you want, Herr Professor?" McGarvey asked.

"To complete the record," Dr. Hesse said. He sounded sincere. "Those German boys, Fräulein Schimmer's grandfather included, have been waiting for their final service since 1945, nearly fifty years."

"Where is the boat?" Maria asked.

Dr. Hesse turned to her. "I don't know," he said.

"But you have the naval records. You said—"

"Look at them if you wish. In fact you must before you leave. The submarine U2798 departed the yard at Bremen at one o'-clock in the morning on February fourth. Her destination was given simply as 'patrol operations in the Atlantic.'"

"You said her ordered destination was Argentina," McGarvey said.

"The Kriegsmarine simply ordered her into operations in the Atlantic under the discretion of what was called the 2/SKL ... the second department or division of the SeeKriegsLeitung, which was the Naval War Command. More specifically, the U-Boat Intelligence Service."

"What did those records reveal?" McGarvey asked.

"Another bit of legerdemain that wasn't made clear until the board of inquiry convened after the war. It seems she was turned over to the RSHA at Major Roebling's convenience for operations in the South Atlantic."

"Argentina?" MaGarvey prompted.

Dr. Hesse took a bound volume of typescript out of his brief-case. The massive book had to contain at least a thousand pages.

"These are transcripts of interviews with RSHA officers in Nuremberg just after the war, and then at various prisons in 1949."

"Was all of this prior to the first murder?" McGarvey asked.

"Yes," Dr. Hesse said. "As a matter of fact the chief interviewers there, Horst Holtz and Motti Mueller, both members of the board of inquiry, were the first to die. One in his bed at home, the other in an auto accident."

"They later turned out to be homicides?"

"Suspected homicides," Dr. Hesse said. He opened the bound volume at a marked spot. "This is from an interview with RSHA Oberleutnant Rainer Mossberg, on March 17, 1949, at Prison Camp Twenty-seven A, outside of Bonn."

Q.: You are saying that U2798's destination was somewhere in Argentina. South America.

A.: Yes, but that was Roebling's baby. We had nothing to do with it. It was an arm's-length operation, if you know what I mean.

Q.: Roebling was carrying something with him?

A.: That guy (*pause*) was always carrying something with him. You know, a regular fucking opportunist. He had all the answers. Knew Schellenberg. They were like this (*prisoner uses obscene gesture*), if you know what I mean.

Q.: What was it he was carrying, exactly? Major Roebling, that is.

A.: I don't know. I wasn't in that circle.

Q.: Was this cargo important?

A.: I don't know (*pause*) I don't know. Given the time, the circumstances, probably very important. They were all crazy down there, you know. They were going to carry on from the National Redoubt in the mountains. And from Argentina. A lot of the (*pause*) inner circle got down there before it was impossible to leave. Hell, I should have gone myself. At least to Switzerland.

Q.: But you don't know what he, Major Walther Roebling, might have been carrying with him aboard U2798.

A.: No.

Q.: Or where in Argentina they were bound.

A.: Well, that's a big (*pause*) mystery.

Q.: What do you mean, mystery? What kind of a mystery. Do you know?

A.: I know nothing for sure. But there were rumors, you know. In those days (*pause*) always rumors. May I have a cigarette?

Q.: What rumors, specifically?

A.: Well, there was supposed to be some kind of trouble. Someone was waiting for them or something. So their primary destination may have been changed. Maybe even their secondary destination was changed too.

Q.: These destinations were in Argentina?

A.: Yes, of course.

Q.: Where?

A.: Well, that's just it, you see. I don't know. There's no one around now who knows.

Q.: What did you mean, then, by saying primary and secondary destinations?

A.: Just that I'd had heard that alpha and beta were questionable, which left only gamma, delta, and epsilon. Nothing more. May I have the pack?

"That was the end of the interview," Dr. Hesse said. "Within the month both Holtz and Mueller were dead."

"I don't understand," Maria said.

"What about Mossberg?" McGarvey asked, his mind racing well ahead.

"He escaped from prison at the end of June of that year. And as far as the records go, he is still at large."

McGarvey got up and went to the window. He looked out over the snow-covered garden as he tried to think this out. "How old was Mossberg at the time of the interview?"

"They were promoting them young at the end," Dr. Hesse said. "He was just twenty-one."

"He'd be sixty-three today."

"Practically a boy ..." Dr. Hesse mused.

McGarvey turned. "He knew where the submarine went, and so do I. Or at least I think I can narrow its location to a searchable area."

"How ..." Maria started to ask, but then changed her mind.

"Mossberg never got to her," McGarvey said.

"Was he behind the killings?" Dr. Hesse asked.

"Probably. And he might be dead himself now. The murders stopped in 1978, and no trace of the sub has turned up."

"Where is it?" Maria asked, a deep burning glow in her eyes.

"That's what I intend finding out," McGarvey said.

"No ..."

"You and I, Fräulein Schimmer, are going to find it together."

*   *   *

It was very late when Dr. Hesse heard his housekeeper cry out once, the sound distant and muffled. He lay awake in the dark for several minutes listening for the cry to be repeated, but the house was silent.

It had probably been a nightmare, he told himself. In the morning he would chide her about it.

In the meantime there was Kirk McGarvey and the extraordinary young woman he'd brought with him. Something would have to be done about that situation as soon as possible. In the morning he would have to make his call, an action that had not been necessary for a number of years. This time, however, something might come of it.

There was a noise in the corridor and Dr. Hesse started to sit up, but his bedroom door was thrown open and a strong light shone in his eyes, obliterating his night vision and blinding him.

"What is it?" he cried out.

"You are in no danger, Herr Professor, if you cooperate with me," a man told him in English. The voice was cultured, possibly British educated, but there was another accent there too. Well hidden.

"What do you want with me?"

"A few moments of your time. I wish to speak to you about Mr. Kirk McGarvey."

And then Dr. Hesse had it. The hidden accent was Russian. He knew now that he was going to die.

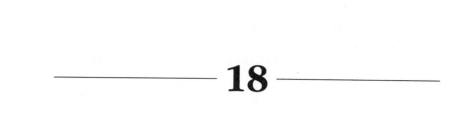

18

THE GEORGETOWN HOME OF Secretary of Defense Donald Hamilton was lavish even by Washington standards. So were his parties, held every Saturday night in season. Half of Washington, it seemed, was there.

"Here comes your boss," Dominique Carrara told her husband.

Phil Carrara looked over his shoulder as Lawrence Danielle took a drink from a passing waiter and joined them. He didn't look happy.

"I didn't think you came to these kinds of soirées, Larry," Carrara said.

"I don't, as a rule," the deputy director growled. He turned to Carrara's wife. "You're looking particularly radiant this evening, Dominique."

"Thanks. I think it's time to powder my nose," she said, smiling.

"Good idea," Danielle agreed, returning her smile. "I won't keep him long."

"Five minutes?"

"Make it ten."

"Sure thing," Dominique pecked her husband on the cheek and left.

Danielle looked around to make certain that no one was within earshot. "I take it you haven't seen the amended overnights from Europe."

"I usually check them around midnight," Carrara said, a sinking feeling in his stomach. "What's happened that I should know about?"

"It's McGarvey. Phil, the man has definitely gone over. I don't think there can be any question of it now. He's got to be brought in ... one way or the other."

Carrara shook his head. "We haven't established a firm age on those blood samples found in Hewlett's office. I gave you that report. And the fingerprints are next to meaningless."

"I might have agreed with you, except that McGarvey has disappeared."

"I know that."

"Carley Webb got into his apartment and looked around."

"Whose idea was that?" Carrara asked dangerously. The chain of command, as far as he was concerned, worked both ways.

"Take it easy," Danielle cautioned. "I'm told that she did it on her own initiative."

"Included in the amended report?"

"Yes," Danielle said. "I happened to be in the comms center this evening when it came in." He looked around again to make certain no one was listening.

"I'll take Dominique home and get out to Operations."

"Good idea. What she found in his apartment clinches it as far as I'm concerned."

"What was that?"

"He's had C-four plastique. She found a piece of wrapping material that tested positive. No doubts about that. Nor is there any doubt about his typewriter. Technical Services has positively identified the machine as the one used to write the death threat letter to Tom Lord."

What the deputy director was saying was extraordinary, and made even more so because it was out of place and character for Danielle to become personally involved in the bits and pieces of an ongoing investigation. All of that belonged in Carrara's purview.

"Could have been planted," Carrara said, his thoughts racing ahead to a dozen different possibilities.

"In McGarvey's apartment?" Danielle asked. "I give the man more credit than that. He wouldn't leave himself so wide open."

"He might not have been expecting it, Larry. But I agree with you: I give him more credit too. Enough credit to doubt that he would leave such incriminating evidence for anyone to find."

"Ms. Webb isn't just anybody. And the man has disappeared. I checked the Interpol overnights as well. No trace of him yet. Or of the Argentinian woman, I might add."

"What does the general say?" Carrara asked, still thinking ahead. He missed the odd, angry expression that briefly crossed Danielle's face.

"He agrees with me wholeheartedly. McGarvey must be brought in at all costs."

"We don't want to get Interpol involved," Carrara said.

"I agree."

"This is our problem. He was our man, and he's done some great things for the Agency and for his country. I mean to give him the respect and consideration all those loyalties demand."

"Bring him in, Phil, before he does more damage."

"Assuming he's done any in the first place."

"Just bring him in," Danielle said. He turned on his heel and walked off.

In a small, dingy apartment on Trinidad Avenue in Washington's northeast district, Nikolai Morozov yanked off the tape holding the subminiature wire recorder to his chest. The pain was sharper this way, but it didn't last as long as when he peeled it off slowly.

He unplugged it from the highly sensitive directional microphone and handed both to the technician, Dmitri Yerokin.

"How was it tonight?" Yerokin asked. With his blond hair, blue eyes, and tan, he could have passed for a Californian.

"The usual," Morozov said, rebuttoning his formal shirt. "There's always something at Hamilton's parties."

He donned his waiter's jacket as Yerokin plugged the wire recorder into the transcribing machine. Within half a minute the sophisticated machine had compressed the information contained in the wire recorder into an eighteen-millisecond pulse. The pulse was then automatically transmitted to a powerful receiver in the Soviet embassy several blocks away. In the next instant, the information was erased from the wire recorder. If they were arrested here, they would have no incriminating evidence, something that under *glasnost* and *perestroika* could not be allowed to exist.

"Anyone interesting I should flag?" Yerokin asked before Morozov left.

"Maybe," Morozov replied.

"Oh?" Yerokin said, interested.

"I was within range of the deputy director of the CIA, and his deputy director of Operations, during an entire conversation."

"Good." Yerokin smiled broadly. "Very good."

19

THEIR LUFTHANSA FLIGHT FROM Munich had been delayed Saturday evening in Rio de Janeiro, and the airline had put them up overnight at the Hilton. They were well rested when they finally arrived in Buenos Aires.

Ezeiza International Airport, fifteen miles southwest of the city, was very busy. Three international flights had arrived within minutes of each other. Hundreds of people crammed the main concourse in the ultramodern terminal building, and customs and passport control were mobbed.

As an Argentine citizen, Maria went through a separate, much faster, line than McGarvey. By the time he was through and had retrieved his single bag, she was waiting for him with a tall, dark-haired man dressed in a classic white linen suit. It was high summer in the Southern Hemisphere and quite warm.

Maria beckoned to McGarvey, and he went over. The man smiled broadly, revealing a half-dozen gold-capped teeth.

"Ah, this is your North American friend finally," the man said in passable English.

"Captain Eduardo Esformes," Maria said. "Kirk McGarvey."

McGarvey put down his bag and shook hands with the man.

"Any friend of Señorita Schimmer is a friend of mine, Señor McGarvey," Esformes said.

"Captain," McGarvey said, inclining his head slightly. It had been a very long time since he'd last been on the South American continent. Then it had been Santiago, and he had come to kill a man. Old demons, he decided, died hardest.

"Eduardo tells everyone that he is an officer with the federal police, but I know for a fact that he is with army intelligence," Maria said.

McGarvey thought that they had a long-standing relationship, but not necessarily one of mutual trust or even admiration.

Esformes laughed. "She is a kidder, all the time with the jokes. But with important friends ... well, what can one do?"

There was nothing to say. He was in the middle of some kind of dangerous game between them.

"If you will excuse us, then ..." Maria said, but Esformes spoke over her.

"What brings you to Argentina, Señor McGarvey? A vacation, perhaps? Sightseeing? We have a wonderful country."

"Actually, treasure hunting," McGarvey said.

Esformes smiled. "You are an expert in this endeavor?"

"Yes, I am."

"An archaeologist?"

"Not exactly, though I have sometimes covered old ground."

Maria's expression was unreadable, though she held herself very still. She wore a long skirt and a high-necked blouse for the cold in Europe. The outfit was out of place here, yet the clothes and the way she wore them lent her a definitely aristocratic air.

"May I see your passport?"

"Of course," McGarvey said. He pulled it out and handed it over.

"How long will you be staying in Argentina?" Esformes asked, studying the Argentinian tourist visa McGarvey had hastily bought from a forger in Munich.

"A week, maybe longer. Perhaps we could get together for a drink?"

Esformes looked up. "Have you been in Argentina before?"

"Never," McGarvey said.

"What is the nature of this treasure you're seeking?"

"An old shipwreck somewhere off your coast."

Maria inhaled sharply but if Esformes noticed he made no sign. "If you should actually make such a find, Señor McGarvey, my government would have to be immediately notified. We have an interest in ... such things, as Señorita Schimmer will undoubtedly tell you."

"We'll keep that in mind, Captain," McGarvey said. "Now, about that drink ..."

Esformes handed back his passport. "Stop by your embassy and have this attended to, señor. Your passport has expired."

"Thank you."

Esformes looked at Maria, then turned and walked off, disappearing into the crowd.

"Do not underestimate that man," Maria said. "He is very dangerous."

"I won't. Nor will I underestimate you."

The Holiday Inn overlooked the busy Rio de la Plata, which brought giant ocean vessels more than a hundred miles from the sea. The river's distant shore, fifty miles to the north, was Uruguay, its capital city, Montevideo, downriver on the sea.

It was late afternoon, but still very warm. The sun was low in the west, slanting the shadows and reflections of the city's skyscrapers across the harbor. McGarvey, shirtless after his shower, stood smoking a cigarette on his balcony.

Although dinner here never began before nine o'clock and usually not until midnight, the cafés and tearooms were filling up. It was Sunday, but Buenos Aires, the jewel of South America, never truly slept.

Someone knocked on his door. He hurried back into the room, stubbed out his cigarette in an ashtray, and snatched up his gun from beneath the jacket on the bed. It had come through in pieces in his shaving gear.

"Who is it?" he called, standing out of a direct line with the door.

"Me," Maria said.

McGarvey stuffed the pistol in his belt at the small of his back and let her in. She was dressed in a light cotton skirt and an extremely sheer blouse. She wore no bra.

"Don't make a situation out of it," she said, catching his look as she came in.

"It?" McGarvey asked, closing the door.

She went to the balcony and he followed her out. "It's very common for women to dress this way here," she said. "Now, get dressed. We have a man to see. He's anxious to meet you and to learn how you figured out where my grandfather's submarine is located."

"I don't know where it is."

"But you said . . ."

"I said I think I can narrow its location down to a searchable area."

She stared at him for a few seconds, and he was struck for the first time how haughtily beautiful she was. In Europe she'd worn makeup. Here she wore very little, and looked none the worse for it. She looked fresh, new.

He'd always had very bad luck with women, beginning with his ex-wife Kathleen. It was the type, he thought: beautiful, but almost completely self-absorbed. Maybe he was attracted to that type, or worse, maybe they were attracted to him. Whatever, they seemed to find him.

"Then we will discuss your 'searchable area,' Señor McGarvey. Get dressed. I do not wish to keep my friend waiting."

McGarvey remained where he was. "I think I liked you better buried upside down with your skirt up around your ass. At least you were civil."

"I said get dressed," Maria ordered through clenched teeth.

McGarvey went to the bureau, lit a cigarette, and dialed room service. "This is McGarvey in Eighteen-oh-seven. Send up a bottle of American bourbon, some ice, and whatever newspapers you have from the States and Europe."

Maria had come up behind him. She snatched the telephone from his hand. Before she could cancel his order he grabbed her wrist and took the phone back. "Thank you," he told the order taker. He hung up.

"Let go! You're hurting me," Maria said, trying to pull away from him.

"Perhaps I'll break your wrist, Señorita Schimmer. But first we're going to have a little chat. I'm going to ask you a question, and you are going to tell me the truth."

Her complexion had turned pale with anger. If she'd had the means, he believed that she would have killed him at that moment. But she said nothing.

"What was your relationship with Carleton Reid?" he asked.

She tried to pull away, and he bent her arm back. She winced, but she did not cry out. The pain she was undoubtedly suffering did not bother him in the least. She had lied to him from the beginning, and there were a lot of good people dead in Paris. If she had somehow been part of that, he would kill her.

"Carleton Reid," he said reasonably.

"If you had bothered to make a simple telephone call either to Maurice Gavalet or to Horst Höehner, you would know that I had never laid eyes on the man until that night at the Inter-Continental."

"What's the mysterious cargo aboard your grandfather's submarine?"

"I don't know."

"Who do you work for?"

"No one. Myself. What do you mean?"

"Does the name Arkady Kurshin mean anything to you?"

Maria looked at him blankly. She shook her head. "No. Should it?"

It was the very first thing, he decided, that she had been honest about. He let her go, and she immediately stepped away from him, rubbing her wrist.

"If you ever touch me like that again, I shall kill you," she said, her voice low with emotion. She meant it.

"There won't be a next time," McGarvey said. "I'm leaving in the morning."

"Why?" she cried out. "You said you were willing to help."

"I've changed my mind."

"Why?"

"I'd rather not get involved in whatever you have going with Esformes. That's your fight, not mine."

"You can't leave just like that."

"Yes, I can, and I will," McGarvey said. "I made a mistake coming here like this, getting myself involved in your problems."

"But what about me?"

McGarvey had to smile inwardly. Her almost complete self-centeredness seemed innocently childlike.

"I'm sure you and your friends will persevere. Dr. Hesse gave us the clue. You'll figure it out if you put your mind to it."

"Goddamnit! I won't let you leave!" she shouted.

"There's nothing you can do about it," McGarvey said, looking at her evenly.

"We'll see," she snapped coldly. She turned on her heel and went to the door.

"Sorry about your wrist," McGarvey said.

She hesitated a second, then yanked open the door and was gone.

The concierge booked him a seat on the morning flight to Miami. From there he would have to decide whether he would return to Paris or continue up to Washington to straighten out the mess he was apparently in.

It had been a mistake, after all, to run from Paris. Like it or not, his name had been involved in the embassy attack, making him very much a part of the situation.

Pushing Carley away had provided no solution to his dissatisfaction. Nor had following Maria Schimmer halfway around the world on a wild-goose chase been sensible. He didn't think she was connected with the Russians.

And yet the loose ends in this business bothered him.

He could accept for the moment the possibility that Maria's meeting with Carleton Reid had been happenstance. He could even accept her explanation as to why she'd been in the embassy.

But a comment Dr. Hesse had made stuck out in his mind. The old man had not only gone to the naval archives for them, he had brought back a series of files on the submarine. Not copies of the files, but the actual documents themselves.

"*Look at them if you wish,*" Dr. Hesse had told them. "*In fact, you must before you leave.*"

It made no sense to McGarvey. Why had the old man been so insistent that they look at the files? They had, but they'd found nothing else useful, unless he'd wanted their fingerprints on the documents, for some reason.

At eight that evening he placed a call to Dr. Hesse's home in

Freiburg. It was midnight there, but the old man had told him that he never got to sleep until one in the morning, and sometimes later.

An unfamiliar male voice answered on the first ring. "Yes, who is this?"

"A colleague," McGarvey said in German. Something was wrong. "I am calling for Dr. Hesse. Is he there, please?"

"Yes, which colleague? Where are you calling from?"

"Dr. Fritz Webber. I am telephoning from Mexico City. May I speak with the professor, please?"

"I'm afraid not, Dr. Webber. Dr. Hesse is dead. He has been murdered."

"My God," McGarvey whispered.

A key grated in his lock. He slammed down the telephone and snatched his pistol as the door opened and Maria Schimmer came in. She was wearing sandals and a white cotton off-the-shoulder dress. Without a word she closed and chained the door, kicked off her sandals, and unzipped her dress, letting it fall to the floor. She stood before him nude.

20

MCGARVEY SLOWLY LOWERED HIS gun and laid it on the table. Dr. Hesse was dead, and Maria was offering herself to him. He was beginning to lose his capacity for surprise.

"What do you want?" he asked quietly.

"Is that all you can say?" Maria flared.

She was a beautiful woman. Her long dark hair fell from her shoulders to her breasts. A small, intensely red strawberry birth-mark on her left breast was matched by a similar one on her belly, just beneath what was obviously a bikini line.

"You're even more beautiful than I thought you would be," McGarvey said. "But what are you doing here like this? What do you want?"

"You may make love to me if you wish," she replied, lowering her voice but looking directly into his eyes.

"Why?" he asked.

Her left eyebrow rose. "What, are you a queer? Don't you want to make love to me?"

"I'd like very much to make love with you, but why now? Like this?"

She stepped forward, away from her dress. "I never thanked you for saving my life."

McGarvey went across the room, picked up her dress, and handed it to her. For a moment she'd thought he was taking her up on her offer, and he'd seen a tiny glint of triumph in her eyes that faded when she understood what he was doing.

"Get dressed," he said.

She grabbed the dress from him, and turned away to put it on. Her back was also beautiful.

"You're going to have to tell me why you came here like this."

"Go to hell," she said.

"Someone has killed Dr. Hesse, very possibly because of your submarine."

Clothed, Maria whirled around, genuinely shocked. "When?"

"I don't know. The police were there when I telephoned."

"Did you give them your name? Did you tell them where you were calling from?"

"No."

Maria no longer looked angry or embarrassed. "You said we'd been followed in Freiburg. Could it have been the same man?"

"It's possible. Were you expecting this?"

Maria was startled. "Of course not," she said. "But you heard him. He said there had been killings."

"That stopped in 1978."

"Because the inquiries stopped. Maybe he stirred up an old hornets' nest."

"There are a lot of them in Germany," McGarvey said.

"Yes," Maria answered, momentarily lost in thought. "Especially now that the wall has come down and the light of day has risen in the east."

"Which brings us back to the submarine and what was aboard her," McGarvey prompted after a beat.

Maria looked up. "It was the first time I'd ever heard of a cargo."

"Bullshit!" McGarvey said harshly.

"No, listen to me, please. I have been lying to you about some things. I'll admit that."

"Now you're going to tell me the truth?" McGarvey asked, his skepticism obvious in his tone.

"There is something aboard that submarine that I'm looking for."

"I'm listening."

"Major Roebling was bringing something with him to Argentina. Something terribly important. In this you must believe me."

"I'm still listening."

Maria nodded. "He brought no cargo with him, Kirk. All he brought was a small notebook with the names and cover identities of twelve men. The 'Council.'"

"Nazis?"

She nodded again. "Schutzstaffel. They were to be organized. Argentina was to become their Fourth Reich, and Roebling was to be their link between the old world and the new."

"It was forty-five years ago. No one cares any longer."

"Simon Wiesenthal does."

"Before long all those old Nazis will be dead. As it is, most of them are already so old they can offer no threat."

"With a restored Germany?" Maria asked with emotion. "Think about it. They have the money, the power. They could become the core of a new government, or movement."

"I think not," McGarvey said.

"Christ!" she said. "What do I have to do to convince you to help us?"

"Us?" McGarvey asked.

"I'm not alone, Kirk," she said tiredly. "There aren't many of us, and people like Captain Esformes would like to see us destroyed because we upset the status quo here, but we are determined to continue."

"By doing what, exactly?"

"If we can find the submarine, and Roebling's book with the names, then we can expose whoever is left. They won't hold up to scrutiny, Kirk. They're bad men. Mass murderers, some of them. Doctors who experimented on children, pregnant women. Monsters."

"Old men now."

She laughed harshly. "Don't disparage the power of old men. Unless I miss my mark, your Dr. Hesse had something to do with them. And now he is dead."

McGarvey said nothing.

"I want you to meet someone," Maria said. "He is the assistant director of the Natural History Museum of Buenos Aires. Tell him about Dr. Hesse, and about what you may have figured out."

"I'm leaving first thing in the morning."

"I know. But that doesn't prevent you from coming with me tonight. Please."

"And then what?"

"Then you can go back to your friends in Paris, or your ex-wife in Washington. Whatever."

McGarvey looked at her. One of his teachers at the Company training camp outside Williamsburg had told him that a good spy could spot the anomalies a mile away.

He'd never mentioned Kathleen to her. He'd never mentioned Washington or his past life. None of that.

"I'll meet you in the lobby," he said.

"Five minutes."

"Right."

She picked up her sandals, and at the door she looked back. "If you had touched me, I would have had to kill you eventually."

"Are you a lesbian?"

"A black widow spider," she said, and she left.

"His name is Albert Rothmann," Maria told him in the taxi.

It was a few minutes after nine and the city was starting to come alive for the evening. Traffic was heavy along the broad Boulevard Córdoba, and already there were long lines waiting outside the more popular restaurants and nightspots.

"A co-conspirator of yours?" McGarvey asked. He was feeling irascible. He did not like being lied to, and he liked being spied on even less. Maria and whoever she worked for, or represented, had done both.

"He was a friend of my father's. Like an uncle to me, actually."

"Convenient."

"I need your help, Señor McGarvey. And I will take it any way I can get it. If taking shots at me is your price, then so be it. I'll not shoot back."

They rode the rest of the way in silence, turning ten minutes later down a tree-lined lane that led off the Avenida San Martín into a small park. The main section of the Natural History Museum was housed in a large, ornate building reminiscent of some of the neoclassic structures in Paris.

The cabbie left them off at a staff entrance that was open, and they took an elevator up to the fourth floor. The museum was long closed for the evening, and no one seemed to be around. The dinosaur displays were eerie in the darkness.

"He often works late," Maria explained.

"Does he know we're coming?"

"Yes. I called him earlier this evening. He's very interested in meeting you."

An office door at the end of the corridor was ajar. No light came from within.

"That's odd," Maria said as they approached. "He said he would wait for us."

McGarvey stopped her. "Was there supposed to be anyone else up here tonight?"

She looked at him in confusion and alarm. "No, just him."

McGarvey pulled out his gun and motioned for her to hold back. He cautiously approached the door, flattening himself against the wall to the right, and listened. There were no sounds.

He pushed the door open with his foot, and a moment later reached around the corner for the light switch. He flipped it on and rolled through the doorway, sweeping his pistol left to right.

There was no one in the small office except for a dark-haired man seated at the desk. He had been shot in the middle of the forehead with a small-caliber weapon. His head was flung back against the back of his chair, and his arms were outstretched in front of him as if he were propping himself up.

Maria let out a little cry from the door. McGarvey turned back to her.

"Rothmann?" he asked.

She nodded.

McGarvey went to the desk and felt for a pulse at the side of the man's neck. There was none, but the body was still warm, the skin still pliable.

"Is he dead?"

"Yes, but not a long time. Who else knew we were coming here tonight?"

"No one," Maria said. "Unless my telephone at the hotel was tapped ..."

They both heard sirens in the distance. "Esformes," McGarvey said.

"The bastard!"

"We'd better get the hell out of here," McGarvey said, holstering his gun and taking her by the arm.

Out in the corridor she pulled away from him. "You were going to tell us where the submarine might be."

"Later."

The sirens were already much closer.

"Now!" she cried, her eyes wild.

"Goddamnit!" McGarvey shouted. "Look, there were five Greek letters in the code, according to Mossburg's testimony: alpha, beta, gamma, delta, and epsilon. Starting with the Rio de la Plata right here as alpha, the next place a submarine could make a rendezvous along the coast would be Bahia Blanca."

She stared at him open-mouthed.

"I can read a map too," he said. "Mossburg told his interrogators that alpha and beta were out for some reason. Which leaves gamma as the next possibility."

"Golfo San Matías," she said.

"That's what I figured. Can you get us there?"

She looked at him. The sirens were very close. "Why the change of heart again?"

"Him," McGarvey said, glancing at the door to Rothmann's office. "And Dr. Hesse. And Paris."

"There may not be a connection ..."

"I think there is," McGarvey said dangerously.

She studied his face for another second, then nodded. "I have access to a small airplane at the airport. If we wait until dawn to take off we won't attract any attention."

"We'll have to get out of here first."

The sirens were just outside now.

"There's a back way," Maria said, and together they hurried down the corridor, taking the stairs two at a time to the ground floor.

The night watchman or someone had let the police in the

front door. McGarvey and Maria could hear them coming through the museum, one of them shouting orders.

They slipped out into the corridor and had just managed to reach another door that led to a vast storage area and duck inside, when the staff entrance door at the end of the corridor banged open.

"This way," Maria whispered urgently. She took McGarvey's hand and guided him through the darkness, past big piles of wooden crates, pallets of what appeared to be fiberglass insulation or packing material, and something very large that loomed up on their left.

The sounds of pursuit faded, until they came to a window at the rear of the building. From there they could hear more sirens outside converging on the museum.

Maria quickly ran her fingers around the inside edge of the windowframe, stopping at a point halfway up on the left.

"Alarmed?" McGarvey asked.

"Yes," she said. "Give me a credit card, or something like it."

McGarvey took his American Express card out of his wallet and gave it to her. Carefully she inserted it between the bottom of the windowframe and the casement, sliding it to the left until it stopped. She bent it forward, then slid it another quarter inch to the left.

"Open the window slowly," she said.

McGarvey unlocked the latch and slowly raised the window while she held the alarm system's trip switch in place. He climbed out the window, and once outside he reached back and held the credit card in place as she climbed out. Sliding the card almost all the way past the switch, he nodded to Maria, who lowered the window so he could pull the card out.

Straight across from the loading dock area and access road to their right was a heavily wooded park, evidently part of the museum's grounds.

Without a word he followed Maria across, and they reached the safety of the trees as several sets of lights came around from the front of the museum. Without looking back they hurried through the darkness, coming ten minutes later to a broad avenue filled with shops and cafés and people and traffic.

They hailed a taxi and told the driver to take them to the airport. As they sped away McGarvey wondered who set them up. If it had been Esformes, he wondered exactly what the man's problem was with Maria. It was something, he suspected, that he would find out about sooner or later. That and the obvious fact that Maria was not an amateur. She'd had training somewhere. She'd known about the alarm on the museum window and how to bypass it. It was curious.

21

THE SUN WAS HIGH in the morning sky when they flew over the Punta Rasa and got their first glimpse of the vast Golfo San Matías. Bounded on the south by the Valdés Peninsula, the bay was more than a hundred miles on a side, with few cities or settlements along its coast.

"Ten thousand square miles of water for a submarine to stay hidden," McGarvey said, looking up from a chart. "And no prying eyes ashore to see a thing."

Maria was an expert if somewhat distracted pilot. The plane was a twin-engine Cessna 310 that belonged to a company called International Traders, Ltd. She said it was a dummy corporation that had been set up by her and two others to funnel funds into their search efforts.

The explanation, like most of the others she'd given him,

seemed too pat to be entirely true. There was more to her and the mysterious group she represented than she was ready or able to reveal.

"If it's there we'll find it," Maria said with conviction. She had perked up since they'd gotten airborne. They'd spent the night in the commercial pilots' ready room at the airport, and neither of them had gotten much rest. McGarvey's mouth was foul from too much strong Argentinian coffee and too many cigarettes. Maria's complexion seemed sallow beneath her normal olive coloring.

"If it's not?"

"Then we'll go farther south to delta and epsilon. Sooner or later we'll find it, now that we know where to look."

"What if it never made it this far?" McGarvey asked, playing devil's advocate to her certainty. "It might never have got out of the North Atlantic."

"It did, Kirk," Maria said, glancing at him. "It must have."

"In the meantime you're a fugitive."

She nodded. In the distance they could see the town of Viedma on the Rio Negro. A couple of miles south of the city was the only airport on the gulf.

"What about your friends? You said there were others besides Rothmann."

"We have to stay away from them now. You can't believe how many bodies are buried in the hills around Buenos Aires and out on the pampas and in the jungles. It never stops. Now Esformes and his gang will be watching very closely."

"They killed Rothmann without hesitation," McGarvey said. "What's stopping them from killing the others? Or you and me, if they catch up with us?"

She said nothing, concentrating on her flying for the moment. She'd reduced their speed, and they began a slow descent toward the airport still twenty miles away.

"We could stay and fight them," McGarvey said. "I have friends who might be able to help."

She remained silent for a little while, but then she turned and looked into his eyes. "I still don't know what you're doing here, or why you decided to help me in the first place. But now I need you. I don't think I can do this alone. Albert would have come with me ... but ..."

"We've already covered that ground," McGarvey said, looking

out the window toward the gulf. The white-capped waves looked like ripples on a tiny pond. Harmless at this distance.

"If it gets too bad, and you want to leave, I'll understand."

"We'll find your submarine," McGarvey said. "And we'll find whatever it was that Major Roebling brought with him."

This part of Argentina was Patagonia, desolate, windswept, and cold year-round. Steep cliffs plunged into the sea from a landscape that was nearly desert until the thick forests began some distance inland, beyond which were the Andes, South America's spine.

Twenty-five years ago Viedma had been a cowtown struggling for its existence in the bleak region. But when the former president of Argentina, Raul Alfonsin, had suggested that the federal capital be moved there because of what were believed to be untapped mineral and oil deposits in the region, the town had begun to grow.

Now, with a population of nearly fifty thousand, Viedma was in stasis. No minerals or oil had been found yet.

A clerk at the airport told them, "We are a city waiting to become a capital. We have the libraries, the office buildings, the shopping centers, the hospitals, and the cultural facilities. All we need is the government."

They'd arranged to store the plane and McGarvey had rented a Ford export-model Escort with yellow headlights and a loud muffler.

"We'll need a boat and equipment," McGarvey said on the way into the city.

"I've been thinking about that," Maria said. "There's no real harbor here at Viedma. Most of the fleet that operates within the gulf is based in Puerto Madryn behind the Valdés Peninsula."

"The navy is still there, isn't it?" McGarvey asked. He thought he remembered that from some CIA briefing years ago.

"Yes, it is," she said, looking at him. "Which is one of the reasons I picked Viedma. There are some boats to be had here. But what's more important, there are Europeans who will have access to the equipment we're going to need, as well as the skill to use it and the good sense to keep their mouths shut."

"What about money?"

"I have plenty," she said.

"Are these 'Europeans' expatriates or Argentinians?"

"Expatriates, a lot of them. Waiting for the big boom."

"In the meantime?" McGarvey asked.

Maria shrugged. "I don't know much about this place. I've heard it described as a pocket of poverty in the middle of an oasis. A few tourists come here from time to time, I suppose to gawk at Argentina's answer to Brasilia."

"That never quite was."

"No one will bother us here, I think."

"Esformes will find us."

"Perhaps," Maria said. They had come to a small boat basin just upriver from the sea. The docks were on floats because of the huge tidal range, and the tidal flats stretched nearly a mile on either side of the river before they were contained by levees.

The marina had the scruffy, down-at-the-heels look of work-boat harbors the world over. Almost all the boats here were utilitarian. Not many pleasure cruisers.

Even the shabbiest boats, however, were equipped with radar. It was a good sign.

"We'll get our boat here," Maria said. "Pull in."

McGarvey turned off the main highway, went through an open gate hanging on one hinge, and bumped across a broad field down a rutted dirt track to the marina office. A dog was sleeping in the sun, and a hundred or more sea gulls were perched on the ends of the docks. There seemed to be no other life.

"These are my kind of people, Kirk," Maria said when they pulled up. "Unless you've had experience dealing with them, let me do it."

"It's your country," McGarvey said, watching her eyes. There was no reaction he could see.

"Get us rooms at the Hotel Matías. Downtown. I'll meet you there as soon as I can."

There was much about her that was extraordinary. McGarvey was struck with the notion that she was not South American, though her Spanish seemed authentic. Perhaps it was her English. The accent was wrong, somehow.

"We're going to need clothing," McGarvey said. He looked up at the perfectly clear blue sky. There was a metallic tang to the air, and it was windy by the water. "Unless I miss my guess, it's going to be cold out on the gulf."

"I'm a thirty-eight tall," she said. "Forty shoe or boot. But don't go overboard. Don't get conspicuous."

He just looked at her.

"Sorry," she said. "I'm very nervous now that we're this close."

"We may not be."

She looked out the window. "We are," she said. "I can smell it."

"It's your show," McGarvey said.

"Yes, it is." She got out of the car and headed down to the docks.

"He's a fellow North American," Maria said, introducing the blond-haired, husky man she'd brought with her. It was nearly three in the afternoon. They were in the hotel's pleasant coffee shop. "Captain Steven Jones, Kirk McGarvey."

They shook hands. Jones's grip was iron hard, his hand roughly calloused. McGarvey figured him to be in his mid-to late thirties, with the too-early-to-be-burned-out look of the roustabout and professional adventurer.

"I'm an oil engineer by trade," he explained in a Texas drawl. "Leastways I used to be. Came down to work the Tierra del Fuego fields on the big island."

"What happened?" McGarvey asked.

"It got a little rough for my blood, what with the fight going over Chile's claim. And the goddamned weather—" He glanced at Maria. "Sorry, ma'am," he apologized. He was like an over-grown puppy. "The weather started to get to me, so I cashed in, bought a boat, and set up shop here in the gulf."

"Doing what?" McGarvey asked, amazed that he was believing what he was hearing.

Jones smiled broadly. "Well, now, the marlin fishing ain't so bad in the right season, if you know what you're doing. And I do. And if you got the connections with the fat cats up in Dallas and Houston who like that sort of thing. And I do. Then you can make a respectable living."

"But we're out of season now?"

"Pretty much. So I'd be willing to take a look for this meteorite of yours."

McGarvey exchanged a look with Maria. She'd been inventive.

"But I won't dive. I told that to the lady up front. I don't know many workboat skippers who will." Jones leaned forward and tapped a blunt finger on the table. "There's a damned sight more under the sea than's ever been cataloged. And most all of it is hungry most all of the time."

"We'll do the diving," Maria assured him. "But you have the tanks and compressor?"

"Sure thing. And I'll get that other installed yet this afternoon. We can start first thing in the morning if you want."

"We'll leave tonight," Maria said.

"Which 'other' is this?" McGarvey asked.

"The magnetometer. I'm borrowing it from one of the old exploration rigs. It's the only way you're going to find a ferrous mass out there. And even then it's going to be like looking for a needle in the haystack."

"But we will find it," Maria said.

Jones shrugged. "It's a lot of water, and at the speeds we'll have to go to cover it all before the marlin begin to run, we could miss it easy unless it's big."

"It's big," Maria said.

"I mean *really* big," Jones said.

"We won't have to search the entire gulf," McGarvey said. Maria glanced sharply at him.

"Yeah?" Jones said.

"I think I might be able to narrow it down a bit."

"Do you know where she went in?"

"Maybe," McGarvey said.

McGarvey had rented only one hotel room. They used it to clean up and change into the clothes he'd bought for them. There were plenty of shops in town, but most of them were empty. He'd had to settle for cheap Mexican corduroys and rough woolen sweaters. It would be cold out on the gulf.

Jones had agreed to round up his mate and let them aboard at six sharp. They would stay out five days. Based on what they'd found or not found by then, they would reevaluate not only their approach, but their contract as well.

Maria had gotten a chart from Jones. She spread it out on the bed. It showed the entire gulf and a section of the shoreline.

"We're here," she said, pointing to their location. "What did you mean when you told Jones you could narrow down the search area? How?"

McGarvey was looking out the window toward the ocean. At this latitude it wouldn't get dark until after nine in the evening. "If we find your submarine, we're going to dive on it. You want to find Roebling's notebook."

"That's right."

"How deep can you safely dive?" he asked. "A hundred feet? Two hundred feet?"

"I see," she said after a moment, understanding that it would do them no good to search waters too deep for them. "What else?"

"If they were here to make a rendezvous, it would have been set up for a deserted stretch of coast."

"Somewhere between San Antonio Oeste in the north, and Puerto Lobos in the south. Eighty miles."

McGarvey turned around. "So we start in the middle, say a few hundred yards offshore, and work our way north and south."

"Hell," Maria said half to herself. "Why didn't we think of that?"

McGarvey didn't answer. The question hadn't been for him.

22

AN INCREASING SWELL HAD been building from the east for the past two days. As long as they ran with it, the motion aboard the old but well-maintained wooden Chris-Craft wasn't so bad. But each time they turned onto a course parallel with the shore they began to roll and wallow.

"This is not so good for the lady," Jones said to McGarvey over the chart table below. The navigation station was tucked in the starboard corner in the passageway that led back to the engines. It was hot and stuffy and smelled of diesel fuel, but it was well lit and well equipped with good VHF and single-sideband radio equipment, a direction finder, LORAN, and even an old Magnovox satellite navigation receiver.

"She'll manage," McGarvey said.

They had already covered an area more than ten miles north

and ten miles south of a center line between San Antonio Oeste and Puerto Lobos, and nearly two miles offshore.

On their first morning out they had spotted two wrecks, neither of which was large enough to be their submarine. But just in case, Maria had donned a wet suit and tank both times and had made the initial dives.

The first had been the hulk of an old steel fishing boat, and the other had been a railroad locomotive, sitting upright on the sand bottom in about one hundred feet of water. It had been amazingly intact, she'd said, and McGarvey had made a dive down to it with her.

It had been a waste of time, but Jones and his compact Argentinian mate, who spoke no English and whose only name seemed to be Jorge, needed to do some work on the engines anyway.

They'd discovered nothing since then.

The food aboard the thirty-eight-foot boat was surprisingly good. Jorge was an excellent cook, and the provisions Jones had laid in were first class, as was his "wine cellar" in the bilges.

"The people who hire me won't eat goat and *chipas*," Jones had explained with a broad grin. "And neither will I. Besides, you're paying for it."

"What about the weather?" McGarvey asked, looking up from the chart.

"It will hold for another thirty-six hours, perhaps a little longer, or a little less."

"And then?"

"The wind will blow, the seas will build, and life will become uncomfortable."

"How about your equipment?"

"The weather won't stop our search, although it will make keeping to the pattern difficult, and the diving perhaps impossible."

McGarvey studied the chart. He tried to put himself in the submarine captain's place. This was a hostile coast. The war was winding down, perhaps even over by now. After such a long voyage they would be nearly out of provisions and perhaps fuel. There was the RSHA passenger, Major Roebling, to consider as well, along with whatever he'd brought with him. The mission would have been of supreme importance.

There was no record of the submarine after her departure.

She'd not returned to Germany, nor had she turned up anywhere else. The Allies had not captured her. And no submarine had been sunk in the Atlantic during that specific period.

But there was a lot of water between here and Bremen, and the chances were that the boat had never made it this far. There was no reason to think that it had. No evidence that Roebling or the U-boat's crew had shown up in Argentina. Nothing had washed ashore. Even as desolate as the Patagonian coast was, had anything washed ashore in 1945 it would have been found eventually.

But then Maria had not told him everything. Nor, he was beginning to suspect, had Dr. Hesse. Which led to a number of interesting speculations.

"We're nearly finished with this pattern," Jones was saying. "Do you want to expand the search to the north and south, or shall we work farther offshore?"

"North and south," McGarvey said.

"This meteorite must have hit very close to shore. It must have made quite a splash in its day."

"Yes," McGarvey said. "It must have."

"*¡Capitán, aquí, aquí!*" Jorge called down from the bridge.

The boat came hard to starboard as McGarvey and Jones rushed topside. Maria was braced in the corner in front of the magnetometer. Her eyes were glued to the machine.

"This could be it," she said excitedly. "I think we found it!"

Jorge had brought the boat completely around so that they were running along their own wake.

"It's big, whatever it is," she said, showing them the readings on the strip chart coming out of the magnetometer. A series of very dark lines rose well above the normal background and bottom traces, showing that they had passed over a significant mass of ferrous metal.

"Here it comes again," she said as the trace suddenly began to bloom.

"*Lento*," Jones told his mate, and Jorge immediately throttled back so that they were nearly dead in the water.

Jones tossed a marker buoy over the side, the bright orange float spinning around as its small anchor and line automatically paid out.

When they had drifted completely over the object, Jorge again turned the boat hard to starboard, throttled up a little so that they would not be pushed off station by the swell, and ran back slightly west of their buoy.

This time they were on the object almost immediately, coming off it again within yards.

Jorge repeated the maneuver, turning outward toward the west each time, until they were no longer detecting anything beneath them.

"*Babor*," Jones said calmly, and Jorge immediately turned to port.

"How deep are we?" McGarvey asked.

"Seventy-five meters," Jones said. "Two hundred fifty feet. But the bottom slopes toward the west and south."

They came over the submerged object again, and Jones made several notations on the chart. As soon as they had passed it, Jorge turned again to port.

On the sixteenth run they had passed over the complete length of the object and Jorge turned back toward their marker buoy, again throttling back so that they were nearly stationary against the swell.

Jones made a few calculations and when he looked up there was a glint in his eyes. "That's some meteorite down there," he drawled. "I think it must have distorted very badly when it hit."

"It's big, isn't it?" Maria said.

Jones nodded. "I'd say about two hundred and thirty feet long, but very narrow. Maybe fifteen or twenty feet on the beam. And she's down toward the southwest." He glanced at the paper strip chart. "She's a ship of some kind, I think."

"You're not being paid to think, Captain," Maria said menacingly. McGarvey took a step back. Jorge turned around and looked at them. There was no reading his dark, deeply weathered face.

"Your name is Schimmer," Jones said. "What's down there?"

"Shut up," Maria said.

"Is it the U-boat?" Jones asked, ignoring her.

"What U-boat is that?" McGarvey asked, careful to keep his tone conversational, his manner light. Jorge had released the strap that held his big skinning knife in its sheath at his hip.

"The one that was here in 1945."

"What are you talking about?" Maria asked, the words not quite even.

"One of the old fishermen said he saw the periscope. No one believed him, but he insisted."

"Where is this fisherman of yours?" McGarvey asked.

"Dead."

"What do you suppose a German submarine was doing here at the end of the war?"

Jones grinned. "You haven't been in Argentina very long, have you?" he said. "There've been two big German immigrations to this country in this century. One in 1918 and 1919, and again in 1944 and 1945."

"So?"

"A lot of them didn't come empty-handed. A lot of money changed hands. An Argentinan passport in those days was very expensive."

"So what we have here is a German submarine filled with the bodies of Nazis trying to escape Nuremberg," McGarvey said.

Maria was white with anger.

"And money," Jones said. "Gold, I'd suspect. Maybe diamonds. Artwork. A lot of stuff was never found."

"But you don't dive," McGarvey said gently.

Jones shrugged. "Within forty-eight hours, probably less, I could have a topnotch marine salvage team here. And you two would be shit out of luck."

"But then you wouldn't get as big a share, assuming there is gold down there," McGarvey said. "In fact you might attract enough attention to get the government interested, in which case you might get nothing."

Jones glanced up at the sky. "Less than an hour's good light yet. You'll have to wait until morning to dive. That is, if you're up for a dive that deep."

"We are," Maria said, and she turned on her heel and stalked down to her cabin.

23

PHIL CARRARA CAME THROUGH the glass doors on the seventh floor as Thomas Doyle, deputy director of Intelligence, was coming out of Murphy's office.

"Hope you're prepared," Doyle said half under his breath in passing. "He's loaded for bear this morning."

"When isn't he?" Carrara replied, and the DCI's secretary waved him through.

Lawrence Danielle and the Agency's general counsel, Howard Ryan, were seated across from Murphy. Ryan had a yellow legal pad balanced on his lap.

Murphy looked up and motioned for Carrara to take the lone vacant chair in front of his desk. "Coffee?"

"No thanks, General," Carrara said, sitting down.

It was just nine in the morning, and it had begun to snow

again a couple of hours ago. The light coming from outside was a flat gray. It matched Carrara's mood.

"Well, where is he?" Murphy asked, a dangerous edge to his voice. Carrara didn't think what the DCI was about to hear would cheer him up.

"We have reason to believe that he's in Buenos Aires. At least he was there four days ago."

Murphy was surprised. He exchanged a look with Danielle. "What the hell's he doing in Argentina?"

"Apparently he went down there with Maria Schimmer, the woman he dug out of the embassy—"

"Yes, yes, we know all about that. But what's he up to, and more important, why isn't he in custody by now?"

"He's a dangerous man," Ryan added. "Surely you must agree with that, Phil."

Carrara avoided the general counsel's eyes. He had never liked or trusted the man, but Murphy had come to depend upon Ryan's advice more and more over the past year.

"There have been three additional murders," Carrara said, "with strong circumstantial ties to McGarvey and the woman. But I must stress that the evidence to this point is circumstantial."

"Since we spoke Saturday evening?" Danielle asked sharply.

"Our knowledge of them has come since then," Carrara said. "In fact we're only just now unraveling what may have happened in the first instance. And in the second the reports are still uncertain."

"Let me ask you something before you continue," Murphy interrupted. "Have your people come up with any ties between these killings and Iran? Iranian interests, Iranian citizens?"

"No," Carrara answered, mystified.

Murphy was definitely disappointed. "Well, who has he killed now?"

"We don't know for a fact that he's guilty of killing anyone," Carrara said.

"We will take note of the 'circumstantial' nature of your evidence, Phil," Ryan said.

"Interpol out of Bonn are looking for McGarvey and the woman for questioning in connection with the murders of Dr. Heinrich Hesse and his housekeeper sometime Friday evening or early Saturday morning in Freiburg."

"That's where the Germans keep their naval records from the war, I believe," Ryan said.

"That's correct," Carrara said. "McGarvey and the Schimmer woman were evidently seen at the professor's house Friday afternoon. But they were not seen after that time."

"But you have traced them to Buenos Aires," Ryan said. "Which means you know how and when they left Germany."

"The next morning," Carrara said. "Lufthansa out of Munich."

"Giving McGarvey and this woman time to sneak back to Freiburg, kill the professor and his housekeeper, and get out."

"Presumably," Carrara admitted.

"What did they want with this German professor?" Murphy asked.

"Unknown," Carrara said.

Danielle had been deep in thought. He looked up. "Did Dr. Hesse have access to the naval archives in Freiburg?"

"I don't know. But I presume he would have."

"What is it?" Murphy asked.

"We have a report from the SDECE that the woman met with a French intelligence officer, a man from Simon Wiesenthal's office, and Carleton Reid at the Inter-Continental just prior to the explosion. She told them that she was looking for a Nazi submarine but was getting no cooperation in Freiburg."

"Evidently she convinced McGarvey to help her," Carrara said. "That doesn't mean McGarvey killed the man."

"Who was the third victim?"

"Dr. Albert Rothmann, the assistant director of the Natural History Museum of Buenos Aires."

"When?"

"Sunday evening."

"Were McGarvey and the woman in Buenos Aires at the time?" Ryan asked.

Carrara nodded.

The general counsel turned to Danielle and Murphy. "At least in this, there can be no doubt. For whatever reason, he and Maria Schimmer are on some sort of an operation . . . a rampage might be a better description."

"For what purpose?" Danielle asked.

"God only knows," Ryan replied. He sat forward to emphasize his point. "But you can be damned sure of one thing," he said.

"Whatever McGarvey is up to this time, it will ultimately involve some sort of revenge against the Agency."

"For Chrissake, why?" Carrara asked angrily.

"Because of John Lyman Trotter, Jr., McGarvey's pal. The man was a traitor and a murderer. He damned near managed to kill McGarvey," Ryan said, turning again back to Murphy. "And in part because of you, Mr. Director. Or at least because of how you treated McGarvey after his involvement with Dr. Abbott a couple of years ago."

"We treated the man shabbily," Carrara said. "But only a madman, a maniac would blow up an embassy merely out of revenge."

"I agree," Ryan said with a slight smile.

There was a tight silence for a few long seconds, Ryan's statement hanging in the air, until Danielle spoke.

"You say they were in Buenos Aires four days ago. Where are they now, Phil? Any hints, any leads?"

"No. They simply disappeared."

"Let me guess," Ryan said. "They dropped out of sight immediately following Rothmann's murder."

"That's enough, Howard," Murphy said. "Are they still in the country to the best of our knowledge?"

"As far as we can tell, General."

"Have we the resources down there to find them?"

"Probably not," Carrara admitted. "Argentina is a big country. Lots of places to hide if you know what you're doing. Presumably Maria Schimmer does."

"And McGarvey," Ryan said.

"How about the Buenos Aires police?" Danielle asked.

"The federal police are apparently interested, but we don't have much on that. I've told our people to stay at arm's length. It wouldn't help our operations down there to advertise our presence."

Again Danielle had drifted off for a moment. "Makes one wonder about the connection between this woman's search for a Nazi submarine and her disappearance in Argentina."

"What do you mean?" Murphy asked.

"A lot of Nazis went down there at the end of the war to escape retribution from the Allies. A lot of money went with them. Gold. Artwork. Diamonds. All taken from the bodies of their Jewish victims, or looted from museums across Europe. A lot of it has never turned up."

"She's a treasure hunter?" Murphy asked.

Danielle shrugged.

"Which has nothing to do with the attack on our embassy," Ryan said.

Murphy nodded. "He has to be brought in, Phil."

"What about the girl?"

"Her, too, if getting her out of Argentina poses no serious threat to our operations down there. But McGarvey has to be brought in at all costs. It wouldn't do to let the Argentinians get their hands on him."

"We'll do what we can," Carrara said, rising.

"See that your people do," Murphy said. "Light a fire under them if need be, but get it done. Soon."

At the door Carrara turned back. "What about this Iranian connection, sir?"

"You'll hear about it soon enough," Murphy said. "There've been rumblings about an assassination attempt on Richard Abbas."

"My chief of station in Tehrān?"

Murphy nodded. "Doyle thought there might be a connection with McGarvey."

"Where'd we hear about this?"

"I'm not sure," Murphy said, turning to Danielle.

"Came from Mike Oreck's office, I think," the DDCI said.

"Yes, sir," Carrara said, and he left.

Back in his own office, Carrara looked up Oreck's number in the headquarters directory. The man headed what was called the Office of Economic Research; Thomas Doyle was his immediate superior.

He telephoned the man directly, even though he should have gone through the Directorate of Intelligence.

"Phil Carrara. Wonder if you could spare me a couple of minutes this morning."

"Yes, sir," Oreck said. "Have you spoken with Mr. Doyle?"

"Saw him this morning in the general's office," Carrara said.

"Yes, sir. Could you tell me what this is in reference to?"

"I'm told that your office has heard rumors of a threat against one of my people."

"Oh, that, sir," Oreck said, his voice suddenly guarded. "I think you're right: it would be better if I came up and personally briefed you."

"Has my man been warned?"

"Ah, yes, sir," Oreck said. "I believe that message went out with the overnights. I'll be right up."

Oreck was a heavily built man with dark hair, thick black eyebrows, and a square face. His handshake was bone-crushing.

"Sorry to have been so mysterious on the telephone, sir, but this has an extremely tight distribution list, if you know what I mean."

"I don't know," Carrara said. "I was told this morning that a death threat against my chief of Tehrān station was uncovered by your office, which I found odd."

"Not so odd, sir, considering the project."

Carrara said nothing.

"You'll be receiving your briefing package today or tomorrow sometime. A planning and implementation conference will be scheduled for early in the week."

"Go on."

"Well, sir, the President has apparently signed a secret agreement with the Iranian government to return monies we have been holding in frozen bank assets. Oil payments mostly, from what I gather."

"What does Dick Abbas have to do with this?"

"The Iranians have demanded payment in gold. We've agreed, and the gold will be shipped to Bushehr on the Persian Gulf sometime within the next ten or fifteen days."

"By ship?" Carrara asked, surprised. "Why not by air?"

"Because we are sending them approximately four million ounces, sir. One hundred twenty-five tons of gold."

Carrara sat back.

"Yes, sir, it affects all of us that way. On the present market it's worth a bit more than one and a half billion dollars."

"What about my chief of station?"

"He's to make certain that the shipment makes it overland from Bushehr to Tehrān. There are certain people within the Iranian army who would like to get their hands on that gold."

"No doubt," Carrara said. "But Abbas is under deep cover."

"Yes, sir. His job is simply to keep a watchful eye. If anything should begin to develop, he's to use the SatCom system to call for help. We need the impartial observer there. And we need the secrecy, of course."

"Once it's on Iranian soil it's their problem, so why are we involved? And why wasn't I informed earlier?"

"This just developed, sir. And it came from the White House. I believe the current thinking is that with everything that's been going on in the region, we need a friend, even if it is Iran. Or maybe especially. At any rate, apparently we've guaranteed delivery at Tehrān. We're looking for stability in the region, and we'll do whatever it takes to insure it."

"Then it should have been shipped by air. Our air force could have brought it in."

Oreck said nothing.

"But you're also trying to tell me that someone may have gotten wind of the shipment and Dick's role as a watchdog, and they want to eliminate him because of it. Is that correct?"

"That's what we believe."

"I see," Carrara said absently, his mind racing to a dozen different possibilities and problems.

"If there'll be nothing else, sir . . . ?" Oreck said.

"No," Carrara replied. "Thanks for coming up this morning."

"Yes, sir," Oreck said, and he let himself out.

Where were the connections? Carrara asked himself. There had to be connections. A gold shipment to Iran. The possibility of a treasure aboard a Nazi submarine that an Argentinian woman was seeking. The attack on the U.S. embassy in Paris. McGarvey's initial fears that somehow Arkady Kurshin, the chameleon, was alive and involved. Of course, there had been the rumors out of Moscow.

Or was it all simply revenge, as Howard Ryan argued? Revenge and insanity. And was everything else merely coincidence?

He didn't think so.

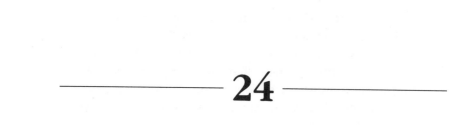

24

THE DAWN BROKE COLD and gray over the Golfo San Matías. In the night the wind had risen sharply, and it was now kicking up steep six-foot waves from the east. The motion aboard the Chris-Craft was unpleasant.

McGarvey got a mug of coffee from the galley on the starboard side of the main saloon directly across from the dining table, and bracing himself against the pitch and roll made his way topside.

Maria was going over their scuba gear with Jones. Jorge was back on the bridge, preparing to bring them into the wind to make the boat a more stable platform for the dive. Angry dark clouds scudded in very low from the open ocean.

"How long will this weather hold?" McGarvey asked.

Jones looked up, then at the horizon and the sea. "Not long," he said. "You will get one dive this morning. After that it'll be too rough."

"It's enough," Maria said. She'd been in a taciturn mood since yesterday afternoon's confrontation with Jones, after they'd found what they took to be the submarine.

Jones had not elaborated on what he knew of the U-boat's sighting forty-six years ago, nor had they asked him to do so. But the mystery would be solved in the next hour or so, McGarvey figured, and then he would be able to return to Paris.

He'd known all along that sooner or later he was going to have to go back to Europe. Whether or not the embassy attack had anything to do with the murders of Dr. Hesse and Albert Rothmann—a long shot, he thought, but nagging nonetheless —he was starting to have the same over-the-shoulder feeling that he'd had in Freiburg.

Someone was behind him. The awareness was like the throb of a mild toothache. Insistent. A presence.

Turn around, he'd been telling himself for the past few days. This adventure with Maria was becoming even less than a diversion. He did not care about Argentinian politics, and he cared even less about Nazi war criminals of nearly a half century ago. Yet at times he found that he was almost afraid to look over his shoulder lest he come face-to-face with himself. Something his sister said he'd never done, especially not since the deaths of their parents. But that had been years ago. Where had his life gone? Into what place had it leaked?

"Bring me back a sample," Jones said dryly.

Maria didn't bother answering him. "We're just going down to take a look. Confirm that it's what we're looking for. I don't think we'll be able to do more in this weather."

"Can we stay here until it passes?" McGarvey asked.

"That's probably not such a good idea," Jones said. "We're in for a big blow. The barometer is down and going farther."

"We'll come back," Maria said, an odd note in her voice.

She was lying again, which McGarvey found disturbing. They'd come this far, had gotten this close, yet she said she was willing merely to take a look and then leave.

Jones had caught it too, and he looked sharply at her. "If need be, I'll bring my own crew back here."

"Let's find out what's down there first," she said. "Shall we?"

Jones nodded thoughtfully, then glanced up at Jorge and mo-

tioned for him to bring them into the wind. "The bow of whatever is down there is lying at just under two hundred thirty
feet. The stern, unless it's the other way around, is in two
hundred eighty feet of water. But there's a protuberance of some
sort rising about fifteen, maybe twenty feet above the level of
the main mass. No matter what, you'll be diving to two hundred
feet or more. You're going to have to take precautions."

"Yes?" Maria said, listening attentively.

"You'll have only five minutes at that depth. On the way up
you'll stop at forty feet for three minutes, thirty feet for six
minutes, twenty feet for eleven minutes, and ten feet for twenty-
one minutes."

"I thought you didn't dive," McGarvey said.

"I don't," Jones said. "But I'm not stupid."

"Go on," Maria said.

"You'll need lights. It'll be very dark, and cold. My wet suits
are good, but you'll start to feel the cold almost immediately.
You're going to have to stick together. Watch each other not
only for signs of hypothermia, but for nitrogen narcosis as well.
This is no Bahamian sport dive you'll be making."

"Navy?" McGarvey asked.

After a beat, Jones nodded. "When I got out I worked on an
oil rig in the North Sea. About the third time I'd nearly bought
the farm, I promised I'd be good to myself."

Jones would be all right, McGarvey figured.

"Anything else?" Maria asked.

"No," Jones said.

"Then let's get started," she said.

It had been many years since McGarvey had last made a dive,
and then it had been the type that Jones typified as "Bahamian."
Warm, crystal-clear water, in depths of less than one hundred
feet.

This was completely and ominously different. He followed
Maria's bubbles down along the buoy anchor line. The water
was penetratingly cold, and just under the surface visibility
dropped to less than ten feet. It was like swimming in pea soup,
or in a fog, or, the thought caused him to shiver, in a very deep
cave.

When he'd been changing into his wet suit in the main saloon,
McGarvey had happened to glance aft at the nav station, where

Jones had been studying the strip charts from the magnetometer. The captain had made a pencil sketch from the readings. The drawing was crude but recognizable as a submarine, its conning tower rising up at an angle, the boat down by the stern.

How much of the sketch was an accurate depiction of the magnetometer readings, and how much of it was speculation on Jones's part, was a moot question. McGarvey figured he would be seeing it for himself very soon.

At seventy feet he had to stop for a moment and clear his ears before he could continue.

At one hundred feet the water suddenly got warmer and visibility dramatically increased to forty or fifty feet. It was as if he were in an airplane that had just descended out of one cloud bank and he was now looking down at another.

Maria was disappearing below him, still following the buoy anchor line, and he kicked down after her, increasing his speed.

Below 150 feet it began to get much darker, as if it were the very late afternoon or early evening of a thickly overcast day. The water temperature again dropped, and he could feel his strength beginning to ebb. Jones had warned them that beyond 200 feet they would begin to experience nitrogen narcosis, what was called "rapture of the deep." Breathing ordinary compressed air at that depth created a state much like drunkenness. The victim's coordination and judgment were impaired; some divers decided that they no longer needed to breathe air, that breathing water would be just fine, so they took out their mouthpieces and drowned.

"Watch yourselves and each other," Jones had repeatedly warned.

Maria had seemed unconcerned, but McGarvey had taken the warnings to heart.

At about two hundred feet there was another thermal inversion and the water cleared. It was dark, but McGarvey could see that something very large lay on the bottom, stretching left and right into the blackness.

At first he was unable to see Maria, but then he spotted her trail of bubbles leading downward and to his left. She was far below him, barely visible.

He swam down, slowly angling toward where she had disappeared into the gloom, stopping a minute later when her hand light came on. She was at the submarine's conning tower. He

could make out the periscope and snorkel now, and as he
watched, her light flashed on a large white *U* painted on the
side of the sail. The beam shifted to illuminate a figure two, and
then the seven, the nine and the eight. It was her submarine.

McGarvey swam a little closer until he was just about at the
same depth as she was, but well aft of the conning tower. She
still had not spotted him. She kicked off and swam around the
front of the sail, disappearing on the other side.

McGarvey swam the few yards across the afterdeck to the
starboard side of the boat. Maria was just entering the submarine
through an open hatch at the base of the sail. The escape trunk,
he figured. But it was open. Someone had probably gotten out
of the boat that way.

He had started to swim forward when he spotted another
open hatch directly below him. He stopped, then swam down to
it. Switching on his light, he shined the beam into the interior of
the U-boat. At first he could make little sense out of what he was
seeing. He was looking down into the boat's machinery spaces,
probably into the engine room itself. But everything was in a
jumbled mess. One of the bulkheads was twisted and nearly torn
away from the inner hull. The decking beneath it was buckled.

There had been an explosion aboard.

Backing out of the blown hatch, McGarvey looked forward.
Maria was still inside the boat. He turned and swam the rest of
the way to the starboard side of the boat and followed the
steeply curving hull down.

A very large hole had been blown out of the side of the
submarine. He could look all the way through the pressure hull
into the machinery spaces.

His lips were beginning to feel thick, but the water temperature no longer seemed to bother him, and he was not feeling
so claustrophobic.

He held up his right arm so that he could see the depth gauge
strapped to his wrist. He could read the numbers, but for a long
second or two they didn't seem to make any sense.

More than two hundred feet. He recognized the first number.
Then he understood that he was at 268 feet, and that he was
feeling the effects of nitrogen narcosis.

Time to leave; the thought struggled to form in his head.
Warning bells were beginning to jangle at the pit of his stomach.

A Company psychologist had once told him that the reason

he was so good at what he did, the reason he had survived for so long in a profession whose mortality rate was extremely high, was because he had an overdeveloped instinct for survival.

"You don't know when, or probably even how, to give up," the doctor had told him.

There was a certain humor in that notion, McGarvey thought, that he'd never seen before.

He pushed away from the submarine's hull and hung there ten feet above the sandy bottom. He looked down. Something had fallen out of or had been blown from the submarine and littered the bottom. He languidly swam the rest of the way down, the air from his regulator thick and sour-tasting.

With great effort he managed to switch on his light and shine the beam on one of the bricklike objects, while with his other hand he fanned the silt from it.

For a seeming eternity he had trouble understanding what he was looking at. But the object was shiny, reflecting the harsh light. And it was gold. That fact slowly penetrated the fog in his head.

With exaggerated care, McGarvey picked up the gold bar, fumbled it into the mesh bag clipped to his waist, and pushed himself upward.

It was difficult swimming up from the bottom with the extra weight. When he reached the sub's afterdeck he sank to his knees to rest for a moment, his head already clearing.

The beam of Maria's light flashed across him, and he looked up as she descended to him from above the conning tower. When she got close he could see that her eyes were very wide behind her face mask. She was frightened.

She gave McGarvey the thumbs-up sign, and he repeated it for her. Then he pointed upward. She nodded.

He waited until she'd started up to transfer a little air from his two tanks into the buoyancy-compensator vest to counteract the extra weight he was carrying, and then followed her at an angle toward the buoy anchor line that rose in the gloom, his head becoming clearer with each foot as they approached the surface.

Kurshin watched as the canvas-covered truck pulled up on the quay alongside the *Común*, a hundred-foot aluminum pleasure vessel. The same two men he'd spotted at the airport climbed down from the cab and were joined by three crewmen from the ship.

The Puerto Nuevo section of Buenos Aires, which was just a couple of miles southeast of the U.S. embassy, was busy this morning. No one paid any attention to Kurshin, who was seated in his rental car, or to the crewmen who quickly unloaded the aluminum cases from the truck and started bringing them aboard the sleek ship.

McGarvey and the woman had come to Buenos Aires, according to Dr. Hesse. And Kurshin figured that sooner or later the CIA would come looking for them. By now they would have discovered the evidence he'd planted not only at the Paris embassy, but in McGarvey's apartment as well. At the very least they would want to bring the man in for questioning. The Company had the organization and the manpower to do in a few days something that might take him months to accomplish if he had to work alone.

His planning and patience had finally paid off.

CIA interests in Argentina were not conducted out of the embassy as they were in many other countries. Here the Company operated out of Mercator Air Freight, Ltd., at Ezezia Airport, and to a more limited extent out of the Tomas Vestry Import/Export Co., GmbH, ostensibly a German firm here at Puerto Nuevo.

With everything that had been going on in Latin America in recent years, the CIA would be taking care not to advertise its presence here.

Kurshin had reasoned that the preliminary search for McGarvey and the woman might be carried out by local operatives, but that any real search would of necessity involve imported talent. Talent that would arrive in Argentina aboard a Mercator Air Freight flight.

He'd finally gotten lucky this morning. The two men were obviously American by the cut of their clothes and their looks. They'd brought with them a dozen large aluminum cases that had been passed through Argentinian customs without question before being trucked into the city to the Vestry Company docks.

They were here to find McGarvey, and apparently the Nazi submarine he and the woman were seeking.

The only question that remained was exactly where they intended to begin their search. A question Kurshin intended asking one of them at the earliest possible moment.

25

THE WEATHER HAD DETERIORATED drastically during the past forty minutes. When McGarvey surfaced just behind Maria he was propelled violently upward and to the west on the crest of a fifteen-foot wave.

For one moment Maria was rising above him on another wave, and in the next she had disappeared in a trough.

He'd caught a brief glimpse of the Chris-Craft about fifty yards downwind, hobby-horsing wildly in the rough seas. The deep low-pressure system had developed much faster than Jones had predicted.

Rising on the next crest, McGarvey caught sight of Maria again, well downwind from him. She seemed to be struggling with her mouthpiece and face mask. She was in trouble, and as he watched helplessly, a breaking wave buried her.

Immediately McGarvey released a little air from his buoyancy vest and dived beneath the surface as he took a snap compass course on where he'd last seen her.

Thrusting powerfully with his fins, and no longer impeded by the conditions on the surface, he managed to cover the distance between them in a couple of minutes, coming up once when he was within ten yards to make sure she had surfaced, and then diving again.

He surfaced within reaching distance of her and grabbed her tank harness, pulling her to him.

She struggled wildly until she realized what was happening. Her mask was half off her face, and she had spit out her mouthpiece. Her lips were blue, and spittle and mucus ran freely from her mouth and nose. She was in panic and on the verge of drowning.

McGarvey tried to shove the mouthpiece back into her mouth, but she pushed it away.

"No ... no ..." she cried, gagging and sputtering as she swallowed water. "Air ... no air ... tanks empty ..."

McGarvey took a deep breath, spit out his mouthpiece, and, holding Maria close put it in her mouth.

She nearly vomited, but almost immediately she forced herself to calm down. She drew in three measured breaths while looking directly and resentfully into his eyes.

McGarvey took the mouthpiece back, breathed deeply a couple of times, and returned it to her.

The wind was so strong that the division between water and air was almost nonexistent. Breathing was next to impossible.

They had drifted nearly down to the Chris-Craft, which was now barely fifteen yards away. The boat's stern landing platform rose and fell so violently that there was no way to approach it, let alone clamber aboard. McGarvey could see Jorge on the bridge, and he tried to signal, but the Argentinian was intent on keeping the boat at an angle into the wind. He did not see them as they bobbed in the huge waves.

There was a real danger, McGarvey decided, that they would drift past the boat and be impossible to find. Their wet suits were black and their faces white, the same colors as the dark water and cresting waves.

Jones appeared at the rail and spotted them. He shouted something to Jorge, who turned and saw them. Almost instantly the boat began to angle slowly toward them.

Jones pointed toward the landing platform at the stern, shook his head, and crossed his arms making the figure X, all of his movements and gestures exaggerated so that they could be clearly understood. Boarding by the swim platform was out. McGarvey waved his understanding and took another couple of deep breaths from his mouthpiece, handing it back to Maria.

McGarvey could not see how Jones was going to get them aboard under these conditions, but he had underestimated the man. The stern of the boat had been modified so that it looked almost like the aft section of a trawler, with a narrow deck above which rose a mast and sturdy boom.

Jones swung the boom out over the port side of the boat, then tossed a bright orange life jacket out over their heads, upwind of them. The jacket was attached by a nylon line to the boom.

As it drifted down on them, McGarvey snagged it and hurriedly tied a loop around Maria's waist, and another around her legs, making a crude sling for her to sit in.

She took a deep breath from his mouthpiece and handed it back.

There was enough slack in the line so that the boat's motion was not pulling at her yet. But as soon as McGarvey signaled, Jones took up the slack on the boom winch. Maria was violently yanked out of the water, swinging toward the wildly gyrating boat. She would have smashed into the hull, except that Jones had figured the length of line and the period of the waves just right, so that at the last moment she was dunked half into the water, coming up short.

Moments later the boat rose on the next wave at the same instant Jones hauled in on the boom line and Maria was yanked out of the water and dumped on the deck. It was like fishing.

In the precious seconds it took Jones to free Maria from the line, McGarvey had already drifted well behind the boat, and Jorge had to bring it around downwind of him. For ten or fifteen seconds he was out of sight of anyone aboard the Chris-Craft. Hurriedly, he pulled the gold bar from the mesh bag at his side, unzipped the front of his wet suit, stuffed the gold bar inside, under his left arm, and zipped up his suit.

This time it took two tries before Jones could get the life vest and line near enough for McGarvey to grab. But the boarding went as smoothly as it had for Maria, though McGarvey felt as if every muscle in his body had been yanked from his bones.

"Welcome aboard," Jones said.

"What the hell's wrong with her tanks?" McGarvey shouted. "She ran out of air."

"She has plenty of air. Her regulator just hung up, that's all," Jones said. "Did you find what you were looking for?"

McGarvey looked over at Maria, who was lying on the deck, still gasping for air. "It's down there."

"The German U-boat?"

"Yes."

"Jesus," Jones said softly. He looked out at the sea and shook his head. "We'll be back," he said. He looked at Maria. "We'll be back," he repeated.

"It's the second time you've saved my life," Maria said.

It was early afternoon, but already the day had turned very dark. Motion aboard the boat was so violent that almost everything had become impossible; cooking, eating, bathing, even moving from one part of the boat to the other entailed great risk. Jorge and Jones remained on the bridge. They were making for Puerto Lobos to the southwest, but the going was very slow.

Somehow Maria had managed to clean up and comb her hair, but she still looked battered and tense, braced in the doorway to McGarvey's aft cabin.

"It's getting to be a habit," he said, looking up. He had wedged himself in his bunk with a bottle of brandy.

"Thank you," she said. "But I'm going to need your help again. Now more than ever before."

"Sorry," McGarvey said, "but you're on your own. You've found what you're looking for. I'll leave it to you to work out the details between Jones and your Captain Esformes, and whatever assorted Nazis are still running around Argentina looking for their property."

Her eyes narrowed. "What are you talking about?"

"I found what you've been looking for all this time. What you were really looking for."

"I don't understand—" she said, stopping in midsentence.

McGarvey had wrapped the gold bar in a towel. He pulled

himself up and got it from the shelf beside his bunk, then unwrapped it and laid it on the blanket.

"There was an explosion aboard," McGarvey said. "Aft. Probably in the engine room. There's more of this down there on the ocean floor, and presumably even more inside the boat."

The gold bar was stamped with the swastika.

Maria stared at it, an unreadable expression clouding her features.

"I'd suspect this is the recast dental work from the Jews they killed. A little nest egg for your friends here in Argentina. But you're going to have to fight a lot of people for it."

Maria shook her head. "It's not what you think," she said thickly.

"No? Are you denying that this is what you came looking for?"

"I'm not denying anything, Kirk. All I'm trying to tell you is that what you think you see isn't necessarily so."

"Look, I don't care any longer. I shouldn't be here. I belong back in Europe, where I left a very large mess that needs to be straightened out. At first I thought you were somehow involved with it, but now I know better. As soon as we reach Puerto Lobos I'll leave you to it." He nodded toward the gold. "Now, if you'll get that out of here, perhaps I can get a little rest."

"Don't be stupid," Maria snarled. "I'm trying to tell you something." She flipped her hair back. "Now that you've found this, you can know the rest."

"Let me guess," McGarvey said dryly. "You're an Israeli in search of Nazi gold."

Maria's eyes flashed, a little color coming to her cheeks. "I'm an Argentinian of German descent, and my grandfather was the skipper of that submarine down there."

"But?"

"My father killed Jews for the Odessa—"

"The organization of former SS officers."

"Yes," she said. "Which was somehow gruesomely funny because he was part Jew himself."

She had lied to him from the beginning, but this now was the most fantastic. "Your father killed Jews, even though he himself was a Jew, and your grandfather, also presumably a Jew, commanded a Nazi submarine. And they were related to Hitler, who was probably a Jew, right?"

"I'm telling you the truth. My grandfather's mother was a Jew, but she married a Gentile and converted to Christianity, and later the records were lost."

"Then how did you come to find out about your heritage?"

"Because my great-grandfather told his son, and my grandmother told my father, who told me."

"But your father killed Jews."

Maria nodded. "By the time he'd been told, he was too old to accept it, or he didn't care. I don't know. But he was a Nazi and he simply could not be Jewish, so he lashed out. He killed Jews to prove he wasn't Jewish. He told me that he had no feelings about it, and that I shouldn't, either."

"I see," McGarvey said after a pause, not certain if he believed her, though in this story she seemed sincere. "So now, in an effort to clear your family's name, you want to find this gold which you will turn over to the government of Israel for humanitarian purposes. You want to wash your own hands as well. Cleanse your soul."

"Yes," Maria said defiantly, her nostrils flared. "But not with that." She pointed at the gold bar. She pulled out a narrow-bladed dagger from the waistband of her trousers and lurched forward, falling against the bunk.

For a second McGarvey thought she was attacking him, and he raised up to defend himself. Instead she used the knife to score a line on the bottom of the gold bar.

"There's your gold," she said.

McGarvey cautiously sat forward and examined what she had done. The bar he'd brought up from the bottom was lead, as far as he could tell. It had been covered with a thin layer of gold.

"That's what my grandfather brought over from Germany," she said. "He and Roebling were to be used as decoys while the real gold, much more than could have been hauled by a dozen submarines, was hidden somewhere else."

"How do you know this?" McGarvey asked. She had his interest now.

She sheathed her knife. "Because Major Roebling escaped from the submarine after setting the explosives that sank her. He'd fixed the watertight doors so that they were jammed open, and he even fixed the escape trunk hatch, making it tamperproof. He was the only one to escape. Everyone else aboard, including my grandfather, drowned."

"Why did he do it? He thought he was bringing over a fortune. Why sink it?"

"Somehow he found out about the ruse, and he knew that they had been betrayed."

"Did he know by whom?"

"Yes," Maria said. "He was a brilliant man, but he was very greedy and ruthless. If the gold wasn't to be used to establish the Fourth Reich, then he wanted it for himself. He made his way up to Buenos Aires, where he began killing everyone he figured knew about the switch."

"Then he must have also known where the real gold was stashed," McGarvey said.

"He said he did."

"What happened to him?"

"He was killed in a shoot-out in the city," Maria said.

"What happened to the gold?"

"It was never found."

"But you know where it is," McGarvey said. "You found something in the submarine."

"In the escape trunk," Maria said, her eyes bright. "Major Roebling's bag snagged on something in those last dark, frantic moments. He had to leave the boat without it in order to save his own life. And I found it."

McGarvey sat back. He lit a cigarette in order to give himself time to think. It was an extraordinary story she was telling him, true or not. Yet it was nothing more than a treasure hunt.

"Contact the Mossad. They'll help you," he said.

She laughed disparagingly. "What, help the daughter of a Jew killer?"

"Then retrieve the gold yourself. You said you've found Roebling's bag, presumably containing the . . . treasure map. That's what you found, wasn't it?"

"No," Maria said, looking away for a moment. "The man had been lying. He didn't know where the gold was hidden."

"Then, what?"

"But he knew the men who'd hidden it."

"So what?" McGarvey said. "The gold is gone, then. Spent. Invested."

"That much gold? We would have heard about it. There was simply too much of it."

"We?" McGarvey asked.

"The world. People. The Allies after the war. The Israelis. Hell, even the Russians."

"But the men who Roebling suspected knew its whereabouts must be dead by now."

"Maybe not, Kirk. It's what I'm asking you to help me with. The group was called Der Amt Sechster Anbau—the Office of the Sixth Annex."

"Based where? Berlin?"

"Lisbon," Maria said. "Admiral Canaris had set up the network during the first war under the Office of Special Submarine Intelligence Operations. He knew the Spanish and Portuguese coasts like the back of his hand. His knowledge was no doubt passed along to Walther Schellenberg, who took over from him near the end of the second war. Kirk, there are millions of places along those coasts for the gold to have been hidden."

"The chances are a million to one that it was ever there, or is still there, or that there are any members of the Amt Sechster Anbau still alive who would know about it."

"Maybe a million-to-one chance, but this is billions of dollars in gold. Tens of billions."

"I'm not a treasure hunter."

"You must help me."

"No," McGarvey said. "Not this time."

A storm had developed from the southeast during the late morning and early afternoon, so that by four o'clock the sky was deeply overcast, and cars in Buenos Aires had to run with parking lights. Kurshin noticed that no one in the city ever used headlights.

Work on the docks began to slow down, and a group of men gathered in the foreman's shack at the end of the quay, the light from within dim and yellow.

At six, the shorter of the two Americans came off the ship, walked down the quay to an old Chevrolet, got behind the wheel, and took off.

Kurshin followed him in his rented Taurus, careful not to lose him in the dense traffic downtown, until it became clear that he was heading to the U.S. embassy. The man was taking his time, either because he was in no hurry, or more likely because he was uncertain of the traffic in a strange city.

On the broad avenida Santa Fe, Kurshin was able to speed up

and get a half block ahead of the American, pulling over sharply and parking in the first available spot.

He yanked his pistol out of its holster and stuffed it in his jacket pocket, jumped out of his car, and, as the Chevy approached, stepped out in front of it.

The American slammed on his brakes, coming to a complete halt as he laid on his horn.

Kurshin pulled the gun from his pocket and darted around to the passenger side. He yanked the door open and slipped inside before the American had a chance to react.

"Drive," Kurshin ordered, showing the American the gun.

"What the hell is this . . ." the CIA agent sputtered. He looked military: short-cropped hair, closely shaved face, khaki trousers and shirt.

"Drive, or I will kill you here and now," Kurshin said.

Traffic was piling up behind them, and other drivers were honking their horns.

"If a cop shows up, I will shoot you," Kurshin warned.

The American took off. At the next intersection Kurshin instructed him to turn left, away from the river and the embassy.

"If this is some kind of a stickup, I don't have very much on me, and besides, you'd be making a big fucking mistake."

"On the contrary, it is you who have made the mistake, coming here to look for McGarvey and his woman," Kurshin said in a reasonable tone.

The CIA officer nearly lost control of the car. When he recovered, he said, "What the hell is this? What do you want? Who the hell are you?" He was tan, but his complexion had begun to pale.

"A friend. I want to know where McGarvey is keeping himself these days. I want to have a word with him."

"I don't know what you're talking about. McGarvey who?"

"You do know, and you'll tell me, either the easy way or the hard way. Personally, I don't care which."

After a half-dozen blocks they had come to one of the many slums called *villas miserias*. It was a densely packed area lined with tin and cardboard shacks, with open sewers along the sides of the narrow, filthy streets. The slum was crisscrossed with dark alleys and dead-end streets.

Kurshin had the American pull over, shut off the engine, and kill the lights.

"I don't know what the fuck you're talking about. I swear to Christ."

"Let's go for a walk," Kurshin said, motioning with his gun for the agent to get out of the car.

"Christ . . . Christ, don't do this. What do you want? Just tell me. Money? Whatever."

"You and your partner showed up at Mercator with a dozen aluminum cases, which you trucked to that ship at the Vestry docks. Mercator and Vestry are both fronts for Central Intelligence Agency activities in Argentina. You are here to find Kirk McGarvey, whom you suspect was involved with the attack on your Paris embassy. You believe he is currently somewhere along the coast searching for a Nazi submarine that may have been sunk at the end of the war."

The American was breathing rapidly through his mouth. He was impressed.

"All I need to know is, where will you begin your search? Where do you believe McGarvey and the woman are at this moment?"

The American was shaking his head. "If you know that much, then you know that I can't tell you anything. You're the opposition. Okay, pal, you've got me. But the goddamned cold war is over. Let us clean up our own house."

"Get out of the car," Kurshin said.

"Bullshit."

Kurshin cocked the pistol's hammer.

The American hurriedly opened the door and slid out, Kurshin right behind him.

"What the fuck do you think you're going to do?"

Kurshin lowered his aim and fired, the bullet catching the American in the left kneecap. The man screamed in pain as he collapsed in the filthy street.

No one came running; no one sounded the alarm. No one would, in this section of the city.

Kurshin hunched down beside the American and jammed the barrel of the pistol into the man's scrotum. "Where do you believe McGarvey has gotten himself to?"

The American was sobbing in pain and fear. "Christ, Christ . . ."

"Where?" Kurshin asked softly.

The American looked up, pleading. "Viedma. The Gulf of San Matías."

"I hope you're not lying."

"No, no, I swear to God. We're leaving in a few hours. We're supposed to be there sometime tomorrow. God, I swear it."

"I believe you," Kurshin said, and he stood up and shot the man in the head at point-blank range.

26

IT HAD TAKEN THEM nearly ten hours in the steadily rising wind and seas to make the forty-five nautical miles southwest to the breakwater off the town of Puerto Lobos.

They'd had nothing to eat during the long day. Except for the one visit, Maria had kept to her cabin forward of the saloon. As far as McGarvey knew, Jones and his mate had remained topside on the bridge, trying to bring them in to safety.

McGarvey had actually managed to get a few hours of sleep, despite the extreme motion and uncertainty about their chances. But he had pushed himself dangerously close to collapse on the dive. At forty-six he was no longer a kid, and despite his good physical condition, his age was beginning to catch up with him.

His dreams were jumbled and confused, and involved erotic

pictures of Maria, naked on a huge pile of gold bars, all stamped with the swastika. She was beckoning to him, but someone else out of the range of his vision was calling to him, trying to tell him something. He could hear the desperation in the person's voice, but he could not tell who was calling, nor even the speaker's gender, which left him frustrated and disturbed.

When he woke it was pitch-dark in his cabin. If anything, the motion of the sea had gotten worse, and for several seconds, disoriented, he was on the verge of becoming seasick.

He pulled himself out of his bunk and, bracing himself against the bulkhead, cupped his hands around the small porthole and looked out into the night. He glanced at his watch; it was nearly ten.

At first he could see nothing, but then he thought he spotted lights ahead to the south, and a second later he caught the flash of the navigational beacon on the end of the Puerto Lobos breakwater. They had arrived, but this close to shore the waves were tremendous and extremely dangerous.

Pulling on his foul-weather jacket, McGarvey lurched out of his cabin into the empty main saloon, which smelled strongly of diesel fuel, sloshing bilges, and the heads. Dim red and amber lights on the navigation equipment above the chart table aft, and a thin line of white light from beneath Maria's door forward, provided the only illumination. The companionway hatch leading topside was partly open, but the night above it was utterly dark.

He hesitated for a minute. Perhaps he should speak to Maria again, try to explain to her why he was leaving. But then he decided that he owed her no explanation. In fact, it was she who owed him the truth.

He had started for the companionway when Jorge suddenly appeared at the hatch and came down the ladder, a broad grin on his dark face.

"Where is the woman?" the Argentinian demanded in clear English.

"So, he does speak after all," McGarvey replied carefully. This was trouble. His gun was holstered at the small of his back beneath his foul-weather gear.

Jorge glanced at her door. "Get her. The captain wants both of you topside immediately."

"What does he want?"

"Get the woman," Jorge repeated. "Immediately. There is no time."

"Time for what?" McGarvey asked.

Jorge pulled out a big gun, cocked the hammer, and pointed it at the center of McGarvey's chest. It was a .357 magnum, and the Argentinian's hand was steady. "Hurry."

"Maria," McGarvey shouted without taking his eyes off Jorge. "Maria. Come out here," he called. "And bring the . . . gold with you."

"That is not necessary—" Jorge began, but abruptly stopped.

"You know," McGarvey said to him. "Maria!" he shouted. He turned and lurched across the saloon, bracing himself against the dining table as the boat swung around broadside to the waves for a moment before coming dead into the wind. They were heading back out to sea.

The door to Maria's cabin opened and she came out. "Are we almost there?" she asked, and then she spotted Jorge beyond McGarvey. "Oh," she said, reaching for the doorframe for support.

"They want the gold," McGarvey said, looking into her eyes.

"No!" Jorge shouted from behind him.

"We're going to give it to them. Now," McGarvey said.

"All right," Maria said, and before Jorge could do anything she turned and went back into her cabin.

"Get away from that door," the Argentinian yelled. He was suddenly very agitated.

Maria was back a second later. She handed the heavy gold bar to McGarvey, who turned and held it up.

"This is what you want, isn't it?"

Jorge's black eyes grew large, his greed obvious on his lined face. It was a universal look, unmistakable. His gun hand wavered.

"We don't want any trouble," McGarvey said, taking a step closer.

Jorge's aim steadied.

"You can have this, and the rest aboard the sub. Just put us ashore."

"That's up to the captain."

McGarvey smiled reassuringly and took another step closer. The boat was rising and falling by the bow now. It felt as if they had nearly stopped and were maintaining their position somewhere off the breakwater.

"If you want to share it with him and his pals, that's up to you. But we just want to make it to shore."

"It's not my business," Jorge said.

McGarvey took another step closer, and stumbled, dropping the gold bar.

Jorge instinctively moved forward in an effort to grab the gold bar. At that moment he was open and vulnerable. McGarvey shifted his weight to his left foot and kicked out with his right, catching the Argentinian's gun hand.

The pistol discharged, the noise deafening in the narrow confines of the saloon. McGarvey was on top of the man in the next instant, driving him against the companionway stairs.

Though short, Jorge was extremely strong. Almost immediately he had the advantage, bodily forcing McGarvey back, turning the gun inward.

"Kirk!" Maria cried.

The boat dropped into a trough with a tremendous lurch, and McGarvey let himself go limp, falling back under Jorge's attack.

The Argentinian was suddenly propelled forward by his own strength, and before he realized what was happening to him, he went completely over McGarvey, the wrist of his gun hand snapping with a loud pop.

Jorge bellowed in pain and rage, scrambling to his feet as he pulled out his skinning knife.

McGarvey snatched up the gun. "I don't want to kill you," he shouted.

Jorge stopped short, fury in his face.

Maria rushed across the saloon. "*¡Bastardo!*" she screamed, and before Jorge could react, she plunged her dagger to the hilt in his back.

The Argentinian cried out, stumbled forward, and then went down.

Kurshin got lucky. An Austral flight to Viedma put him in the Patagonian city a little after nine in the evening. He was able to rent a car at the airport, and in the city it took him only five telephone calls before he'd found that McGarvey and the woman had stayed briefly at the Hotel Matías, but were gone.

It was what he'd expected. They would be out on the water searching for the submarine. Or at least they had been out there. He didn't think they'd be out on a night like this, however. The weather here was even worse than it had been in Buenos Aires. The flight down had been rough.

He reasoned that they would have had to hire a workboat to take them out. They'd need the equipment and the crew to operate it if they expected any chance of success.

Such a boat and crew, he was told, could be hired at only one marina in the city.

It was ten-thirty by the time he got there, and except for a dim light or two on a couple of the boats, the place seemed deserted.

He drove down the long dirt track and pulled up in front of the ramshackle marina office. Shutting off his lights, but leaving the engine running, he got out of the car.

The air smelled of the sea, of creosote, and of diesel fuel. Nothing moved in the night wind except for tree branches and boats' rigging. Someone aboard one of the boats laughed and shouted something, and then was quiet again.

It was possible that McGarvey and the woman had come back here, and were at this moment aboard one of the boats. But somehow he didn't think that was the case.

He was reaching inside the car to turn off the engine when someone came up out of the darkness behind him.

"¿Que pasa, señor?"

Kurshin spun around, reaching for his pistol. But it was just an old man with dark, leathery skin and whispy white hair.

"I'm looking for my friends. I was told they might be here," he replied in Spanish.

"Are they fishermen, these friends of yours?" the old man asked pleasantly.

"No. The man is American and the woman is an Argentinian."

"Oh, yes, they are with Captain Jones aboard the *Yankee Girl*. But they are not here. They have been gone for three days now."

"Where?"

The old man shrugged, and glanced toward the docks and the river. "On the gulf."

"But not tonight," Kurshin suggested.

"No, of course not."

"Did they head north?"

"No, it was south."

"But they are not here?"

"No," the old man said.

"Where, then?"

"Perhaps not so far south as Golfo Nuevo."

"No?"

The old man shrugged. "They have no doubt gone to safety at Puerto Lobos. It is the only sensible thing to do. And Captain Jones is a sensible man."

"How far is this city to the south?"

"By water or by highway?"

"By highway."

Again the old man shrugged. "Two hundred, perhaps three hundred kilometers. But the road is good."

"*Gracias,*" Kurshin said.

The old man nodded, and stepped back as Kurshin climbed into his car, flipped on the headlights, and headed back to the highway. If he pushed it, he figured he could make Puerto Lobos in less than three hours. The timing would be perfect.

There was a lot of surge in the small harbor. They had to put out automobile tires to save the boat from beating herself to death against the docks.

Jones had been extremely wary ever since McGarvey, and not Jorge, had come topside to help bring the boat through the breakwater. But he'd said nothing, and McGarvey had maintained the silence until they were safely docked. It was nearly one in the morning. Nothing moved on the streets of the small port town, although a couple of the waterfront bars were open and seemed to be doing a lively business.

"Your mate is dead," McGarvey said.

"I see," the man said expressionlessly.

"You wanted the gold for yourselves," McGarvey said softly. "But there is none down there."

Jones said nothing.

"What I brought up was a solid lead bar, with a coating of gold to make it look authentic. Somebody was playing a trick."

Jones's eyes narrowed. "You won't get out of Argentina alive," he said.

"I think you are in more trouble here than you realize, Captain," McGarvey continued. "This is your boat, and he was your mate. You'll have to do something with the body."

"The police—"

"Will do nothing. In Buenos Aires there are people who would be upset to learn that you have been dredging up old Nazi secrets. Powerful people who have influence with the police."

"Then I will kill you myself."

"You might try," McGarvey said. "But I have a better solution for you."

Jones said nothing. Finally he inclined his head slightly.

"There are a lot of lead bars down there to be salvaged."

"Lead is not worth the effort."

"But each bar is covered in gold. Maybe a few ounces each. Maybe eight hundred to a thousand dollars apiece. Not a fortune, but worth the effort."

"What about Jorge?" Jones asked.

"The submarine holds many secrets," McGarvey said. "One more will make no difference. Does he have family?"

Jones shook his head. "How do I know if you're telling the truth?"

"The lead bar I brought from the bottom is in the saloon."

"I mean about what's left on the bottom."

"Go see for yourself."

"I don't dive . . ."

"I think you do if the rewards are there."

Jones remained silent for a moment or two. He glanced at the companionway hatch. "What about you and the woman?"

"We'll leave tonight. Immediately."

"What's to prevent you from turning this over to the police —or to your friends in Buenos Aires?"

"For what reason?" McGarvey said. "We came looking for gold, and we did not find it."

"But you found something," Jones said. "Something worth more than a submarine filled with gold."

"Don't press your luck," McGarvey warned. "I'm offering you an easy way out. Take it."

"If I don't?"

"You won't like the consequences. Believe me."

For a long time Jones just stared at McGarvey. Then he moved away from the companionway hatch. "I don't want trouble."

McGarvey nodded. "Maria," he called.

She appeared at the hatch with their things. But she hesitated, not quite certain of the situation.

"Go," Jones said.

McGarvey motioned for Maria to get off the boat. Quickly she crossed the deck and, timing her move to coincide with the boat's motion in the surge, scrambled over the rail and onto the dock.

"I heard the shot," Jones said. "Did you kill him with his own gun?"

"No," McGarvey said at the rail. "Maria killed him."

"He was a friend," Jones said, but McGarvey had clambered over the rail, and he and Maria were hurrying off the long dock into the town.

27

KURSHIN STOOD IN THE shadows at the end of the Puerto Lobos dock. A couple of the portholes were lit aboard the *Yankee Girl*. Other than that the rest of the tiny harbor was in darkness, except for the four-and-a-half-second flashing green light at the end of the breakwater.

The wind was very strong. Even inside the harbor waves rose to three and four feet.

He checked his watch. It was a few minutes after one-thirty. He'd stood in the darkness for a full five minutes to make certain no one was hidden either on the deck of the thirty-eight-foot converted pleasure craft or on the dock somewhere.

Satisfied that there was no one, Kurshin took out his pistol and started for the boat.

In his mind was a jumble of confused thoughts and images and emotions with McGarvey at the dark center of each.

All of his failures—his disfavor with Baranov while the former KGB chief was still alive, and his own near death—could be attributed to McGarvey. But not to the American alone. In Kurshin's mind, McGarvey always had an army of backers behind him. Soldiers. Highly trained CIA operatives. Fieldmen. Shooters. Technicians. He had the cooperation of all the Western intelligence services. He knew the federal police forces in every Western nation. And most galling of all, the man had been incredibly lucky.

All of that had changed. Now the CIA was not his ally, nor were the police here in Argentina, or in France or in Germany. They all were looking for him.

He had the girl, but as far as Kurshin knew she was no professional. Which left only the captain and crew of the small boat he'd hired. They'd have only as much loyalty as a few dollars would buy. They would not have the stomach for an all-out fight when the time came.

Which left only McGarvey. This time it would be just the two of them. Head to head.

The boats and the floating dock were heaving on the waves, sometimes violently. Kurshin had to time his move as he scrambled aboard, and as it was he lost his footing and fell heavily to the deck, banging his right elbow.

He shifted the pistol to his left hand as the companionway hatch slid open and a heavyset man with pale hair looked out.

"What the fuck . . . !"

Kurshin was on Jones in an instant, jamming the barrel of the big pistol into his face. "Where is he?"

"What are you talking about?" Jones rasped, but Kurshin could see in the man's blue eyes that he was hiding something.

Kurshin cocked the hammer. "I want McGarvey. Where is he?"

"Gone. I swear it. Mother of God, the son of a bitch is gone."

A sharp stab of disappointment hit Kurshin's chest. "Gone? Where? Where is he?"

"I don't know. He and his woman just left. I swear to God. What are you, the police? They killed my mate. Stabbed him in the back."

This was impossible. He had come halfway around the world, betraying Didenko and even killing the general's soldiers in the process. He had come so fucking close. He tried to think it out. He'd passed no one heading north. The highway had been totally deserted.

Unless they had seen his headlights first, and had shut theirs off before he spotted them. They could have pulled over to the side of the road and he might have missed them.

But that was paranoia. They were still here. They had to be!

"How long ago did they leave?"

"A half hour. Maybe less. I swear to God, there's no one here except me. Jorge is dead."

It had been more than two days since Kurshin had last slept, and he was having trouble keeping his thoughts straight.

He could almost hear McGarvey's laughter. The thought of it, the sound of it in his head nearly drove him crazy.

"Jesus Christ, man, what's the matter with you?" Jones said.

Kurshin shot him in the head, driving him backward down the ladder into the saloon with a tremendous crash.

For a full minute Kurshin remained at the companionway hatch, listening for a sound from below. Any sound. But there was nothing other than the wind howling in the rigging, and the boat's hull banging against the rubber tires and the dock.

Cautiously Kurshin went below, swinging his pistol left to right, sparks jumping in front of his eyes as he came from darkness into light.

Jones lay on his back in a puddle of blood, his left eye destroyed. He was dead; there was absolutely no doubt about it. But there was a lot of blood. Too much blood, some of which led forward through an open door.

Kurshin hesitated a moment. The man had told him that his mate was dead. Stabbed in the back. His body could have been dragged forward.

Stepping carefully over Jones's body, and around the blood, Kurshin looked in the forepeak. A short, swarthy man, dressed in dungarees and a yellow slicker, lay facedown in the lower bunk. The back of his jacket was covered with blood. He had been dead for some time.

But why? Kurshin stepped back into the main saloon. What had happened here to cause McGarvey to kill one man, leave the other alive, and simply walk off with the woman? It didn't make sense.

Suddenly his eyes fell on something swaddled in a towel on the galley floor. He went over to it, bracing himself against the counter, and flipped aside a corner of the towel. It was a gold bar, a swastika and serial number stamped into the surface.

They'd found the submarine and the gold. They'd apparently dived down to it and retrieved ... what? He looked up. This gold bar at least. Others, perhaps? A lot more gold?

Working quickly, it took Kurshin less than ten minutes to search the entire boat from the forepeak to the aft cabins, and from the bridge to the bilges. But there was no more gold, although he found the scuba gear, a couple of .223-caliber automatic rifles, the magnetometer equipment, and below, at the chart table, Jones's calculations and sketches on the magnetometer readout strips. The navigational chart of the gulf showed not only their search pattern over the past three days, but the spot where they'd discovered the U-boat.

He still wanted McGarvey, but this now offered another possibility.

After memorizing the exact latitude and longitude of their find, he found a large plastic bag into which he stuffed the gold bar, still wrapped in the towel, the magnetometer strip graphs, and the gulf chart. Sealing the package with tape, he brought it topside, and making certain that no one was watching, he tossed it overboard.

Kurshin was not particularly interested in wealth; he'd never been interested in having more than he needed for survival and a modicum of comfort. But there were others who thought differently. Once McGarvey and the woman were dead, presumably no one else would know about the treasure. It could be a powerful bargaining chip. Very soon he was going to have to face General Didenko.

McGarvey would be dead, but the gold would be an offering. The KGB, especially in these times, was desperate for hard Western currencies to fund its foreign operations.

Didenko would be interested. And the general had what Kurshin needed for survival: assignments, targets, kills.

28

THE STORM INTENSIFIED THROUGH the night, blowing sheets of rain against the windows of the Victory Hotel in Puerto Lobos. Even the bars along the waterfront had closed, and there was no traffic below on the street.

McGarvey and Maria had gotten separate rooms for the night. In the morning they would rent a car and drive back to Viedma, where they would retrieve the airplane for the flight back to Buenos Aires. They would have to keep out of Esformes's way until they could get a flight out of the country, but McGarvey foresaw no trouble from the *federales*. Nor did he expect Jones to try anything. The man had been sufficiently intimidated to keep his mouth shut. And he had the prospect of making a fair sum of money from the fake gold bars from the submarine.

McGarvey had not been able to sleep. He stood in the darkness by the window, looking down on the deserted street as he smoked a cigarette.

He had not bothered to ask Maria what her plans were. He figured she had only two options: remain in Buenos Aires to straighten out the mess with the federal police over Rothmann's death, or pursue her search for the gold. He expected she would do the latter, and would fly to Lisbon at the first opportunity.

A dark blue Chevrolet came down the street from the general direction of the waterfront, made a U-turn in front of the hotel, and parked at the end of the next block.

It was nearly impossible to pick out details in the blowing rain, but after a moment the car's lights went off and a lone figure got out.

There was something faintly familiar about the person, and McGarvey's stomach began to knot.

He stubbed out his cigarette in the ashtray and watched as the figure walked back toward the hotel.

There was something. . . . But it was impossible, he told himself. It could not be.

He reached for the telephone and dialed Maria's room number, keeping his eyes on the approaching figure.

And in the end the legions from your past shall arise to strike you down. The agent come out of the field will spend his final days looking over his shoulder. It is axiomatic.

The figure stopped below and looked up. McGarvey pulled away from the window, his heart hammering. Christ!

It was Arkady Kurshin! Alive! Here!

The telephone began to ring in Maria's room down the hall.

It was impossible. And yet there was no doubt in McGarvey's mind that the man below was Kurshin. He'd known it from the moment the man got out of the car, from the way he walked, the way he held himself. He'd known it since Paris, when Carley had described the man who'd come to the embassy with the fake passport.

It had been Kurshin behind him all this time. In Paris, in Freiburg, and again in Buenos Aires.

The phone in Maria's room rang again. "Come on," McGarvey whispered urgently. He looked down again, but there was no one there now. Kurshin was inside the hotel.

The man had come here for revenge. That part was clear. But what about Paris? Why had he gone through all of that? And what about Maria? Was there a connection between them after all?

Her phone rang a third time.

To each fieldman comes the moment when he must face himself through his past. The more extreme his dossier, the more violent his acts, the more terrible this showdown will likely be. For some it is a matter of honor, or dishonor. For others it is a life's summation that adds up to less than zero. For still others it is a nemesis come back to be reckoned with.

The son of a bitch had traced them to this hotel. How?

Maria's phone rang again, and she answered it. "What is it . . . ?" she mumbled sleepily.

"Get the hell out of your room right now!"

"What?" she demanded, coming fully awake. "Kirk?"

"We've got trouble. Get out of your room. Go up to the third floor and wait in the maid's closet. But do it now!"

"What kind of trouble?"

"Russian," McGarvey said. He slammed the phone down, then grabbed his jacket and pistol, opened the door a crack, and looked out into the corridor. There were five other rooms on this floor. Nothing moved for the moment. But Kurshin was certainly on his way up.

The man had somehow tracked them to Viedma, and he could have learned from someone at the marina where they'd gone. Figuring that they would not remain at sea in this storm, he'd come to the only other logical spot where they might put in, and he was checking all the hotels in town.

Which meant he'd already been to the docks. To the *Yankee Girl*. Jones, by now, was almost certainly dead.

McGarvey slipped out into the corridor and hurried to the stairs. It would take Kurshin only a minute or so to find out what rooms they were in.

Maria came out of her room as someone started up from the lobby.

"Kirk," she called, and he turned and frantically motioned for her to be silent, but it was too late. Whoever was on the stairs below had stopped.

Kurshin stood pressed against the wall between the first and second floors, fingering the safety catch of his gun. It had been a woman's voice calling the name. Unmistakable. They knew he was coming and they were waiting for him. He had lost the element of surprise, but it was of no matter.

Someone would die here tonight. It would be either McGarvey or him. Somehow, now that he was this near, he didn't think he really cared which. The final confrontation was all that mattered.

"McGarvey," he called softly.

Below in the lobby the night clerk lay dead behind the counter. There was no one to interfere this time.

"I thought you were dead, Arkasha," McGarvey's voice drifted down to him. That the American had used the diminutive form of his first name did not bother him as he thought it should.

"I very nearly was," Kurshin answered. "But I'm back."

"What do you want?"

"You."

"What about the woman?"

"Send her away. This is between you and me."

There was silence from above. Kurshin moved away from the wall and leaned forward so that he could see farther up the stairs. McGarvey, he figured, was on the landing just above.

McGarvey fired, the noise of the unsilenced pistol shockingly loud and intimate in the confines of the stairwell, the bullet smacking into the plaster wall well above Kurshin's head.

"You missed," he said, ducking back.

"It was you in Paris, wasn't it," McGarvey said.

"Yes."

"Why?"

Kurshin chuckled. The question was satisfying. McGarvey hadn't figured out what was happening. "If you survive this night you will see."

"A lot of innocent people died in your attack. It was a senseless gesture."

"There are no innocents, you know that."

Someone else on the second floor said something, and a woman stifled a scream. "Get back," McGarvey called urgently.

"Oh, no," Kurshin said. "I'm coming for you, McGarvey." Keeping his back against the wall he eased himself up a step, and then another.

McGarvey fired a shot, the bullet splattering plaster dust. His fleeting shadow flashed against the wall, and Kurshin fired three shots in rapid succession.

"It was an act of insanity, Arkasha," McGarvey said after a few moments. His voice was distant and yet sensually close. "Baranov is dead, Arkasha. I killed him. Shot him in the back of the head. Tell me, who is your circus master these days?"

Kurshin laughed again, but this time he felt the beginnings of a constriction in his throat, in his chest. "I've been to the boat. I know about the gold."

There was only silence from above. He could hear the wind-driven rain against the building. McGarvey was testing him. Waiting for him to make a mistake. His grip tightened on his pistol as he moved up another step.

The situation was getting totally out of hand. There were too many people up and awake now. Three doors on this floor were open. Kurshin would not hesitate to kill anyone in his path, anyone who tried to interfere with him. A lot of people were going to get hurt, unless the fight could be led away from the hotel.

McGarvey wanted to end it here and now. He had waited a very long time to be sure about the Russian. This time he wanted no uncertainties. He wanted to see Kurshin falling; he wanted to see the man's blood. He wanted to feel for a dying pulse in his body, feel the flesh growing cold.

Maria was watching him, wide-eyed. "Who is it?" she mouthed the words silently.

McGarvey motioned for her to go upstairs, but she shook her head.

"We'll both go up to the roof," McGarvey said just loudly enough so that he was certain Kurshin could hear him.

"The notebook is in my room. I didn't get a chance to bring it with me," Maria protested.

"Fuck the notebook," McGarvey said. "Upstairs! Now!"

He stuck his gun arm around the corner and fired two shots down into the stairwell, then lunged across the corridor, grabbed Maria by the arm, and roughly propelled her up the stairs.

Kurshin came after them in a rush, firing as he came, one of the shots plucking at the back of McGarvey's pants leg. McGarvey cried out in pain, and fired two more shots back.

They rounded the corner halfway up to the third floor, and

continued up, stopping at the top to listen for footsteps from below. Nothing.

"Are you hurt?" Maria asked.

McGarvey shook his head. A thin man in a bathrobe had come out of his room halfway down the corridor. McGarvey frantically waved him back, and the man ducked into his room and shut the door.

"I want you to go up to the roof," McGarvey whispered urgently. "Find a way down, or at least find a hiding place and stay there until I come for you."

"I'm not going to leave Roebling's notebook downstairs," she argued. "You heard him—he says he knows about the gold."

"He doesn't care about that, goddamnit," McGarvey whispered. He ejected the spent clip from his gun, pulled his only spare out of his pocket, and snapped it in place. He had no other ammunition.

It was quiet in the stairwell. Too quiet. McGarvey reached around the corner and fired a shot down, Kurshin's answering fire coming so fast and accurately that McGarvey felt the bullet passing his head.

"Time to die," Kurshin called. "What do you say?"

"What does he want?" Maria asked.

"Me," McGarvey said. "He wants me dead. But he'll kill anyone with me. I want you up on the roof. Now, before it's too late."

"And you're going to stay here, waiting for him?" she asked incredulously.

McGarvey nodded, his jaw tight. This time there would be no mistakes, no questions after the fact. This time he would know for sure.

"You're insane," Maria said. "Who is this man?"

"Russian."

"KGB?"

McGarvey nodded. His head was light. Twice Kurshin had nearly succeeded in killing him. He'd lost a kidney to one of the man's nine-millimeter bullets.

"The war is over," Maria said desperately. "At least what I'm doing means something—" She stopped herself in midsentence, realizing that she had gone too far.

"I don't care about your gold either," McGarvey said. "This

man has killed a lot of people. It was Kurshin who attacked our embassy in Paris."

"And you have killed, too," Maria said.

"Go up to the roof, dear," Kurshin said, his voice just around the corner, not more than five feet away. He had snuck up on them. McGarvey hadn't heard a thing; he hadn't been listening carefully enough. It had been a terribly foolish mistake.

He pulled Maria around behind him, and shoved her down the corridor.

"All right, Arkasha," he said in a reasonable tone as he backed off a couple of paces and raised his pistol. "I wonder if one of us is out of ammunition. Let's see, shall we?"

Kurshin started to laugh, but he cut himself off abruptly. For just a moment McGarvey thought it was another of the Russian's tricks, but then he heard the sirens in the distance. A lot of sirens, sometimes loud on the wind, then fading, but definitely getting closer.

Someone from the hotel must have called the police to report the shooting. But a town this size would not have so many police. There were a dozen sirens out there, maybe more.

But if Kurshin had traced them this far, perhaps Captain Esformes had done the same.

"Goddamnit, what are you waiting for?" McGarvey suddenly shouted. He was not going to be cheated! Not this time!

There was no answer from the stairwell, and the sirens were definitely coming closer.

"Kurshin!" McGarvey shouted.

"What is it?" Maria asked, frightened.

"It's your friend Esformes, I think. Maybe the army as well."

"After us?"

"I think so," McGarvey said through a red haze. Girding himself, he rushed the stairwell, extending his arm around the corner and firing two shots, then rolling into the open, firing a third shot.

But there was no one there. Kurshin was gone.

"Arkady!" McGarvey shouted. "You bastard! Come back!"

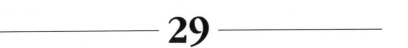

29

KURSHIN COULD BARELY CONTROL his rage enough to think straight. He wanted to turn back and rush up the stairs firing as he went, until McGarvey lay in a bloody heap at his feet.

But once again the American had been saved by luck. Kurshin did not want to commit suicide, after all. In the end his own life was more precious to him. There were other things in the world he wanted to see, and do. If nothing else, he wanted to be alive to savor McGarvey's death.

For just a moment he was torn with indecision. Go or stay. McGarvey above and the approaching police below. He did not want to be caught in a cross fire.

But the woman had been concerned about a notebook. It was apparently very important to her. A key of some kind?

Before he'd killed the desk clerk he'd gotten McGarvey's and the woman's room numbers. There was time, he told himself.

He rushed down the corridor and burst into Maria's room. Her overnight bag lay open on a chair in front of the window. Her purse was on the dresser.

Glancing over his shoulder to make sure that no one was behind him, Kurshin quickly went through her things. The leather-bound notebook was in her purse. A gold swastika was stamped on its cover beneath the letters R.S.H.A., for the German Reichssicherheitshauptamt, the Nazi secret service.

He pocketed the notebook and slipped back out into the corridor, his mind racing ahead to a dozen different possibilities. Less than thirty seconds had elapsed since McGarvey had fired his last shots, but already the sirens were nearly out front.

A door across the corridor opened and a portly bald man looked out at him.

For an instant Kurshin froze, but then he heard someone on the stairs. McGarvey! The bile was bitter in his throat. The bastard!

But there would be another time and place. There would have to be.

Before the confused hotel guest could react, Kurshin leaped across the corridor and burst into his room, shoving him off balance as he shut the door. The man had stumbled backward against the bed. Kurshin shot him in the head with his last bullet, then turned to face the door.

Nothing moved in the second-floor corridor. McGarvey crouched in a shooter's stance, his pistol in both hands, his heart hammering, the muscles of his legs twitching.

"Is he there?" Maria asked softly behind him.

"No. I don't think so."

The sirens were on top of them now. Someone downstairs in the lobby was shouting something, and elsewhere, perhaps outside, a woman was screaming.

"Kirk, I must have my passport. I can't get out of the country without it. And we need the notebook."

If it was Esformes outside and he caught up with them, it would be a long time before they went anywhere. But it was hard for McGarvey to keep his thoughts in order.

Kurshin had survived. He had tracked them all the way here

for revenge ... and what else? Paris meant something. It had to mean something, but to McGarvey it made no sense.

"Come," he said, straightening up and pounding down the corridor to her room.

She came right behind him, and slipped inside while he waited. Now all the doors were closed. No one wanted to risk trying to see what was going on.

Maria collected her purse and bag. "What about your things?" she asked, but the sirens were out front now, and there was a huge commotion in the lobby.

It would take the police, or whoever they were, a minute or two to get organized and seal off the entire hotel, front and back. It would take them even longer to seal off the small town. Precious minutes that they would have to use to their best advantage.

McGarvey grabbed her arm and propelled her down the corridor to the stairwell. Downstairs a man was shouting orders in Spanish.

"It's him," Maria whispered. "Esformes. I know the voice. He knows we're here."

Someone started up from the lobby.

McGarvey shoved Maria up the stairs, and they barely made it around the corner before the police were on the second floor.

At the head of the stairs Maria pulled McGarvey forcibly into the third-floor corridor. "There," she said, pointing to the window at the opposite end. The glass was painted red. "*Escalera de incendios*," she said. "The fire escape."

"Go!" he said.

They raced to the end of the hall, where Maria yanked open the window. This side of the building was in the lee of the storm, so the wind and rain weren't as bad, and the sounds of the still arriving sirens were suddenly very loud.

Slinging her bags over her shoulder, Maria climbed out onto the metal-runged ladder and immediately started down. McGarvey followed her, closing the window behind him.

The ladder led down into the dark alley behind the hotel. The ground-floor windows and doors of all the buildings were tightly shuttered against the night and the storm.

At the bottom Maria crouched in the darkness as the lights of an army Jeep flashed past on the street at the end of the alley. McGarvey joined her a second later.

It would take Esformes another minute or so to realize that they had gotten out of the hotel, but then he would be expanding the search.

"We're not going to make it very far on foot," Maria said. "We'll have to steal a car to get to the plane."

"That's where Esformes and his men just came from," McGarvey said, starting down the alley. He had holstered his gun. No matter what happened, he didn't want to get into a shootout with the Argentinian authorities. Yet if Kurshin had gotten out of the hotel and was waiting in the darkness for them, they would be caught in a no-win situation: a cross fire between the Argentinians and the Russian.

"What are you talking about?" Maria demanded, catching up with him.

McGarvey pulled up short of the corner and flattened himself against the building. There was a lot of activity on the street in front of the hotel. More sirens were approaching from the south. The navy had probably been asked to lend a hand.

"What are you talking about?" Maria repeated. "We have to get to the plane. It's our only way out."

"Esformes knows about your airplane. That's the only way he could have tracked us to Viedma. From there he probably talked to someone at the marina."

"What are we going to do?"

McGarvey looked around the corner. To the left was the front entrance to the hotel, a dozen police cars and army Jeeps parked in the street. To the right, at the end of a dark block, Kurshin's dark blue Chevrolet was parked. A police car, its lights flashing, raced past. Kurshin had not gotten out of the hotel after all. He'd hidden, knowing that Esformes was not looking for him. He was safe inside.

The wind blew the rain in long sheets down the street toward the hotel. It was to their advantage. Anyone standing outside in the storm would have his back to the wind.

McGarvey turned back. "Will your Argentinian passport give us a problem getting across the border into Chile?" His passport was in his jacket pocket.

Her nostrils flared. "No," she said. "But we'll need a car."

"The American car at the end of the block. We're going to walk directly to it and get in. Don't look around, and no matter what happens, don't run."

"What about the keys?"

"They'll be in the car."

"How do you—?"

"Trust me," McGarvey said, and before she could argue, he stepped around the corner and started down the block.

It was possible that Kurshin had made it as far as the lobby and ducked into the restaurant moments before Esformes showed up. His escape would be blocked until the Argentinian authorities moved out. That could take several hours.

Two more police cars raced past on the street, their sirens blaring, their lights flashing. McGarvey caught just a glimpse of one of the cops looking his way, but then the patrol car was pulling up at the hotel.

"He saw us," Maria said urgently.

"Don't run," McGarvey repeated.

At the corner Maria went around the front of the Chevrolet and got in on the passenger side, tossing her bag in the back. Without looking around, McGarvey opened the door and slipped in behind the wheel. The keys dangled from the ignition, as he knew they would. Moments spent fumbling a key into the ignition could sometimes mean the difference between life and death.

As he started the car, he looked in the rearview mirror. A knot of men had formed on the sidewalk in front of the hotel. Some of them were soldiers, with Uzi submachine guns slung over their shoulders.

For a moment McGarvey toyed with the idea of turning himself in. He could explain to Esformes what Kurshin was, and together they could stop the man. But he didn't think the Argentinians were in a mood to talk. They had a long-standing reputation of shooting first and asking no questions later.

Kurshin would escape from Argentina. And whatever he'd been up to in Paris was not over. Langley would have to be warned. And so would Carley. She had seen Kurshin. She had talked with him. Sooner or later he would be coming after her.

McGarvey put the car in gear and pulled away from the curb, not switching on his lights until he was around the corner.

He kept watching in the rearview mirror, expecting at any moment to see the lights of a pursuing police car. But they made it out of town without seeing another moving vehicle, and they headed west into the black night toward the Andes and the Chilean border some four hundred miles away.

"Oh, my God," Maria cried minutes after they'd cleared the town. She'd been rummaging in her purse.

McGarvey looked at her. She was shaking. Her eyes were wide, her mouth open.

"Roebling's notebook. It was in my purse. It's gone. Someone took it."

"Are you sure?"

"Yes," she said softly. "It was him. The Russian. He knew about the gold. He must have gone to my room . . . just before us. . . . We have to go back!"

McGarvey shook his head as he tried to think it out. What possible interest could Kurshin have in gold? Unless it was to finance some sort of operation. And what did this have to do with Paris?

"We must go back!" Maria screeched.

"And do what?" McGarvey asked sharply. "Get arrested by Esformes? Or get shot by his men? Or by Kurshin?"

"We must . . ." she protested weakly.

"Do you remember any of Roebling's contacts in Lisbon?"

"There were more than a dozen."

"Do you remember any of them?"

"A couple. Maybe three."

"Then it's a start," McGarvey said, his own plan forming. "I'll help you."

"In Lisbon?"

"Yes," McGarvey said. "But first Paris."

"Why?"

McGarvey looked over at her. She was still deeply shaken. "If you want my help, it'll be on my terms. No questions asked. This time we'll do things my way."

After a silent few seconds she finally nodded. "As you wish," she said. "But we have to find it. We have to!"

BOOK THREE

30

MOSCOW

GENERAL DIDENKO WAS REMINDED of an old Russian proverb he'd heard his grandmother use: *In Moscow they ring the bells often, but not for dinner.* It was a Stalinist-era catchall acknowledging the two salient facts of the time: a lot of people were getting killed, while for everyone else there was never enough to eat.

Well, he thought, facing the twelve old men who comprised the Politburo of the Communist party, the Moscow bells were ringing again. This time they were tolling the end of socialism. In fact, they seemed to be signaling the end of the Union.

"The party no longer enjoys the power it once had, Comrade

General," Yurii Pavlichenko said from the end of the massive, ornately carved table.

"Nor do we have such influence, Vasili Semonovich, that we can interfere with KGB funding," Missile Defense Forces General Feodor Obolentsev said. "The government has taken even that away from us and placed it in the hands of the Council of Ministers, and of course the Presidium."

"Our budget has been slashed nearly in half, and the cut in hard Western currencies effectively hamstrings our foreign operations," Didenko replied, careful not to raise his voice. But he knew that this had been a wasted afternoon.

"Do not overstep your bounds," Obolentsev warned. He was a huge man, with massive fists that he had a habit of clenching when he was under stress. They were clenched in front of him now. "Take heed. You are only a department chief. There are many rungs remaining on your ladder. Down, as well as up."

"The winds of change are even sweeping through these old halls," Pavlichenko said. His pale, wrinkled skin was parchment thin. The other men nodded sagely.

"Good advice, comrades, and I thank you for it," Didenko said.

"And we thank you for coming here so frankly with your concerns," another of the Politburo members said. "We will not forget."

No, Didenko thought, this would not be soon forgotten. He smiled and nodded, inwardly seething. He had come for help, but had received nothing but platitudes and worthless advice.

He left the conference room, gathered his coat and hat in the anteroom, and hurried downstairs to his waiting car and driver. The soldiers at the door snapped to attention as he passed.

"Take me home," he said, climbing into the back seat.

He opened the compartment in the back of the front seat, poured himself a stiff measure of French cognac, drank it, and then poured himself another. He sat back as they headed out of the Kremlin, a light snow falling, muffling all the sounds and perhaps the sins of the city.

He had pinned too many of his hopes on one man—Arkady Kurshin. But there was no one else he could trust now. Baranov had used him to great success. But as the assassin had put it, Didenko was no Baranov. Nor was the Union the same. Nor was the world. Everything was different now.

For the very first time Didenko could see the end of Russia as a major world power. The *rodina* had lost her European buffer zone, and now she was losing her republics one at a time.

The weapons were still in place, but the will was gone from the party as well as the government.

Where were the men of vision and of action? he asked himself. The question had been plaguing him for months. A question to which he had no answer.

With gold, which could be converted into Western currencies, the Komitet's foreign operations could be adequately funded and the changes could be reversed.

Could have been, he thought bitterly. But Kurshin was gone. Disappeared off the map. And there was no one he could trust. No one left who could carry out his plan to save what was left of the KGB. The day of the Komitet assassin was gone.

Short of turning his field officers into ordinary bank robbers, there seemed to be no solution. One thing was sure, however. Kurshin should die. He could not be allowed to continue as he was, out of control. Besides, he knew too much. But who was there to do the job? Who under Didenko's command was good enough?

He shook his head. Killing Kurshin would be impossible unless he showed up here in Moscow. And maybe it would be impossible even then.

The limousine turned onto Kutuzovsky Prospekt, and five minutes later Didenko rode up in the elevator to his eighteenth-floor apartment. His building was not too far from Gorbachev's. It had always been a point of pride with him. Until this afternoon, that is. Now he felt that he had lost. Once and for all, he had lost.

Everything had been in place for his salvation. Everything, that is, except for one element: Kurshin in Tehrān. One man. How could he have been so stupid as to pin all of his hopes on one man?

His housekeeper was gone for the evening, and he had dismissed his secretary before he'd left the office. His apartment seemed very large and very empty.

Tossing his overcoat and uniform tunic over the back of the couch, he went into his study, closing and locking the door. He loosened his tie, undoing the top button of his shirt, and poured himself another stiff measure of cognac from a sideboard. Behind his desk he took a key out of his pocket, unlocked the top drawer, and looked at the loaded German Luger. It was a spoil of war. His brother's son had taken it from the body of a Nazi general in Berlin.

His brother was dead. The boy was dead. Everyone was dead. Paris would be blamed on him.

As Didenko reached for the pistol the telephone on his desk rang. For a moment he debated not answering it, but on the second ring he picked it up.

"Yes," he said.

"It's me, you cunt," Kurshin said. "I'm in Rome and I need your help. I'll do anything you want to get it."

Didenko closed his eyes and sat back, a great sigh escaping his lips. There was hope after all.

"Are you there, you bastard?" Kurshin shouted.

"I'm here, Arkasha. Believe me, we are going to help each other."

31

PAN AM FLIGHT 214 TOUCHED down at Charles de Gaulle Airport a few minutes after seven-thirty in the evening, nearly on time, and taxied to the terminal building.

It took the passengers less than fifteen minutes to clear passport control, retrieve their bags, and get through customs.

Carley Webb was waiting just within the main doors, her cheeks flushed and her hair glistening from the thickly falling snow, when Phil Carrara came across to her.

"You're a pleasant surprise," he said.

"Mike is tied up with the SDECE. He asked me to come fetch you," Carley said. She looked exhausted, as if she hadn't slept in days.

"Besides, you wanted to spend a few minutes alone with me on the way into town," Carrara said, not unkindly. He thought he knew how she felt. He was glad for both of them that Ryan wasn't here.

"Something like that," she said. "My car is outside." She managed a smile. "By the way, welcome to Paris. How was your flight?"

"Thanks," Carrara said. "Long. How are you holding up?"

She looked at him. "Okay. But it's a big mess here. Mike is doing a wonderful job, though. He's got a lot of enthusiasm."

Carley's car was a dark brown Peugeot. She drove fast with the traffic, and very competently.

"He's on his way back to Europe," Carrara said when they'd cleared the airport. "At least we think he is."

"I saw the weekends. It couldn't have been him, Phil."

"I want to agree with you. But the fact remains that Ken Bellows is dead. They found his body in one of the slums. The dogs had been at it."

"Not Kirk."

"The Argentinian federal police have issued arrest warrants for him and the woman he's been traveling with. There were other killings, too. Another man, an Argentinian in Buenos Aires. A ship captain and his mate in a small coastal town south of Buenos Aires. A clerk and an Italian tourist in a Puerto Lobos hotel." Carrara looked out the window. They were passing a big roadside ad for Perrier water. It was a huge bottle.

"How do you know they're coming here?"

"They crossed the border into Chile Friday afternoon, and then disappeared. I'm guessing they're on their way back here. Paris is where it all began."

Carley drove for several minutes in silence, concentrating on what she was doing. She was a very good-looking young woman, but essentially naïve. It was wrong to have hired her, he decided. She was perfect for certain aspects of the job, aspects he'd never discussed with Dominique, but her career was killing her.

"Are you all right?" he asked.

She glanced at him. "Is he coming here to see me?"

"It's possible."

Again Carley fell silent. Then she said, "If he's guilty, Phil, why come to see me? I mean the only reason he'd come back here would be to clear himself. To make sure that his name was cleared in connection with the attack on our embassy."

Carrara nodded. "That's what I figured, kid," he said. "But out of sixteen thousand employees in the Company, you and I may be the only ones to think so."

"What do you want me to do?"

"There isn't much you can do until he shows up."

"*If* he does."

"Right," Carrara said. "In the meantime, we have a lot of work to do here. It's the main reason I've come over."

"It's the scheduling and communications that are killing us. We've lost direct contact with half of our networks."

"We'll have to send out runners. Go back to the old field procedures."

"That's what Mike thought, but he's got his hands full with everything else at the moment," Carley said.

Traffic was heavy, which was normal for this time of the evening, but despite the snow no one had slowed down.

"The general is after his scalp, isn't he?" she asked after a time.

"He wants him brought in at all costs. But at this point he only wants to have a parley. It's Ryan who's after his ass."

"Howard Ryan?" Carley asked, glancing over.

Carrara nodded. "He's after you, too. He thinks you may have helped McGarvey ... wittingly or unwittingly. He thinks you were sleeping with him, and he thinks you're in love with him."

"I see," Carley said. "What do you believe?"

"Whatever you tell me."

"And then?"

"I'll hold Ryan off from my end and let you and Mike get on with the business of rebuilding Paris."

"Fair enough," Carley said. "Yes, I was sleeping with him, and yes, it's true I'm in love with him. But that's as far as it goes, Phil. I swear it."

"It's good enough for me," Carrara said gently.

It was snowing heavily when McGarvey and Maria emerged from the Gare du Nord after their six-hour train–hovercraft–train trip from London. It seemed as if they had been traveling for months rather than a few days, partly because they were on the run, and partly because they had crossed from the Southern Hemisphere into the Northern, from summer into winter.

After crossing the border into Chile, they had gone to the small airport at Osorno, where they'd caught a flight up to Santiago.

They had spent the remainder of Saturday and all of Sunday in the capital city, purchasing new clothes, a couple of pieces of luggage, and—through McGarvey's old contacts—new identification papers. To McGarvey it had seemed strange and even claustrophobic to be there. This had been where his fall from grace had begun. He'd been sent here to kill a man.

But Santiago had not changed in those interim years. Coming into the city had been like entering the land of his own dreams, at once unreal and frightening. Leaving it had been a relief, even though by doing so he was returning to the real, much more dangerous world.

Maria shivered and hunched up her coat collar as they got in line at the taxi rank.

"Is anyone following us?" she asked, looking up at him.

"I don't think so." McGarvey glanced over his shoulder at the people still coming out of the station. "Not yet, anyway, but he'll be there. I can guarantee it."

"What does the bastard want? And just who are you?"

"An interesting question," he said. "Do you want the truth?"

"Yes," she said.

"All right. I'll tell you who I am, and then you'll tell me who you really are, and who you work for."

"We've already gone over—"

"Who owns International Traders, for starters?" McGarvey interrupted. "My guess would be the Mossad."

"No."

"Who, then?"

"Some people in Argentina who want to see . . ."

"What?"

"Justice done."

"By finding this hoard of gold, and doing what with it?"

"Returning it to its rightful owners," Maria said defensively. "What are you after?"

Life, he wanted to say, but he didn't. "The truth," he said instead.

32

IT WAS SNOWING VERY HARD. All of western Europe was gripped in the storm. The Channel ferries and hovercraft were being closed down. Charles de Gaulle and Orly had also been closed. Even the trains were being delayed. All travel was being discouraged for the next twenty-four hours.

As McGarvey had learned from Dr. Hesse, Interpol wanted them for questioning in connection with the embassy bombing. For the CIA to have turned over their names to the civilian authorities was a drastic step.

Alone, on the way over to Carley's apartment in the First Arrondissement, McGarvey carefully watched his back to make certain he wasn't being followed. But this time no one was behind him. The feeling wasn't there. Kurshin was not here. Not yet.

"It's him," Carley said softly from the window. "He's in the doorway just across the street."

"Son of a bitch, he made it," Carrara said admiringly from the bedroom door. "Is he alone?"

"I think so," Carley said. McGarvey stepped out of the shadows and started across the street. "Wait. He's coming. He's alone." She turned away from the window.

"Don't clutch up now. You know what has to be done."

Carley shook her head. "I don't know if I can do this, Phil. If he asks me something, I'll have to tell the truth."

"None of us is going to get hurt by the truth, Carley. Not even McGarvey. Remember that."

"If he's innocent."

"Yeah," Carrara said. "But if he's guilty, playing fair won't matter. I'll nail the bastard myself."

Carley looked at him. He was an administrator, not a fieldman like McGarvey. The spark was missing from his eyes, from his bearing and stance, from his attitude. His wasn't the kind of look you expected to see from a killer. He was tame; McGarvey was feral. There was no comparison.

"He's innocent," she said.

She opened the door for him on the first ring, and entering her apartment McGarvey got the impression that she'd been waiting for him.

"I saw you from the window," she said, closing the door behind him. She wore a pair of blue jeans and an old UCLA sweatshirt, and no shoes.

"How are you, Carley?" McGarvey asked. She looked strung out and very nervous, he thought.

"Okay," she said.

McGarvey went to the window and looked out. A car passed on the street below but did not stop. Nothing else moved.

For a moment he studied Carley's reflection in the dark windowpane. She glanced at the bedroom door, then quickly looked away.

By your tradecraft you shall be known. The old line from the Farm came back to him. They'd been expecting him to come here. To make contact. It was the nature of the beast. His move.

He turned back to her and unbuttoned his overcoat. His pistol was in the left pocket. "So, who've you got in there, Carley? A good one, or a bad one?"

Her eyes widened. "Kirk, I—"

The bedroom door opened and McGarvey pulled out his gun. Carrara appeared in the doorway.

"I guess I should have known better than to try to fool you," the DDO said.

McGarvey slowly lowered his pistol and uncocked the hammer. He put the gun back in his pocket. "Did you trace us from Chile?"

"We lost you after you crossed the border. The federal police in Buenos Aires have issued warrants for your arrests. Yours and Maria Schimmer's. You knew that?"

McGarvey nodded. "For the murder of Albert Rothmann."

"There are others. Steven Jones and Jorge Vallejo aboard a boat in Puerto Lobos. A hotel clerk in the town. And one of the hotel's guests, an Italian tourist. SISMI is interested in you now. We got a twixt from Rome yesterday."

"We killed Vallejo in self-defense."

"The others?"

"Arkady Kurshin."

Carrara swore, half to himself. "Are you sure? Absolutely sure, Kirk? I mean, did you actually *see* the man?"

"Yes," McGarvey said, his jaw tightening. "I saw him. There's no doubt."

"He's alive after all," Carrara said in wonder. "But how the hell did he trace you to Buenos Aires?"

"There's a professor in Freiburg."

"Hesse. He's dead."

"Right."

"And it was him at the embassy?" Carley asked.

McGarvey nodded tiredly. "Almost certainly. But I don't know what he wants. I don't know what he hoped to accomplish by killing Tom Lord and the others. It makes no sense to me."

Carrara's tie was loose, but he still wore his jacket. He stepped out of the bedroom doorway, and McGarvey moved back a pace, his hand going into his coat pocket.

Carrara, startled, stopped short. "Easy, Kirk," he said. "There are no other surprises tonight. No one else hiding in the closet."

"But you knew I was coming."

"We knew you were on the move, and I figured you'd show up here sooner or later. The general wants to talk to you."

"Not now," McGarvey said. "I came to warn you about Kurshin, and have you call your dogs off me."

"I can't do that. Not now."

There was something else. McGarvey could see it as a dangerous glint in the man's eyes. "What?" he asked softly.

"One of our people was killed in Buenos Aires. Kneecap first, then shot in the head. With a Walther PPK. You're high on everyone's list."

"What was he doing there?"

"Looking for you and the woman. And the submarine."

"I didn't kill him."

"The woman?"

McGarvey shook his head. "It would be my guess that Kurshin found out where we were from him."

"The man gets around," Carrara said dryly.

"What are you saying, Phil?" McGarvey asked, his voice flat. Carley recognized the tone, and she stiffened. Carrara did not.

"The general wants to talk to you, as I've already said. But I have a feeling that if I tried to take you by force, you'd prevent it."

McGarvey nodded.

"Perhaps it was the same with Ken Bellows in Buenos Aires."

"No," McGarvey said. "I wouldn't have come back here like this."

"For Carley's sake," Carrara suggested.

A pained look crossed her face.

McGarvey shook his head. "No. Not for Carley's sake. Whatever there was between us is over with, Phil. I returned to warn you that Arkady Kurshin is on the loose. He's on his way to Lisbon, I think, and I'll be waiting for him. But there's no telling what the man will do to get there. If your people get in his way, he'll kill them. I think he's already demonstrated that ability, and willingness."

"Why Lisbon?" Carrara asked.

McGarvey just looked at him.

"If it has something to do with gold or artwork or whatever from the war, I think we know what he's after."

"It's gold," McGarvey said. "At least I've been led to believe it is."

"A lot of gold?"

"Yes."

"The KGB is in big trouble. Its budget has been deeply cut. Gorbachev is controlling it that way, especially by limiting its foreign currency. If they can get their hands on money, or something that can be easily converted, they'll go after it."

"Who's Kurshin's runner?"

"A man by the name of Vasili Didenko."

"General Didenko," McGarvey said. "Baranov's number two man in the old days."

"The same."

"Still takes us back to the embassy attack, Phil. Makes no sense from where I stand."

"It might," Carrara replied, and before McGarvey could ask he continued, "The general will explain it to you. I'm not authorized. But there might be a pattern to his movements."

"Is it anything that would stop Kurshin from coming after me in Lisbon?"

"A few days ago I might have said yes. But now ... I don't know."

"Then Lisbon it is."

"I can't let you leave," Carrara said. "I will stop you, Kirk."

"I don't think so," McGarvey said. He turned and walked to the door.

"You'll have to kill me, then," Carrara said.

McGarvey looked back in time to see the DDO pull out a pistol.

"No!" Carley screamed, leaping between the two men. She wrapped her arms around Carrara and wrestled him back against the bedroom doorjamb before he could make a move. "Run!"

McGarvey hesitated for just a second, then slipped out the door and down the stairs, and out into the snowstorm.

33

TEHRĀN WAS A DANGEROUS PLACE, and Richard Abbas had known for some time now that his days here were numbered. SAVAK, the secret police from the shah's era that still survived under the ayatollahs, was on to him again.

As director of the CIA's front organization, the Compagnie Général de Picarde, S. A., he expected to come under daily surveillance. And did. They sold computers and computer software, which the Iranians badly needed, but they were Westerners, and not to be trusted.

But over the past few months SAVAK had stepped up its surveillance. Now they watched him almost continuously, tapping his telephones, opening most of his mail, and staking out his apartment almost every night.

Then there had been the threat on his life. He'd received assurances from Langley via high-speed satellite burst transmissions that he was safe. Yet he had the over-the-shoulder feeling that the threat was still valid. It was the same feeling that all good operatives developed . . . or at least the ones who survived very long in the field did.

Getting ready to leave the office, he called in his number two, Shahpur Naisir. "Is everything set?" he asked in French. It was six in the evening.

Abbas was a well-built man of six feet two, towering over the much smaller, much slighter Shahpur.

His assistant COS nodded, glancing pointedly at the telephone. They'd discovered the new SAVAK bug three days ago during a normal sweep. Abbas had personally taken care of it.

"We're clean," Abbas said.

"Your gear is in the car," Shahpur said. He was still very tense. Everyone in the office was tense.

"Has the *City of Tallahassee* entered the Gulf of Oman yet?"

"She was reported past Ras al Hadd two hours ago. And I got that from the horse's mouth. The KH-11 pass couldn't have been timed more perfectly."

"She's on schedule, then."

Shahpur nodded. "She'll make the Strait of Hormuz in another twenty-two or twenty-three hours, and dock at Bushehr twenty-six hours later."

"Escort?"

"Our navy, of course, until she actually enters the Persian Gulf, then the Iranians take over. But if someone is going to hijack that gold, it won't be at sea, I think. The navy is all right. It's the army that has me worried."

"Me, too," Abbas said. "But it's a fool's mission we're on."

"Yes" Shahpur agreed.

Like Abbas, he'd been born and raised in Tehrān. He had left at the age of fifteen in 1978 shortly before the fall of the shah. He, too, had been recruited by the CIA in the early eighties and now considered himself to be an American, as Abbas did. Here, however, they presented themselves as French, as did the other key employees in Picarde.

"The government won't thank us for saving the gold, if it comes to that," Abbas said.

"Most certainly not. But if you're caught out there in the desert, they won't hesitate to kill you. Not the army, and certainly not Captain Peshadi."

Hussain Peshadi, an officer in SAVAK, had a personal vendetta against Americans. His older sister had been having an affair with an American consular officer. When the embassy had been stormed, she'd been caught inside. She'd been executed immediately following her five-minute trial by the People's Court.

The Americans had caused her downfall, and Peshadi, who'd been one of the men responsible for holding the hostages in the embassy, had vowed death to Americans. Death to *all* Americans.

It was he and his people who had stepped up the surveillance on Abbas.

"I won't leave Tehrān until I shake him," Abbas said.

"Will you try tonight?"

"Midnight. If all goes well, I should be on the coast sometime tomorrow afternoon. It'll give me plenty of time to get set up before the ship docks and they start unloading the gold."

"Don't forget to activate the telephone-answering equipment in your apartment."

"No," Abbas said. "As of tomorrow morning when you telephone me, you'll hear a definitely under-the-weather Frenchman."

Shahpur nodded. "Take care, then, Richard."

"You, too," Abbas said.

Although they both considered themselves to be Americans, their upbringing still made them maintain a certain polite distance. It was extremely impolite and rude to do otherwise.

They neither embraced nor shook hands. Instead, Shahpur lowered his eyes, turned, and left. Abbas followed him out a few minutes later, retrieving his Renault from the locked parking area behind the building, and headed across town to his apartment near the Mehrabad International Airport.

He picked up a two-man tail almost immediately, but he did nothing to avoid them, or lead them to believe that he'd detected their presence. He was an innocent Frenchman, after all. He had no reason to suspect that he was being followed.

He stopped at a druggist's shop near the university where he purchased several over-the-counter cold remedies, and then continued home. They would check out the shop, and the minor subterfuge would help maintain the fiction that he was ill.

With any luck he would be finished with his baby-sitting business sometime on Sunday, when the gold was safely in the vaults of the Bank of Iran, and he'd be able to slip back into his apartment that night.

It wouldn't be a restful weekend, but he'd not signed on with the Company for rest and relaxation. He'd joined the CIA for the simple reason that he believed then, and still did, that the Americans were right, while very nearly everyone else was wrong.

His American wife, Sandra, believed the same. But she was no spy, so he had kept her at home in Alexandria with their seven-year-old son.

Six months, he told himself as he parked behind his apartment building, and he would be back in the States. This, he'd been assured, was to be his last posting to Iran. He would be assigned to the Iranian desk at Langley. A boring job, but a safe one.

The elevator was out of order again, as were the lights in the stairwell, so he had to trudge up to the fifth floor in the dark.

At forty-two he was getting old for field work. At least that was what his wife said. And sometimes he felt that way himself.

The lights in the fifth-floor corridor were off as well. He swore to himself as he fumbled his key into the lock. Inside, he shut the door and flipped on the light switch, but nothing happened. The electricity to the entire building was apparently out.

"Goddamnit," he said out loud.

"Not a very French thing to say," someone said in the darkness.

Abbas reached for his pistol, but the beam of a flashlight was switched on in his face.

"If you touch your pistol I will kill you," the man warned. He spoke English with what Abbas took to be a non-American but definitely cultured accent.

"Who are you? What do you want?"

"Who I am is of no matter," Arkady Kurshin said. "But what I want is your help."

"With what?"

"Why, with the gold, of course. What else?"

Kurshin laughed, the sound low and menacing, and Abbas knew that he was in mortal danger.

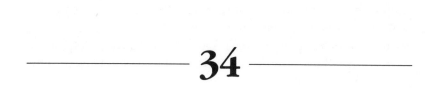

34

KURSHIN REPLACED THE BREAKERS in the circuit box in the front closet, and the lights came on in the apartment. The lights in the corridor would remain out.

He'd forced Abbas to strip naked and then had tied him securely to a straight-backed chair that he tipped up on two legs against the wall. He didn't bother taping the man's mouth. The American would not call for help because of his illegal status in the country.

Back in the living room he pulled up another chair and set it in front of Abbas. He sat down and smiled pleasantly.

"Time for a little chat now, I should think," he said.

"I have nothing to say to you," Abbas growled.

"Well, we have a long night ahead of us. The gold isn't

due at Bushehr for nearly forty-eight hours. We have lots of time."

"You're not Iranian," Abbas said. "Which means time is on my side. SAVAK will nail your ass to the wall the instant you try to pull me out of this apartment. They're a nervous lot."

"Ah, then that's who followed you here. Means you're doing a sloppy job. You know, the Iranians still don't like Americans very much. It would be a pity if something were to happen to the gold ... and then it was blamed on you."

Kurshin got up and went to the window where he carefully parted the curtains and looked down. The same gray sedan that had followed Abbas into the parking lot was still in front.

He'd worked with pricks like them before. Their field officers never had any imagination. If they'd been told to stake out the front of this apartment building, they would do exactly that, never thinking about the back way out. Losing them would be child's play. And that in itself would be another nail in the American's coffin.

In the bedroom he retrieved the long extension cord he'd found earlier, and out in the living room plugged it into a wall socket behind Abbas.

The CIA station chief watched him through half-closed eyes. If he had any idea what was about to happen, he didn't show it. Kurshin admired him for at least that much.

"The mains here in Iran are at two hundred twenty volts," Kurshin said. "Dangerous sometimes." He unplugged a table lamp and ripped the cord from its base. Setting the lamp aside, he used a pocket knife to strip the insulation from the first six inches of the cord.

Abbas's eyes were wider now.

Kurshin sat down in front of him and gently wrapped one of the bare wires around his flaccid penis.

"Son of a bitch, don't do this," Abbas said, trying desperately to struggle away.

Kurshin straddled the chair, holding it in place with his body weight, and managed to wrap the other bare wire around the American's testicles.

"There's nothing I'm going to tell you," Abbas said breath-lessly. He was choking on his own words, and his chest was heaving.

Kurshin sat down again, pushing his chair back a little bit. He picked up the extension cord and brought its plug and the lamp cord plug nearly together.

"Don't do this," Abbas pleaded, his voice rising.

"If you make too much noise, they'll arrest you. And they will kill you."

Abbas was breathing heavily through his mouth.

"Your name is Richard Abbas and you are the chief of station for Central Intelligence Agency activities here in Iran. I know this. I would simply like to hear you admit it."

Abbas said nothing, his eyes fixed on the two plugs.

Kurshin touched them together for just an instant. Abbas's body spasmed so violently that the chair he was tied to crashed to the floor. But he did not cry out. The only sound to escape him was a low, animal moan from the back of his throat.

"That must hurt," Kurshin said, moving his chair over so that he could look into Abbas's eyes. Sweat had beaded on the American's forehead. Kurshin hit him again with a short jolt.

A thin, high-pitched wail came from Abbas, his eyes screwed shut. When he finally opened them he looked up at Kurshin with a violent, nearly out-of-control hatred.

"Fuck you, too," Kurshin said, and he joined the two plugs and left them together.

Abbas's body spasmed again and again, the keening wail from deep in his throat like a distant air raid siren, and still Kurshin did not unplug the cords until he began to smell the odor of burning flesh. He finally disconnected them.

The American's legs continued to jerk spasmodically and his chest rose and fell rapidly, but he appeared to be unconscious or at the very least, insensate.

Kurshin went into the kitchen and poured a glass of cold water. He felt absolutely nothing about what he was doing to the man, although he knew that there were those who derived pleasure from such things.

Abbas was merely a means to an end. The gold would be taken from under the Iranians' noses, and the Americans would be blamed for it. It was the price he was paying to General Didenko in exchange for a clear shot at McGarvey.

"Listen to me, Arkasha," the general had said over the telephone. "These are merely the opening moves. There will be so much more for you and me to accomplish together. Ours will be the triumph of the century."

With the way things were going in the *rodina*, the nation was ripe for the emergence of a new despot: a Hitler, another Stalin. Didenko hoped to be such a force.

Kurshin had to smile. Someday he would have to kill the general. The man was mad. But in the meantime there was work to be done.

Abbas was just regaining consciousness when Kurshin came in and sat down in front of him.

"Time for our little chat now, yes?" Kurshin said amiably.

"I work for the CIA," Abbas whispered. "So what? It's common knowledge."

"Thank you," Kurshin said. "You brought cold medicines home with you tonight, but you do not appear to be sick. Why?"

Abbas said nothing.

Languidly Kurshin reached down and picked up the two cords.

"I'm not going to my office for the next few days. My excuse will be that I was ill."

"Yes? Why is this?"

Again Abbas hesitated. Kurshin hit him with a very brief jolt. This time no sound came from the American's throat, but for several seconds afterward he shivered violently, his eyes closed, his jaw clamped tightly shut, the veins bulging on his neck.

"I was to drive south . . . to Bushehr . . . to meet the gold," he said after a long time.

"For what purpose?"

"We believe there is a possibility that an Iranian army unit plans on hijacking the shipment."

"How were you to prevent this if it began to develop?"

"I wasn't supposed to prevent it. My orders were to observe the convoy. If something started to go down, I was to report what I saw."

"To whom? And how?"

"To Langley by radio."

"Radio? What radio? I found nothing in this apartment."

"It's a handie-talkie. In my car. Hidden."

"Not enough power."

"It's set to the up-and-down-link frequencies of one of our

satellites. Virtually undetectable by anything other than another handie-talkie."

"Yes, I see," Kurshin said. It would be perfect for his plans. "Why were you ordered to baby-sit the shipment? Once the gold arrived on Iranian soil it is no longer the problem of the United States."

"It was thought that if the gold were to be hijacked here in Iran, no matter by whom, the Iranian government would blame America. We need a friend here. Especially now. We were will-ing to do whatever it takes to insure they got their gold. To Tehrān. No one wants another Iraq-Kuwait incident. Iran will be the watchdog once again."

Kurshin looked at Abbas. The man was pitiful. "No more torture tonight. Nor will there be any further need of such things if you continue to cooperate with me."

"Who are you?" Abbas croaked.

"It doesn't matter," Kurshin said. "Believe me in this."

It was dawn by the time Kurshin was finished. Abbas had been good to his word and had cooperated with everything that had been done to him. In fact at one point he had even smiled slightly, a gesture Kurshin missed.

"Hold very still now," Kurshin said.

Abbas, still strapped to the chair, held his head up and didn't move as Kurshin cut the latex rubber in a long seam up from the back of his neck to the top of his head.

Very carefully the Russian peeled the entire mask from Abbas's face, and then stepped back. For just a moment or two Abbas was confused, until suddenly everything that had been done to him this night, everything that Kurshin had said, and this now, made a terrible sense to him, and he shivered.

Kurshin had pushed the latex mask inside out so that Abbas was looking up at his own image. It was a life mask. Kurshin was his same general build. His English was good.

If he'd had any doubts before, Abbas had none now. He knew for a fact that he was a dead man.

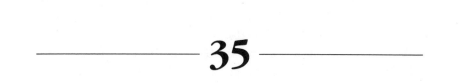

35

AT 9:00 A.M., Shahpur Naisir dialed Abbas's apartment. The telephone rang three times, but instead of the expected recording with which he would have a prearranged conversation, the telephone rang a fourth time, and then a fifth, and kept ringing.

After fifteen rings, Shahpur hung up and dialed again. It was possible, he told himself, that he had misdialed. The connection was made, with the same results.

No one else in the office knew about the operation. An espionage team working in a country like Iran, with which there was no diplomatic relationship, had to compartmentalize so that no matter who might be arrested, they could not compromise the entire station.

No matter who, that is, except for himself and Richard Abbas.

Shahpur got up from his desk and went into Abbas's office, closing and locking the door behind him. The shutters were closed against the glare of the early-morning sun, and the room was cool, the way Abbas liked it.

With shaking hands he opened the safe, having to make two tries at the combination before he got it right. He took out a .380-caliber Beretta automatic, a clip of ammunition, which he loaded into the butt of the gun, and a silencer tube that he screwed onto the end of the barrel. He levered a round into the firing chamber, eased the hammer down, and stuffed the weapon into his belt beneath his jacket.

Next he took out one of the satellite-frequency handie-talkies and put it in his jacket pocket. Abbas had one just like it.

To be caught in Iran with the communications device, and especially with the pistol, meant death. There would be no appeal. No chances for a reprieve. No possibility of an exchange of spies.

Locking the safe, he let himself out of Abbas's office and told the receptionist that he would be out of the office for most of the morning.

"Yes, sir," the young man said. "But I've not seen Monsieur Abbas yet this morning."

"He's been delayed," Shahpur said. "In fact, I'm on my way over to see him now. Is there anything pressing?"

"No, sir."

"Very well," Shahpur said. "I should be back by noon. If something comes up in the meantime, it'll hold."

Shahpur got his car from the back and made two circuits of the office building, coming in from the east the first time and from the west the second. He picked up no tail on either pass.

This was his home . . . or it had been. He'd understood these people, their customs, their desires, their fears. He'd even understood why they hated America and Americans so vehemently, and it had nothing to do with what the mullahs told them. It had to do with the envy and raw hate that someone extremely poor had for someone extremely rich. The two came from different universes. There was no common language.

But now he felt out of place. He felt as if he were in a foreign land. He no longer understood.

He headed out past the university, traffic fairly light at this hour, so that it was easy for him to watch his back. Still no tail.

No one was interested in him this morning. That in itself deepened his apprehension.

There were drills for this sort of thing. They all knew that sooner or later their luck might run out. It would be one thing to be arrested as native-born Americans. But to be in the hands of SAVAK as Iranians who'd gone over to the infidel meant more than a simple firing squad. They would be held up as public examples, their deaths particularly long and painful as a warning to other would-be traitors.

Rely on the three Cs, he'd been taught at the Farm. Remain Calm. Maintain a Clear head. And most important, stay within your established Cover identity.

He worked for Richard Abbas at the offices of the Compagnie Général de Picarde. His boss had not shown up for work, nor had he answered his telephone. As a concerned employee, Shahpur would naturally investigate.

Such a fiction would immediately break down if the Iranian authorities decided to detain him and he was searched, or if Abbas himself had been arrested. But the entire station was in serious jeopardy at this point. Something had to be done. And he was the only one for the job.

Passing the Ministry of Health and Social Welfare building, he turned left down a dusty dirt road that led to a complex of tall apartment buildings housing mostly foreigners. Depending upon the type of demonstration, the police would either lead the mobs down this road, or block their access to the area.

This morning nothing moved, except for a jet taking off from the airport to the southwest. At that instant Shahpur sincerely wished he were aboard the airliner, no matter what its destination might be. Anywhere, he thought, would be preferable to here and now.

He didn't spot the Iranian surveillance team until he was practically on top of their gray Morris. They looked over at him as he passed, one of them recognizing him for sure. He parked about thirty feet away, and trying to act as nonchalant as possible, he went up the walk and entered the building. He half expected them to come after him, but they did not.

An old woman wearing a chador came out of the stairwell as he approached the elevators. "Pardon, sir, but the machine is not working this morning," she said in Farsi.

"Thank you, mother," Shahpur replied pleasantly. Farsi was a much prettier, much gentler language than English. Too bad, he thought, that it had been used to gloss over heinous crimes committed in the name of Islam.

She left the building. Shahpur went back to the door and watched as she went down the walk. She headed past the two men in the gray Morris. They hadn't moved, nor would they, he suspected, until Abbas left.

Shahpur turned and looked at the stairwell door. Which meant Abbas was still here for some reason. Immediately he thought about the threat on the station chief's life.

Was it possible, he asked himself, that someone had come here last night and killed Abbas? This was Iran, and any act of violence was possible. Especially against Westerners and Western interests. He thanked heaven that his family had left Iran when he had. It was one lever that SAVAK would never be able to use against him.

Entering the stairwell, he listened for a full minute before starting up. There wasn't a sound. The lights were out, but someone had propped open the doors on each floor so that the corridor windows could provide some illumination.

He had a very ominous feeling about this.

He took out the pistol, cocked the hammer, and went the rest of the way up to the fifth floor, gingerly stepping through the doorway into the corridor.

Again he stopped to listen, but there was absolutely no noise of any kind. The building could have been deserted. Or evacuated, the thought suddenly struck him. He looked back the way he had come. This could be an elaborate SAVAK trap to lure him and Abbas into some kind of a compromising situation.

For a moment he hesitated, but then shook his head. He was here now and he would see it out. Abbas should be on his way down to Bushehr, and his answering machine should have been switched on.

He went down the corridor and put his head to Abbas's door. Did he hear something from within? Someone murmuring, perhaps. The sound of running water in the bathroom? A shuffling sound.

Or nothing at all. Merely his imagination.

The faint sounds stopped. Shahpur was about to knock, but then he took a key out of his pocket and let himself in. Either

Abbas was gone, or he was in trouble. Either way, knocking on his door would do no good.

Stepping into the apartment he was confused for a critical second or two, unable to understand exactly what it was he was seeing.

Abbas, naked, was tied to a chair propped against the wall. But Abbas, in shirt-sleeves, stood at the bathroom door.

"Why, hello, Shahpur," the clothed Abbas said. "Why are you here?"

There was something wrong with Abbas's voice, and there was definitely something wrong with the question.

All of that took no time at all. He saw the pistol in Abbas's hand at the same moment the Abbas tied to the chair cried out.

"Run ... !"

Shahpur raised his own pistol as a thunderclap burst in his head. . . .

Kurshin hurried to the doorway. Nothing moved. Apparently no one had heard the single shot from his silenced pistol.

Shahpur's body had been flung half out into the corridor. Hurriedly Kurshin dragged it into the apartment, and getting a towel from the bathroom wiped up the blood from the corridor floor. He closed and relocked the door, then turned to Abbas.

"There is something you forgot to tell me," he said. "It has cost you your number two's life. What is it?"

Abbas was staring at Shahpur's body.

Kurshin went to the window and looked down at the gray sedan. It hadn't moved. A figure in black was walking away down the road. He thought it was a woman.

Turning, he went to Abbas. "Will you tell me, or will we have to go through the same procedure as last night? Frankly I don't care one way or the other, you must understand this. But I will have your answer."

"I understand," Abbas said, looking up at him.

"Yes?"

"It's the answering machine. Attached to my telephone."

Kurshin glanced over at the machine. "What about it?"

Again Abbas looked at Shahpur's body. "I'm supposed to be out sick for the rest of the week. I've recorded several messages on my machine. Shahpur was to telephone here this morning and have a conversation with me. He was supposed to call again tomorrow and on Friday morning as well. I was scheduled to be back here Sunday evening."

"When he called this morning and there was no answer either by the machine or by you, he got suspicious."

"Yes," Abbas said heavily.

"By why?" Kurshin asked. "Unless you expect your telephone calls to be monitored. Is that it? Is SAVAK investigating you?"

Abbas nodded.

"Good," Kurshin said, nodding. "That's very good."

36

PHIL CARRARA TRUDGED DOWN the stairs into the damp basement of the U.S. consulate on the rue St.-Florentin, his mood
heavy despite the fact that the sun had come out this morning.

He was met at the bottom by Carley Webb. "Could I have a
word with you before we get started?" she asked.

He was meeting with his abbreviated Paris staff on a twice-
daily basis, at 10:00 A.M. and at 10:00 P.M. The others were
already gathered in the basement conference room. It was still
a few minutes before the hour.

"What is it?" he asked coolly. He'd done nothing about what
had happened at her apartment, though he could have had her
arrested or, at the very least, fired. He still hadn't worked it out
in his own mind, but he suspected that she had saved his life.

"It's been a full thirty-six hours. I just checked the A.M.S. There's been no word out of Lisbon."

"Maybe he didn't go there after all. Maybe he was lying. Maybe he hasn't gotten there yet. Maybe Don Sneade has got his hands full, or maybe he slipped by, or maybe he's wiped out the entire station single-handed."

"Send me down there, Phil."

Carrara looked at her closely. "To do what, Carley?"

"Find him."

"Warn him?"

"No, dammit. Find him."

"If Don hasn't run him to ground yet, what makes you so sure that you'll be able to do it? We've got a lot of people out in the field looking for him."

"I'll just have to show up. Make myself visible. Kirk will come to me."

"It's over between you two, or was he lying about that as well?"

Carley's nostrils flared. "Do you want my resignation? Because if you do, I'll give it to you right now and go down to Lisbon on my own."

Carrara turned away, but she grabbed him by his jacket sleeve and pulled him back.

"Goddamnit, Phil, what do you think would have happened if I hadn't interfered?"

"I never thanked you for saving my life . . ."

"No," Carley cried. "Or maybe yes. I don't know. But someone would have got hurt, I do know that. And I also know that he wouldn't have fired the first shot."

"Then you were saving his life."

"Yes, Phil, because he's innocent."

"You're telling me that you believe his story about Arkady Kurshin?"

"Why not?" she asked. "You do. You warned Sneade about it."

Again Carrara stared at her. "No," he finally said.

"No what?"

"No, I don't want your resignation, and no, I'm not sending you to Lisbon."

"What if I got down on my knees and begged you?" she said.

"Don't make me fire you," Carrara replied coldly. He stepped a little closer to her and lowered his voice. "I hope to God it wasn't Tom Lord who put you up to sleeping with McGarvey. I hope it was your idea alone. But since it's happened, and you've admitted that you're in love with him, don't get hysterical on us. It's bad for business, yours as well as ours."

She said nothing, but her eyes were beginning to glisten.

"If you do your job properly, you might get out of this hole you've dug for yourself. But do us all a favor, Carley, and confine your sex life to your own hours."

"You bastard," she said, and she slapped his face, the noise almost as loud as a pistol shot in the narrow corridor.

Mike Wood, the interim chief of Paris station, came to the door. "Carley?" he said.

She turned on her heel and stormed up the stairs. They all heard the door slam at the top.

"What is it?" Wood asked.

Carrara turned to him. "I blew it," he said heavily.

"Do you want me to send someone after her?"

Carrara shook his head. "I'll go myself. Be right back."

"No, sir," Wood said. "The director is on the line from Langley for you. I had it transferred next door."

Carrara glanced up the stairs. "All right," he sighed.

"Before you take the call, there's something else you'd better know. It's at the top of this morning's agenda. It's about Tehrān station."

Something clutched at Carrara's gut. "What's happened out there?"

"No one seems to know, except that Dick Abbas and Shahpur Naisir seem to have disappeared. No one's been able to raise them. Ghfari is getting damned worried."

"Christ," Carrara said softly. "Send someone after Carley. I want her down here, no matter what it takes. And put the meeting on hold. I'll be right back."

He went into the secured office next to the conference room and picked up the telephone. "This is Carrara," he said.

"I have your call, sir," the operator in the communications center upstairs answered, and a moment later the DCI's gruff voice was on the line.

"Phil, what the hell is going on out there? I'm told that McGarvey was in Paris and you let him slip through your fingers."

Carrara had filed a highly amended report on what had happened that night. "Nothing I could do about it, General, short of engaging in a shoot-out. Some innocent people would have been hurt."

"Where is he now?"

"Lisbon. We're working on it. But we've got another, more serious problem developing in Iran."

"What is it?"

"My chief of station, Dick Abbas, and his number two are missing."

"Dick was supposed to monitor the shipment from Bushehr."

"That's right. We're going to have to insert someone over there, and right away."

"Spell it out for me."

"McGarvey has been on a wild-goose chase with the Argentinian woman."

"Yes, and the son of a bitch killed one of our people," Murphy bellowed.

"I don't think so. I don't know. McGarvey is convinced Arkady Kurshin is behind all of this. He said he came face-to-face with the man."

"Kurshin is dead."

"Perhaps not. You said yourself that the KGB is being hamstrung because of a limited budget. Especially its sources of Western currencies."

"What are you telling me?"

"I think Kurshin has been reined in, and has been redirected to Iran. I think he's after the gold. If General Didenko can pull off this coup, no one will be able to dislodge him. We'll have another Baranov on our hands."

"Go on."

"I want to send McGarvey after Kurshin."

Hate rode like a cancerous tumor on McGarvey's shoulders, weighing him down, causing a great weariness to descend on him. But it was like a powerful engine, driving him forward, no matter the costs.

It was just noon when he and Maria arrived at the Lisboa Penta, Lisbon's largest hotel. It had taken them a full day and a half from Paris, first by train to Madrid, and then overnight by rental car. McGarvey had wanted to come into the city clean. He wanted to pick his own sight lines before it was too late, before the cross hairs of some gunsight were centered on him.

"Give me your passport," he told Maria as the hotel doorman approached their car.

She looked sharply at him, but dug out the U.S. passport she'd been traveling on since Santiago. It identified her as Margaret Sampson. She gave it to him, and he slipped it into his pocket.

"We're here for your gold," he said. "I promised you that much. But you're going to have to do this my way. Arkady Kurshin will show up sooner or later, and my own people may be gunning for me."

"What happened in Paris?" she asked.

The doorman had stopped a few yards away, and stood respectfully waiting for them to finish their conversation.

"You're going to have to keep your head down," McGarvey said. He decided that he felt numb. Maybe his sister had been right all these years; perhaps he wasn't a full-time member of the human race. Once in a fit of anger she'd told him that whatever made a person good and decent and caring was dead in him. He had called her a name, but her words had hurt. And still did.

"I don't care," Maria said. She looked away. "I'll do whatever you say. But I'll hold you to your promise." She turned back. "It's all I've got now."

Carley would be in trouble because of what she'd done. But every woman he'd ever been close to got into trouble because of him. It was as inevitable as the death of a moth circling an open flame.

"We're going to register under our own names and use our real passports. One room. Less ground to defend."

"They'll find us."

"Probably." He got out of the car, the doorman smiling profusely as he rushed to the other side of the car to help Maria out.

The hotel was huge, but the rooms were small. Theirs was on the eleventh floor in the back, looking down through the glass ceiling of the solarium. In the distance was the airport, and nearby was the Gulbenkian Foundation's art museum.

A pleasantly warm breeze ruffled the curtains. Maria waited on the tiny terrace as McGarvey signed for the wine from room service. He brought a glass out to her.

They'd bought a few things to supplement their meager wardrobes in Paris and more in Madrid, some on his credit cards—by the time the charges could be traced back to him, he figured this operation would be long over—and some with Maria's money.

She wore dark slacks and a fisherman's sweater. The knit was bulky and made her look tiny, almost frail; her long dark hair and olive complexion were in high contrast to the off-white of the wool.

"I've written down the four names I remember, and parts of three others," she said.

"Your Nazis."

She looked up at him. "Yes."

"Are these from the Amt Sechster Anbau, or are we dealing with a new group this time? Perhaps the 'Council,' the twelve old men you told me about in Buenos Aires? What?"

Maria said nothing.

"A reunited Germany, I think, had you the most worried. We're going to keep these riches out of their hands. Or was it your father—stepfather?—the Jew killer whose memory you want to expunge? Maybe it's some permutation or combination of all those? Maybe Hitler is still alive. What? Are you ready to tell me?"

She didn't look away from him, nor did she flinch or show any reaction, but he could tell that his words were hurting her.

"We'll start now. This afternoon," he said. "We'll try the newspapers, the tax records, property deeds. If they're still alive and here in the Lisbon area, their names will show up in some document somewhere."

"I was seven years old the first time I was raped," Maria said, no inflection in her voice. She could have been making a statement about the weather. "My father, my real father, Rolph Reiker, had been gone for nearly a week. When he came back that night, he brought a half-dozen of his friends with him. They sent the housekeeper and my nanny away and started drinking. They made me bring them their wine and whiskey."

"Were they ex-Nazis, all these men?" McGarvey asked, though he didn't know what difference it made.

"Most of them. One of them was a general in Argentina's army. He was an old man, with white hair and a huge belly. I remember he smelled of cigars and whiskey. I was dressed only in my nightshirt and he kept watching me."

At some point, she went on, the other men noticed the general's interest in Maria and started making jokes about it. As she passed, one of them even grabbed at her nightgown, and another of the men pawed her chest. "Nothing there, Juan," someone said, and they all laughed.

But the general wasn't going to be put off. He liked little girls.

"So my father held an auction," Maria said evenly. "I was to go to the highest bidder. Of course no one else wanted me, I was just a baby, but they all knew that the general did, and they wanted to have a little fun at his expense."

When the bidding got to a certain point, her father made her take off all of her clothes and stand in front of the men.

"That fat man actually licked his lips," Maria said. "He made me turn around slowly. Once, twice, and then a third time. He doubled his bid. And won."

Maria finally looked away, out across the rooftops of the city bathed in the afternoon sun. A thin haze had settled in, and smelled of the sea.

"My father told me to do whatever the general wanted, and if I did I would be rewarded. If I did not cooperate, then I would be punished. He would lock me into the small room in the dark basement."

Her shoulders sagged a little.

"There were rats in the basement. I hated rats. I was more afraid of the darkness and of the rats than I was of that fat man."

"Your father used you like that from then on," McGarvey said.

"Yes. Of course in a few years, when I began to develop, I was more in demand. My father even slept with me in the beginning. I got pregnant three times before I was sixteen. My last abortion ruined my ability to bear children."

"I'm sorry," McGarvey said, and he meant it. In a small measure he was beginning to understand her.

"So from that moment on I was not only sterile of body, I became sterile of mind," she said. "Except for one thing, and that was the gold. My grandfather brought the submarine from Germany, and my father killed Major Roebling out of revenge, and for the gold. It was all he could talk about for years. I remember it from when I was a small child. It was my father's dream. But he was frightened of another group who wanted the gold. He said that they would stop at nothing to get it."

"Who were they?"

"I don't know. I don't know whether my father ever knew for sure, but they were probably the same people Dr. Hesse spoke about. The ones who had done the killings."

"What happened?"

"When I was sixteen my father came to me drunk, demanding that I sleep with him. But I could no longer do it, so I killed him."

"What about your stepfather, Schimmer?"

"Not my stepfather, although I tell people he was," Maria said. "My husband. He was one of my father's friends. We were married when I was seventeen, and two years later I poisoned him."

"He had money."

"And connections, all of which fell to me, naturally. Since then I've been looking for the gold, as one by one the old men have died off."

"Did you kill them?"

"No."

"Not even the fat general?"

She shook her head. "He was dead by then. Died in bed with his wife, a much respected man in Argentina."

McGarvey thought about what she'd told him. He did not think this story was a lie. And he also understood why she had done the things she had.

"What about the gold? What happens if and when you find it?"

"I don't know, Kirk," she admitted. "I've never let myself think beyond that point. But I know one thing: for some reason everyone is frightened out of their minds about it. I think that when we find the gold, and find out exactly why it has caused so much fear, I'll have an idea what to do."

"Then let's start now," McGarvey said.

"I need to rest now," Maria said. "We'll begin tomorrow."

37

"HAVE YOU SEEN NOTHING since Shahpur Naisir entered the building this morning?" Captain Hussain Peshadi asked from the open window of his car.

The stakeout officer at the wheel of the gray Morris shook his head. "An old woman came out just after he went in. And now many of the foreigners are returning from work."

It was a few minutes after six in the evening. A very cool wind blew from the mountains.

"Richard Abbas has not left his apartment since yesterday?" Peshadi asked, hardly believing what this idiot was telling him.

As a young man, Peshadi had trained for nine months at London's Scotland Yard. He'd learned not only police procedures, but also a streetwise cynicism that every cop develops. Nothing since had done much to soften his views.

"That is correct, Captain."

"And then Naisir showed up this morning, and he, too, is still inside?"

"Yes, sir," the driver said complacently. "As you can see, his automobile remains where he parked it."

"The shits that you relieved told you that Abbas had not left his apartment, and that no one else left? They saw nothing either? They were as blind as you?"

The surveillance officer blanched. His partner on the passenger side started to speak, but Peshadi cut him off viciously.

"Didn't you think something was odd? Didn't it ever occur to you to go into the building and check with your own eyes that Abbas and Naisir were still there?"

"No, sir," the driver said fearfully.

"By Allah, I will have your balls if they have walked off," Peshadi said through clenched teeth, climbing out of his car and pulling out his pistol. "Cover the back of this building," he told the two men. "If anything moves, shoot it." He turned back to his own driver, Sergeant Mohammed Turik. "Watch the front entrance. If I'm not out of there in five minutes, call for backup units."

Peshadi was a slightly built man with a wiry frame and muscles like steel cords. He'd played rugby for a short time in England, and many an opponent, badly underestimating his strength, had found himself flat on his back. After he'd sent the third man to the hospital, he was barred from the team for unnecessary roughness, but by then he was already developing his seeds of hatred for things Western.

The elevator was out of order, so he had to take the stairs up to the fifth floor. The building was permeated with the odors of frying meat, and on the third floor he was certain he could smell the raw odor of alcohol.

Intellectually, he understood that life without international commerce was impossible. But still his stomach turned when he thought of what Western influence had done and was doing to his country.

He himself had been badly tainted by association. It was something he fought against every single day of his life.

He hesitated at the fifth-floor landing, remaining around the corner, out of sight, as he studied the corridor. Nothing moved, but he could hear the sounds of music, and laughter. Ordinary sounds . . . Western sounds.

Tightening the grip on his pistol, he rolled out into the corridor and went directly to Abbas's door. He put his ear to the wood.

There were no sounds from within. He stepped back and pounded on the door with the butt of his pistol.

Almost immediately the music from one of the apartments down the hall stopped. A door opened and a man stuck his head out.

"Go back!" Peshadi barked in English, and the man disappeared. The door slammed.

Peshadi banged the butt of his pistol on the door again. The fifth floor had suddenly become very still.

Cocking the pistol, he fired three shots into the door lock, destroying the wood around it, and the door opened a few inches, caught only on a splinter.

Peshadi kicked it open and stepped out of the possible line of fire as he extended his gun hand into the apartment.

Naisir lay on his back just within the living room. Although he was recognizable, he'd obviously been shot in the face at close range. The bullet had entered his head just below his left eye. Long strips of cut-up bed sheet lay crumpled in front of a chair situated about six inches from the wall. An electrical cord, its wires stripped at one end, snaked across the floor to an extension cord that was plugged into a wall socket behind the chair. There was an odor of human waste, and something else. Something very odd. Yet an odor that Peshadi remembered from a very long time ago. A pungent smell. Cloying, almost.

Glue. Rubber cement.

Within the hour the Criminal Investigation Division of SAVAK had arrived at the apartment, and its team members—most of whom had trained in the West—had begun taking the place apart under Sergeant Turik's precise direction. Other investigators were questioning everyone in the building, and a team had been dispatched to the offices of the Compagnie Général de Picarde to watch for any activity out of the ordinary.

Peshadi was down at his car, talking to his office via radio-telephone.

His immediate superior, Colonel Seyyed Bakhtir, snarled, "Listen to me, Captain, I want that man found within the next twelve hours. Do whatever it takes to get the job done. I'll give you anything you need. But under no circumstances—absolutely none, do you hear me?—is that man to be allowed to leave Iran. Am I clear?"

"Yes, sir. But may I ask why this particular one is so important?"

"You may not," the colonel said. "But he is important. Very important to Iran. To our national interests."

"Yes, sir."

"Find him, Peshadi," the colonel ordered. "You of all people understand the price of failure. Find him."

Peshadi replaced the handset in its bracket and went back inside. It was late, well after ten. The technicians had gotten the elevator running again, and the lights in the stairwell were back on. They had simply been switched off, as had the corridor lights. Sabotaged for some reason.

A lot had happened here that he did not understand. Abbas was missing, but his car was still parked in the rear. His number two, Shahpur Naisir, was dead. Shot in the head with a medium-caliber pistol. He'd had his own gun out, evidently believing that he was walking into a deadly situation.

Someone had been tied to that chair, and had been tortured with electricity. They'd found some blood and a small amount of fecal matter on the chair seat, indicating that the victim had not only been in a lot of pain, but that he or she had probably been nude.

A strange business, he thought, riding up in the elevator. Made even stranger by Colonel Bakhtir's instructions.

Sergeant Turik met him on the fifth floor. He was a large man by Iranian standards, with a barrel chest and thick neck. "I was just coming down to fetch you," he said.

"Something new?"

"We've definitely uncovered a nest of spies. There can no longer be any doubt of it. All of them downtown must be arrested before they're allowed to get into more mischief."

The sergeant's large gray eyes gleamed. He loved his work, and admired Peshadi, although he didn't particularly hate Westerners.

"What is it?"

"First of all, the walkie-talkie that we found on Naisir's body is not an ordinary machine. It's set to communicate with a satellite. An American spy satellite. He could have talked to Washington with it."

Peshadi's suspicions were confirmed. Abbas, and in all likelihood the others in the computer firm, were CIA.

"What else?"

"The answering machine. It's been set up to make anyone monitoring his calls believe that he is sick at home. He recorded a one-sided conversation, with pauses at all the right spots. His accomplice could call the apartment and have a little chat with him. We'd think he was here all the time, when in reality he was gone."

"He's a clever bastard," Peshadi said.

"Yes," Sergeant Turik said. "So where is he now?"

38

MCGARVEY STOOD ACROSS THE street from the U.S. embassy, watching the front and side entrances. It was early evening, and since six o'clock activity had all but ceased.

He'd hoped by coming here like this to see someone he recognized. One of the old hands from the Company. Someone with whom he could make contact. He and Maria were going to need some local help if they were to have any real chance of finding the four Germans whose names Maria said were written in Roebling's notebook.

Forty-six years was a very long time, and so much had changed since the end of the war that hardly anything in Europe was recognizable for what it had been. In all likelihood the old men were dead by now and the gold either long gone or its hiding place lost.

In addition, McGarvey had the feeling that when Kurshin showed up in Lisbon—and he had no doubt that the man would come here sooner or later—it would be to make an attack on the embassy. Perhaps it was a lure to bring McGarvey out of hiding. To isolate him from his own people so that their fight would be an even one.

McGarvey wanted the fight once and for all. But he wanted no one else hurt. Not this time.

But he'd seen no one he recognized. Nor did the embassy seem any busier than normal, as it would if it had been placed on an emergency footing. There were no indications that the front entrance and back gates were guarded. Either they were being extremely low-key about their expectations of trouble, or Carrara had disregarded his warning and nothing was being done here.

It was depressing.

A cool wind was coming off the water. McGarvey stuffed his hands in his pockets and walked back to the hotel.

By registering so openly in Lisbon's largest hotel, and so near the embassy, he was making it easier for anyone to find him. In the morning, he decided, he and Maria would begin looking for her gold, and whatever secret that surrounded it.

Kurshin would come to Lisbon. He had to.

When he got back to their room Maria was sitting in the middle of the bed watching television. She'd switched off the lights and her complexion in the pale glow from the screen seemed chalky. "Where did you go?" she asked.

"To the embassy." He went to the window and looked down the way he had come. There was nothing but ordinary traffic. He couldn't see the front of the embassy from this angle.

"Did you tell them that we're here?"

"No."

"But they will find out sooner or later. So will Interpol, as soon as the police pick up the hotel registration cards and match them against their wanted lists."

She'd changed into a pair of jeans and a loose pink shirt. After the story about her past, she'd withdrawn. When he'd left she'd been lying in bed, facing the wall. Now she seemed to have come back a little. Again he wondered how much of what she had told him was the truth. And he wondered how she knew so much police procedure and tradecraft.

"Do you mean to let the authorities take us?" she asked. "Or do you think your Russian will show up first?"

He'd placed her in danger by so openly coming here. But she seemed inured to risk. Was it her past? Or something else?

"I suppose I can't say anything. You saved my life in Paris and again in Argentina. So I owe you my support. But you can't imagine how important this is to me. I've worked for this all my life. A lot of blood has been shed. I want it to end, finally. It's too much."

He watched her lips as she talked. They were full and sensuously moist, both sides of her face framed by wisps of her long dark hair that had escaped the pins.

"It has become such a part of my life, I can't imagine another way to live. It's as if I've been in jail for all those years." She shook her head. "I don't remember a time when I was ever really happy, though I suppose when I was very young and didn't understand what was happening around me I must have been at peace."

"Maybe you have no future. Maybe you have only a past."

She looked away. "What a cruel thing to say to me."

"Maybe you should think about turning your back on the entire thing. Say the hell with it. Get on with your own life. A husband. Children."

"I told you that I cannot bear children."

"Adopt a child. Give instead of take."

She shook her head again. "I don't think so," she said. "I told you, it's more than my body that's dead."

"I don't believe it," McGarvey said gently.

Someone knocked at the door. Maria reared back, but McGarvey motioned for her to be quiet. He pulled out his gun and moved out of the firing line.

"Kirk, are you in there?" a woman called from the corridor. McGarvey recognized her voice. It was Carley.

Maria's eyes were fixed on the door.

"Are you alone?" McGarvey said.

"Yes. I have to talk to you. Please let me in."

"It's all right," he told Maria. He holstered his gun, unlocked the door, and opened it.

Carley, dressed in boots and a red coat, smiled uncertainly. "Hello," she said.

"Did you get here clean?" McGarvey asked, looking past her down the corridor.

She nodded. "Who are you expecting?"

McGarvey looked at her. "You know."

"Not here, Kirk. He's in Iran. It's why I came. Phil wants your help, and the general has authorized it."

McGarvey stepped back so she could come in. She stopped short when she saw Maria on the bed.

McGarvey closed the door. "You know each other, I believe."

"Maria Schimmer," Carley said.

Maria was confused for a moment, but then she remembered. "You were at the embassy in Paris, after the explosion."

"There are quite a few people who would like to have some words with you," Carley said.

"Is that why you are here?" Maria asked defiantly.

Carley stared at her for a second longer, then turned to McGarvey. "Send her away. We have to talk."

"How do you know he's in Iran?" McGarvey asked. "And what is he doing there?"

"I can't talk about this with her in the room, Kirk. I don't care if you and she are.... I have my orders."

Maria got up from the bed and languidly went into the bathroom. Before she closed the door she looked a last time at Carley.

"She's very pretty," Carley said.

McGarvey didn't reply.

"I've come with a message from Phil. It's very important."

"How'd you find me?"

Carley smiled wryly. "Didn't you want someone to find you?"

McGarvey nodded. "What makes Phil think Kurshin is in Iran? The man knows I'm here. He'll come after me."

"Our chief of Tehrān station, Dick Abbas, and his number two have disappeared. Abbas was on a very delicate assignment for us. It was about a shipment of gold—a lot of gold—from New York to Tehrān through the port of Bushehr."

"How much gold?" McGarvey asked.

"In excess of one billion dollars, U.S. More than would be

aboard a World War Two submarine, if that's what you and she are after."

"Phil thinks that General Didenko pulled Kurshin from Argentina to go after the Iranian shipment?"

"It makes sense, Kirk. The Soviet Union is right there. Abbas was supposed to keep tabs on the shipment overland to Tehrān. There've been rumors about an army plot to take it. He was going to watch for it."

"With Abbas gone, Kurshin could pull off the snatch, blaming it on us. The Iranians would love to believe it."

"Exactly," Carley said. "Will you do it?"

McGarvey glanced at the bathroom door. "What about her?"

"You have our word that she'll be left alone."

"Interpol is after her."

"It'll be taken care of. She could come into the embassy."

"No."

"Will you do it?"

"What about backup in Iran? I don't know my way around the country."

"The number three, Bijan Ghfari."

"What about SAVAK?"

"They're watching our people like hawks. It's why Phil wants to send you. You're an unknown to them."

"Besides, I've got a thing for Kurshin."

"You know his methods better than anyone else," Carley said. "Will you help us?"

McGarvey didn't have to think about it. "Wait for me at the embassy," he said.

"Now," Carley insisted, but McGarvey shook his head.

"I'll come as soon as I can. But you're going to have to give me a little time. Get us transportation."

"I have a jet waiting for us at the airport."

"I'll be there in a little while, Carley."

"When?"

"Soon."

She looked at the bathroom door, her jaw tight. Then she turned on her heel and left. McGarvey watched from the door as she got on the elevator. She never looked back.

Maria stood at the open bathroom door when he came back into the room. "So. You're going just like that," she said. "Then go now."

"You listened at the door."

"Of course."

"When I'm finished in Iran I'll be back."

She was shaking her head.

"Yes. I promise you, I will return."

"If your Russian doesn't kill you. If the Iranians don't capture you. If your own people don't betray you in the end. I have seen this thing before. The Americans have invented their share of dirty tricks."

Her past had flawed her beauty, McGarvey decided. Just as ambition had flawed Carley. In many respects they were the same woman, except that Maria for all her outward toughness was vulnerable. Her need was so palpable it had been obvious to him from the moment he'd dug her out of the Paris embassy.

"I'll be back," he said softly.

She came into the room and pulled off her shirt, then peeled off her jeans. She was naked beneath.

"I told you before you don't have to do this," McGarvey said. He could not take his eyes off her. She was beautiful. If she was scarred internally from her terrible past, none of it showed on the outside.

"I'm doing this for me," she said. "This time I'm being selfish."

In the light from the television her body glowed like polished marble, yet McGarvey could practically feel the heat coming from her. Even at this distance, standing in front of her was like being in front of an open hearth. And when he finally went to her, and took her into his arms so that he could feel her heartbeat against his chest, she wasn't at all like marble. And her warmth was comforting.

In bed he entered her without preliminaries, and she drew up her legs, pulling him deeply inside of her, clinging so tightly to him that he could feel her desperate need in every cell of his body.

"I'll come back," he said.

39

"WHEN DOES THE *CITY OF TALLAHASSEE* dock in Bushehr?" the President asked. "Do we still have time to divert her?"

The events of the past twelve hours were stunning enough, CIA Director Roland Murphy thought, but with the addition of Arkady Kurshin the situation was developing into a full-scale disaster.

Murphy was meeting with the President, his National Security Adviser Thomas Emerson Haines, and Chief of Naval Operations Admiral Maurice Stans in the Oval Office.

"She arrives in port within the next two hours," Murphy said. "But since she entered the Persian Gulf she's been under the protection of the Iranian navy. I don't think we'd do anything but exacerbate the situation by trying to divert her."

"Besides, Mr. President, we don't have the resources in the

area," Admiral Stans said. He was a heavy-jowled man with a bulldog face and ramrod-straight appearance. "The nearest ship that could do the job is twelve hours to the south."

"How about a naval air strike? We could put a couple of jet fighters over the ship within two hours, and order her to stand off, couldn't we?" the President asked.

"Yes, we could do that, sir. But think of the consequences," Haines said.

The President turned to him coolly. "Yes, I've thought about the consequences, Tom. But have you thought about what will happen if that gold shipment is hijacked? The entire region will swing violently anti-West. We can't afford that now."

"I don't believe it will happen at sea," the admiral said. "Our sources show no hostile vessels within striking distance. The gold will reach Bushehr, all right."

"And once on Iranian soil it's their problem," Haines said. "We will have held up our end of the bargain by delivering it to the port of their choice via the mode of transportation of their choice. What more can we be expected to do?"

The President turned back to Murphy. "General?"

"I'm afraid it's not going to be that simple, Mr. President," the DCI said heavily.

"Give me the bottom line."

"Arkady Kurshin. We have reason to believe that he is in Iran."

"Do I know the name?"

"You may recall, Mr. President, that Kurshin was the Russian who hijacked one of our nuclear submarines and nearly succeeded in firing a missile on that target in Israel."

"Two years ago," the President said, recalling the incident. "He was killed."

"We never found his body. It's possible he's back in action, this time working for General Vasili Didenko, the head of the KGB's Department Eight. The dirty tricks people."

"Baranov's old gang."

"Some of them, yes, sir."

"Go on," the President said grimly.

"Our chief of station in Tehrān is missing. He was supposed to bird-dog the shipment overland from Bushehr to Tehrān. There have been rumors that an army faction might try to snatch it. Dick was to have blown the whistle."

"Still don't see that it's our problem—" Haines began, but Murphy interrupted him.

"Our number two man in Tehrān was found shot to death in Dick Abbas's apartment. On his body was found a pistol and a handie-talkie set to one of our satellite frequencies."

Haines groaned out loud. "Christ. SAVAK has got hold of this? They know that we're active out there with such communications equipment?"

"Let the general finish with what he was saying, Tom," the President said.

"To answer your question, Tom, yes, they do know. Which is the crux of the matter. If something were to happen to the gold between Bushehr and Tehrān, the United States could be blamed. We'd be in a tough spot."

"They'd be easily convinced," the President said thoughtfully.

"You say this Russian may be behind it?" Haines asked.

"We think it's possible," Murphy replied.

"We're talking more than a hundred tons of gold, General. That's a big load for one man to cart off." Haines turned to the President. "We know for a fact that the Soviet's Air Force–South Commander Yevgenni Zirkovsky is a moderate. One of Gorbachev's handpicked people. He'd have to be in on such an operation."

"Assuming such a strike would involve airborne units," the President said.

"There'd be no time to haul it overland across the Soviet border," Murphy pointed out. "Not without giving themselves away. No, they'll come by air, in aircraft with U.S. markings."

"Zirkovsky would never go along with such a risky scheme," Haines argued.

"Didenko has his own air force. Did you know that?" Murphy asked.

There was a stunned silence.

"KGB border guard units for the most part. He's been skimming the force for the past year or so. He could pull it off."

"Has there been any evidence that this 'air force' of his has been moved into place?" Haines asked skeptically. "He can't launch such an operation from Moscow."

"Azerbaidzhan," Murphy said quietly.

"Gorbachev's got his hands full there," the President said, understanding exactly what Murphy was getting at. "This time he sent in the KGB to quiet things along the border. Including what are supposed to be surveillance aircraft."

"Exactly," Murphy said.

"But why take such a risk?" the President asked. "If they failed, the backlash would be horrendous. It could undo everything Gorbachev has tried to do. He'd lose all the way around."

"It's the KGB," Murphy said. "It needs hard Western currencies in order to operate its foreign stations. It's as simple as that, and Didenko is the man for the job. He's sent Kurshin into Iran to set up the hijacking and blame it on us."

"What about Abbas?" Haines asked.

"His body will be proof that the United States was involved in the hijacking. We sent them the gold and now we're taking it back."

"Then we must warn them," Haines said, but Murphy shook his head.

"I don't think the Iranian government would believe us. It would just be one more nail in our coffin."

"We still have resources in the country, don't we?" Haines asked.

"Yes."

"Contact them."

"By handie-talkie?"

"If there's no other way, yes. The Iranians, even if they have got one of the machines, won't monitor it every minute of the day, will they? Nor will they be able to monitor every single frequency."

"I don't know. It would be a risk. The situation is explosive at the very least."

"I agree," the President said. "What do you suggest?"

"Fight fire with fire, Mr. President," the DCI said. "Send an assassin to stop an assassin. Kirk McGarvey is on his way to Iran now. He knows Kurshin better than anyone and he has a vendetta against the man."

"God help us if he's caught by the Iranians," Haines said.

"It doesn't appear as if we have any other choice," the President said. "But I agree with Tom: God help us."

40

A DRY, DUSTY WIND raked Egypt's capital city of Cairo as the Alitalia Airbus from Rome touched down at Alamaza Airport west of the city. The aircraft taxied ponderously to the main terminal, the setting sun casting long shadows behind it down the apron. A lot of people lined the rail of the observation deck, all of them brown-skinned Arabs.

A tall, exceedingly thin Egyptian waited on the far side of customs until McGarvey's passport was stamped and his single bag cleared, and then came over.

"Kirk McGarvey, permit me to introduce myself," he said. "I am Anwar Jaziraf, and I am here to serve you in any way that I can."

No one streaming past them, or in the crowds that filled the terminal, paid them the slightest attention. But there was no reason for the opposition to be here. For the moment, all eyes would be directed toward the east.

"When does my flight for Tehrān leave?" McGarvey asked.

"In less than three hours, so you can see that we must shake a major leg to have the time to properly brief you," Jaziraf said. "So you will please come with me."

He turned and headed off in a long, loping stride. McGarvey fell in behind him.

"I'll need papers."

"It is being taken care of even as we speak. You will be a Frenchman, naturally. They are expecting you."

"Where are we going now?"

"We have secured an apartment very near this airport. It was felt that no time should be wasted in transportation. At times Cairo's traffic can be impossible. At all times, that is," he added, smiling broadly at his own little joke.

"The apartment is safe?"

"Oh, yes, very safe indeed. For tonight."

Jaziraf's car was a noisy, battered, venerable Morris Minor that seemed on the verge of exploding, or at the very least falling apart in the middle of the highway. The Egyptian drove very fast and recklessly with one hand on the wheel, the other gesticulating out the open window at the sights of ancient Egypt that mingled with the slums of modern Cairo. The safe house was in a block of modern apartments directly across the highway from an Egyptian army barracks. As they pulled into the parking lot, a column of canvas-covered trucks, led by three Jeeps, roared out of the compound and headed at high speed into the city.

"Oh, don't worry about that. It's only the Sadat Brigade. The army's emergency readiness team. Their colonel loves to show off, so they run their little exercises into the city at all hours of the day or night. They're not bad, actually, although in a real fight most of them would probably shoot their own foots ... feet."

Inside, they took the elevator up to the sixteenth floor. As the door slid open Jaziraf motioned for McGarvey to hold back as he checked the corridor.

"Clear," he said. McGarvey followed him to one of the apartments.

Jaziraf was the deputy chief of Cairo station. It was felt that

McGarvey should be isolated from the COS on the off chance that the station, or McGarvey, had been compromised. Jaziraf, who was very good, was, however, expendable. It was the law of the jungle.

He knocked on the door to 1607 and it was opened almost instantly by a very large man with well-muscled arms, a thick neck, and a beet-red complexion.

"Bob Wills," he said, introducing himself. "Langley." He and McGarvey shook hands. "Did you have any trouble getting here?"

"I can't guarantee Lisbon, but I cleared Rome without a tail."

"Good," Wills said. Jaziraf had gone to the window.

"We're clean," the Egyptian said, turning back. "Anyone for a drink?"

"Coffee," Wills said.

"Cognac?" McGarvey asked.

Wills chuckled. "You owe me five bucks," he told Jaziraf.

"My drinking habits have preceded me," McGarvey said. He put down his bag and took off his jacket.

"I peeked at your file on the way over. You've done some credible work. But this one is going to be a tough son of a bitch. Problem is, we didn't have enough time to put something together. I'm afraid you're going to have to play it by ear over there."

"Did Phil Carrara send you?"

"Actually, no," Wills said. "I work for Mike Oreck. Office of Economic Research."

"Intelligence."

"Right," Wills said. "We worked a co-op with Operations on the project. Tehrān station was supposed to watch for bad guys, and blow the whistle if and when they showed up."

"Has there been any further word on Abbas or Naisir?"

Jaziraf came back with the coffee and cognac. "The number two is dead," he said. "Shot in the head."

"We just learned that," Wills said. "His body was apparently found in Dick Abbas's apartment. By SAVAK."

"Which means they'll be watching our front operation in Tehrān like hawks."

"Unfortunately, yes," Wills agreed. He led McGarvey over to a large table that was filled with maps, reports, files, and dozens of photographs, some of them from satellites and others ground-surveillance shots.

He picked up one of a slightly built, dark-skinned man coming out of a Scotland Yard building. "Hussain Peshadi. Trained with the Brits in the late seventies. He's SAVAK's chief investigator in Tehrān. A tough bastard. You're going to have to watch out for him. He's rabidly anti-West. Especially anti-American. And he's sharp as nails."

McGarvey studied several other more recent photographs of Peshadi. "How does he get along with the Russians?"

Wills shrugged. "Okay, I suppose. Just like most other Iranians. They're neighbors."

"When does the gold arrive in Bushehr?"

"Should be there within a few hours, if it's on schedule. It'll take them several hours to load it onto the convoy of trucks. We're assuming the group will leave immediately. I've got the maps for you showing their route. It's fairly straightforward stuff."

"How about my contact in Tehrān?"

"Bijan Ghfari, the number three. He'll be watching for you. He'll arrange your transportation, communications equipment, and, of course, weapons. But it's essential that you get out of Tehrān as quickly as possible. We'd like to salvage what we can of our operation."

"What about my passport and other papers?"

"They will be ready within the hour," Jaziraf said.

"You mentioned my cover would be as a Frenchman?"

"Anything wrong with that?" Wills asked.

"Everything," McGarvey said. "SAVAK found a body in Abbas's apartment. It means they're watching Picarde. Which also means they're going to keep a watchful eye on any stray Frenchmen who show up just now."

"You're right, dammit," Wills said.

"I want Russian papers," McGarvey said.

"Sir?" Jaziraf asked.

"Internal and external passports, lots of visa stamps, lots of entry and exit marks. And I want a KGB identification booklet. Moscow office—" McGarvey had a thought. "Make that KGB out of Baku."

"Why there?"

"It's Azerbaidzhan."

"So?"

"If the Russians are planning on snatching the gold, it's the nearest border for them to run to."

"Right, but so what? Why do you want to pose as a KGB officer from Baku?"

"Kurshin is going to try to steal the gold and blame it on us," McGarvey said. "I think turnabout is fair play, don't you?"

"What have you got in mind?"

"Let's see that route map," McGarvey said.

Wills dug a large map from the pile and spread it out on top of everything else. "We don't expect you to carry anything like this into Iran, of course. Ghfari will have everything you need."

The convoy's route had been penciled in red. It went directly inland from Bushehr, not turning north until it reached the mountain city of Kazerun.

"As you can see, they'll be in the mountains and high elevations for ninety-five percent of the distance," Wills said.

"How far is it from Bushehr to Tehrān?" McGarvey asked, studying the map.

"Nearly five hundred miles as the crow flies. But almost twice that by the route the convoy will be taking."

"A million places for an ambush to take place."

"Exactly."

"But not so many places for their transport planes to set down."

"Or ours," Wills added.

McGarvey looked up. "What are you talking about?"

"We have a Delta Force strike team standing by in Turkey. If the Russians make a move, they will be inserted."

"Not until I give the signal," McGarvey said.

Wills just looked at him.

"If you want me to go in there, I'll have to have your word on it."

"I could tell you anything you wanted to hear . . ." Wills faltered at the look on McGarvey's face.

"I'd come looking for you afterward if you lied to me. I want your word that the Delta Force will not be called on scene unless or until I give the signal."

Wills nodded after a moment. McGarvey was left with the

impression that it had been too easy. That the man had been told to expect the demand and to meet it.

"Exactly how much gold are we talking about here?" McGarvey asked.

"Four million ounces," Wills said. "One hundred twenty-five tons."

"Three heavy transport aircraft, maybe four, just for the gold. Another one or two for the assault troops. My guess is that Kurshin will set up the ambush spot as near a secluded landing area as possible, and then lay out a beacon or beacons for them to home in on. They'll be coming in at night. Low, to avoid radar detection, and because of the mountains their own on-board radar and navigation equipment will be practically useless."

"They've got the planes," Wills said.

"I'm surprised the Soviet air force is getting involved."

"Not the air force," Wills said. "They'll be KGB aircraft, with American markings, of course."

"Didenko," McGarvey said.

"That's right."

"It means Dick Abbas is still alive, then."

"That's not very likely, is it?" Jaziraf said.

"Yes, it is," McGarvey replied, looking up from the map. "The Russians will snatch the gold, and among the casualties, killed by the Iranians, will be Dick Abbas, chief of station for CIA activities in Iran. The proof SAVAK wants."

"The Delta Force—" Wills started.

"No," McGarvey said. "I intend to supply SAVAK with Kurshin's body and Russian identification, along with at least one of their aircraft."

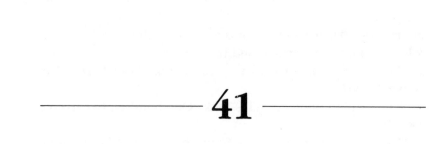

41

MCGARVEY, TRAVELING UNDER THE name of Valeri Vasilevich Bayev, arrived in Iran a few minutes after midnight. His Russian passport had raised a few eyebrows on the Lufthansa flight, but he'd been treated no differently from any of the other passengers, many of whom were French or German.

Coming into Mehrabad International Airport, he'd gotten a good look at the city. It was mostly in darkness, unlike the old days under the shah when Tehrān had been an open, reasonably westernized capital with an active night life.

Just inside the terminal, everyone holding a French passport was shunted into a separate line where their papers were carefully scrutinized by a team of a half-dozen grim-faced men in civilian clothes. It was an examination McGarvey figured he would not have passed.

When it was his turn in the normal line, McGarvey handed over his passport to the Iranian official. The man looked up sharply when he realized what nationality McGarvey was.

"Do you speak Russian?" McGarvey asked in Russian.

"I speak a little Russian. Do you speak English?" the official countered, his Russian poor.

"Yes, I speak English," McGarvey said in a broad Slavic accent.

The official nodded. "What is the purpose of your visit to Iran?"

"I am engineer. Industrial engineer. Heavy equipment. Motors for factories."

"Yes, I understand, but why have you come to Iran?"

"To do engineering," McGarvey said. "With Iranian businessmen, we will build factories. I am here to find out if it is"—he seemed to be groping for the right word—"possible."

"Do you have a sponsor here in Tehrān?"

McGarvey shook his head, a look of consternation clouding his features. "Is necessary?"

"No. How long will you be staying in Iran?"

"One week, perhaps ten days, no more. Then I must return to home."

The Iranian official stamped the passport and handed it back. "Your luggage will come from the aircraft soon. When you have cleared customs you must take a bus or a taxi directly to your hotel. It is not permitted for you to be on the streets at this hour. Your hotel will advise you of our laws."

"Yes, I understand this," McGarvey said, nodding.

The official looked beyond him to the next person in line and McGarvey walked through the doorway into the customs area where the baggage from the flight was just coming in, a dozen nervous people waiting for it.

As McGarvey took his place at the carousel, one of the Iranian officials in civilian clothes came in from the other room and said something to one of the customs men. They both looked pointedly at McGarvey. The civilian was a SAVAK officer; there was little doubt of it in McGarvey's mind. A simple call to the Russian embassy would shatter his cover identity.

He looked around the hall as if he were merely idly curious about his surroundings. The only way out that wouldn't involve an immediate confrontation with an Iranian official would be through the luggage opening. But what was on the other side of the wall? In all likelihood there would be a couple of armed guards to watch the incoming baggage.

He did not speak Farsi, he did not have a weapon, and he didn't even have any Iranian money. If he had to run now, he would be in serious trouble. Ghfari was doubtless being closely watched by SAVAK. If McGarvey was on the run, making contact would be doubly difficult.

Back in Cairo, while Wills had been finishing the briefing and awaiting McGarvey's Russian identification papers, Jaziraf had somehow managed to dig up a cheap cardboard suitcase and several changes of clothing, all of Russian manufacture. He'd also found a couple of engineering texts, in Russian, and the names of six Iranian engineering firms, which were jotted down in a notebook in Russian and in English.

The yellow cardboard suitcase came out onto the carousel. McGarvey grabbed it and went across to the three customs counters. The SAVAK officer stepped back but remained within earshot.

"Do you have anything to declare?" the uniformed customs official asked. They'd been told about him.

"*Nyet*," McGarvey said.

The official opened the suitcase and pulled everything out of it, checking the lining and the hinges before he turned to the clothes and finally the books and notebooks.

"No cigarettes or liquor?"

"*Nyet*."

"Pornographic magazines or photographs?"

"*Nyet*."

"Weapons?" the customs official asked evenly.

McGarvey shook his head. "I am engineer, here to help with building. I have no need of . . . weapons."

The customs official looked up as the SAVAK officer came over and held out his hand.

"I would like to see that notebook," he said, his voice stern. He also spoke English.

The customs official handed it over, and the officer quickly thumbed through it. "Have you already spoken with these companies?"

"No," McGarvey said.

"But you are hoping to begin tomorrow?"

"Yes."

The SAVAK officer looked up coldly, his eyes large behind thick glasses. "I think Gorbachev is a very dangerous man. What do you think of that?"

McGarvey shrugged. "I know people in Georgia and Azerbaidzhan who would agree."

"How about you, comrade?"

Again McGarvey shrugged. "I am engineer, not politician."

The plainclothes officer looked at him for a moment or two before he returned the notebook. "Go directly to your hotel, comrade. The rules will be explained to you."

"Yes, thank you," McGarvey replied.

The SAVAK officer left, and the customs official went down the counter to inspect the next person's luggage.

McGarvey hastily stuffed his things back into his suitcase and hurried into the main hall of the terminal. There he exchanged a few hundred dollars in British pounds for Iranian rials. Even here the Russian ruble was no good.

As a Russian, he should have taken one of the shuttle buses, but he was impatient to get started, so he took a taxi to a small hotel in Vanak, near the old Sheraton, Hilton, and Hyatt Regency hotels.

The attention he'd gotten from SAVAK had altered the plan. The agency would check the engineering firms he was supposed to be contacting tomorrow, and find out that no one had heard of him. They would come looking for him immediately.

The *City of Tallahassee* would be in port by now, but it would take the better part of the next twenty-four hours for the gold convoy to reach a good position for a Russian ambush. Probably longer. McGarvey had wanted to use the time to poke around Tehrān on the chance that Abbas was still in the city.

But that was changed now. He was going to have to make contact with Ghfari tonight.

Wearing the dark, Russian-cut clothes he'd brought with him, McGarvey slipped out of the hotel a few minutes before three in the morning, easily eluded the two sleepy policemen posted in front, and made his way through the nearly pitch-black alleys the four blocks to Ghfari's apartment.

There was no one out on the streets at that hour. No delivery vans, no ambulances, not even the police or military. Stepping to the end of an alley, he looked out across a broad boulevard fronted by shops and narrow little stalls that during the day sold hammered brass and copper goods. Above the shops were apartments.

Ghfari's flat was above a shop selling translations of the Koran and approved foreign-language books. As a safety precaution Wills had made a sketch of the building's layout in case McGarvey was coming in on the run.

"Only as a last-ditch effort, you understand," Wills had cautioned. "Under normal circumstances Ghfari is watched, but now he'll be very closely watched."

From where McGarvey stood, he could not spot the SAVAK surveillance team that he knew would be there. The only possibility, he decided, was that they were stationed in one of the buildings or shops on the opposite side of the avenue from Ghfari's apartment. If he crossed the street here he would be spotted.

A very narrow alley ran behind the shops on this side; he thought it likely that one backed the stalls on the other side, too. If the alleys were also being watched, he would at least have the cover of greater darkness here than on the broad street.

He turned and hurried back the way he had come, crossing a side street a block away, and taking the alley the long way around. He crossed the broad boulevard a block and a half west of Ghfari's apartment and covered the rest of the distance in a few minutes.

This alley, like the other, was not much wider than a cart path. Filled with a foul-smelling jumble of litter and debris, it was more of a refuse dump than a deliveryway. Garbage was evidently tossed out on a regular basis and never collected. Even the smell of human waste was strong. There were probably open sewers nearby.

Nothing human moved in the alley; only rats skittered here and there in the filth. McGarvey remained in the darkness watching the back of Ghfari's apartment house fifty yards away. The ground-floor doors and windows of all the apartments were tightly shuttered.

Gradually he began to realize that no one could get out of the buildings from here. The steel security shutters were all locked from the outside. Short of climbing out a second-story window and jumping down into the alley, the only exit at night would be from the front. Therefore it wasn't likely that SAVAK would have posted a surveillance team back here. There would be no need for it.

Nevertheless he approached Ghfari's building with caution, keeping well within the darker shadows.

He took a ballpoint pen from his pocket, quickly unscrewed the barrel, and slid out the slender steel pin concealed inside. Jaziraf had given it to him on the way out to the airport.

"Who knows, maybe it will be of some handiness to you," the Egyptian had said, grinning.

It took McGarvey a full ten minutes to get the heavy Yale lock open. He unlatched the hasp, and replaced the padlock on the staple with the hasp up so that when he closed the shutter it would look as if it were still locked.

Very carefully he lifted the metal shutter up on its tracks slowly enough so that it didn't make much noise. Behind it was an ordinary wooden door, also locked. This lock was rusty and it took McGarvey twenty minutes to get it open.

He had spent too much time outside, exposed. He had to get into the building.

A narrow passageway ran front to back, a security shutter on the front door. The bookshop was on the left, and a stone stairway lead up to Ghfari's apartment on the right.

There were no sounds from the shop or from the apartment above. The only light in the passageway came through the front shutter from the main boulevard.

He closed the back shutter and shut the door, leaving it unlocked in case he had to get out in a hurry. Anything was possible. SAVAK could have arrested everyone at the station and could be waiting upstairs now in ambush.

At the front door he glanced up the stairs, and then peered through the cracks in the shutter at the buildings across the street. At first he saw nothing, but as he was about to turn away he spotted a glint of light from something metal or glass in an upstairs window. He waited patiently for a few minutes longer. Another movement, and then a brief glimpse of a face in the window. SAVAK was there, as he'd figured, watching this place. Which meant there was no ambush waiting for him here.

Crossing the passageway, he hurried up the stairs on the balls of his feet, making absolutely no noise. There was only one door at the top, with what appeared to be an ordinary tumbler lock. But Ghfari would be very gun-shy just now. If somebody barged in, he might shoot first and ask questions later. And he had probably fail-safed his door.

McGarvey knocked very softly, hoping that Ghfari would have the presence of mind not to turn on a light.

There was movement from within the apartment. McGarvey knocked again, softly.

"*Qui est-ce?*" someone asked softly.

"It's me," McGarvey answered in English. "From Cairo. There's trouble."

A moment later the lock clicked and the door swung inward. The apartment was very dark. McGarvey stepped inside and stopped short as the barrel of a pistol was pressed against his temple.

"Your name, quickly now," the man said in English.

"McGarvey. Kirk McGarvey." He could smell gun oil.

"Who sent you?"

"Wills briefed me."

"A name from Cairo. One name. There is no time now. Tell me or you will die."

"Anwar Jaziraf," McGarvey said without hesitation. SAVAK did not work this way. Only frightened men, backed into a corner, demanded such information in such a melodramatic fashion. Jaziraf had told him the French-born Iranian was good, but young, and at times excitable.

The gun barrel was withdrawn. Ghfari stepped behind McGarvey and closed the door.

"Don't turn on the lights," McGarvey said.

"You spotted my friends across the street, then," Ghfari said, taking McGarvey's arm. "I will lead you."

McGarvey let himself be led across the totally dark room and through a doorway. Ghfari closed this door, then switched on a dim light.

"How did you get past them?" Ghfari asked. He was a tiny man with a full black mustache. It was obvious he was deeply frightened.

They were in what appeared to be a very small storeroom or closet. A piece of black cloth had been attached to the bottom of the door. There were no windows. No light would escape. He probably used the place as a darkroom.

"From the back. I picked the locks on the shutter and the door."

Ghfari nodded nervously. "No one saw you come here?"

"No," McGarvey said. "But we're going to have to get out of the city sooner than planned. I came in under a Russian passport."

"Very good. I tried to tell those idiots not to send anyone carrying French documents. SAVAK is all over us now. I think they will close our office in the next few days. But why are you here tonight like this?"

"It couldn't wait until tomorrow." McGarvey quickly explained what had happened at the airport.

"There is no doubt the *salopard* was SAVAK. You were not on any of his lists. He will check out your story."

"Which won't hold up."

"No, of course not," Ghfari said. He considered the problem for a moment. "You cannot go back to your hotel. They will be back first thing in the morning to keep an eye on you."

"Is it Peshadi?"

Ghfari looked up, his eyes narrowing. "Yes. You have heard of this one?"

"From Wills."

"Well, he's behind all this, all right. It was him and his sergeant who found Shahpur's body. I had to identify it, and that prick was standing right over me, ready for me to make a mistake."

"Did he ask you about the gun and handie-talkie they'd found?"

"No, but that's coming."

"Then you'll have to come with me," McGarvey said. There was no way he was going to leave the man behind for Peshadi. It wouldn't take SAVAK very long to open him up.

"This is my station now."

"They'll have to send someone else in under a different cover. What's left at the office to take care of?"

Ghfari was shaking his head. "Nothing," he said. "All the paperwork has been destroyed. I took the only other gun and handie-talkie over to the safe house for you."

"How about personnel?"

"Iranian contract people who know nothing."

"No one else who worked for the Company?"

"There were only three others. They took off for the Turkish border yesterday afternoon."

"Sounds like you were ready for this."

"It's been drummed into my head since Lyon," Ghfari said. "But if I leave, there will be nothing to start with. We have worked damned hard to get to this spot."

"They'll send someone else, different cover, different everything. Picarde is contaminated beyond repair now. You're going to have to turn your back on everything."

"We have a lot of assets in the field."

"Unless they're compromised, which they will be if you are caught and interrogated, they'll lie dormant until a new agent handler shows up. It's happened before."

Ghfari sighed deeply, as if he were glad to be convinced. "We will have to leave here tonight."

"I'd like to be out of the city by daybreak," McGarvey said.

"Impossible. We will have to spend the rest of the day at the safe house."

"Why?"

"No car until after dark. It will also give our satellite two more passes over the region. We will get another update on the convoy's position."

"So will SAVAK if they monitor our transmissions. They've got the handie-talkie."

"We have always taken enormous chances here, Mr. McGarvey. This is simply another. We have no choice."

It was loose, but they had no other choices. At least spending the day in the safe house rather than out on the desert would expose them to much less risk. "This is your city," McGarvey said.

Ghfari shook his head. "No. But it could have been."

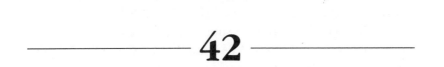

42

AWAY FROM THE CITIES, especially Tehrān, the interior of Iran was wild, more like a lunar landscape than a place on earth. Bounded to the east by Afghanistan and the rugged Elburz mountains, and to the west by the even taller, more inhospitable Zagros range, much of the ancient nation of Persia was a desolate, windswept high salt plateau.

Since the reign of the ayatollahs had begun, the populated regions of the country had slid backward by five hundred years. The climate of Islamic fundamentalism had stifled almost all progress. And the eight-year war with Iraq had sapped the economy at a time when a healthy rial was needed the most.

But nothing had changed in the interior for two thousand years or more. Moses, Christ, or Mohammed would have felt perfectly at home in ninety percent of modern-day Iran.

Within an hour after the assistant chief of Tehrān station had shown up at the apartment, Kurshin had led an unresisting Dick Abbas out the back way, and they'd climbed into a green Triumph sedan that had been supplied to Kurshin by his Russian embassy contact. The two SAVAK officers in front of the building had not even looked up as they'd driven by, and within the next hour they were outside the city, heading south on the main highway to Qom.

By that evening they had climbed well above the salt desert and were in the mountains. Kurshin had pulled off the highway into a cul de sac. They'd spent the night in the car.

All day Thursday they had worked their way farther southwest. The going was very slow because of the poor condition of the roads, and the great amount of military traffic they'd encountered south of Qom.

It had taken them five hours to skirt the city, which had a population of more than one hundred fifty thousand and its own SAVAK barracks.

By then, Kurshin had figured, Naisir's body would have been found in Abbas's apartment, and the search would be on. But for Abbas alone.

They'd spent Thursday night in the car, again parked off the highway in the mountains. The temperature had dropped to below freezing, and sleep had been almost impossible for both men, and especially for Abbas. Abbas was not dressed for the cold and he had not eaten in forty-eight hours.

The sun was coming up now, and it seemed thin and cheerless even to Kurshin, who knew he had won here. The gold would already be aboard the trucks, and the convoy would be on its way northeast. It was only a matter of time now; in twenty-four, perhaps thirty-six hours the gold would be in Russia and he would be on his way back to Europe.

He urinated at the side of the dirt track and then went back to the car where he pulled one of the full canteens of water from the trunk and drank.

Next he filled the gas tank with the last of the fuel from the jerry cans, closed the trunk, and went around to the driver's side.

Abbas was awake in the back seat and was staring at Kurshin, his eyes dark, his complexion wan. He didn't look well.

"May I have some water?" he asked, his voice weak.

"No," Kurshin said, getting in behind the wheel and starting the car.

"If I die from dehydration, I will be of no use to you," Abbas said.

Kurshin considered him in the rearview mirror. He shook his head. "I don't think you will die so soon. But if you pass out I will give you some water to revive you."

"I can't go on much longer like this," Abbas said.

"You will manage."

"Please," Abbas croaked. "I'm begging you in the name of human decency. Just a little water."

Kurshin turned in his seat and looked closely at the American as if seeing him for the first time. His lip curled a little. "You're not much of a man, are you," he said conversationally. "I could kill you now and it would make very little difference to my plans. Or I could keep you alive a little while longer. In the end it is up to you."

Abbas's Adam's apple bobbed up and down and his eyes were blinking furiously. He was clearly on the verge of losing control. "What kind of a monster are you?"

"You can't imagine," Kurshin said. He took out his pistol, levered a round into the firing chamber, and calmly reached over the back of the seat and placed the muzzle against Abbas's forehead.

The American flinched.

"What is it to be?" Kurshin asked. "Death now, or life?"

Abbas said nothing.

"With life there is hope. Who knows, perhaps something will go wrong at the last minute. Perhaps I will be killed and you will get your chance to escape. Die now and that would be impossible."

"I want to live," Abbas said.

"Then you will cooperate with me?"

"Yes."

"Very good," Kurshin said. He withdrew his pistol, eased the hammer down, and laid it on the seat beside him. He had absolutely no respect for men such as Abbas, even though this type made his work easier. The man was weak, and deserved to die. And he would.

The only two men who had ever earned his respect were Valentin Baranov, and Kirk McGarvey. Baranov was dead, and McGarvey would be soon.

He eased the car into gear and headed back down to the main highway. "We will get ready to take the gold now," he said.

It was getting dark again, and for a little while Richard Abbas thought he might be going blind. He was lying in the cramped back seat of the Triumph as they bumped slowly over an extremely rough track. It was the motion that had awakened him. They were once again off the highway.

It took a long while for his brain to begin to function properly, but finally he managed to sit up and look outside.

They were following what appeared to be the dry bed of a mountain stream that would contain water only in the spring. They were very high in the mountains, but above them the even taller peaks were covered with snow. This was a no-man's land. Nothing lived here except for the eagles. No one would ever want to come here.

Kurshin was concentrating on his driving. Ten minutes later, after they had gone another half mile, the stream's course opened onto a narrow defile that had to be a mile or so long and perhaps several hundred yards wide. The ground, from what Abbas could see, was reasonably level and free of large boulders or holes or drift piles.

It would make a perfect landing spot, Abbas slowly realized. The site was completely hemmed in by taller mountains. Once the aircraft got in, they would be virtually invisible to Iranian radar, and certainly invisible from the highway below. SAVAK would never suspect a thing. Neither would the guards on the gold convoy.

It was ingenious. The Russians would get the gold, and the Americans would be blamed for it. The Iranians were always ready to believe ill of the Americans.

Kurshin pulled up at the edge of the landing area, shut off the car's lights and engine, and looked back at Abbas. "So. You are awake. How do you feel?"

"Very . . . bad," Abbas said, feigning much more weakness than he actually felt, although he was frightened at how little strength he did have.

Kurshin studied him. It was late afternoon and would be night before long. They were much higher in the mountains here than they had been last night, so already the weather was much colder. Abbas didn't know if he would be able to hold up much longer.

"Get out of the car," Kurshin said, opening his door and climbing out.

Abbas pretended to fumble with the door handle for a long time, and took even longer to pull himself out. Meanwhile Kurshin had opened the trunk and had taken out a metal canister about twenty inches long, and half that wide. A short whip antenna was attached to its top surface.

"There's water for you in the trunk," he said. "And some food in the box. But I would drink and eat with care lest you make yourself ill."

Abbas dragged himself to the back of the car as Kurshin walked off a few yards with the canister and set it down on the ground. He hunched over it and began fiddling with the base of the antenna.

Abbas snatched a canteen from the trunk, and for just a moment he wavered on his feet, dizzy even from that slight effort. His fingers felt so thick and numb that he had a difficult time simply removing the cap. With shaking hands he raised the canteen to his lips and drank, spilling more than half the water all over the trunk and himself before he managed to get some down his throat. It was lukewarm and tasted metallic, but it was wonderful, the relief to his dehydrated system almost immediate.

A second later his stomach knotted up, and he almost vomited, but he held it back by force of will.

He took another drink, this time more cautiously, and his eyes fell on one of his shirts rolled in a ball in the corner of the trunk. His own gun was half wrapped in the cloth, its butt and trigger guard exposed.

Abbas glanced over at the Russian, who was still occupied with the canister. It had to be some kind of a transmitter, Abbas thought. It was the only explanation that made sense. He reached inside the trunk and grabbed the pistol, the feel of the metal like a shot of adrenaline to his system.

He cocked the gun, and then holding it behind his right leg, he straightened up and turned around. Kurshin was still doing something with the transmitter.

Abbas walked on unsteady legs toward the Russian. The man seemed completely absorbed in what he was doing. It was the mistake he had talked about. Only it was going to cost him his life.

"You son of a bitch," Abbas growled, raising the pistol and aiming it at the back of Kurshin's head. He pulled the trigger, and the hammer slapped on an empty chamber.

Kurshin turned around and grinned up at him. Abbas stumbled backward, off balance, the Russian's laughter rising and finally echoing off the sheer cliffs around them, a red light blinking atop the transmitter.

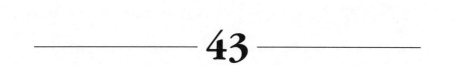

43

MCGARVEY HATED THE INACTIVITY. He'd paced the tiny downtown apartment all morning and most of the afternoon, not
daring to turn on the radio or television for fear someone in
the building would hear it and come to investigate.

The apartment belonged to an Air Iran international pilot, and
was very rarely occupied. Although the man was completely
above any sort of suspicion, the paranoia that gripped Tehrān
was all-encompassing. Anyone could become a suspected sym-
pathizer of things Western under the correct circumstances.
McGarvey didn't want anyone knocking on the door. Not now.

Ghfari had gone out around three-thirty in the afternoon, and
although it was already after six, he had not returned. McGarvey
was becoming concerned.

He had weapons now. A Russian-made TK automatic and an

AK-47 assault rifle. He also had one of the satellite handie-talkie transceivers, maps, and fresh papers that identified him as Danish. But until Ghfari returned with the car, he had no transportation.

For the past hour he had watched the street from the window, half expecting at any moment to see SAVAK, or the police, or even the military pulling up below. He had visions of Ghfari being arrested and interrogated. The young man would crack easily.

McGarvey checked his watch again. He'd give Ghfari thirty more minutes before he would have to write him off.

The convoy was already on its way north, and depending upon where Kurshin had set up his ambush point, the attack could come any time within the next twenty-four hours.

The street was still clear. McGarvey went into the bedroom where he got his jacket and stuffed the pistol in his belt at the small of his back. The AK-47 had been disassembled and was loaded into a leather overnight bag along with several thirty-round clips of ammunition, a second pistol and ammunition, the handie-talkie, and the maps, which included the convoy route, in itself a highly secret piece of information.

They would face immediate trial and execution if they were caught with any of that. And, as Wills had warned in Cairo: "It would be more evidence to the Iranians that the U.S. was behind the hijacking. So don't let yourself get caught."

The last of the afternoon light had faded, and the few cars and trucks on the street below all ran with headlights. In a couple of hours it would be curfew, and getting out of the city would be next to impossible.

McGarvey closed the heavy bag and brought it out to the tiny living room, where he set it by the door. It would be cold in the mountains at this time of the year. In addition to the car, Ghfari was to bring them warm clothing, extra fuel, and food.

But anything could have gone wrong. If Ghfari had been stopped and the car searched, he would have been put under immediate arrest. Innocent people did not drive around with such things in their cars. At least they didn't in Iran these days.

"Ghfari is a good man," Jaziraf had told him. "I know him well. We trained together."

"But?" McGarvey had asked. They were nearly at the airport.

The Egyptian had been giving him last-minute instructions and hints all the way out.

"He is a young man. There is much that he has not experienced in his life. Therefore there is much that he does not understand."

McGarvey's life would depend on Ghfari's abilities and judgment. He was grateful for Jaziraf's candor. "Can he be trusted?"

"Oh, yes, most completely he can be trusted. But he is only the number three, he is alone in a hostile country, and he is terribly frightened. I have heard it in his last transmission."

Frightened men did extraordinary things. But they also did stupid, dangerous things.

Ghfari drove past in a battered Range Rover with big, knobby, off-road tires, two very tall whip antennae at the back, and some sort of symbol painted on the door.

He stopped at the end of the block and pulled the big station wagon half up on the curb. He got out, the headlights still on, and walked to the back of the car where he seemed to check something at the base of one of the antennae.

Before he got back behind the wheel he looked down the street the way he had come, up at the apartment, and then back down the street.

It was a signal. He'd managed to get their transportation, but something had evidently gone wrong, and he wanted McGarvey to get out of the apartment. They would have to meet out on the streets somewhere.

Ghfari pulled away from the curb and turned the corner at the end of the block. McGarvey checked to make sure the pistol was secure in his belt, then picked up the leather bag and let himself out of the apartment.

Downstairs he waited for a few moments in the relative darkness of the doorway to study the street. Traffic was light, but as far as he could tell, normal. No one seemed to be lingering nearby. No one seemed particularly interested in the building. The few shops on this street seemed to be getting ready to close for the evening.

McGarvey stepped out onto the sidewalk, the early-evening air very cool, and walked in the opposite direction Ghfari had gone.

At the corner he headed east, directly away from what had once been called Argentine Park. He had no idea what it had been renamed since the revolution, but there seemed to be some kind of a demonstration going on there. A bonfire had been lit and it looked as if the crowd was burning some effigy, though at this distance it was impossible to tell just who or what the straw figure represented. Such occurrences, he'd been told, were common these days in Tehrān.

In the next block, the Range Rover pulled up beside him. He tossed the bag in the back seat and climbed in beside Ghfari.

"It's SAVAK," Ghfari said, immediately pulling away and heading up toward the Tarasht Highway just south of Vanak.

"Did they follow you?"

Ghfari glanced in the rearview mirror. "I have lost them for the moment. But they know this car. They were at the meeting. I do not know if the others got away."

"These others," McGarvey said, "do they know our plans?"

"No," Ghfari said grimly. "But if SAVAK catches them, they will die."

"There's nothing we can do for them now," McGarvey said.

Ghfari looked at him. "I know."

"Then let's get out of the city. We've wasted enough time."

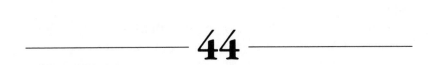

44

THE PRESIDENT AND Thomas Haines were bent over a small-scale map of Iran spread out on the President's desk when Roland Murphy was shown into the Oval Office. It was two forty-five in the afternoon, Washington time.

The situation in Iran was coming to a head now. The President had asked to be briefed the moment the operation, which they were calling PLUTUS after the Greek god of wealth, went critical. In Murphy's estimation, it had.

Both men looked up when Murphy came in.

"We have fifteen minutes, General. Then I have a news conference," the President said.

"Anything to do with Iran?" Murphy asked, joining them.

"No," the President said. "At least I hope not. But if it comes up, I intend stonewalling it. For the moment, anyway."

"Every president since the Second World War who has tried to keep something from the media has been crucified," Haines cautioned.

"I know," the President said glumly. "But it's my call. What's the latest, General? The convoy is off and running?"

"Yes, Mr. President. At least I can give you that much good news," Murphy said.

The President gave him a sharp look. "Spell it out."

"There've been no troubles so far, and our last report was that the gold was at the halfway point, about here." Murphy stabbed a blunt finger at a point well into the mountains.

The President and his security adviser looked at the spot. "That's pretty wild country, isn't it?" Haines asked.

"That's an understatement. The area is about as remote as they get."

"We don't have time," the President warned.

"Arkady Kurshin is there, all right, at least according to McGarvey."

"We've gotten word from him? He's in place?"

"There was evidently some sort of trouble in Tehrān, but he and our number three man in the station managed to get out of the city and use the satellite link with us. He wanted us to look for heat traces off the main highway south of Qom, and for any kind of a narrow-beam high-frequency beacon in the same area."

The President's eyes narrowed. "In English, General."

"He didn't stop to explain, but we think he believes that Kurshin will set up a radio homing beacon to allow low-flying aircraft to land at some remote spot in the mountains. They'd be able to come in under Iranian radar, set down, hijack the gold shipment, and fly out before anyone knew what was going on."

"Well?" the President asked.

"We just found the beacon," Murphy said. He took out his glasses, put them on, and studied the map for a moment or two before he drew a small circle in the mountains well north of the convoy's present position.

The President's eyes were bright. "Are we sure it's a Russian beacon?"

"No," Murphy admitted heavily, "but it's where it should be if Kurshin has set it for the reasons we think he did."

"Has this information been transmitted to McGarvey?"

"Not yet, Mr. President. We told him to wait until twenty-three hundred hours Greenwich time, which is when our satellite will be overhead. Gives us another three hours to decide what to tell him."

"In the meantime the convoy is heading into a possible ambush," Haines said. "And the Iranians may have intercepted your transmission to McGarvey."

"It's a chance we have to take," Murphy said. "But we've got as much as twelve hours, depending upon how fast the convoy moves. Which places the Russians at the disadvantage. Iran keeps time eight and a half hours ahead of us. It's coming up on eleven-thirty in the evening over there. The convoy isn't due to pass the ambush spot until sometime tomorrow morning. During daylight hours. Unless it speeds up, which is possible."

The President exchanged glances with Haines. "Which also puts *us* at the disadvantage if we want to send our Delta Force team in."

"McGarvey was quite specific about not making such a move. At least not for the moment," Murphy said.

"We may have no choice, General," the President replied. "I simply will not allow that gold to fall into Russian hands. Not after your warning."

"Perhaps you should call President Gorbachev on the hot line—" Murphy stopped when the telephone on the President's desk chimed softly.

The President picked it up. "We'll be through in a few minutes," he said sharply. He looked at Murphy. "Who?" he asked. "Send him in." He hung up the phone. "Your deputy director of operations. He says it's of vital importance."

All three men turned toward the door as Phil Carrara, carrying a briefcase, came in. He was very nervous, and he looked all in. He'd been back from Paris less than eighteen hours.

"I'm sorry, General, but this couldn't wait," he said apologetically.

"That's all right," the President told him. "This is my office. What have you got for me?"

"Oh, yes, Mr. President. I'm sorry, sir. All hell has broken loose in Moscow and in Azerbaidzhan. My people think it's extremely significant as concerns PLUTUS. I agree."

"What's happened, Phil?" Murphy demanded.

"General Vasili Didenko was arrested three hours ago at his apartment on Kutuzovsky Prospekt by officers from the Special Investigations Division of the militia."

"On what charge?" a stunned Murphy asked.

"Treason," Carrara said.

"Then it's finally over," Haines interjected, but Murphy ignored him.

"Where'd we get this?"

"Thomas."

Murphy nodded. "Then it's true," he said softly. He turned back to the President. "'Thomas' is the code name for what we call a 'gold seam' in Moscow. He's very highly placed, and his intelligence is completely beyond reproach. It always has been. But I don't think you want to know the details."

"No," the President agreed. "But we're out of the woods. You can recall McGarvey now. And we can have the Delta team stand down."

"I'm sorry, Mr. President, but I don't think that would be wise," Carrara said. "Not just yet. We have another problem that is probably related."

The President turned his cold, gray stare toward the DDO. "What else have you brought?" he asked.

"We think that a revolt has begun in Baku, the capital city of Azerbaidzhan along the Iranian border. I have some satellite shots which seems to show fighting downtown and at the air base to the west of the city."

Again the President and his national security adviser exchanged glances. "Any word from the Kremlin on this?" the President asked.

"We've heard nothing, sir," Carrara said. "But this has just begun. The photos came to us in real time."

Haines had picked up a phone and was calling his office.

"Let's take a look at these photographs," the President said, and he picked up one of the other telephones. "Get me Jim Bardley over at the National Security Agency, General Powell at the Pentagon, and call my cabinet."

Carrara had begun laying out the satellite photographs and the president hunched over his desk to look, the phone still to his ear.

"No, we'll be meeting downstairs in the situation room," he said. "Fifteen minutes."

Carrara handed him a magnifying glass and the President took a closer look at one of the shots. It showed the fighting going on at the air base.

"Cancel it," the President said into the phone. "Didenko's aircraft are still on the field?" he asked Carrara. Then he said into the phone, "I don't care what excuse you make, Jon. They'll know what's going on within the hour in any event. Oh, and call Dan—get him back here on the double. He should be in San Antonio by now."

The President hung up and turned his full attention to the photographs.

Murphy snatched up another of the telephones on the President's desk and called Lawrence Danielle.

"These are the seven aircraft we're assuming Didenko's troops are going to use," Carrara said. "All Soviet-made military transport aircraft. Actually, they're old converted Badger bombers the KGB was given."

The President studied the photographs for a full minute longer. "Unless I'm missing something here, the fighting has been kept away from that area of the base," he said, finally looking up.

Carrara nodded. "Yes, sir, we came to the same conclusion ourselves."

"What's that tell us?"

"Some of the other photographs show that the Azerbaidzhanis have apparently closed their borders, or at least they've started at all the main highway and rail crossing points."

"What about General Didenko's forces at the airfield?" the President asked, a dangerous edge to his voice. His telephone rang. He picked it up. "Hold it for a moment," he said sharply.

"We're certain that the number of people in Moscow who even knew about the force, let alone that it had been diverted to Baku, must be very small, Mr. President. We also have reason to believe that the KGB field commander in charge of the force was given at least some autonomy in the event he ran into a snag."

"Let's hear it all."

"With Didenko's arrest and now the apparent uprising in Azerbaidzhan, we think two things are possible. The KGB commander won't want to return to Moscow. He would face certain arrest with his boss. So he might stay there in Baku and help the new government. Or"—Carrara glanced at Murphy—"or he means to continue."

"To snatch the gold?" Haines asked, looking up from his phone call.

"Yes, sir."

"Why?" Murphy asked. "Even if they pulled it off, and got back to Baku with it, what then, Phil?"

"I don't know, General," Carrara said. "But I do know that a billion and a quarter dollars' worth of gold is a very powerful incentive. And at this moment that field commander has everything going for him. He has the force and the ability to go after the gold. There aren't many people who know what he's up to. His boss has been taken out of the picture. And he finds himself in the middle of a confusing situation in which normal law and order are probably breaking down. No one there knows what's happening from minute to minute."

The President was still holding the phone to his ear. "He could throw in his lot with the Azerbaidzhan government. A billion plus in gold would be a powerful bargaining chip across any table. No matter what happened afterward, he would end up on top."

"Or he wouldn't have to return to Azerbaidzhan at all," Carrara said. "Iraq would welcome him with open arms. So would Syria. Even Lebanon. There, with his money and his force, he could carve out his own fiefdom. The possibilities aren't endless, but they're certainly sufficient to keep us in the dark."

The President nodded thoughtfully. "Who is it?" he said into the phone. "Put him on."

Murphy had finished with his call and he looked again at some of the photographs.

"Jim, yes, I just heard. The general is over here from Langley. Are your people ready to confirm?" The President looked at Murphy and Carrara and nodded. "How about Soviet military traffic?"

"Are we still watching the Baku airfield in real time?" Murphy asked Carrara.

"Yes, sir. The moment those planes take off and head for Iran we'll know about it."

"All right, I want you over here right away. We'll meet in the situation room. But it's important that I be kept up to date. I want to know what's going on over there. In detail, Jim."

Haines finished his call at the same time as the President and they both hung up. "Powell is on his way over," the security adviser said. "He called my office."

"Besides our satellite surveillance of the region, who is watching things over there?" the President asked.

"We have Bob Wills standing by in Cairo with our station people," Murphy said. "And of course McGarvey and Bijan Ghfari in Iran."

"How about that Delta Force team?"

"They're en route from Ankara to Van, a city of some sixty thousand people in eastern Turkey about fifty or sixty miles from the Iranian border," Carrara said.

"When will they arrive there?"

"Within the hour, Mr. President."

"And how soon could they be on site? In Iran. At that Russian beacon, I mean."

Carrara started to shrug, but then thought better of it. "The straight-line distance is about five hundred to six hundred miles. But assuming we wanted to get there without being detected by Iranian radar, or by the Russian forces, we'd have to take a more indirect route. Let's say double the distance. Three to four hours from liftoff at Van until touch down on site."

"And the Russian forces out of Baku?" the President asked.

"Almost the same distance, Mr. President," Carrara said, understanding exactly what he was being asked. "But the Soviet aircraft are a little slower than ours."

"Let me get this straight," the President said. "If our Delta team is placed on standby in Van, there would be enough time for them to reach the target even if we didn't give them the go-ahead until the Russians lifted off from Baku?"

"It would be tight, Mr. President, but I believe we could beat the Russians to the punch."

"I'm glad to hear that," the President said. "I was beginning to believe that everything was going to depend upon one or two men alone in those mountains."

45

THE DARK BLUE PEUGEOT with government plates was admitted through the gates of Qasr Prison and drew up at a side entrance to the main administration building. Captain Peshadi was alone in the car. It was a few minutes past midnight, and he had been without sleep for two days and two nights. His mood was black.

The prison was a squat gray stone fortress. Peshadi looked up at the thick walls, rolls of electrified barbed wire glinting in the harsh lights. Get behind these walls and there was no hope, the thought came unbidden into his mind, and he shivered.

His assistant, Sergeant Turik, was waiting for him in the downstairs staging room. He was noisily drinking tea from a tall, chipped glass, and when he saw Peshadi he put the glass down and grinned.

"I think our birds have flown the coop," he said.

"Abolhasan has finally talked?" Peshadi asked, the first glimmering of hope coming alive. Colonel Bakhtir had been relentless ever since he'd learned that Abbas was missing. His twelve-hour deadline had come and gone, and he was out for blood now. Anyone's.

"He gave us the one name we wanted," Turik said. "But we got even more than that. It was real police work."

"You said the 'birds' have flown the coop?"

"South on the Tarasht Highway. They're long gone by now. Probably in Qom, or somewhere south. Maybe they're heading for Turkey."

Peshadi was becoming impatient. "But you just told me Abolhasan gave us the *one* name we wanted."

"Yes?" Turik asked, incomprehension in his eyes.

"One name. Where'd the other one come from?"

"Oh," the sergeant said, nodding. "There are two of them now, but we don't have a positive ID on number two."

Peshadi waited.

"We're working on it," Turik said.

Peshadi maintained his patience as best he could. "But how do we know that there are two of them, instead of the one Abolhasan identified?"

"The Range Rover was spotted twice. Once when it picked up the tall Westerner downtown, and the second time on the highway south."

"Now we're getting somewhere. I want to talk to Abolhasan," Peshadi said.

A pained look came over Turik's face. "He's dead."

"You killed him?"

"Not me. One of the shits in back. The man was a diabetic. Weak heart. There was no way for us to have known."

"But you taped his interrogation?" Peshadi asked, half believing for just a fraction of a second that the British might be right. Perhaps theirs *was* the only civilized police force in the world.

"Of course."

"And the name he gave us?"

"Bijan Ghfari."

"Picarde," Peshadi said, a little thrill rising in his chest.

"Yes, and that's not all," Turik said. "The office has apparently been closed for good. Everyone is gone. Vanished into thin air."

"What about this man with Ghfari? This Westerner? How did we come to learn about him?"

"Several witnesses spotted the man getting into the Range Rover on a street downtown. They noticed him not only because he was obviously Western, but because he was carrying a big leather bag, and he seemed to be in a great hurry."

"Did you get a description?"

"Yes."

"What about the sighting on the highway?"

"The police. But since there was no reason to stop them, they did nothing."

"Then why the report?"

"Because the Rover turned up on the stolen list, and they happened to remember seeing it earlier."

"Heading south."

Turik nodded. "It's out of our jurisdiction now. We can notify Qom and let them handle it."

"Did the highway police get a look at our mystery man?" Peshadi asked.

"Not enough of a look to match a description," the sergeant said. "But they were sure that there were two people in the car."

"Good work," Peshadi said, and Turik beamed. "Now I would like to talk with these witnesses who spotted the Westerner with the big leather bag."

Again the sergeant's face fell. "They're not here. We let them go home. There was no reason to hold them. They'd done nothing wrong."

Peshadi sighed deeply. It was the lack of sleep, he told himself. "Well, at least we have their descriptions, I hope."

"Yes," Turik said. He plucked a file folder from the table and handed it to Peshadi. "I had them combined and transcribed. They match well."

Peshadi opened the file and glanced at the typewritten notes, then closed the folder. "I think that's all for tonight," he said.

"Shall I notify Qom?"

"I'll take care of that, Mohammed. You go home and get some sleep. I'll see you at the office in the morning."

"You should get some sleep yourself, Captain," Turik said, and he grabbed his coat and left.

* * *

Peshadi's small, overstuffed office was on the third floor of the Ministry of Justice building in the southern part of the city. His was one of the few with lights on.

It was late. His eyes were on fire, and his throat felt raw; he'd read and reread the description of the Westerner a dozen times, and still he felt that he was missing something ... or, better yet, that he knew this man. Tall, husky, obviously Western. Self-assured, but definitely in a hurry. A stranger in a strange land. An alien on another planet. An exotic. Where had he heard such a description?

Three questions were foremost in Peshadi's mind. How had the Westerner entered Iran? What was his purpose here? And where had he and Ghfari gone?

Picarde, S.A., was almost certainly a front for CIA activities in Tehrān, which meant that Ghfari worked for the Americans, and that the Westerner who'd been spotted was an American.

Here to close down the Picarde operation? Peshadi had had his suspicions, but he'd done nothing out of the ordinary against anyone on the staff. At least nothing out of the ordinary for Iran. What, then, had made them decide to close up shop? And why had they taken the risk of sending someone in to help?

That line of thinking was getting him nowhere. The man had obviously come to Iran to do something. To accomplish some goal.

The primary question, Peshadi thought, was what exactly were the Americans up to this time?

And what about Richard Abbas and the body of his assistant in his apartment? Someone had been tortured up there. What sort of sense did that make?

Turik came in and went to the tea urn, but it was empty. He looked forlorn.

"What are you doing here?" Peshadi asked.

"Couldn't sleep. I kept thinking about that bastard with Ghfari." Turik, who'd also been trained in England, only spoke in such a Western fashion when he and Peshadi were alone. One day he would slip up, though, and Peshadi knew that he would not be able to help the man.

"I think he's an American. Probably CIA."

Turik nodded.

"But how did he get into Iran?"

"By air?" Turik mused.

"Probably. Under false papers, of course. Perhaps one of the Frenchmen slipped by ..."

Suddenly Turik made a connection. "Russian!" he blurted. He hurried out of Peshadi's office and raced across the corridor to the operations room, where from a startled night duty officer he grabbed the Open Files book.

Peshadi had followed him. "What is it, Mohammed?"

Turik looked up a file number, then retrieved the file from one of the cabinets lining the far wall. He opened it and quickly scanned the notes as he came back to Peshadi. His eyes were shining. "I was right," he said, handing the police report to Peshadi. "Valeri Vasilevich Bayev. A Russian engineer here to drum up business."

"So what?" Peshadi said, but then he read the description.

"The Russian disappeared from his hotel room last night. He hasn't been seen since. Or at least he hadn't been seen until he climbed into that Range Rover."

"Maybe not a Russian," Peshadi said, but then he had another chilling thought, and he looked through the report for information about the man's passport. Bayev was from Baku. Azerbaidzhan.

"This is trouble, isn't it," Turik said.

Peshadi looked up. "Considering what's happening along our northern border right now, I'll have to agree. But I don't know what's going on here. It's something."

Turik was watching him.

Peshadi turned to the night duty officer, a young man with wisps of a beard on his chin. "I want you to telephone Colonel Bakhtir, wherever he is. Get him out of bed and tell him he is needed here."

"Later this morning?" the young man asked, wide-eyed.

"No, right now," Peshadi said. "Tell him we have an emergency of the greatest magnitude."

46

WHEN DICK ABBAS AWOKE it was very dark, but he could not
see the stars overhead. Again the thought flashed through his
brain that he was blind, but gradually he began to see the car
off to the left, the flashing red light on the radio beacon twenty-
five yards away, and the towering mountain peaks, dark and
ghostly in the night.

The sky was overcast, he realized. That was why there were
no stars. Now he could faintly make out the moving clouds
obliterating some of the peaks to the west. Whatever weather
was moving in on them was coming down the great funnel
between the mountains, all the way from Turkey.

That afternoon Kurshin had given him more water to drink
and a thin paste of rice and what was probably curried lamb.

He'd thrown up his first mouthful, but he'd kept eating, finally managing to hold some of the food in his stomach.

By nightfall he was feeling somewhat better, though the pain in his groin was a constant reminder of what had happened to him in Tehrān, to what he had become at the hands of the Russians. As far as he knew, there would be nothing to stop them from carrying out their plans. Shahpur was dead, and Ghfari was too young and inexperienced to be of much help. He might have made contact with Langley, but they would have no idea where he'd been taken.

By now Peshadi and his people would have found Shahpur's body, and they would know that something concerning Picarde, S.A., was going on. The entire staff was probably behind the walls of Qasr Prison by now. There would be no saving them. Nor was help coming for him.

Abbas struggled free of the two thin blankets he'd been given and sat up. His back was stiff and sore from lying on the hard ground, and he was so cold that he shivered uncontrollably for at least five minutes before the episode passed, leaving him breathless and frightened.

Kurshin was nowhere in sight. Abbas figured he was probably asleep in the back seat of the car.

His own strength was seriously diminished because of the torture he had endured, and because of the lack of decent food and water over the past . . . how many days? It was hard to keep track.

Stumbling to his feet, he stood for a long time until he regained his balance, and then he took a couple of tentative steps toward the car. He expected at any moment to be confronted, or shot.

He had no doubt that his captor was Russian. No one else could have had the intelligence about the gold shipment, nor would any other country have had the expertise to mount what was turning out to be a sophisticated operation.

And there was something about the man's eyes, about his manner in Tehrān. Unlike most Westerners, he'd not been in the least nervous about being in Iran. He'd acted naturally. As a Canadian might act in the United States. So naturally, in Abbas's estimation, that he could only be Russian.

He took another few cautious steps toward the car, angling to the left so that he would come up from behind.

Assuming it was a Russian operation, and this valley was to

be used as a landing site, the Soviet aircraft would have to come down the mountain ranges at extremely low altitudes to avoid detection by Iranian radar. That was the reason for the beacon Kurshin had put out: it was meant to guide the aircraft in.

If Kurshin were dead, or if the beacon itself were put out of commission, the Soviet pilots would not be able to find their way in, and the plan would be wrecked.

He had no idea what time it was. Kurshin had taken his watch. But he figured it had to be very late, probably well after midnight. The beacon had been operating for more than twenty-four hours. The gold convoy would be close by now, and the Soviet aircraft would be coming in at any time.

He cocked his head to listen, but the night was silent except for the faint, faraway sighing of the wind through the high passes.

A few yards from the car, he ducked down below the level of the rear window and half crawled, half scrambled the rest of the way. He carefully tested the trunk lid, but it was locked as he had expected it would be.

He made his way around to the driver's side of the car and slowly rose up so that he could see inside. Kurshin was not there. Neither in the back seat nor in the front.

Abbas slowly rose up so that he could see over the roof of the car. The beacon's red light winked on and off in a two-second interval. But nothing else moved in the night. Absolutely nothing. Even the distant wind seemed to have suddenly been stilled.

He remained where he was, standing against the side of the car, for a long time—perhaps ten minutes—waiting for something to happen. Anything.

Kurshin had not simply walked away. He was here somewhere. But he was invisible. What had happened? What was happening?

Again he cocked his head to listen. He figured he would be able to hear incoming aircraft from a long way up the valley. But there was nothing.

Once more he focused on the flashing beacon. It was an electronic device, its circuits certainly delicate. If they were smashed, there would be no repairing them here. Nor had he seen another such device in the trunk.

Moving around to the other side of the car, and keeping low, he worked his way the twenty-five yards across the stony ground at the head of the stream bed. His heart was pounding heavily, and he was light-headed with the effort.

Still there was no sign of the Russian. And yet Abbas thought he could feel the man somewhere very near, almost as if there were a terrible odor on the night air.

He found a fairly large rock, which he brought over to the beacon.

The feeling that Kurshin was close was becoming almost over-powering. Abbas raised the rock over his head. Suddenly he was startled by a light, and he stumbled backward a couple of paces.

For a second he didn't know what he was seeing. There seemed to be lights all the way up the long, narrow valley. But then it came to him all at once.

The lights had been strung in two parallel lines, and stretched for a very long distance. Kurshin had laid them out. They were like flashlights, used as landing markers for the incoming aircraft.

It meant the planes were on their way in. They would be here soon.

Raising the rock again, Abbas hurried forward, girding himself to the only action open to him, even though he was too late. If the landing lights were on, surely the aircraft had already found this place.

He started to bring the big rock down with every ounce of his strength, when something shoved him violently off balance from the right, sending him sprawling on his back.

Kurshin, wearing the latex mask he'd made from Abbas's face, loomed overhead. "Sorry, but I still need that beacon," he said reasonably. "And I'm going to need your clothing as well."

Kurshin held up a small remote-control device and pushed a button. The runway lights went out, and the night disappeared from Abbas's eyes.

47

FROM QOM THE RAILROAD went to Kāshān, while the main highway split straight south to the ancient city of Isfahan, which also was the capital of the province of Isfahan. Here the road climbed and twisted its tortuous way into the massif of the Zagros Mountains, peaks rising to fifteen thousand feet and more.

McGarvey and Ghfari were well into the range above the city by two in the morning. The weather had begun to turn ugly, with what appeared to be a major front moving in on them from the northwest. They both felt a sense of urgency now; so much time had passed since Abbas had been taken. This was an unforgiving land at any time of the year. But it was especially harsh in the winter.

An hour out of Tehrān, they had pulled over to the side of the road and had established contact with Langley Center via satellite. They had been told to get off the air and remain off until 2300 hours Greenwich mean time, which was three and a half hours ahead of Tehrān's timekeeping. There had been no explanations. When McGarvey had insisted on speaking to Carrara, the channel went dead. Ten minutes later they'd not even been able to establish an uplink with the satellite. They'd been locked out.

It was nearly time now for their scheduled on-air rendezvous, and McGarvey was not happy about the arrangement. If SAVAK had captured a handie-talkie, it was possible they were monitoring Langley's broadcasts. It was why he'd wanted to limit contact to the one time.

He rolled down his window, the frigid air instantly filling the car. "We need to find a place to pull off," he told Ghfari who was driving.

"Is it nearly time?" the Iranian asked. He'd done all of the driving because it would have looked very odd for a Westerner to be chauffeuring an Iranian. And besides, Ghfari knew the country and McGarvey did not.

"Another twenty minutes or so."

"There is a place very soon, I think."

The highway was built along a narrow ledge that plunged a thousand feet or more to their left, and abutted a wall of stone that rose even higher on their right. There was no place to pull off here. And earlier there had been enough traffic, most of it military, to make it risky even at this hour for them to park at the side of the road. Someone would stop and ask questions they could not answer.

The gold convoy had to be well inland by now. In fact, by McGarvey's reckoning it was barely six hours south of them at this point, which meant that the Russian ambush could be very close. He considered the possibility that they might have already passed it.

He could almost smell Kurshin's presence on the night air, and the sensation made the hair at the nape of his neck stand on end.

The road suddenly crossed a long suspension bridge that spanned a dramatic cleft in the mountains, and then climbed sharply to the right, the escarpment finally giving way to a mountain valley that rose on the right gradually to the distant snow-capped peaks.

A deep drainage ditch ran along the upper side of the macadam, and Ghfari slowed down until he found a shallower spot to cross.

He put the Range Rover into four-wheel drive, eased up onto the stony valley floor, and headed directly away from the highway.

McGarvey watched out the rear window until he thought that they could no longer be spotted from the road. "Here," he said. "Turn off your lights."

Ghfari pulled up and switched off the car's lights, the immense darkness instantly closing in on them. This valley got narrower the farther up it ran, finally ending in a snow-covered bowl between two peaks not more than a thousand feet above where they had stopped.

McGarvey got out of the Range Rover and hiked down about fifty yards along the track they'd taken up, and then stopped and looked back. The car was nearly invisible even at this distance. The highway was another thousand yards below them. There would be no possibility of being spotted up here by a passing patrol, unless their location had already been pinpointed, and someone were to stand on the road and look through binoculars at the exact spot. Which was not likely.

There had been something ominous in Langley Center's peremptory response to their plea for information. Something had happened since he'd left Cairo. Something had changed, and it had worried him all the way south.

By the time he returned to the car, Ghfari had gotten out and had keyed up the handie-talkie.

"Any response yet?"

"No," the Iranian said. "The satellite's repeater has not even kicked on. But we are a few minutes early, yes?"

McGarvey nodded, and looked up toward the mountain peaks, and then back down the dark valley beyond the highway to the harsh, forbidding salt plateaus that dominated the interior of the country.

"When this is over, you're not going back," he said.

"I know," Ghfari replied. "But this situation will not last forever. Nothing does, except for Allah."

"It might take a while."

Ghfari managed a thin smile. "I do not think so. Not considering everything else that's happening in the world. Change is coming, and it will reach Iran as well."

The handie-talkie beeped twice, and a rapid string of morse code that identified the particular repeater channel followed.

McGarvey took the handie-talkie from Ghfari and keyed it. His mission code name was "Tinker." "Center, this is Tinker, copy?"

"Roger, Tinker. Stand by for urgent message from Punjab," the radio operator at CIA headquarters outside Washington said. "Punjab" was the mission code name for Phil Carrara.

"Tinker, Punjab. Copy?"

"Copy, Punjab."

"Is your present position secure?" Carrara's voice was small and very far away, but recognizable.

"For the moment. But we're getting a little worried here, if you know what I mean. We're running out of time."

"Yes, I understand. But the situation has changed. The bad guys are en route now. I repeat, the bad guys are en route. ETA beacon position estimated at oh-one hundred hours UTC. You copy that?"

It was barely two hours from now. "Yes, Punjab, I copy oh-one hundred UTC. What about the shipment?"

"The timing couldn't be better for the bad guys," Carrara radioed, which meant that the Russian forces would be on the ground and in position for the ambush by the time the convoy reached them.

"Say beacon position," McGarvey radioed.

"We think you should remain in place until the situation is secured, Tinker. We are working up a rescue scenario."

"Negative, negative," McGarvey said. "Say beacon location. Our present position is not tenable after first light."

There was a slight pause on the frequency. "Listen to me, Tinker. The situation has changed. Warbucks has ordered our strike team from Van. They are already en route. They will take care of our problem."

"Warbucks" was the mission name for the DCI, Roland Murphy.

"They won't make it in time."

"We think they will."

"There is a major storm front moving in from the west. The bad guys may make it, but our people will be right in the middle of it now. Say beacon location, goddamnit!"

"It's imperative that you not be captured."

"We will be if we are forced to stay here. Where is the beacon?"

There was another pause on the frequency. "All right, Tinker, we have your position now. You're close. The beacon is about fifty miles south of you. But it is well off the highway, in a long defile. Our maps show it as Qashqai Valley."

Ghfari had pulled out a map, and a moment later he pinpointed the valley with his narrow-beam penlight. "Here," he said.

"All right, Punjab, we have it located. We can be up there before oh-one hundred."

"We will instruct our forces to look for you, Tinker, but there is something else you need to know."

"Recall them. We'll destroy the beacon."

"We can't," Carrara said. "The bad guys are Didenko's people. They're coming down from Baku."

"Yes, I know this."

"Didenko has been arrested for treason."

The news was stunning. It took McGarvey a few seconds to recover. "Why haven't his people been recalled, Punjab? What else is going on?"

"There is armed rebellion in Azerbaidzhan. Our best estimate is that bad guys mean to snatch the goods and make for Libya, or Syria. Do you understand?"

McGarvey understood completely. It meant that Didenko's people were going to cut themselves loose from Moscow. Coming in here this morning, they would be desperate men with absolutely nothing to lose. Each man would fight like ten. There would be no quarter given by any of them.

"Does Kurshin know?" McGarvey radioed in the clear.

"That's unknown," Carrara replied. "But we don't think so."

"We'll start immediately."

"Who is with you?"

"Number three," McGarvey said.

"Any sign of number one?"

"Not yet, Punjab," McGarvey radioed. "But with any luck there'll be three of us coming out."

"That's a roger," Carrara said. "Keep your head down."

McGarvey switched off the handie-talkie and looked at Ghfari. "That's not going to be so easy if SAVAK has monitored this transmission."

48

"*NOT YET, PUNJAB,*" the first voice said in English. "*But with any luck there'll be three of us coming out.*"

"*That's a roger,*" the second American said. "*Keep your head down.*"

Captain Peshadi shut off the tape recorder. "The transmissions ceased at that point," he said.

Colonel Bakhtir looked extremely troubled. Peshadi faced him across his desk. It was a little past two-thirty in the morning. Most of Tehrān slept, but SAVAK's headquarters was fully staffed, on emergency footing.

"Do we know where this valley is?" the colonel demanded.

"Yes, sir. It is south of Isfahan."

"How far from Tehrān?"

"Five hundred kilometers."

"Too far, too far," Colonel Bakhtir muttered. "Get me a map. I want to see for myself." He picked up his telephone as Peshadi opened the office door and called for Sergeant Turik to bring the map.

"Get me General Dadgar," the colonel told the operator. He put his hand over the mouthpiece. "The map, Hussain?"

Sergeant Turik came over from the operations room with a large-scale map.

"Have there been any other transmissions?" Peshadi asked from the doorway.

"The frequency has been silent," Turik said. He glanced in at the colonel, and lowered his voice. "What's going on?"

"I don't know yet, Mohammed. But I want you to get us a helicopter and pilot."

"Peshadi!" the colonel roared.

"A fast helicopter, Mohammed," Peshadi said. "And a good pilot."

"Right now?"

"Right now," Peshadi said. He went back inside and spread the map on the colonel's desk. After a moment he found the valley, and circled it with a pencil. "Here," he said. "This is the Qashqai Valley."

Bakhtir studied the map, tracing a line from the valley down to the highway, and then south. When he looked up Peshadi could see genuine fear in the man's eyes.

"Yes, I'm still holding for the general," he snapped into the telephone.

"The Americans are involved with something down there," Peshadi said carefully. "And so, too, are the Russians, unless the transmission we overheard was only a ruse. It's possible."

The colonel waved the suggestion off. "It is no ruse, believe me, Hussain. We have received reports that a people's revolution may have begun in Baku and a few of the other cities of Azerbaidzhan."

"But the communications device is American, as is the satellite its signal reaches. That is what our technicians tell me."

"The Americans are involved, there's no doubt about that. But so are the Russians now."

"There is to be a war between them on Iranian soil?" Peshadi asked, amazed at what he was hearing.

"Not if we can prevent it," Bakhtir said. "And prevent it we must, at all costs. You can't know the importance of this."

"No, sir," Peshadi said.

Bakhtir suddenly stiffened. "Yes, General. I do understand what time it is. But by Allah this is urgent. Iran needs its air force tonight. Immediately."

Peshadi went to the door. Across the hall, Turik in the operations room, was perched on the edge of a desk. His sergeant looked up from the phone and nodded: he'd managed to get them a helicopter.

"No, General, I have not spoken with the imam. There is no time for that. It is why I called you with this. We must hurry —or what is coming from Bushehr tonight will be lost."

Bakhtir looked up at Peshadi and genuine relief cleared his features. He nodded. "Of course, General. We believe it may be a two-pronged threat. One from the Soviets, who may have sent an air force of unknown strength through the mountains from Baku. And the other from the Americans themselves."

Peshadi could hear the general's shouts from across the room.

"Of course it may be an elaborate plot by the Americans themselves, but we cannot deny the reports we've been getting out of Baku, and Moscow. Nor can we ignore this threat."

Sergeant Turik came to the door, and Peshadi turned to him. "Did you get us a machine?"

"Yes. By the time we get out to Doshen Toppeh it will be warmed up and standing by. It's an American-made Cobra. Very fast, and loaded with weapons."

"Hussain," the colonel called, and Peshadi turned back.

"Yes, sir?"

"Close the door."

Peshadi did as he was told. Bakhtir had his hand over the telephone's mouthpiece.

"I want you to get down there as fast as you possibly can. The general is checking with his radar squadrons, but considering the mountainous terrain, I don't think they will see much. Also he says that the weather is deteriorating in the area."

"I understand," Peshadi said. "We can leave immediately."

"Good," the colonel said. "It's possible that the air force cannot do anything for us, in which case we will have to rely on the army units coming up with the convoy."

"Convoy?" Peshadi asked.

"Yes, I'll continue to hold," Bakhtir said into the phone. "You must know something," he told Peshadi. "An agreement has been reached with the United States government to release all Iranian money that they have illegally held in their banks since the revolution. Plus interest."

Peshadi said nothing. No mention of this had been made on the television or in the newspapers. The news, if it was true, was momentous. Iran's economy had been badly damaged by the war with Iraq.

"The payment in the form of gold bullion arrived in Bushehr and is on its way here by convoy. At this moment it is approaching that valley."

Peshadi was momentarily confused. "But the amount. . . . It must be huge!"

"More than one hundred metric tons of gold, Hussain. Gold which Iran desperately needs. Gold which the Russians would like to have."

"Gold that the Americans would like to take back, blaming the Russians for its theft if they can."

Colonel Bakhtir was nodding. "Stop them, Hussain."

"I will," Peshadi promised. "But radio the convoy leader and warn them."

"It's not possible," the colonel said. "There has been no communications with them. Equipment trouble, or some such. One would think that precautions would have been taken given the nature of the shipment. But it is up to us now. To you."

"I understand," Peshadi said.

"Kill the Americans and the Russians, Hussain," Bakhtir said. "Kill them all."

"Yes," Peshadi said. "With pleasure."

49

THE BIG AIRCRAFT LURCHED heavily and dropped into an air pocket, coming up short with a loud, bone-jarring bang. KGB Colonel Alexei Berezin looked on unconcernedly as the piss-ant copilot picked himself up from the deck and continued back to him. This was better than Baku. Anything was better than that.

The seven aircraft in the wing were Tu-16 Badger bombers that had been decommissioned from the air force in 1980, converted to fly airlift missions, and given to the KGB for strike force operations. They had been used to some success in Afghanistan for spot missions, their fuselages and especially their landing gear beefed up for rugged off-runway landings and take-offs.

For this mission the red stars had been painted out of their camouflaged tails and replaced by the white star on blue background of the U.S. Air Force. An unnecessary deception, the colonel thought. It no longer mattered what the Iranians saw.

Berezin's elite force of sixty fighting men was divided between two of the aircraft, his executive officer, Major Yurii Myakov, in charge of the second group. There had been no communication between them since takeoff. Nor were communications necessary. Myakov knew his job. Nothing would go wrong on his end.

The copilot finally made it back to where Berezin was strapped to his canvas seat. He had to shout to be heard over the engine noises.

"Captain Sulitsky would like to speak with you on the flight deck, sir."

"What does he want?" Berezin asked, without bothering to raise his voice.

"It's the weather, sir," the copilot shouted. He was clearly nervous. He looked at the troops seated along either side of what had once been the bomb bays in which nuclear weapons were transported.

"What about it?" Berezin asked.

"It's getting worse."

"Yes, we can tell," the colonel said. A few of the troops nearest, who heard his comment, snickered.

The aircraft gave another powerful lurch. "We may have to divert to an alternate landing site."

"*Nyet*," Berezin snapped.

"It may not be possible to land where you wish, sir," the copilot said.

Berezin waited for several seconds to allow his blood pressure to drop a little. Then he languidly released the buckles that held him in place. The copilot backed up a couple of paces as the colonel rose to his impressive height of nearly six feet six, the battle gear strapped tightly to his chest and back extremely deadly-looking.

"I will come with you to speak to Sulitsky," he said.

The copilot turned, and moving from one handhold to the next, he worked his way forward. Berezin followed him without holding on, as if the aircraft wouldn't dare knock him over. His men loved it.

And they were going to have to continue loving it, he thought, because there would be no going back for any of them. Even with General Didenko under arrest, Azerbaidzhan had been in revolt, and it had been up to them to help defend the *rodina.*

But they had not. In fact, the two militia officers from Moscow who had come to arrest Berezin had even thought that under the circumstances he should be allowed to remain free to fight.

And fight he had. But the only two deaths that could be attributed to him were those two militiamen.

There was no going back. Only forward to pick up the gold, and then onward to the only place fit for a fighting man and his forces: Lebanon. He figured that with his men, and with the weapons the fabulous wealth that would soon be theirs could buy, he could strike a few key targets and set himself up in a stronghold that his few troops and vast fortune could hold until something better could be planned.

Grandiose plans, perhaps, but then Berezin had not gotten to this point in his career by being timid.

He climbed up onto the flight deck, and then pushed the copilot roughly aside and climbed down into the right-hand seat. Outside, the night was invisible. The only thing to be seen was a swirling white fog. Nothing more.

Captain Sulitsky was an extremely competent KGB pilot who'd flown a lot of difficult combat missions in Afghanistan, yet it was obvious that he was having a hard time controlling the aircraft.

"How does it look for us, Mikhail Alexandrovich?" Colonel Berezin shouted.

"Not so good, Colonel," Sulitsky shouted back without taking his eyes off the instruments. "If the fucking wind shears in these mountains don't tear us apart, we might just fly into the side of one of the taller peaks."

"What are our chances of making it to the target?"

"Fifty-fifty, maybe less."

"Have we still got a good lock on the beacon?"

"*Da.*"

"Has Iranian radar discovered us?"

"*Nyet.*"

"Are you frightened?"

Sulitsky laughed. He risked a quick glance at Berezin. "I'm pissing in my pants, Comrade Colonel."

"But we have a chance of making it?"

"*Da.*" Sulitsky had turned back to the panel.

"How about the other pilots?"

"If I take us the rest of the way, they'll follow."

"We have no other choice. You understand this?"

Again Sulitsky glanced at him. "Yes, I understand perfectly. I just wanted you to confirm how important this was. I wanted you to tell me that we'd have less than a fifty-fifty chance if we didn't pick up the gold."

"You were right to ask, Mikhail Alexandrovich, because without the gold, we will have no chance. None whatsoever."

Abbas was sitting on the ground, out of the wind behind the car, when he thought he heard the sounds of aircraft up the valley. He pulled himself to his feet and looked over the top of the car, but there was nothing to be seen, and now the sounds were gone, blown away on the stiff wind.

He tottered around the side of the car, his legs like rubber beneath him. After he'd tried to destroy the beacon transmitter, Kurshin had beaten him with his bare fists. It felt as if every bone in his body was broken, and what little strength he'd had was gone.

"You heard it too?" Kurshin asked, materializing out of the darkness.

"I didn't hear a thing." His voice was weak even in his own ears.

Kurshin looked skyward. "They're coming."

"They won't make it. Not in this wind."

Kurshin looked at him. Staring into a replica of his own face gave Abbas a momentary chill.

"Curious thing about valleys like this—the wind always funnels between the mountains. No matter what's happening up there, the wind is going to blow straight up and down the valley."

"They'll never get lined up—" Abbas began, but then they both heard the sounds of the aircraft overhead.

Kurshin raised the remote-control device and pushed the button. Instantly the string of portable runway lights he'd brought from Tehrān came to life, crudely outlining the landing area.

"Who are you?" Abbas asked.

Kurshin smiled. "You could not have been a very effective chief of station," he said. "Certainly not even as good as Thomas Lord."

For a moment the name meant nothing to Abbas, but then it suddenly clicked in his head, and he staggered back, stunned as if by a physical blow. "Paris," he said. "It was you."

"Yes."

"Why?"

"It was necessary to keep your organization in Langley very busy. We wanted to deplete your personnel. We wanted to kill your best, or at the very least keep them involved with cleaning up the messes, with investigating the attacks, and with answering to your president and congressional committees."

It was almost beyond comprehension. "Who is 'we?' Who are you?" he demanded.

"The KGB, of course. Who did you think?"

"But it's over. We don't do this anymore. Your people don't do this. It's over!"

"Oh?" Kurshin said.

The aircraft were directly overhead now, turning at the end of the valley so that they could make a second pass, this time lining up with the runway lights. The noise was very loud, roaring off the mountains. And there were a lot of planes. But there would have to be, to transport so much gold, and the troops needed to take it from the convoy.

Abbas stumbled backward in despair. The entire monstrous situation was overwhelming. There was nothing he could do about it. There was nothing anyone could do about it.

"Go if you wish," Kurshin shouted over the wind and the tremendous roar of the big aircraft overhead. His disdain was monumental.

Abbas had half turned and was looking down the dry stream bed, the way they had come up.

"But long before you could reach the highway we would overtake you."

Abbas looked at the man.

"You're going to die this morning," Kurshin said. "And there isn't a thing you can do to prevent it."

Abbas started walking toward the stream bed, half expecting a bullet in the back of his head. If Kurshin was calling to him, he could not hear over the roar of the planes. In any event he no longer cared.

The approach of Soviet aircraft was totally unknown to General Mashoud Dayati in the lead Jeep of the gold convoy, but all evening, and into the early morning hours, an unease had grown within him.

By everything that was holy in heaven and on earth, he would be glad when they were past Isfahan and out of these wretched mountains. He had pressed his people for more speed. He was a military man and knew that if there was to be trouble, it would happen here. The region was ideal for an attack. If it was going to happen, he thought nervously, it would come within the next hundred kilometers.

The convoy, which consisted of eighteen identical canvas-covered trucks and two Jeeps—one at the rear, and the general's in the lead—stretched for over a kilometer. Twelve of the trucks contained the gold bullion, and the six other trucks, dispersed throughout the convoy, contained 84 of the 114 troops under his command. The others were the drivers and relief drivers of the gold trucks, as well as the drivers and passengers of the two Jeeps.

A .50-caliber machine gun was mounted on each of the Jeeps, and the fourteen men in each troop truck made up separate fire teams armed with AK-47 assault rifles, American-made LAW antitank weapons, grenade launchers, and Russian-made SA-7 SAM portable rocket launchers.

They were a formidable force; but more than a hundred metric tons of pure gold was a powerful incentive. There had been rumors that someone within the Iranian military itself might mount an attack on the convoy.

It saddened the general to think that such greed still existed in his country. Western greed. American-spawned greed. Hate bubbled up inside of him at the thought of what the Americans and their puppet shah had done to Iran. The damage was still being repaired, especially the damage to the attitudes of women in the bigger cities. It would take decades, perhaps centuries, before they achieved their ideal.

"You are troubled, my general," the convoy's mullah, Abdollah Sabzevār, said from the back seat where he was wedged in beside the machine gunner and his metal boxes of ammunition.

The general looked over his shoulder, at the religious leader. "If there is to be an attack on us, it will come between here and Isfahan."

Sabzevār looked almost comical in his thick clothes, his wool cap pulled over his ears. The Jeep was open to the cold mountain air.

"Will we be attacked, do you think?"

The general shrugged, then looked ahead, down the deserted highway. "I hope not. By Allah, I sincerely hope not."

50

MCGARVEY HUNG HALF OUT of the Range Rover's window, his eyes tearing in the wind as he tried to penetrate the darkness along the road for a way up into the valley.

Ghfari had driven very fast down from the high valley where they'd made contact with Langley Center, bumping onto the highway, and then raced south as fast as the old oil company vehicle could manage.

They'd been on the highway for nearly an hour now. If Carrara had been right about the beacon location, and if the satellite fix on their handie-talkie signal was accurate, they should have been directly below the valley minutes ago. From what McGarvey could see, however, there was simply no way up. The road was blocked by sheer rock walls, by huge boulders, or by impossibly steep gullies that not even the Range Rover could manage to cross.

"I don't see a thing," Ghfari said.

"Neither do I," McGarvey shouted. "But they're up there, and their forces are going to have to make it back down the hill to stage the attack. There has to be a way."

"There," Ghfari said, braking as the headlights found a narrow concrete bridge over a shallow gully. It was a dry riverbed; in the spring melts it would be a torrent.

They came to a stop just before the bridge. McGarvey snatched a flashlight, jumped out of the car, and hurried up the road to the near end of the bridge. Tire tracks led across a narrow ditch on the right side of the road, crushing the sparse mountain grass along two parallel tracks and then disappearing into the stream. What snow there had been here was scoured away by the wind.

Ghfari got out of the car. "Do you see something?" he called.

"Shut off the engine," McGarvey called back, and he stepped down off the highway and made his way fifteen or twenty yards to the stream bed.

The Range Rover's engine died, and McGarvey held his breath to listen. The wind roared in the peaks towering somewhere far above them, lost in the swirling clouds. But there was something else. Something he could feel more than hear. Something deep-seated and heavy. A rumbling sound almost like thunder, fading in and out on the wind.

Aircraft. Big, lumbering, transport aircraft. Heavy enough to transport troops and haul more than a hundred tons of gold out over the mountains. Heavy enough to be heard at this distance over the wind.

McGarvey hurried back up to the highway. "This is the place," he shouted on the run. "They used the dry riverbed."

"What is that sound?" Ghfari asked. He too had cocked an ear to listen. "It sounds like—"

"Russian transport aircraft," McGarvey shouted. "Get in!"

"They are here already?"

"They can't do us any harm if they don't land," McGarvey said. "Get in and drive!"

The track was extremely rough, and the Range Rover bounced all over the place. A couple of times they almost tipped over, but Ghfari was a good driver, and he managed to recover nicely without losing time.

McGarvey had reassembled the AK-47 and checked its action. He stuffed the extra clips of ammunition in his belt and jacket pockets, and then cycled a round into the firing chamber of his TK automatic pistol. He did the same with Ghfari's pistol and laid it on the seat next to the Iranian.

"If those planes land and we're outgunned, I want you to get the hell out. No screwing around, just run."

"What are you talking about?" Ghfari asked through clenched teeth as he concentrated on his driving.

"There are going to be some angry people when I start shooting at their airplanes. If the situation falls apart, I want you to run."

"Where?"

"Your choice," McGarvey said. "If you head south to warn the convoy, you'd face almost certain arrest and possibly execution as a spy. But you might save the gold. The other way, toward Turkey, would mean freedom."

Ghfari started to say something when their headlights flashed on a figure stumbling down the stream bed less than a hundred yards above them. Ghfari automatically pulled up.

"Kill the headlights," McGarvey ordered, snatching the AK-47 and jumping out of the car.

Now he could clearly hear the sounds of incoming aircraft. A lot of them. Not very far away.

Ghfari leaped out of the car and walked out ahead a few feet. He was hearing the aircraft too, but he held up his hand for McGarvey to keep silent.

He walked a few feet farther up the stream bed. "Richard?" he called.

"Bijan?" the answering cry came weakly from above.

"Is it Abbas?" McGarvey called softly.

"I think so." Ghfari hurried up the slope, McGarvey holding back to cover him in case it was some kind of trick.

A few moments later Ghfari came back out of the darkness helping an extremely battered Dick Abbas.

"It's the Russians—they're coming in now," Abbas said in a breathless rush. He looked as if he had been in a street brawl, McGarvey thought. He was dressed in a Russian military jump suit with KGB border guard markings.

"Who set the aircraft beacon?" McGarvey asked. "Who did this to you?"

"I don't know," Abbas croaked. "But he's Russian, I think, and damned good."

"Kurshin," McGarvey muttered. The incoming aircraft were very loud. It sounded as if one of them was coming in for a landing.

"We've got to stop them," Abbas said, grabbing McGarvey's arm. "They're coming for the gold and they mean to blame it on us. The Russian is wearing my clothes."

"How far is it?" McGarvey asked.

"Quarter of a mile—maybe a little farther. Half a mile at most. The slope opens into a long narrow valley."

McGarvey turned to Ghfari. "Take him back down to the highway and get the hell out of here. You should be in Turkey within twenty-four hours."

"What about you?" Ghfari asked.

"I'll take the handie-talkie. Langley Center will work out something to get me out of here once the show is over."

"No way," Abbas interrupted forcefully. "Give me a weapon. I'm going back up there."

"You can't—"

"I will!" Abbas insisted. "You owe me this. I want a weapon. I want at least a chance against that son of a bitch."

They were running out of time. There was no room now for argument. Abbas had apparently been hard used by Kurshin. But he was luckier than most who came up against the man: he was alive.

McGarvey handed him his pistol. "If we can bring down one of the planes as it's landing, it will ruin the strip for the others."

"I want just one man," Abbas said.

McGarvey didn't answer him.

In the Range Rover, without headlights, they headed up the slope. The sounds of the incoming aircraft were right overhead now, reverberating off the higher mountain walls. Near the top the runway lights cast a faint pinkish glow, and suddenly the night was brilliantly lit when one of the big planes' landing lights came on.

"I'll try for one of the planes," McGarvey shouted. "You guys take care of the beacon. But if we find ourselves outgunned, don't try to stand and fight. They came here for the gold, and no matter what happens, if you get out of their way when they start down the hill, they'll ignore you."

McGarvey drew the AK-47's ejector slide back, released it, and switched off the safety as they burst over the crest of the hill and bounced violently up from the lip of the stream bed onto the valley floor itself.

There seemed to be noise and lights everywhere. Noise so deafening it was nearly impossible to think, and lights so strong they were blinding.

But then McGarvey could make out the individual runway lights strung along the valley, and the brilliant landing lights of one large plane nearing touch down, and at least two others coming in behind it.

He motioned for Ghfari to make directly for the incoming plane, and the Iranian jammed the accelerator pedal to the floor, the big Range Rover surging forward.

They shot past a parked automobile, and Abbas began firing rapidly from the back window.

McGarvey glimpsed a man running at an angle toward them, shooting as he came, the bullets from the automatic weapon smacking into the side of the car.

"It's him!" Abbas screamed.

Kurshin. For a split second McGarvey fought the urge to tear the wheel out of Ghfari's hands and go back, but then they were past, and Abbas stopped shooting. Perhaps he was out of ammunition.

Several hundred yards up the valley, Ghfari skidded to a halt at the same moment the converted Russian bomber touched down, bounced once, and twice, and came roaring toward them.

McGarvey leaped out of the car and began firing at the big plane, one shot after the other in a rapid but measured sequence of about five shots a second.

At first nothing seemed to happen. Ejecting the spent clip, he slammed a second thirty-round clip into the weapon and continued firing as the plane came nearly even with where he stood.

It was barely one hundred feet from him when the landing gear in the nose suddenly exploded in a shower of sparks, and as if in slow motion the bomber tipped forward, plowing dirt and rocks in a huge furrow.

The port-side landing gear collapsed, pulling the aircraft to the left. That wing brushed the ground, then dug in and ripped away from the fuselage, pulling things out of the interior in a screeching, tangled, nightmarish scene.

McGarvey glimpsed a long row of canvas seats, bodies still attached to them, tumbling on the ground, and then the aircraft rolled over on top of them and began to slow down as it continued breaking apart.

Ghfari and Abbas watched with open mouths. There was no fire, but there would not be many, if any, survivors.

The second and third aircraft had immediately increased power and pulled up sharply. They roared directly overhead, making a tight turn just above the peaks to the east.

There would be no possibility of using this landing site, and the pilots knew it. For them, at least, this mission was over.

"Are they all dead?" Ghfari asked in awe.

"I don't know," McGarvey replied.

The downed bomber had finally come to a halt a thousand feet beyond them, the main section of the fuselage ripped from the nose all the way back to where the tail surfaces had broken off. Parts of the plane were scattered for two thousand feet or more.

"No matter what, they won't be taking the gold," Abbas said harshly. He looked up at the sky.

Already the sounds of the other aircraft were fading in the distance. They had circled around to the northwest. They wouldn't come back.

"Now Kurshin," McGarvey said.

Abbas looked at him. "Is that what he's called?"

"We'll do it together," McGarvey said. "And then we'll get the hell out of here before SAVAK shows up."

"I want him," Abbas said, his voice shaking with emotion.

"Don't underestimate the man," McGarvey said.

Abbas suddenly fell to the ground, blood spurting from a bullet wound in his left leg.

It was Kurshin! McGarvey shoved Ghfari down behind the Range Rover and snapped off a couple of shots.

At the same moment, the sounds of a helicopter somewhere down the hill became audible on the wind.

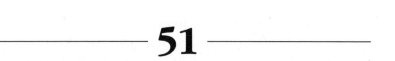

51

KURSHIN WAS ENRAGED THAT success had been so suddenly and decisively turned into disaster by the one man he had least expected to see in Iran. McGarvey's presence here was almost beyond belief, yet Kurshin had seen the man with his own eyes.

He should be in Lisbon with the Argentinian woman, searching for Nazi gold. What was he doing here?

"You are correct, Arkasha, in saying that I am no Baranov," Didenko had told him. "He was a man for his times, and he was nothing short of amazing. But these now are different times, with their own peculiar difficulties and problems."

"I will kill you if you fail to live up to your promise to me," Kurshin had told the general.

"Ah, and you would be right to do so," Didenko had said smoothly. "It is up to us now to save the Union before it is too late."

"Don't underestimate McGarvey ..."

"I do not, believe me in this, Arkasha. I have a great deal of respect for that one, just as I have for you. But there is no reason for him to abandon his search in Lisbon and come to Iran. No reason whatsoever. What happened in Paris was enough to keep the CIA after him for the moment."

Kurshin stared through the AK-74's powerful night vision scope at the Range Rover three hundred yards up the valley, but there was no movement.

He'd aimed for McGarvey, but Abbas had gotten in the way, and he hadn't had a chance for a second shot before McGarvey's return fire had caught him off guard. It was as if the man could see in the dark.

And now the rest of the strike force was leaving, the sounds of the big planes fading on the wind.

Turning his scope on the downed aircraft, he studied the wreckage for a moment. It wasn't likely that any of the troops had survived, and even if they had they would be injured and in shock, useless as an assault team.

Which meant the gold was lost to them.

But he'd never really cared about that. All he'd ever wanted was to face McGarvey. Just the two of them. Well, he had gotten his wish. One of them would not leave this mountain valley alive.

He brought the scope back to the Range Rover. Still there was no movement. Abbas was down, but Kurshin did not know how badly the man was hurt. He did know, however, that the chief of station was a driven man now. Abbas would be a dangerous opponent with a weapon in his hand. Kurshin had seen the look in his eyes.

And there had been a second man with McGarvey. An unknown. Too many variables, but he had come too far to simply turn and run.

He heard a helicopter, and for a split second before he recognized the sound for what it was, he thought the other planes were coming back.

He looked over his shoulder from where he lay, behind the ridge of a small depression about ten yards from his car, in time to see a big transport helicopter coming up from the east.

The markings on the tail identified it as an Iranian air force machine, but Kurshin was almost certain it belonged to SAVAK.

The beam of a powerful spotlight flashed across the end of the runway and then stabbed out toward the wrecked aircraft, and the helicopter banked sharply to the right and headed directly across the landing strip.

Kurshin brought his rifle around to aim at the machinery just beneath the rotor. A hand-launched rocket leaped up from the wrecked Badger on a fiery orange tail. The chopper swerved sharply left as it dived for the ground, but an instant later the missile struck its tail and blew with a sharp report, the flash momentarily blinding.

It was almost impossible to believe, but someone had survived the crash of the Russian aircraft and had brought down the helicopter. And almost as impossible to believe was the fact that anyone could have survived in the chopper, yet McGarvey could make out the figures of at least a half-dozen men emerging from the wreckage, silhouetted in the dark against the flames rising fifty feet into the night.

At first the only sound they could hear was the steadily rising wind, strange after the roar of the big airplane and the chopper, and the sounds of the crashes and explosions.

But they heard automatic-weapons fire clearly from the general vicinity of the Russian plane, and at least one of the Iranians went down.

"*Merde*! Let's get the hell out of here!" Ghfari said.

"There's no place to go, for the moment," McGarvey muttered not taking his eyes off the battle scene. The chopper had come down about five hundred feet away, almost directly between them and the downed Russian plane.

The helicopter had probably brought SAVAK troops up from Qom, but how did they know about this spot? Unless Iranian radar had spotted the incoming Soviet aircraft despite their precautions.

It didn't matter. There would be more coming. The entire country would mobilize, if need be, to protect the gold shipment. It was their lifeblood. Meanwhile Kurshin was still out there.

Even more troops were scrambling out of the wreckage of the helicopter, deploying themselves in a tight semicircle to the south, effectively cutting off the Russians from escape down to the highway.

Whoever was leading the SAVAK unit was damned good, but the few Russian survivors, though they were badly outnumbered, were even better. And they were determined. They had nowhere else to go. They would either fight their way past the Iranians or they would die there in the mountains.

In a way McGarvey had to admire them.

He turned back to Abbas. Ghfari had gotten a first-aid kit from the Range Rover and was hastily bandaging the man's wound. Kurshin's bullet had hit Abbas high in the left thigh, exiting cleanly in the back. He'd been lucky.

"How do you feel?" McGarvey asked.

Abbas looked up, his eyes glinting. "He's the devil," he rasped. He pushed himself up on one elbow and grabbed McGarvey's arm.

"Take it easy, and we'll get you out of here."

"Kill him," Abbas said. "Kill the son of a bitch! For me. You must do this, for me!"

Ghfari's eyes were wide and he was swallowing rapidly.

McGarvey glanced again downfield, toward the still raging battle. From what he could tell, neither side had the advantage yet, but the Russians would have to make their move soon if they were to have any chance of breaking out. Other SAVAK and Iranian army units would be streaming toward this valley even now.

A huge explosion lit the night sky, and a second later the heavy crump rolled across the floor of the valley, a warm pressure wave following directly on its heels. The Iranian helicopter had blown. Even more flames whipped by the increasing winds leaped more than a hundred feet into the air, and two Iranians, their clothing on fire, raced out into the open like human torches.

The Russians immediately laid down a heavy curtain of weapons fire, mercifully hitting both of them before they had gotten ten yards.

The other Iranians held their ground and returned a steady barrage of answering fire, raking the Russian aircraft and everything around it.

"That's not going to last very long," Abbas said through clenched teeth.

"I agree," McGarvey said. He looked at Ghfari. "Get him into the car and head back up into the valley as far as you can go."

"No, wait!" Abbas said, trying to struggle the rest of the way up.

"We're probably going to have to hold here out of sight until the dust settles. At least through the day. With any luck the Iranians will be so busy picking up the mess, and so relieved that their gold got through, that they won't come looking for us. Tomorrow night we might be able to get the hell out of here."

"What about you?" Ghfari asked.

"I'm going after Kurshin."

"But how will you catch up with us? How will you find us if we're hidden?"

"I'll manage," McGarvey said. He peered up over the hood of the car in the direction Kurshin's shot had come from, but there was nothing to be seen. The darkness was made more intense by the furiously burning helicopter.

"What if you don't make it?" Abbas asked.

"Call Langley for help. Carrara knows the situation. In fact they've already got at least one rescue scenario worked out."

"He's very good," Abbas said. "The Russian."

McGarvey nodded. "Yes, I know."

"You've been up against him before?" Abbas asked, his skin almost rosy in the flickering light of the distant flames.

"Once or twice," McGarvey said, laying down the rifle. "I'll give you a hand."

He and Ghfari carefully lifted Abbas, and keeping the Range Rover between them and Kurshin's last position, they managed to get the station chief into the back seat of the car.

"It's up to you," McGarvey said.

Ghfari nodded uncertainly.

"Jaziraf said that you were okay. He was right."

"*Merci*," the younger man said.

Again McGarvey looked down the valley from where Kurshin had fired. Nothing could be seen. He picked up his rifle. "Give me a couple of minutes to get clear before you go."

"Yes, sir ..." Ghfari said, but McGarvey had left abruptly,

disappearing into the night, and the French-born Iranian shivered.

If the Iranians did not receive reinforcements very soon, the KGB troops from the downed Badger would overrun their position. It gave Kurshin a certain satisfaction, and a faint surprise at the back of his head that he cared.

He'd managed to work his way to within seventy-five yards of the Range Rover, giving a wide berth to the fighting on the field, when over the wind he heard the car starting.

For just an instant he was confused. He rose up from behind the small hummock where he'd been crouching. The Range Rover started away. He brought the AK-74 to his shoulder, and something slammed into his side, sending him sprawling, a hot feeling spreading from his left hip to his armpit.

He'd been hit.

A second and third shot kicked up dust and small rocks next to his face, cutting his cheek. He scrambled farther down the hill to get out of the direct line of fire.

McGarvey.

McGarvey had sent at least one of the others away in the Range Rover while he remained behind in ambush. It was so like him.

Once again a dark rage rose up from Kurshin's gut. He wanted to leap up and rush forward, killing everything in his path. But that was exactly what McGarvey wanted him to do.

Slowly he brought himself back under control. His entire side was numb. He realized that he was beginning to hear the sounds of battle from across the field again. He'd temporarily lost his hearing. The wind roared in the high passes again.

Fuck your mother, what was happening to him? What had happened?

He rolled over and crawled to the crest of the low rise, mindless now of the blood leaking down his side, and the stinging sensation in his cheek.

For some reason he remembered a scene from his childhood. They'd played Red Army–White Army. It was the Revolution all over again, and they were good Communists, Komsomol members then. He'd finally earned his red scarf, yet he preferred to play the enemy. The maverick. He'd always preferred that. There'd been another hill, behind which he'd

waited for the army colonel to come along. He was supposed
to join the army and report what he had learned behind enemy
lines. Instead he had leaped down on the unsuspecting officer
and killed him.

"Kirk McGarvey," he called into the wind.

After a second or two, McGarvey called back. "Arkady Aleksandrovich, I thought I had killed you this time."

"I don't think you allowed for the wind. I'm here and I'm
going to kill you. But I won't do such a poor job of it as you
did."

McGarvey's laughter drifted over the wind. "You'd better
hurry. Those Iranian reinforcements will be here at any moment."

"That will not be to your advantage, I think. We Russians are
their neighbors. Your people are their enemies."

"It's not an American plane over there."

"American markings . . ."

"Russian troops fighting SAVAK. It'll be tough to explain. And
this time you won't have your general to help you out, to provide
your cover and your contacts and your operating expenses."

What was the man talking about? Was it some sort of a ruse?
Something to throw him off guard?

"Or haven't you heard, Arkasha?" McGarvey continued.

Had his voice shifted farther to the left? Kurshin rolled over
on his side and pointed his rifle in that general direction.

"Heard what?" he shouted.

"About the people's revolt in Azerbaidzhan. And General Didenko's arrest in Moscow. He's being charged with treason, of
course. Your KGB pals were coming here to snatch the gold for
themselves. Most likely they would have killed you. No one
wants a man like you underfoot."

McGarvey was definitely to the left. But close.

"Or you," Kurshin shouted back, turning his head away so
that the direction of his voice would be confusing to McGarvey.

"That's right," McGarvey replied after a long time. "So now
it is just us, Arkasha. Two assassins come to pay their mutual
respects."

"If you kill me and somehow manage to get out of Iran, where
will you go?"

"That's none of your business, Arkasha," McGarvey said dis-
dainfully.

"Lisbon, I should think, so that you can be with your little Nazi whore."

"At least I attract women, Arkasha. I wonder what kind of scum interests you?"

Kurshin's jaw tightened. No other man on earth could get to him this way.

"They're not women, they're policemen. When they fucked you it was because they'd been ordered to do so. It must make you feel like quite the man, McGarvey."

A rocket suddenly streaked from above and behind them and struck the downed Russian Badger just over its remaining wing. The plane blew with a tremendous earth-shattering explosion that threw debris hundreds of feet into the air.

A half-dozen Iranian air force helicopters swooped in low over the valley, the flash of machine-gun fire raining down on the Russian position.

Moving as fast as he could, Kurshin scrambled farther to the right around to the other side of the hillock in the opposite direction McGarvey might think he would go.

Suddenly he jumped up, swinging the heavy assault rifle right to left. McGarvey was just getting to his feet twenty yards away. Kurshin fired on full automatic, the bullets raking the dirt to the left of McGarvey and then slamming into his body, shoving him aside like a rag doll.

He saw the American falling, in slow motion it seemed, everything else that was going on in the valley blotted out of his consciousness. He started to run forward so that he could get a better angle, to finish the job, and he pulled the trigger again, but nothing happened. The gun was empty or jammed.

Somehow McGarvey was turning over onto his back, his own rifle coming up. Kurshin tried desperately to sidestep, but at least three bullets tore into his body, lifting him off his feet and propelling him back behind the hill, his assault rifle falling harmlessly to the dirt.

He was crawling. Helicopters seemed to be everywhere overhead and on the ground. The sounds of gunfire were intense.

Like a moth in reverse, Kurshin sought out the darkness, crawling always away from the spotlights stabbing the night, the flames rising over the wreckage of the Russian Badger and the Iranian helicopter, and the flashes and heat traces of weapons fire.

"My life for yours," he'd promised Baranov so many years ago. As long as there was breath in his body he would not go back on his promise.

Darkness was life. Light was death.

This night was not his time to die. Not yet.

52

THE COBRA ATTACK HELICOPTER with SAVAK markings touched down about fifty yards from the still smoldering wreckage of the Russian transport aircraft. The wind was strong and gusty, but the pilot was an expert. The valley was crawling with air force troops and SAVAK officers up from Qom.

The hatch opened and Captain Peshadi and Sergeant Turik jumped down. A command post of sorts had been set up in one of the big transport helicopters nearby. They walked over to it.

Dawn was coming, and beneath the thickly overcast sky the light was flat, lending a curiously one-dimensional air to the long valley and sheer cliffs. This was a brutal land. Nothing human could or should live here.

All resistance of any sort had ceased. One Iranian helicopter had been completely destroyed, and a second had been badly damaged. There were more than four dozen bodies, most of them Iranian, laid out in three ragged rows on the cold ground.

"It must have been some fight," Sergeant Turik said in awe.

"Yes, but thankfully it was confined to this valley," Peshadi said, staring down the runway.

Wreckage from the Russian aircraft was strewn for over a thousand yards. Evidently the plane had crashed on landing. He shook his head and looked up into the thick sky. Insanity, he thought. All of it had been designed by lunatics and carried out by maniacs.

"Captain Peshadi," someone called from the command helicopter.

Peshadi looked around. "Colonel Masijed?" he asked.

"That's right." The air force colonel jumped down from the open hatch. He'd been one of the officers who'd trained at the shah's military academy and survived the revolution. He commanded the air wing at Qom, and he was no friend of SAVAK —past or present.

They shook hands.

"The situation here seems secure," Peshadi said.

"It is," Masijed said. "Your people did a fine job. Without them we might have been too late."

Peshadi acknowledged the compliment. "The convoy is in the clear, from what I understand."

"They will be in Qom within the hour. The danger is past."

Again Peshadi glanced down the runway, and along the trail of wreckage that led to the Russian aircraft. "What happened here? I was told that you have taken prisoners."

Colonel Masijed said nothing.

Peshadi turned back to him. "Colonel?"

"This is an air force operation."

Peshadi's eyes narrowed. "The convoy . . ."

"Is safe."

"If there are prisoners, they will be turned over to SAVAK for transportation to Tehrān, where they will be placed on trial."

"These were Russians here to steal our . . . to attack the convoy."

"How many of them did you capture? Did you get any of their officers?"

"The Russians are all dead. They refused to surrender. Let me tell you, had their lead aircraft not been shot down, and had their other forces been allowed to land, I do not believe we could have contained them."

"Shot down?" Peshadi asked.

Colonel Masijed nodded. "Yes. By an American. A spy, I think. He and his two companions work for the CIA, no doubt."

Peshadi stiffened. "I want them," he said.

"They were here, Captain, to help protect the shipment."

"No," the word escaped involuntarily from the back of Peshadi's throat, and he stepped forward.

Sergeant Turik grabbed his arm. Two of Colonel Masijed's men suddenly materialized from inside the helicopter. They were armed and looked very serious.

"Two of these men are wounded, one of them quite seriously. As soon as my surgeon is finished we will transport them to the Turkish border near Urmia, where they will be allowed to cross. Unhindered."

"I won't allow this."

"You have no choice, unless you want to die here," the colonel said harshly. He lowered his voice. "Listen, Peshadi, they may have spied on us, and they are the infidel, but this time they were sincerely here to help. They returned our money to us, and they were making sure it got to Tehrān. That *nobody* would take it."

A part of Peshadi could see the logic in what the colonel was telling him, but he couldn't let go. His emotions were too mixed, to muddled by his past.

"I will report this. You will face court-martial."

"I accept that responsibility, of course," Colonel Masijed said calmly. "But you must understand that it could have been much worse here. A number of airplanes we believe were transporting American Delta Force soldiers nearly made it past our radar before they were stopped ... by us and by the storm. There could have been a full-scale war here. Is that what you want?"

Yes, he almost said. No. He didn't know what he wanted. Except for revenge. His sister had been only sixteen when she'd started with her American lover, and seventeen when she'd been executed.

One of the smaller transport helicopters behind them whined into life, its drooping rotors beginning to move slowly, as three men were helped out of a first-aid truck. Two of them were on stretchers.

Peshadi yanked out his pistol, but the sharp sounds of several rifle ejector slides being drawn back and snapped into place made him stop short.

Colonel Masijed took his weapon from him.

The three men came past. One of them on a stretcher looked up. He wasn't Abbas or Ghfari. He was the other one. The tall Westerner in the Range Rover. The one who'd entered Iran on a Russian passport.

"You're going home now, Tinker," Peshadi said to him in English.

"Yes." McGarvey smiled weakly. "Glad we could be of some help, Captain."

BOOK FOUR

BOOK FOUR

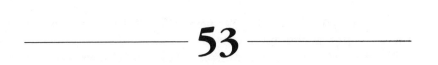

53

WASHINGTON, D.C.

ONE-ON-ONE WITH the President of the United States, the Oval Office had always seemed like an immense room, even to Roland Murphy. This evening, however, it was crammed with most of the cabinet, the advisers, and a number of other key administration people. It was too small.

It was a few minutes before the President's scheduled eight o'clock news conference downstairs, in the East Room, and as usual the air was electric with expectation. Presidents had been made and they had been broken in that room.

Murphy had come over from Langley the moment he'd had word from Turkey. They'd been expecting this ever since analyzing the early-morning satellite passes over Iran. But the actual news was in one respect better than their speculations. As he'd told Lawrence Danielle, "Anything worth doing makes a mess."

He'd thought that saying was especially appropriate when it came to intelligence operations.

The President beckoned Murphy over. "What have you got for me, General?"

"Good news, Mr. President," Murphy said.

The President took him aside, and they put their heads together by the bow windows. "Is it confirmed?"

"We just got word from our people on the Turkish border: Kirk McGarvey, Dick Abbas, and Bijan Ghfari came out of Iran less than an hour ago. McGarvey and Abbas were wounded, but they're expected to recover."

"How'd they manage to get so far so soon?" the President asked sharply, holding his relief in check.

"That's the amazing part. Evidently they were given medical attention and then transported to the border by the Iranian air force."

The President was shaking his head. He glanced over Murphy's shoulder at the others in the room, who were talking quietly.

"There's been no protest from Iran," the President said. "In fact, there's not been so much as a word out of them. The gold is safely in Tehrān. The Russians have been stopped. And no one is pointing a finger at us, for a change. You're right, General, it is amazing."

"Yes, sir."

The President looked at him. "What's left, Roland? Spell it out."

"McGarvey will be flown to the hospital in Wiesbaden to have his wounds tended to, but he is insisting that Arkady Kurshin may still be alive."

"He was shot and left for dead in a hostile environment crawling with Iranian military and SAVAK troops."

"Yes, sir. He was in a worse fix off the coast of Syria two years ago, and he survived."

"Is it possible this time?"

"I don't know," Murphy said. "But all things considered, I wouldn't count the bastard out until the autopsy is over."

The President's press secretary, Richard Wood, motioned from the door. "It's time, Mr. President."

The President hesitated a moment longer. He looked into Murphy's eyes. "I'm going to have to go downstairs now and face the press corps. They're going to want to know what the hell is happening in Azerbaidzhan. It's even possible that one of them has heard of the doings in Iran. What do I tell them, Roland? Is it over?"

"I don't know, Mr. President."

"No," the President said heavily. "But then they're paying me, not you, for this job."

"Ladies and gentlemen, the President of the United States," Richard Wood announced from the podium. He stepped aside as the President entered the East Room and took his place. A hush came over the 237 journalists.

A brief statement had been prepared for the President to read, but he held it up. "I expect everyone has a copy of this."

Some of the journalists nodded.

"Then I'll dispense with the usual reading," the President said. "But before we get to the questions, let me just say that our latest intelligence indicates that the fighting in Baku and along the border has already stopped. And I want you guys to read my lips on this one. There are no—repeat *no*—Russian tanks in any city in Azerbaidzhan. Nor was any force directed from Moscow used in the brief uprising.

"From what I've been told, most of the actual bloodshed occurred at the airport outside of Baku when a KGB installation tried to defend itself. Elsewhere in the country it was the Azerbaidzhani Coalition for Independence that fought with local police—not Russians—for control of the radio and television stations, the telephone exchange, and a number of electric power plants.

"At no time were the two nuclear generating plants in the region in any danger, nor were any of the Soviet Missile Defense installations threatened."

The President pointed to William McKinstry from CBS. "I'll start with you this time, Bill."

"Thank you, Mr. President. Do you have any clear word on the number of casualties yet?"

The President shook his head. "No, and I was just discussing this with Jim Bardley over at the National Security Agency. They've picked up radio reports from the Soviets that claim as few as one or two dead to as many as a thousand. So what we're saying here is that there are casualties, we know that much for sure, but it's going to be a while before we can say for certain how many."

The President pointed to a woman in the middle. She stood up.

"Laura Rodgers, *Denver Post.* Mr. President, do you think that Mr. Gorbachev learned his lesson in Latvia and Estonia two years ago, and if so, will he handle this problem in Azerbaidzhan differently? And a follow-up question: Have you spoken with Mr. Gorbachev since this disturbance began?"

"No, I haven't talked with him in the past forty-eight hours. He's got his hands full at the moment. But you've got to understand that what's been happening in Azerbaidzhan is not the same as Latvia. The trouble was not ordered or in any way sanctioned by the Azerbaidzhani congress. The fighting is independent of the local government."

"But it has the support of the people, isn't that so?" Laura Rodgers asked.

Other reporters were clamoring to be heard, but the President held them off.

"Just a minute," he said. "There's no way of knowing if what's happening there has popular support. There's no Gallup Poll in Baku." The President leaned forward over the lectern. "Listen, all we can go on is what the government of Azerbaidzhan tells us. And they haven't told us very much. As I said, there was no vote in their legislature like there was in Latvia, for independence. They'd declared nothing."

Again the reporters called out and raised their hands to be heard.

"Mr. President, what about operation PLUTUS in Iran?" one voice was clear above the others.

The president groaned inwardly. Out of the corner of his eye he saw that Tom Haines, his national security adviser, was just as surprised and dismayed by the question.

"What's your question?" the President asked.

"Thank you, sir. Paul Spencer, Reuters. It's my understanding that the United States signed an agreement with the government of Iran to return something more than a thousand million dollars in gold which represents funds the United States had held for nearly fifteen years. Is that true? And in a follow-up question, it's my understanding that the shipment may have been attacked in Iran. Is that true?"

"Where did you hear this?" the President asked, trying to keep it as light as possible. But the other journalists had perked up. They smelled blood.

"I have my sources," the British reporter replied smugly.

"I have to take my hat off to them. The operation you mentioned was highly classified and known only to a handful of people. We were going to make our announcement tomorrow morning. You've jumped the gun."

"Yes, Mr. President," the Reuters man said. "But are these stories true?"

"Yes, and no," the President said coolly.

"I don't understand," the man insisted.

"Yes, the first is true. No, the second is not true."

"Then there was no trouble with the gold convoy on Iranian soil?" the Reuters man shouted, but the President had already pointed to another reporter.

"Perry, you've been patient."

Perry Nichols, from the Associated Press, got to his feet. "Mr. President, I think I can speak for most of us in this room when I say that I am surprised. I hadn't heard a thing. Would you care to expand on this situation in Iran?"

The President sighed audibly. "What do you want to know, Perry?" But then he held up his hand. "Wait," he said. "Before I'm accused here of hiding something, let me tell you that's exactly what we're doing, and intend doing so long as it involves national security."

The Associated Press reporter started to protest, but the President continued to hold him off.

"Let me finish here. In an effort to continue normalizing relations with Iran, we agreed to release certain oil funds that had been frozen here, in this country, and return them to Iran. They specifically requested that the funds be sent over in the form of gold bullion. Which we agreed to. In an effort to insure the safe transport of that much gold, we naturally had to keep the entire operation under close wraps. There was no trouble with the shipment. And in fact at this moment the gold is safely in Tehrān."

"Can you tell us exactly how much gold was shipped, Mr. President?"

"Four thousand ounces," the President said.

There was a collective sigh through the press corps.

The President grinned. "That's enough for them to start their own McDonald's chain."

A few of the reporters guffawed, but the Reuters man was deadly serious. Again his voice cut through the noise.

"Are you denying, Mr. President, that a Soviet-made converted Badger bomber crash-landed in a high valley south of the city of Qom? And that the aircraft had U.S. markings, and brought U.S. troops?"

"As you said, Mr. Spencer, a 'Soviet-made' aircraft," the President said sharply.

"Did the United States try to steal back the gold it was sending to Iran, Mr. President? Can you answer that question?"

"Yes, I can," the President said. "And the answer is no. And now let's let someone else have a chance. After all, everyone here has an editor breathing down his neck. Mine is called the American public." And the President emphasized the word *American*.

54

MCGARVEY'S HEAD WAS ROARING, threatening to split in two at any moment. He became aware that he was strapped into a narrow cot or stretcher. The entire room was moving around, sometimes violently, accompanied by a tremendous noise.

"Mr. Wills," someone shouted at his side. The voice was not familiar. Not American.

McGarvey opened his eyes and looked up as a dark-skinned man dressed in a uniform, a combat helmet on his head, moved aside for Bob Wills. They were aboard a helicopter, McGarvey realized.

"How do you feel?" Wills shouted over the noise.

"Terrible," McGarvey choked. His voice was weak. "Where are we?"

"Turkey. On our way to Van. We would have taken off sooner,

but you'd lost a lot of blood and the medics wanted to stabilize your condition first."

He was beginning to remember. He'd been loaded onto an Iranian air force helicopter. It was extraordinary.

"How is Dick Abbas?"

"His leg is broken, he's badly dehydrated, and he suffered a mild concussion from the beating the Russian gave him." Wills's ruddy jaw tightened. "Did you know that he had been tortured?"

"No."

"The son of a bitch hooked an electrical cord to his balls and plugged it in. At the very least Abbas will be sterile. The medic thinks he'll have to be . . . castrated."

McGarvey closed his eyes. He could see Kurshin going down behind the crest of the hill. And then there was nothing. The Iranians wouldn't answer his questions, and no one had mentioned the Russian. It was just like off the coast of Syria. He knew he'd hit Kurshin with at least one shot. He'd seen the man going down with his own eyes, and yet now he knew that he could not be sure if the man was dead.

It was like a ghost story. No matter what happened, you were always sure of one thing: the evil spirit would be back. Each time bigger and more terrible.

"You stopped them, McGarvey," Wills was saying. "You stopped the Russians. The gold got through. It's in Tehrān already, as a matter of fact."

McGarvey opened his eyes. "Any word on Kurshin?" he asked.

"Not yet," Wills said. "But the Iranians aren't exactly cooperating with us one hundred percent. As it is, everyone was practically bowled over when we got word that they were bringing you to the border. They even let us come across so that we could carry you back. No one wants to press their luck any further."

"What about the rest of the Russian aircraft and crew?"

"Back in Baku. They've evidently rejoined the KGB barracks there as if nothing happened. Did you know that Didenko had been arrested?"

McGarvey nodded.

"The latest word is that he's already been tried in camera and sentenced to death."

"It won't end," McGarvey said. His brain was spinning. He wanted to close his eyes and sleep for the next two weeks. But each time darkness came over his vision, he saw two pictures superimposed: one of Kurshin pitching over the rail into the sea, the other of Kurshin being propelled backward behind the hillock. Each time the image faded out with the single close-up of Kurshin's face. The Russian was grinning at him. He was saying something, his lips were moving, but McGarvey couldn't make out what it was.

"What?" Wills asked.

McGarvey focused on him again. "It's Kurshin."

"What about him?"

"He may still be alive."

"He would never have gotten out of the valley."

"I don't know. Christ, I don't know."

Ghfari was suddenly there beside Wills. "You shot the man, I saw it," he said. His dark eyes were wide. He looked very frightened.

McGarvey looked up at him. "You came back?"

"Yes, Richard insisted that we come to help you. He said that no one could understand about that Russian."

"Did you see his body?"

"I saw you go down, and then I saw him fall back, so I know you hit him. But afterward we were helping you, and then the air force came and arrested us."

"From across the field? On foot?"

"Yes."

McGarvey visualized the battle scene and the spot where he and Kurshin had fought it out. If the Iranians had come across the valley on foot, they had to have discovered Kurshin's body. If he'd still been there.

"Did you see them picking up the Russian's body?"

Ghfari shook his head. "No. But he went down. I can swear to that."

"It's not our problem now," Wills interjected. "At least not for the moment. You've been badly wounded. As soon as we reach Van you'll be loaded onto a jet transport and flown immediately to Wiesbaden. You've still got a bullet in your chest just below your right lung."

"He's alive . . ." McGarvey was starting to drift again. He hoped it was the medication and not his wounds that was causing him the weakness, because there was still something left to be done.

"The important thing is that you're alive," Wills said. "And the mission was accomplished. The general sends his thanks for a job well done."

But McGarvey was no longer listening. He was thinking about Paris and Lisbon, and even more importantly about Washington. One thing left to be done. . . .

The past twenty-seven hours had been a nightmare for Arkady Kurshin. He'd taken two hits from McGarvey's weapon, the first passing all the way through his left shoulder just beneath his collarbone, and the second lodging in his right hip. That was the hit that had done the most damage. He would probably be a cripple the rest of his life.

But he had his life. For that much he was thankful not only to his own pure blind luck, but to Colonel Berezin, who'd carried him on his shoulders up into the mountains, out of that valley.

It was dawn, and the light filtering through the silk fabric of the Soviet army survival tent was mottled and golden, and warm after the night's chill. He could smell woodsmoke from the campfire the colonel had started, and the odor of something cooking. It made his mouth water.

He pushed the thin plastic survival blanket aside and slowly sat up, the pain so excruciating that it made his head swim. His stomach turned over and he fought down the urge to vomit. He would not give in to his injuries. He was alive, by some quirk of fate, and there was only one thing that mattered to him now.

It was the thing that had gotten him across the valley to the hills just above the downed Badger.

It was the thing that had given him the energy to go on. To lie perfectly still in the darkness as the Iranian air force troops marched past him, one of them nearly stepping on him, then to continue, even though he had no strength because he had lost so much blood.

There had been no choice. To give up would have meant to die before he had made certain of his goal.

At one point he'd watched the Iranians carrying two men away on stretchers, while a third followed at gunpoint. But there'd been no way for him to tell whether McGarvey, one of the bodies on a stretcher, was alive or dead.

Somehow, however, within his heart of hearts he knew that the American was still alive. In his mind's eye he saw McGarvey rolling over on his back and firing up at him. The man was inhuman, a monster, a machine.

Colonel Berezin's pack lay open at the foot of his survival blanket. Kurshin pulled it over and went through its contents: a small spiral-bound book containing maps of all of Iran and the entire region; more survival clothing and some rations; a spare clip for a TK automatic pistol; and the colonel's identification and KGB pay booklets.

But no weapon. Kurshin parted the tent flap and looked outside.

The colonel, bare-chested, had just finished splashing water on his face, and he dried himself with a small gray towel. A pot of tea was boiling on the small fire. From the smells Kurshin guessed that the other small pot contained soup. A tin of survival bread was open on a flat rock.

Berezin, sensing someone behind him, turned around and grunted his approval. "So, you survived the night. For a time I didn't think you would."

"Where are we?" Kurshin asked, pulling the tent flap open the rest of the way and crawling painfully outside. Berezin made no move to help him.

"About ten kilometers southwest of the valley. I had to carry you most of the way. This was as far as I could go."

Kurshin was impressed. The man was built like a bull with a thick neck and broad shoulders. He had the will to survive and the stamina to pull it off, even up here in the mountains. He would be . . . dangerous, Kurshin thought.

"The *rodina* is north," Kurshin said, hobbling over to the fire.

"We're not going back," Berezin said. "Didenko has been arrested for treason. If we showed up in Moscow they'd arrest us as well. We'd get our nine ounces for sure."

Kurshin digested this news. An eight-inch survival knife, its blade serrated on one side and razor sharp on the other, was lying on a rock. The colonel had used it to open the bread tin.

"Where, then?"

"Iraq. I have friends there who will help us with new identities." Berezin looked calculatingly at him. "For a price, that is. You have access to money? Western currencies?"

"Some," Kurshin said. There were several operating accounts at his disposal: one in Zurich, another in Brussels, and a third on the Channel island of Jersey.

"I'll get you to Iraq, and you will share your money with me. Afterward we will part company."

Kurshin was slightly amused by the colonel's apparent distaste of him. "We could stay together as a team," he said.

Berezin shook his head. "There's the stink of death all over you."

Kurshin shrugged. "How far is it to the border?"

"A long way, maybe four hundred kilometers across the mountains. It will probably take us a week, if we're lucky with the weather. Maybe longer."

"We have the rations?"

"If we conserve."

"Good," Kurshin murmured. "Now, I am hungry. May I have some tea and some soup?"

"Yes," the colonel said, turning to the fire. "The sooner your strength returns, the sooner I will be able to stop carrying you."

Kurshin reached over and picked up the survival knife. The colonel, feeling the movement, started to duck, but he was too late. With his bad left arm, Kurshin pulled Berezin's head back, and with the knife in his right, he sliced the man's neck all the way back to the spinal column.

Berezin let out a huge, blubbering roar with a spray of blood as he swatted Kurshin aside like a rag doll and leaped past the campfire. He scrambled to his feet and, holding his head with both hands, turned around.

For one terrible moment Kurshin thought the man was actually going to come after him, but then the light faded from Berezin's eyes and he fell backward, already drowning in his own blood.

55

IT HAD SNOWED AGAIN in Paris. When McGarvey came in from
Charles de Gaulle Airport a clean white blanket lay over the
city. Multicolored lights played off the snow, lending a special
air to the City of Light.

He'd checked himself out of the military hospital at Wiesbaden, against doctor's orders.

"You suffered a concussion from the bullet that struck your
head," the doctor had said. "Two of your ribs were broken, and
you were damned lucky the second bullet didn't penetrate your
lung. You were even luckier with the third shot to your right
side. If you'd still had that kidney, you might be dead now. As
it is, the bullet passed completely through your body."

"I'll take it easy, Doc," McGarvey had promised, getting
dressed. He'd lost that kidney two years ago at Kurshin's hands.

The doctor had shaken his head in resignation. "You need bed rest, a couple of weeks of it. Hell, even walking out of here could cause you damage."

"No warranties on your work?"

"Shit."

It was eight in the evening when the cabbie dropped him off at his apartment just off the rue La Fayette. He paid the driver and went up. The television was blaring in the concierge's apartment, and the couple on the second floor were having their usual early-evening argument. Everything was normal. Nothing seemed out of place.

Before he left the hospital he'd telephoned Carrara, who'd assured him that all charges against him and Maria Schimmer had been dropped, except the murder charges against them in Buenos Aires. Esformes was pushing that.

There was still no hard evidence on the embassy bombing, but for now, at least, the Agency was willing to go along with the theory that Kurshin had done it. State was citing a group or groups unknown, but definitely not French. The news media was unhappy, but everyone else concerned seemed reasonably satisfied.

As she had been once before—it seemed like years ago—Carley Webb was waiting in his apartment for him. She was dressed in slacks and a sweater. Her coat lay over a chair, and she'd kicked off her boots.

"Welcome home," she said.

"I'm going to have to change the locks. This place is getting to be like Grand Central Station."

"I wanted to welcome you home, and . . . say that I'm sorry."

"For what?" McGarvey asked, taking off the jacket they'd given him at the hospital.

"For ever believing that you might have planted the bomb."

He went into the bedroom, peeled off his shirt, and slipped out of his trousers. He had been sweating profusely all afternoon, and his entire body ached.

"Did you?" he asked, coming back out in his shorts.

She nodded, the motion of her head barely perceptible.

McGarvey shrugged. "You can make yourself useful. Fix me a drink. Bourbon, rocks, no water." He went into the bathroom where he started the water into the tub. He stepped out of his shorts and eased himself into the tub, closing his eyes and lying back, the porcelain cold at first against his back. He felt as if he were on fire.

"Here," Carley said, coming into the bathroom.

He reached out without opening his eyes and she placed the drink in his hand. "Thanks," he said. "Now go home, Carley, before you get more hurt than you already are."

"Bad grammar," she said. "How are you feeling?"

"Terrible," McGarvey said, taking a long sip of his drink.

"What now?"

He opened his eyes and looked at her. She was perched on the closed toilet lid. "I have some unfinished business in Lisbon. If it's still there."

"She is."

McGarvey looked at her for a moment. She was a pretty girl. But she was a girl, still. Not a woman.

"And then?" she asked.

He shrugged again. "I don't really know, Carley, for sure. But I am fairly certain that I'll be leaving Paris. I might go back to the States. Out west first, then Washington."

"D.C.?"

"Yes."

"I'm being sent back in a couple of weeks."

"Disciplinary action?"

"No. A promotion, actually," she said. "Maybe we'll be able to see each other."

"I don't think so." McGarvey looked away. He hunched forward because it felt better on his stitches.

Carley knelt beside the tub and began washing his back, gently, mindful of the bandages and the bruises.

"You'll have to settle down with someone sooner or later, Kirk," she said. "You need to be happy."

"You, too," McGarvey said. "But not with me." He looked up at her. "Get out of the Agency before it eats you alive. Find a GS-eighteen somewhere and settle down. Make babies. Cook roasts on Sunday. Become a den mother. Take up knitting."

"Pig," she said.

"Yeah," McGarvey replied absently. "And old-fashioned, too, as it turns out."

It was noon Saturday by the time he reached the city center of Lisbon and entered the Hotel Lisboa Penta on the Avenida dos Combatentes. He'd confirmed by telephone before leaving Paris that Maria was still there, although he hadn't spoken to her. But he had left a message that he was coming.

He took the elevator to the eleventh floor and hesitated a moment before knocking. Why was he coming back? The question had been with him since he'd left Wiesbaden, yet he still had no satisfactory answer, except that he had promised Maria.

He didn't like unsolved mysteries. And in part, he supposed nervously, he'd returned to Lisbon for the same reason Carley Webb had shown up at his apartment: he wanted to find out what a certain person meant to him.

He was looking for answers. But he knew that whatever they might be, they would probably not be satisfactory.

She opened the door and smiled up at him, her teeth white against her olive complexion. "I didn't think you would come back. But I was afraid to leave in case you might."

"I said I would."

"I got your message this morning," she said, but then McGarvey took her in his arms.

For just an instant she stiffened against him, but then she pressed her body against his and they kissed deeply, the pain from his injuries excruciating.

When they parted she drew him into the room. He turned back and chained the door and then joined her at the bed where she was already pulling off her clothes. She was excited, almost breathless, as she helped McGarvey pull off his jacket and remove his shirt.

Suddenly she stopped. "*Madre de Dios*," she cried in a little voice. She looked from the bandages up to his eyes. "You are in pain? What happened to you?"

"Not so much pain," McGarvey said. "And what happened doesn't matter now. I'm here." He reached out and touched the cherry birthmark on her left breast. She flinched, but did not move back.

"I found the four old men," she said huskily.

"Here, in the city?" he asked, pushing her gently down onto the bed.

"Yes."

He kissed the tips of her breasts, but she pushed him away.

"Now," she said. "I want you now."

He pulled off the rest of his clothes and entered her at once.

She was already moist as her hips rose up to meet his. Once during their lovemaking she cried out a name, which he didn't quite catch, and afterward he could see in her eyes that she was a long way off, and he had at least one of his answers.

As he suspected, it wasn't very satisfying.

56

THE EXPANSIVE MANSION WAS on a *quinta*, a small estate, some twelve miles west of Lisbon along what was known as the Portuguese Riviera. They'd caught sight of it coming down the long coast road. The casino towns of Cascais and Estoril were a few miles farther west, as were the crowds they drew. Here the night was quiet except for the waves breaking on a rocky beach.

As they turned down the long driveway, Maria said, "His name is Alois Rheinfälls."

McGarvey pulled up short and doused the rental car's headlights just off the highway. There was a partial moon tonight, but clouds driving in off the Atlantic obscured it much of the time.

"If it's the same one mentioned in Roebling's notebook," he said.

"It is," Maria replied.

"How can you be so sure?"

"This bastard is rich, isn't he? It's the same one."

McGarvey decided he would not delve into that logic, though he suspected that she was probably correct. According to what Maria had found in the tax records, the property had been owned by Rheinfälls since 1943. Where had he gotten his money in that day and age?

Twenty yards ahead, the driveway was blocked by a tall iron gate. A large sign warned in Portuguese, German, and English that the property was patrolled continuously by guard dogs. There was a telephone on their side of the fence.

"We're not going to get in unless he wants to let us in," McGarvey said. "Even if there is a connection between him and your Major Roebling, it will have been long buried by now. And if this one knows about the gold, he certainly won't want to discuss it with us."

"Then we go in by force," Maria said hotly. "We can use dynamite or plastique. I don't think either will be too difficult to acquire. He will talk—"

"So will the Portuguese police. And once we're arrested, then what?"

"We'll have the information we came for."

"No," McGarvey said. "We'll do it my way."

Maria looked sharply at him. But then she nodded. Despite what had happened between them that afternoon, he had the feeling that she would put a knife in his back, as she had to the Argentinian mate aboard the *Yankee Girl*, if he crossed her.

He put the car in gear, flipped on the headlights, and drove to the gate. When he got out and approached the telephone a pair of Dobermans appeared out of the darkness on the other side, silently, their teeth bared. They did not approach any closer than three or four feet from the wire itself. McGarvey figured the fence was electrified. They watched him, the stubs of their tails wagging as if they wanted to play.

McGarvey picked up the telephone and a few seconds later it was answered by a man. *"Sim."*

"Ich kom aus Freiburg," McGarvey shouted. "I must speak with Herr Rheinfälls."

"Wer ist das?" the man answered in German. He sounded much too young to be Rheinfälls. But he was a native speaker.

"My name isn't important, but we must speak with Herr Rheinfälls. It is a matter of life or death. They ... know."

"Who is this? What are you talking about?"

"Listen to me, you fool, the secret is out at long last! I have the woman with me. We have come from Freiburg. Do you understand? From Freiburg! From Herr Doktor Hesse!"

"Eine Augenblick," the man said. One moment.

McGarvey glanced back at the car. Maria had gotten out and stood looking at him. The dogs were beginning to get agitated.

An older man came on. *"Ja, hier ist Alois Rheinfälls. Wer ist das?"*

"My name is Kirk McGarvey. I'm here with the granddaughter of Captain Ernst Reiker. I believe you know this name?"

"What is it? What do you want with me?"

"We have been to speak with Professor Hesse in Freiburg, and because of him we found Major Roebling's notebook. Do you know these names?"

"Hesse is dead."

"Yes," McGarvey said. "They killed him. And we all know why. It has begun again."

"What do you want here with me?" Rheinfälls cried in sudden anguish.

"Your help," McGarvey said. "We want the killing to stop."

The line was silent.

"Herr Rheinfälls?" McGarvey said.

"Get back in your car. I will send someone to escort you to the house."

McGarvey hung up the phone and went back to the car. "He's agreed to see us."

"You talked to him?" Maria asked, her voice filled with emotion.

"Yes."

"Dios."

The house was huge and Italianate. It reminded McGarvey of the gaudy villas that had been built in the twenties along the French Riviera by Americans who had the cash but no class. Broad marble stairs rose in front to a balustraded porch that ran the width of the broad, three-story house. Above were balconies, and below on the porch, and out in the front yard, were dozens of statues and fountains, all of them bathed in soft lights.

They were escorted by a pair of burly men who silently frisked both of them before they were allowed inside. McGarvey had figured they would be searched, so he had left his pistol under the seat in the car.

An old man in tails and white gloves led them back to a very large and pleasantly furnished conservatory crammed with growing things. The smells were rich and moist, and they could hear water gently falling on stones somewhere. The rear wall, which was mostly glass, faced south so that in the daytime the large room would be filled with sunlight.

"May I get you something to drink?" the servant asked.

"Get away from me, Nazi," Maria ordered harshly.

The servant didn't flinch. He half bowed. "Very well, Fräulein," he said, and he turned and left.

A few moments later Alois Rheinfälls came in. He was a very tall man with a Prussian officer's bearing and manner. McGarvey judged him to be in his mid-seventies or perhaps even eighty, his hair white, his complexion pale, and his skin wrinkled. He was dressed in evening clothes, as if he had either just come in or was about to go out.

"You have upset my house very badly," he said. "Why have you come here like this in the night? What do you want with me? I know nothing and I cannot help you."

"But RSHA Major Walther Roebling knew you."

"Rheinfälls is not an unusual German name."

"Neither are Dieter Feldmann, or Karl Sikorsky, or Sigmund Müeller," McGarvey said, naming the other three Maria had remembered from the notebook. "Shall I go on?"

Rheinfälls took a deep breath. "I have never heard those names in my life."

"But you knew Professor Hesse in Frieburg."

"I know the name."

"Yes? Well, it was he who told us about the submarine."

"He had no business to—" Rheinfälls began, but stopped himself abruptly.

"We found it," McGarvey went on. "Off the coast of Argentina in the Golfo San Matías. She was sunk in about seventy-five meters of water just offshore. There had been an explosion. A bomb. It was sabotage."

Rheinfälls's eyes were large; a thin sheen of sweat covered his high forehead. He was obviously very frightened.

"Roebling escaped, of course, but he'd left his notebook behind. In the boat's escape trunk. We found it and brought it back to the surface. Along with . . ."

Rheinfälls rocked forward on the balls of his feet.

"A lead bar covered by a thin gold plating. There were a lot of them down there. The sub was filled with them."

"This has nothing to do with me."

"It was an elaborate ruse. Captain Reiker and his crew were sent on a decoy mission to throw off the chase. It was Roebling's job to kill them all and then die himself in Argentina. That way your secret would be safe."

"No."

"But, yes," McGarvey said. "You and your pals figured to wait until after the Nuremberg trials. Until the dust settled. Until the world began to forget."

Rheinfälls was silent.

"But something happened in June of 1949 that you hadn't counted on. At a prison camp outside of Bonn run by the Allies. An RSHA lieutenant escaped. He'd been questioned about the submarine. It wasn't much later that the killings began, starting with his interrogators."

Still Rheinfälls said nothing.

"His name, of course, was Rainer Mossberg."

Now Rheinfälls held out a shaking hand as if to ward off a blow.

"Professor Hesse thought that Mossberg might be dead. The killings, he said, stopped in 1978. But he was wrong. And he lost his life because of his error. So did Major Roebling. They both believed"—McGarvey smiled sadly—"they both believed in you, and what you were hiding."

"No!" Rheinfälls cried.

"Then, what?"

"You don't understand."

"Tell me," McGarvey said relentlessly. "Explain it to me so that the killings will stop."

"We didn't expect this. It wasn't supposed to happen this way."

"No," Maria said, her voice shrill. "Nor did you bastards expect what happened in May of 1948. That had to have been an even bigger blow for you."

"What . . . ?"

"When Israel became a state. On that day you and your friends must have been shitting in your pants."

57

RHEINFÄLLS'S FACE SUDDENLY BECAME animated. McGarvey was amazed at the dramatic change in the old man.

"So, a little Jewess, a Zionist, here seeking retribution for what happened fifty years ago," Rheinfälls spat. "Do you believe that I was a death camp commandant? You think you recognize my face from old photographs? Is that it?"

"No!" Maria shot back. "I may have Jewish blood in my veins, and I may have been born in Argentina, but I'm German, too, and I've learned to be ashamed of it ... of being from the same stock as you."

"Ah, so you believe you carry the guilt of the sins of your fathers. Of your fatherland. You are so clean of sin yourself that you are quite willing to take on the blame for an entire nation of people. It must be gratifying for you."

"I'm no Nazi."

"No, but your people were, I think. And you?" Rheinfälls looked bleakly at McGarvey. "Are you one of Rainer's people come here to kill an old man? Well, let me tell you something. There was no need of you to come here like this. The secret is safe with me, and the others." He laughed. "There aren't many others now. Hesse was wrong. The killings didn't stop in 1978. Nature has taken over where the generals left off."

"The generals?" McGarvey asked, careful to keep his voice even.

Rheinfälls blinked. "What?"

"You said nature took over where the generals left off. What generals are these?"

Rheinfälls stepped back a pace. "You can ask me this now? After what you said?"

"We've come for the gold."

"What gold?"

"You know," McGarvey said.

"Never," Rheinfälls whispered.

"It was collected from Jews," McGarvey said. "From the teeth that were extracted before they were put to death. From the gold chains around their necks, bracelets around their wrists. From wedding bands and watches and watch fobs. Perhaps in some instances of the very rich, from their gold-plated cutlery. Gold-rimmed eyeglasses. Cuff links and collar pins and shirt studs."

"It was sent to South America. For the new Reich. For . . ."

"The Odessa?" McGarvey asked rhetorically. "No, that was merely a diversionary tactic. The real hoard is here, I think. In Portugal. Where you and the others could keep an eye on it. Spend it."

"No!" the old man cried. He looked over his shoulder as if he expected one of his bodyguards to come to his rescue. But the house was silent.

"This life-style is very expensive," McGarvey noted.

"I have always had money. The family has had money. There were mines in Alsace. Vineyards. A steel mill on the Ruhr. Some of the fortune was saved."

"But it's here," McGarvey said. "The gold. There must be millions. Maybe more. A lot more."

"Tell us," Maria demanded.

Rheinfälls looked from McGarvey to her and then back. "You don't understand."

"Explain it to us."

Rheinfälls shook his head. "I can't."

"Then you will die like the others," Maria said. "I'll kill you myself."

The old man stumbled back a few steps and sank down onto a broad wicker chair. His skin looked almost gray, and it seemed as if he were having a problem catching his breath. McGarvey thought he might be on the verge of a heart attack.

"You don't understand," Rheinfälls repeated weakly. Then he mumbled something else, but they didn't catch it.

McGarvey pulled a chair close and sat down. "Let's end it here and now," he said. "Tell us where the gold is ... that is, if it's still intact."

"It is," Rheinfälls said.

"Tell us where."

"Then what?"

"We'll make sure it's returned to the ... Jews. To Israel. To its rightful owners."

Rheinfälls's entire body shook as if he had received a massive jolt to his system. "Impossible."

"No ..."

"It's cursed," Rheinfälls whispered.

"What?" McGarvey asked, not at all sure he had heard correctly. He glanced up at Maria, but she hadn't heard it. Her face was set in a grim mask of hate.

"No one can get near it," Rheinfälls mumbled. "All these years it has been safe from ... everyone."

"Where?"

"It will kill you, too!"

"Where!" McGarvey asked, leaning forward.

The old man's eyes met his.

"Here in Portugal?" McGarvey prompted.

Rheinfälls nodded.

"In this house?"

"No."

"But near enough so that you could keep an eye on it?"

"Yes," Rheinfälls said. "Very near."

"Then tell us where."

"It's been many years since any of us have gone there to see it."

"Where?"

The old man said something very softly. McGarvey leaned even closer so that he was barely six inches away.

"Ponte do Sor," Rheinfälls whispered.

"What?" Maria cried. "What did he say?"

"What is this place?" McGarvey asked.

Rheinfälls turned to look toward the windows. "The lights . . ." he said, when he was flung violently off the wicker chair, a big piece of his skull flying away in a broad spray of blood and brain tissue.

A high-powered rifle, McGarvey thought instantly.

"Down!" he shouted to Maria as he dived off his chair. He hit the floor badly, and something gave way inside his body. It felt as if his incisions had torn open, the pain instant and excruciating.

Through the haze of pain that threatened to obliterate his ability to see or think, McGarvey pulled himself between the big potted plants and the wicker tables and benches to where he could see the back wall of the conservatory.

The back yard was in darkness. No light came from the sides or the front of the big house.

"Kirk?" Maria called from behind him.

"Stay down," McGarvey managed to croak through his pain.

"Rheinfälls is dead," Maria called to him.

Where were the guards or the dogs? The shooter had managed to get onto the property, had turned out the lights, and had fired a shot from somewhere in the back all without raising an alarm.

McGarvey was getting a very bad feeling here. A cornered feeling. In his condition he would not be able to put up much of a fight against whoever it was who had tracked them and had killed the old man before he could tell the entire story.

Rheinfälls had blamed the killings on "the generals." What generals? Who had he been talking about?

"Do you see anything?" Maria asked.

"Not yet. Can you reach the light switch?"

"Just a minute."

"Keep down."

A few seconds later the conservatory lights went out. "There's a guard down in the hall," she called in the darkness. "He looks dead."

McGarvey painfully worked his way across the room, joining her at the hall doorway. He was light-headed and nauseated from the effort. But Maria didn't notice. She was pressed against the wall, her complexion chalky in the light from the hall. But she seemed to be in control. It didn't look as if she would fall apart on him yet.

Cautiously he peered around the doorframe. One of the burly men who had frisked them lay on his back near the stairs. A lot of blood had puddled beneath his head. The front door was open, but McGarvey could see nothing outside except for a section of empty porch.

There were no sounds in the house. And except for the guard's body in the hall, the open front door, and the extinguished lights in front, everything could have seemed normal.

But there was something odd about the downed man. McGarvey stared at the body for a full thirty seconds before he finally had it: the man had not drawn his weapon. He'd evidently come into the hall, or had just come down the stairs, when someone had opened the front door and shot him in the head. He'd made no move to defend himself.

"Are they gone?" Maria asked.

"I don't know," McGarvey answered. "Stay here and keep your head down." He got carefully to his feet, swaying there for a moment or two.

"What's wrong?" Maria asked, alarmed.

"I'm all right."

"No, you're not," she said. "What's wrong with you?"

"There's no time now," McGarvey said. "Just keep down." Girding himself, he stepped into the hall and hurried as fast as he could move across to the stairs, where he ducked down behind the massive oak banister.

From there he could just see into the dining room. The body of the old servant who had ushered them into the conservatory was visible. The man was lying on his back.

McGarvey scrambled over to the guard's body, flipped open the coat, and pulled out the man's gun. It was a large, nine-millimeter Beretta automatic.

He levered a round into the chamber and switched off the

safety as he dashed to the open door. There he flattened himself against the wall.

Still there were no sounds, no movement either from outside the house or from inside.

With care he eased around the corner so that he could see outside. The other bodyguard lay on his side in the driveway. He'd been shot twice, once in the neck and a second time in the head. Like the first guard, he had not drawn his gun.

"Kirk?" Maria called from behind him.

"It's the other guard. He's dead too."

"*Dios* . . ."

He stepped outside onto the porch, and at the railing cocked an ear to listen. But there were no sounds. Absolutely none, until after a few seconds the night insects began to shrill and click.

Somewhere down toward the main road he thought he saw a brief flash of light, but then it was gone. Whoever had killed Rheinfälls and his staff had left.

He and Maria had obviously not been the killer's targets, which somehow gave him absolutely no comfort.

He went back into the house and closed the door as Maria came out of the conservatory.

"Are they gone?" she asked.

McGarvey nodded. "I think so. You take the upstairs. I'll look around down here."

"They weren't after us," she said. "Only Rheinfälls."

"And his house staff."

She looked closely at him. "Are you okay?"

"I'll live," he said. "Now, hurry!"

"What are we looking for?" she asked.

"Telephone directories, files, notebooks, anything that will tell us if any of the other men on your short list are still alive."

"The tax records. I have their addresses . . ."

"It'll be too dangerous to go directly to them. We'll have to talk them out, and meet them somewhere . . . else."

"Where?" she asked.

"Ponte do Sor."

"What is this place?" she asked breathlessly.

"I don't know."

"Where is it?"

"Nearby, I think."

"Is that what he told you?" she asked, glancing back toward the conservatory.

McGarvey nodded.

"The gold is there?"

"Maybe," McGarvey said. "But we won't find it without more information."

"All right," Maria said, and she started for the stairs.

"There's a curse on it," McGarvey said, feeling somewhat foolish.

She spun around, startled."What did you say?"

"He told me that there was a curse on the gold."

"He said that?" Maria demanded, her eyes bright. "He used that exact word?"

"Yes, he did. What is it?"

"My father," she replied distantly. "He said the same thing. I heard him tell someone that there was a five-thousand-year-old curse on the gold. He tried to make a joke out of it, but I could tell that he was frightened out of his mind."

58

THE TAP FLIGHT FROM Crete arrived at Lisbon's Aeroporto da Portela on time at 9:45 P.M. The tall, well-built man who walked with the aid of an aluminum cane was the last off the airliner. His only bag was an expensive leather carryon that he slung over his right shoulder, the same side as his bad leg. He seemed to favor his left shoulder. Wearing a bush jacket, khaki trousers, and soft boots, he looked military.

In the customs hall his passport raised a few eyebrows, but he was admitted with no questions. His single bag was given only a perfunctory check.

"Welcome to Portugal, Colonel Berezin," the customs agent said. "I hope you have a pleasant holiday."

"I will, thank you," Arkady Kurshin said, grinning through his pain, and he went past the gates into the main terminal.

The evening was mild, the air thick and silky with humidity. It was pleasant compared to what he had endured for two days through the mountains of Iran until he was able to steal an old truck for the remainder of his trip to the border, and then to Baghdad.

Kurshin paused just within the main doors and studied the four-lane road that led away from the airport. There were a half-dozen taxis lined up to the right. Directly across from the doors were three shuttle buses, transport to the various hotels in the city. Cars came and went as people streamed out of the terminal.

He could see nothing threatening here. But his tradecraft was slipping, and he knew it. Several times he'd almost blown it with the Iraqis: once at the hospital when in a delirium he called for General Didenko; again with the authorities who demanded to know how he came to be in Iraq with such wounds.

His story to them was a mixture of half truths and lies. He was a Russian on a spying mission against Iran. Agents of SAVAK had caught him and nearly killed him.

"You are a lucky man, Colonel Berezin," the Iraqi officer had told him, and he'd drawn a blank for just a moment. His name was Kurshin, not Berezin. The official gave him an odd, searching look, but then the moment had passed.

McGarvey would not be so forgiving, if he were here and if they came face-to-face. With McGarvey it was going to be a matter of life or death.

My life in your service, he had promised Baranov . . . Didenko. Just lately he was getting the two mixed up in his head. It was bothersome.

All the way out from the Middle East, he had pondered what would happen after he was finished here. He had finally come to accept the decision that there would be nothing after Lisbon. Or at least nothing that mattered. It was a decision that took a big weight off his shoulders. He felt lighter, able to move fast, ready for whatever would happen here between him and McGarvey.

He had come with no excess baggage. With no preconceived ideas. With only one purpose.

He stepped out of the terminal and started toward the taxi rank. Two men dressed in gray business suits jumped out of a red Mercedes sedan and hurried across to him.

They were KGB. It was stamped all over them. Kurshin

stepped back, but this time his reactions were too slow. Before he could turn they were on him, one man at each elbow.

"Arkady Aleksandrovich Kurshin, you are under arrest," the big one on his left said close to his ear. The man's breath smelled of cloves.

"What are you talking about?" Kurshin replied in English. "Who are you? What do you want?"

"Don't give us any trouble, you bastard," the big one snarled. "Check him, Aleksandr."

The second, much smaller agent hurriedly patted Kurshin down as if he were merely happily greeting an old friend. Two of his front teeth were capped with gold, and his left eye was bloodshot. He kept grinning up at Kurshin. "He's clean, Mischa." His smile deepend. "Fuck your mother I'm happy you're here."

"A nice little promotion for you, comrade," Kurshin replied indifferently.

They hustled him across the sidewalk to the Mercedes, Aleksandr relieving him of his cane and bag. Mischa yanked open the rear door, shoved Kurshin inside, and climbed in with him. Aleksandr got in front beside the driver.

As soon as the doors were closed they took off, the driver hunched over the wheel.

"How did you know I would be on that airplane?" Kurshin asked, once they had cleared the airport.

The big man beside him said nothing, and Aleksandr, who had turned around and was watching him, just smiled.

"If I am under arrest, what are the charges?" Kurshin asked reasonably.

Still there was no response from either agent, or from the driver.

"*Fucking farmers*," Kurshin said in Russian. It was anything but a compliment to a Muscovite.

Aleksandr started to say something as his right hand came up over the back of the seat.

Kurshin suddenly grabbed the man's face in both hands, gouging out his eyes with his thumbs. Blood spurted out of the sockets as Aleksandr screamed and tried to pull away, but Kurshin hauled him bodily over the back of the front seat. Mischa had reared back and was reaching for his gun when Kurshin shoved Aleksandr in his lap.

The driver jabbed at the brakes. "Mischa!" he shouted in panic.

Kurshin snatched the big pistol out of Mischa's hand and fired a single shot at point-blank range into the man's forehead between his eyes.

With his weak left arm he shoved Aleksandr away and shot him in the head just behind his left ear.

The man's sphincter relaxed as he died, the stench suddenly overpowering.

Kurshin brought the pistol over the back of the front seat and laid the barrel against the back of the driver's head. They'd pulled over to the side of the road and were just about stopped.

"Find me a dark road so that we can get rid of these bodies, comrade, and you just might live," Kurshin ordered in Russian.

Kurshin was seeing spots and bright flashes in front of his eyes. He had hurt himself; he could feel blood leaking from his shoulder. His head swam. He wanted to be sick.

"Fuck your mother, but you are a dead man unless you do as I say!" Kurshin shouted.

The driver floored the accelerator and they shot back onto the road, horns blaring as passing traffic swerved to avoid them.

"Careful," Kurshin warned, jamming the pistol harder into the man's head.

A few miles further they came to a dirt track that led off to the left, toward the river, through a stand of woods. The driver slowed down and pulled off.

"I was just following my orders, comrade," the man said.

"I know," Kurshin reassured him. "All that will happen to you tonight, if you continue to cooperate with me, will be a long walk back to the embassy."

"We can work this out."

Kurshin's stomach was heaving, and the stench of excrement and blood was thick in his nostrils and at the back of his throat.

"Pay attention and you will live."

"I don't want to die. Oh, please ..."

"Tell Baranov what happened here, comrade—" Kurshin said, cutting himself off. *Was* it General Baranov still? Like the old days? "Tell him. Only him, and you will be rewarded. I promise you."

The driver was sobbing.

"Pull over here," Kurshin said. They were in the woods, at least a half mile, maybe farther, from the airport highway.

The Mercedes came to a jerky halt.

"Comrade—" the driver began, and Kurshin shot him in the back of the head. The man was a fly on a kitchen table. Less.

The car bumped off the narrow track and stopped against a short concrete post.

Kurshin reached over the driver, shut off the lights, and then switched off the ignition. The silence was suddenly stifling, and he vomited over everything.

59

MCGARVEY LET MARIA DRIVE the six miles or so down the coast to Estoril. The effort he had expended at Rheinfälls's had pushed him to the verge of collapse. It felt as if he had torn something inside his gut, and he figured he was probably bleeding internally.

Maria kept glancing over at him as she drove, studying his face in the sudden glare of oncoming headlights. It was clear that she was worried.

"You don't look so good," she said.

"Someone is very interested in your gold," he said, ignoring the comment. He was in considerable pain. He didn't need to be reminded of it. "Enough to kill Rheinfälls to stop him from dealing with us."

She nodded thoughtfully. "But not kill us," she added. "The generals—who do you suppose they are? What did he mean?"

"I don't know yet," McGarvey said. "But from what I can gather, as long as Rheinfälls and the others stayed away from the gold, they were okay. The moment we came snooping around, however, these generals made their move."

"They're protecting the gold," Maria said. "At least that much is obvious. But why don't they take it for themselves?"

"Maybe someone is watching them in turn," McGarvey said. "Someone they're afraid of."

She looked at him. "That's why you didn't call Feldmann from the house, isn't it?"

Maria had found the name in an upstairs bedroom, probably Rheinfälls's. It was jotted down on a piece of paper along with a half-dozen others. The paper had been stuffed as a place marker into an old book of German poetry, lying on a nightstand beside the bed. It was the only name they'd found that matched any of the three remaining names Maria had remembered from Major Roebling's forty-six-year-old notebook.

"If they were watching Rheinfälls that closely, it's likely that his line was tapped," McGarvey said. "We'll call him from town."

"So will Feldmann's."

"Yes, but if he gets out immediately he'll beat them."

"You hope," Maria said.

Estoril was a resort town, and traffic was fairly heavy as they drove up to the casino, the one place they were certain to find a telephone at this hour.

"Why don't we just go out to Ponte do Sor tonight?" Maria asked.

They had found it on a map. It was a town about ninety miles inland from Lisbon.

"And do what? Make a house-to-house search? Dig up the fields? The gold could be anywhere. We need more information."

"Feldmann won't cooperate with us."

"Once he finds out that Rheinfälls is dead, and why, I think he will."

"But what if he won't?" Maria insisted. "What if he's gone? Or what if he's already dead?"

McGarvey turned on her. "What do you suggest?" he asked

angrily. "Maybe you want to call your friends to come rescue you! I've taken you far enough—maybe it's time you go it alone! Or have you already contacted them? Are they on their way here now? Am I going to have to watch my back? Are you going to kill me if I get in the way?"

She'd pulled up and parked just down the driveway from the casino entrance. There were a lot of people everywhere. This place was more than a gambling hall. Inside were many restaurants, a movie theater, shops, courtyards, a nightclub, and an art gallery and museum. It drew a crowd from three in the afternoon, when it opened, until three in the morning, when it closed.

For a minute or so she stared straight through the windshield, her hands gripping the steering wheel so tightly that her knuckles had turned white.

"If need be," she said at last, her voice soft, almost gentle.

McGarvey wasn't terribly surprised by her answer."It means that much to you?"

"Yes."

"But you won't explain to me why."

"Not yet," she said, turning to him. "I can't, Kirk. Believe me." She was earnest. "But you can get out now. We've come close enough . . ."

"No," McGarvey said.

"Why? Can you be honest with me?"

"I don't like being shot at," he said tersely, and he got out of the car and started up the walk to the casino entrance.

Maria caught up with him before he went inside, and together they found a bank of telephones in a broad corridor near one of the restaurants. Neither of them had eaten all day, and the smells of food made his stomach rumble.

He dialed Feldmann's number in the nearby town of Cascais. It was answered on the second ring by a man who gave only the telephone number.

"I wish to speak with Herr Dieter Feldmann," McGarvey said in German.

"Yes? Who is calling, please?"

"There's no time, don't you understand? I am calling from Alois Rheinfälls's home. We must speak with Herr Feldmann. At once. It is urgent."

"He is not here this evening."

"Where is he, idiot?" McGarvey said, cupping his hand over the telephone and raising his voice.

"I'm afraid that I cannot say, sir."

"Don't you understand that there's no time?" McGarvey shouted into the phone. "They know, for God's sake! They're already on their way out to Ponte do Sor!"

The man was suddenly flustered. "At the casino . . ."

"Which casino?"

"Why, Estoril, of course . . ."

McGarvey hung up the telephone.

Maria was furious. "If his phone is tapped, everyone will know."

"They already do," McGarvey said, and he went back out into the main hall, to the desk of the *maître de casino* just to the left of the front entrance, leaving Maria standing in the corridor.

The manager of the casino was in livery, distinctive red piping on the broad lapels of his formal coat. "May I be of some assistance?" he asked imperiously.

"We have been told that Herr Feldmann is here this evening," McGarvey said, palming a thousand-escudo note and laying his hand on the counter.

The *maître de casino* took it. "Yes, I believe I saw him."

"We must speak with him. It is a matter of some urgency."

The man picked up the house phone. "Who may I say wishes to speak with him?"

"We have come from Herr Rheinfälls."

"Yes, I see," the manager said. He spoke softly into the telephone, passing the instructions to someone, and then he hung up. "Herr Feldmann will be given the message."

"Thank you," McGarvey said, and he stepped aside to wait.

Maria came across the entry hall. "Is he here?" she asked.

McGarvey looked back the way she had come, then nodded. "He is being given a message. What kept you?"

"The loo," she said.

"Oh."

A few minutes later a very old man with white hair and blue-veined skin, his back bent in a permanent stoop, came shuffling across the entry hall. He was in evening dress.

McGarvey and Maria intercepted him before he reached the manager's desk. "Herr Feldmann?" McGarvey asked.

The old man looked up at him, his shrewd eyes narrowing. "Do I know you? Was it you who called me from my dinner?"

"Alois Rhienfälls is dead," McGarvey said. "And now it's extremely urgent that we talk."

Feldmann was rocked by the news. His thin, bloodless lips moved but he said nothing.

"We believe it's the generals," McGarvey continued. "They've finally decided to move."

"Move?" Feldmann asked. He looked at Maria.

"I believe they're on their way out to Ponte do Sor this minute."

Again the old man was stunned. "Impossible," he breathed. "They, of all people, would never dare." He shook his head. "No."

"It's true," McGarvey said. "Rheinfälls is dead. If you don't believe me, telephone his home."

Feldmann hurried over to the manager's desk and made a telephone call. As he waited for the connection to be made, he turned and looked at McGarvey and Maria. After a full minute he hung up. He said something to the manager, and then came back.

"There is no answer, but it means nothing."

"It means he is dead, Herr Feldmann," McGarvey said. "We just came from there. Everyone on his staff was murdered as well."

Feldmann ran a hand across his eyes. "It's just that it's so hard to believe . . . after all this time." He looked up, almost pleading. "There's no reason. Not now."

McGarvey took the man by the arm. "We must talk. Now, before it's too late."

"Too late?"

"They'll kill you next."

"I'll run again."

"Where?" McGarvey asked. "There is no place left, Herr Feldmann. The world has become far too small in the last forty-six years."

Again the old man ran a hand across his eyes. When he looked up, there was a new, warier expression on his face. "Who are you? What do you want of me? How do I know that you are telling me the truth?"

"Rheinfälls told me that the gold was cursed. And before he died he told me that it was kept at Ponte do Sor."

"Who are you?" the old man demanded.

The *maître de casino* was watching them. So were some of the others on the staff. They were attracting too much attention here.

"Let's talk outside," McGarvey suggested.

Feldmann tried to pull away. "No."

"Goddamnit, if you want to die like the rest of them, it's your choice. But I'm an American. CIA. And I'm here to try to help you. I'm trying to straighten out this mess so that the killings will finally stop."

"I don't believe you."

"We've been to see Hesse. And we have Major Roebling's notebook from the U-boat off the coast of Argentina. We've seen Rainer Mossberg's testimony. Goddamnit, we've got most of it already. We'll get the rest without you if you don't want to help. But we're also trying to save your life."

Feldmann was overwhelmed. It was as if they'd placed a hundred-pound weight on his frail shoulders; his stoop had become more pronounced, and his legs seemed ready to buckle. "The castle," he said softly. "It's there, where we put it beginning in 1941. All of it. No one has touched so much as a gram of it."

Maria's eyes were shining. She'd heard every word.

"The ledger is there too. No one touched it. We were all afraid to. You understand."

"The ledger—it's still with the gold?" McGarvey asked, not understanding, but afraid if he said so the old man would refuse to go on.

"Yes, of course," Feldmann said, giving McGarvey an odd look. "It's what this is all about. I thought that you—" All of a sudden the old man stiffened and what little color there had been in his face drained away.

"Kirk!" Maria cried.

McGarvey turned. Two men dressed in well-tailored business suits had come in the front entrance. They stood a few feet away from each other, completely neutral expressions on their faces, their stance loose, professional. Each of them held a large-caliber, silenced pistol trained in McGarvey's direction. They were less than twenty feet away. At that range they could not miss.

"Please step away from Herr Feldmann," one of them said. His English was nearly perfect. But McGarvey could still hear a faint accent. German.

"The generals sent you," McGarvey said.

"Step to the side, sir. We have no wish to cause you any harm."

Activity in the broad entry hall was gradually coming to a complete standstill. There were at least a dozen people standing around, some of them with cocktails or glasses of champagne. They'd been talking, but when it began to register that something was happening near the front door, that men with guns had actually entered the casino, a hush fell over the hall.

They could hear the muted hum of conversation from the gaming rooms to the rear of the building, and from the restaurants upstairs.

The *maître de casino* behind his desk about ten feet to McGarvey's right, was speaking urgently into the telephone. The two armed men totally ignored him.

"If I refuse?" McGarvey asked calmly.

"Then we will have to destroy you," one of them said. They were ordinary-looking men. Nothing to distinguish them. Yet their actions and choice of words were chilling. Destroy, not shoot or kill. Military.

"Perhaps I already know too much," McGarvey said. "Perhaps others do as well. Perhaps this can no longer be contained."

One of the men began moving slowly to the side, so that unless the old man moved directly behind McGarvey, he would have a good shooting angle on Feldmann.

A couple came in the front doors and passed the two gunmen without noticing what was going on. They were so intent on each other that they passed through the hall and into the gaming room without once looking around.

"Consider," McGarvey said. "If that's the case, there would be no reason to continue the killing."

"You fucking Nazis!" Maria screamed suddenly, and she fired a single shot that struck one of the men in the side.

Instant pandemonium broke out in the entry hall, people

bolting in panic, crawling over each other in a mad effort to get out of the line of fire.

Feldmann let out a cry and lurched to the left.

"No!" McGarvey shouted, diving to the right and shoving Maria to the side, her second shot going wide.

Both men fired rapidly, hitting Feldmann at least five times before they turned and hurried toward the doors.

Maria jerked away from McGarvey, but before she could fire again he grabbed her gun hand and bodily pulled her around.

She turned on him. "Bastard!" she screeched, spittle flying from her mouth. "You bastard! You bastard!"

"Enough!" McGarvey shouted, wrenching the gun out of her hand.

"Goddamn you!" she screamed, coming at him.

He stepped back and slapped her across the face, stopping her in her tracks.

"They would have killed us both, you stupid fool," McGarvey told her.

Her eyes were glazed and she was shaking in rage. Feldmann was dead, there was no doubt about it. The manager was staring at McGarvey, the telephone still to his ear, his eyes wide.

McGarvey took Maria by the arm and unhurriedly led her across to the doors, outside, and down the walk to their car. He could hear sirens in the distance, and someone was shouting at them from the casino, but no one came out to stop them. Nor did anyone think to give pursuit as they got into the car, McGarvey driving this time, and took off into the night.

60

KURSHIN STOOD BESIDE THE bed in the Hotel Lisboa Penta, the telephone pressed tightly to his ear as he listened to the intermittent ringing. Ten rings now without answer.

Of the eleven other names in the notebook he'd stolen from the woman's hotel room in Argentina, he'd found only three of them here in the Lisbon area. Alois Rheinfälls, Dieter Feldmann, and Karl Sikorsky.

He willed Rheinfälls to answer the telephone now. Someone who would listen to him. Someone who would give him the information that he needed.

This time he was going to win, because this time he was immortal. He smiled to himself as he listened to the distant phone continue to ring.

Hadn't that been proved in the high valley in Iran against

McGarvey, the Iranian air force, and SAVAK? All of them together had not been able to defeat him.

Hadn't it been proved again in the mountains against Colonel Berezin, and against the mountains themselves?

And tonight at the airport. The three KGB officers who'd been sent to arrest him had failed. He could not be touched. He was invincible.

Baranov would understand. And so would McGarvey. They were the only two men for him.

He hung up the telephone, waited a moment, and then picked it up again. When he had an outside line he dialed Dieter Feldmann's number in Cascais.

Finding out where McGarvey and the woman were staying had been child's play. McGarvey had *wanted* to be found. It was as if the man were taunting him: "Here I am, Arkasha. Come and get me, Arkasha. I am waiting for you, Arkasha."

The telephone at the Feldmann villa on the coast began to ring.

It had also not been difficult to find out which room was McGarvey's and to let himself in. He'd been disappointed, though not very surprised, that they were not here. But they had not been gone very long. He could still smell McGarvey's presence here. The soapy, deodorized smells that all Americans left behind lingered in the air, on the pillowcases and sheets, and on the towels in the bathroom.

The telephone rang a second time.

He and the Argentinian bitch were here in Portugal to find the gold that the Nazis had hidden. The RSHA major, Walther Roebling, had thought he was playing a trick on the U-boat's crew, but in the end the cruel trick had been played on him as well. Kurshin wondered what had happened to the man. Had he gone down with the submarine after all?

The telephone was answered on the third ring by a man who, sounding very flustered, gave only the telephone number. His Portuguese had a heavy German accent, and Kurshin easily switched to that language.

"Hello, I wish to speak with Herr Feldmann, please," Kurshin said respectfully.

"He is gone. They are all gone, including Rheinfälls."

"Gone?" Kurshin asked. "Gone where?"

"The police will have to be called ..."

"What has happened?"

"But they won't be able to help, of course."

"Where is Herr Feldmann, please? I am calling for Sikorsky."

"Herr Sikorsky is there?" the man shouted.

"Yes, of course. I am with him now. We had to run. But where have the others gone?"

"I don't know. After the American called, everything has been so confused. No one will answer at the casino."

After the American called.

Kurshin's grip tightened on the telephone and his hip began to throb painfully. "Where have they gone?" he demanded.

"The castle," the man shouted raggedly.

"Where?"

"Ponte do Sor! The castle! The gold! Everything is ruined now ..."

It had taken Chaim Landau nearly ten minutes to track down the two men who'd arrived in Portugal that afternoon from Tel Aviv. He'd been told they'd left the embassy at six, which they had, but he didn't find out immediately that they had returned and were in the basement.

He was out of breath by the time he hit the bottom of the stairs and raced to the security door at the end of the corridor. He prodded the buzzer.

Landau was a special operations case officer, a desk man, not a field agent. His job, among other things, was to make connections between widely disparate facts and data, and from them draw some kind of meaningful conclusions.

One source of his raw data was ongoing projects that the Mossad maintained worldwide. If and when one of these going "concerns," as they were called, wound up in Portugal, it was also his job to act as contact, confidant, and baby-sitter.

One of those "concerns" had just telephoned, giving Landau the thing that the two men had come all the way from Tel Aviv to get.

The window in the door slid back. "Are they here?" he asked.

"Yes," the Lisbon chief of station, Mordechai Lavon, said, unlocking the door. "It's Landau," he called to someone else inside.

Landau stepped into the embassy's safe zone. "She just called." All the offices here were protected from any sort of surveillance, including electronic. They were mostly used for Mossad or

Aman—Israeli military intelligence—operations, but on occasion the Israeli ambassador to Portugal held top-level conferences down here.

Portugal, like Argentina, had always been a safe haven for Nazis.

"In there," Lavon said, motioning to the conference room across the corridor.

Mossad officers Lev Potak and Abraham Liebowitz were studying a map of Portugal when Landau and Lavon came in.

"She called," Landau said.

Potok looked up, a smile on his craggy, weatherbeaten face. "Yes? How long ago was this, Chaim?"

"Ten minutes."

"And?" Potok prompted. Liebowitz was grinning.

"They're on their way out to Ponte do Sor. It's a small town of maybe ten thousand people. About a hundred fifty klicks inland."

"They?" Potok asked. "Kirk McGarvey is here with her?"

"Yes. She was calling from the casino at Estoril. She said she would try to talk him out of it, but she didn't think she could stop him, short of killing him."

Potok suppressed a smile. "What else?"

"There's been a shooting. Outside of Estoril. A man named Rheinfälls. Evidently he was assassinated as the woman and McGarvey were speaking with him."

Potok turned to the chief of station. "Do we know this Rheinfälls?"

"One of the German recluses," Lavon said. "Don't know much about him except that he has plenty of money but very few friends. He lives in a big compound with some hired German muscle. Probably former BND."

"Are the police involved yet?" Potok asked Landau.

"Unknown. Apparently she had only a minute to talk, because she hung up abruptly. But she kept repeating Ponte do Sor. And, 'It's there.'"

"We'll have to do something about this American, first," the chief of station said.

"No," Potok replied sharply. "I've worked with him before. He's a good man. Whatever he's doing in this business will only be to our benefit."

"How can you be so sure, Lev?" Lavon asked.

"I'm sure," Potok said. "The man saved my life, for starters. And I can't even begin to tell you what he did for Israel."

Lavon and Landau were both impressed. Potok was from Tel Aviv. His opinions carried a lot of weight.

"How do we get out to this Ponte do Sor?" Potok asked.

"Car. I'll drive you," Landau said.

"We'll leave immediately. You'd better carry a gun."

"Yes, sir," Landau said. "But may I ask what the 'it' is that she was talking about?"

"Might be nothing at all," Potok said oddly. "It's something she and a few of her friends have been working on for a very long time. Friends of Israel. We all thought it was fiction, and it probably is. But we'll check on it just the same."

"Yes, sir." Landau had the good sense not to ask the next, obvious question: If it was fiction, why had Tel Aviv sent out two of its top agents?

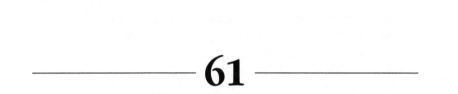

61

THE CASTLE WAS WELL south of the town of Ponte do Sor, and dominated the only hill for miles around. The moon was nearly full, and the night was so bright that the ramparts and spires of the sprawling medieval pile looked like something out of a Disney fantasy. McGarvey half expected to see Crusaders massing in the valley, ready to attack, while dark-skinned Moors, armed with longbows, pots of boiling oil, and piles of rocks were making ready for the siege.

Maria had said very little on the long drive out, but as McGarvey turned off the main highway and started the mile or so up the secondary road to the castle itself, she began to shiver, almost violently.

"Do you want to wait until morning?" McGarvey asked. He felt terrible himself. The wound in his side ached all the way up to his armpit, and he'd found himself drifting off for seconds at a time with no conscious recollection of where he was or how he got there.

"No," she mumbled tersely.

The road began to climb through a dense grove of olive trees that heightened the fantastical illusion. The gnarled trees looked like old men, hunched over, pointing the way in the darkness, wizards showing them the path to hell. Soldiers. The Crusaders, now that they were in among them.

"Is it really here, Kirk?" she asked in a small, awed voice. "I mean, after all this time."

"Unless they were lying to us," McGarvey said. But they hadn't been lying. He'd heard certainty in their voices. The certainty bred by fear.

The hill steepened, and the road began to switch back on itself, once, twice, and a third time, and then their headlights flashed across the massive iron gate just at the crest. It was flanked on one side by what appeared to be a Victorian-style carriage house, and on the other by a stout two-story gatekeeper's house made of gray stone with a slate roof. Windowboxes filled with flowers sat beneath leaded windows that were dark now. A bicycle leaned against a stone wall to one side of the house; beyond it they could see a well-tended garden. Even in February things grew here.

McGarvey switched off the headlights but left the engine running. He got out of the car and, glancing across at the still dark gatehouse, walked the final twenty-five yards up the driveway to the iron gate.

A sign on the gate advised that the Castelo de Oro was open to visitors from 9:00 A.M. until sunset, Tuesday through Saturday; from 10:00 A.M. until 5:00 P.M. Sunday; and closed on Monday. Admission was fifteen escudos.

It was a museum! Either everything they had been told was a lie, or this was a massive joke that the Germans had played on the world. Even the name—Castle of Gold—was a joke.

The main gate was locked, but a smaller gate to one side was not. When McGarvey tested the latch, it swung open noisily.

"*Was ist los?*" a man shouted from the gatehouse.

McGarvey turned around as the beam of a flashlight caught him in the face. He raised a hand to shield his eyes.

"*Wer ist das?*" the man shouted. He was at a second-story window.

"I have come from Herr Rheinfälls and Herr Feldmann," McGarvey said, walking back toward the house.

"Yes? Who are these people? What are you doing here at this hour?"

"I wish to enter the castle," McGarvey called up to the man.

"Impossible. You must return in the morning. At ten o'clock."

"But I must get in tonight," McGarvey said. "Now. It is very important."

"The rules," the man shouted angrily. "You may not enter the museum until morning."

Maria had left the car and had moved silently around to the side of the house, out of the caretaker's sight. Evidently he'd not seen her. McGarvey caught a stray glint of light reflecting from the blade of her knife as she cut the telephone line. Whatever happened here tonight, no one would be able to call for help.

"Go away!" the man shouted.

Maria came back to the front of the house and glanced up at the caretaker as McGarvey returned to the car and shut off the engine. He pocketed the keys.

"The small gate is open," he told her.

"We don't know our way around," she said. "We could stumble around in there for weeks without finding . . . what we came for."

"See here!" the caretaker called out.

They started for the gate.

"Come back!" the man yelled at them. "You mustn't go in there. It is against the rules. I will call the police."

"As soon as he finds out that the telephone isn't working, he'll get dressed and come after us," McGarvey said, going through the gate.

The caretaker was bleating something, but then he ducked back inside.

As they crossed the broad courtyard, their shoes crunching on the white gravel, McGarvey could see that the castle had been built in different stages throughout the centuries, some of the newer sections probably added not more than a hundred years ago.

The older sections of the structure were in poor condition, while the other parts looked almost habitable. He figured that he might not have been far off, imagining Moors defending these ramparts against the Crusaders. The Moors had probably been the first occupants.

They'd made it nearly to the base of the broad marble stairs that led up to the entry veranda, fronting one of the newer sections, when the gatekeeper came running across the courtyard after them. He'd thrown a robe over his pajamas and put tall rubber boots on his bare feet. He was armed with a ten-gauge double-barreled shotgun in one hand and a flashlight in the other.

"You must leave now or I will shoot you," the man shouted. He was out of breath, short and rotund. McGarvey figured him to be in his late fifties or early sixties.

"All right," McGarvey said reasonably. "If you insist." He and Maria started back. As they came even with the caretaker, the man started to swing around, following them with the big shotgun.

McGarvey reached out and gently took the gun from him. The hammers hadn't been cocked.

The caretaker cried out in alarm, and he stepped back and raised his hands over his head, the beam of the flashlight dancing crazily into the sky.

"Put your hands down, mein Herr," McGarvey said with a smile. "No one is going to harm you." He cracked the shotgun and pulled out the two shells. They were very old, and apparently they'd gotten wet at some point. He doubted that they would fire. Security was terribly lax. Too lax, he wondered, for this to be the repository for the gold? Or was this merely another ruse to throw off suspicion? He put the gun down.

"What do you want here?" the gatekeeper asked, his voice cracking.

"We want to see the castle."

"In the morning," the older man said nervously.

McGarvey smiled reassuringly. "You get a lot of visitors here?"

The gatekeeper nodded uncertainly. "In the tourist season there are many people."

"And they are allowed to go anywhere within the castle?"

"Ach, no, of course not. There are guided tours."

"Then there are parts of the castle that are forbidden to the public?"

"Of course."

"Because it would be too dangerous?" McGarvey suggested.

"Yes, up in the towers," the man said, glancing up.

Crumbling towers rose above the Moorish-looking section of the castle.

"And elsewhere?"

"Yes."

"Where?"

The gatekeeper seemed suddenly uncomfortable. "The crypts," he said. "It is a ... sacrilege."

"In the dungeons?" Maria asked.

"The crypts, Fräulein," the old man corrected. "Where there are many bodies. The Moors, the Christians and ..."

"Yes?" Maria prompted.

"And ... the Jews."

"What Jews?"

"From the Inquisition. Many of the bodies were brought here for burial."

"Is that why the Germans bought this castle?" Maria asked sharply. "Is it some kind of a joke?"

The gatekeeper said nothing.

"Show us," McGarvey said.

"Show you what?" the old man squeaked.

"The crypts. We would like to see them now."

"It is forbidden."

"You may tell everyone that a very large gun was held to your head. You had no choice."

Still the gatekeeper hesitated.

McGarvey stepped aside. *"Macht schnell, bitte."*

The old man held back a moment longer, but then headed toward what appeared to be a maintenance road that led from the courtyard behind the main keep and ran toward the older sections of the castle.

They came to a stop in front of one of the sections, before a heavy iron door. The gatekeeper produced a ring of keys from beneath his robe, unlocked the door, and ponderously swung it open on rusting hinges.

Dark stairs led down into the bowels of what, the gatekeeper explained, had been the original keep built in the eleventh century. In another, even more savage age.

The gatekeeper did something with a black iron valve on the wall, and immediately they could smell gas. A second later a flame winked into life, and the gatekeeper stepped back, extinguishing the scratch lighter hanging from a thong on the wall. Another gas light popped to life twenty feet down the stairs. Then a second farther down, and a third, and more, all the way down to the bottom.

The gas lights did little to expel the odors of cold and extreme damp from below. The stairs in some places glistened, and there were puddles on others. At the bottom, water dripped from the walls.

"Why is it so wet down here?" McGarvey asked as they descended. He figured they were now two hundred feet, perhaps a little more, beneath the courtyard.

"We're beneath the castle reservoir. One million liters. In the old days they could hold out against seige forever."

"You mean that we're under water here?" Maria asked.

"Yes, just that, Fräulein," the old man said. "If the walls were to spring a major leak anywhere down here, the rest would crumble and all of this would flood immediately. It is another reason the public is not allowed down here. It is too dangerous."

The tunnel was so low that even the old man had to stoop slightly to avoid cracking his head on the curved ceiling. It led at a slight slope down into the heart of the hill for as far as they could see, the small gas flames fading to a dim blur in the distance.

Fifty feet from the stairs they came to an offshoot tunnel blocked by a massive cast-iron gate.

"The crypts begin here," the old man said uncomfortably.

"Do you have the keys?" McGarvey asked, fingering the thick, square lock.

The gatekeeper handed him the big key ring. "The black key with the cross."

McGarvey located that key among the dozens on the ring and unlocked the heavy gate, pushing it inward. The interior of the tomb was in total darkness. The gatekeeper gave him the flashlight. McGarvey switched it on and shined it inside.

The room was long, and much wider than the tunnel. Stone coffins were placed in a dozen niches cut into the walls.

"Who is buried here?" Maria asked in a hushed voice.

"The Moors just here," the gatekeeper said. "The Crusaders are farther down the main tunnel."

"What about the Jews?"

"Even farther."

"Let's go there," she said.

"It is too dangerous, Fräulein," the old man protested.

"We'll do as the lady wants," McGarvey said. It would be the last of the monstrous joke. It would be exactly where Rheinfälls and his cronies would bury the gold. He could almost hear them laughing about it down here, their coarse jokes echoing off the stone walls.

Every ten or fifteen yards they passed another gate, behind which the gatekeeper said were other stone coffins. There were more than a thousand bodies entombed down here, he told them.

The farther they went, the narrower the tunnel became and the lower the ceiling dropped. At first McGarvey thought it was just an optical illusion, until he realized that he had to bend over almost double in order to walk. It was becoming painful physically, as well as mentally disturbing. He didn't like this at all. The tunnel ceiling couldn't be more than four feet high, and they had descended continuously since the stairs, so that by now he figured they had to be more than three hundred feet below the surface.

"Here," the old man finally said when they had come at least another five hundred yards. Something was different here. For a second or two McGarvey couldn't say exactly why, until it came to him all at once.

He touched the metal gate. "Steel," he said half to himself. He looked down the tunnel. There were other gates for at least another hundred yards. He walked to the next one in line. Here the gates were not made of black cast iron as they had been in the other sections of the tunnel. These were made of steel, rusting steel.

"What is it?" Maria asked.

"Steel," McGarvey said to the gatekeeper. "This part of the tunnel is very new. Maybe even this century."

"It was built in the early thirties, I think," the old man said after a long silence.

"Dios," Maria said softly. "If there are Jews buried here, they were killed by the Nazis."

The gatekeeper stepped back a pace. But there wasn't much room to move in the tunnel.

McGarvey opened one of the gates and stepped inside. The coffins here appeared to be made of granite. There were names on some of them, numbers and dates or cryptic symbols on others. The coffins had been chipped and stained by weather to make them appear very old. He figured they'd been constructed at the same time the Nazis had built the extension to the tunnel. There had to be a dozen in this vault alone.

Maria stepped in behind him. "It's here," she said in awe. "It's really here."

"Hold this," McGarvey said, handing her the flashlight. He put his back to one of the coffin lids. At first it wouldn't budge, and he pushed even harder, knowing that he was doing more damage to himself. But the lid finally began to move.

Maria helped him, and when the lid was open a foot or more she shined the light inside.

There were rags. Old, dirty rags. Were they looking at the clothing draped on the disintegrated remains of a corpse? Maria reached in and pulled the rags away. Underneath was wooden planking, the boards damp and nearly rotted through.

McGarvey pulled away some of the wood with his fingers, and then more, suddenly revealing what the coffin really held.

The flashlight reflected brightly off gold bars packed tightly into the coffin, each of them stamped with a long serial number below the German eagle.

"It's here," Maria said softly. She reached out to touch the gold, but she could not make her fingers come closer than a few inches.

"I wasn't sure what we would find," McGarvey said. He too was impressed, and deeply moved. The lives lost, the human suffering, the pain and anguish that this one coffin filled with gold represented—it was horrible to contemplate. But there was more here. Millions of dollars. Billions of dollars.

Maria turned away from the coffin. She went back out into the tunnel. "There are dozens of gates," she said.

In the darkness, McGarvey pulled away more wood to make certain the coffin was filled with gold. His fingers touched a small package wrapped in oiled paper. He withdrew it, and turned so that he could hold it up to the dim light filtering through the door into the tomb. It was a thick wad of papers.

The top sheet was stamped with a swastika above the initials R.S.H.A., the Nazi secret intelligence service.

A list of some sort started beneath that legend. He couldn't quite make it out in the darkness.

"Kirk!" Maria cried. "He's gone ..."

All the gas lights in the tunnel went out. Maria screamed. Before McGarvey could reach the door, her flashlight went out.

"Maria!" he shouted.

A man began to laugh. He was some distance down the tunnel, the sound of his laughter distorted by echoes. But McGarvey knew who it was.

There could be no mistake.

"Kurshin!" he yelled at the top of his lungs. "Kurshin!"

62

THEY HAD SEEN THE TAILLIGHTS well ahead of them turn off the main highway, but it wasn't until they came to the turn themselves that they realized the other car was heading up to the castle.

"This is it," Lev Potok said sharply. "It has to be." A few miles farther to the east was the town of Ponte do Sor. He'd worried all the way from Lisbon about finding where McGarvey and the woman had gone. But this had to be the place.

They'd passed the access road, so Landau had to back up to it. "Are you sure about this?"

"No, but unless you've got a better idea, we'll try this first," Potok said. "Shut off your lights."

Landau flipped off the headlights, the road momentarily disappearing. But almost immediately they could see perfectly well in the bright moonlight. "Up there," he said.

The other car was already near the top of the hill. They could see its headlights flashing through the olive trees, but in the next moment the lights disappeared.

"Where'd they go?" Liebowitz asked from the back seat.

"He's still there," Potok said, taking out his pistol and checking its action. "He shut off his headlights too."

"Did they spot us?" Laundau asked.

"Probably."

"Is it McGarvey?" Liebowitz asked.

"I don't think so. He had too big a head start on us."

"Then, who?"

"Whoever it was who killed the German," Potok said.

"Here to protect the gold from discovery," Liebowitz said.

"Gold?" Landau asked.

"Drive," Potok ordered.

McGarvey, his gun in hand, groped his way silently in the absolute darkness to the doorway. He paused, his left hand brushing the wet stone wall, listening for a sound, any sound out in the tunnel. Somewhere he could hear water dripping, and in the distance he thought he heard an extremely faint hissing noise. But he couldn't be certain about that.

"Maria?" he called softly. "Are you all right?"

Kurshin laughed again, this time closer. But still it was almost impossible to tell just how far away he was. Sounds were very distorted in the narrow tunnel.

McGarvey had to fight down a rising panic that threatened to blot out all reason and sanity. He was caught now, deep underground in a crypt. A realm of the dead, not the living.

"Is she with you?" he called.

"She's here, McGarvey," Kurshin said. His voice sounded odd, somehow disjointed.

"Let her go, Arkasha. This is just between you and me now."

"No, she will die here with you," Kurshin said. He laughed again, and it sounded to McGarvey as if the man couldn't help himself. As if the laugh had been involuntary. Had he become unhinged? Was he now insane? The thought was chilling.

"What's the point?" McGarvey asked. "Baranov is dead, Didenko has been arrested. There is nowhere for you to go."

"Exactly," Kurshin said, laughing again.

"No one wants you, Arkasha," McGarvey said, carefully edging his way around the steel gate.

"That no longer matters . . ."

"Even if you manage to kill us tonight, and get out of here, then what?"

"I don't care."

"But you should, Arkasha," McGarvey said, moving into position so that he could extend his gun hand out into the tunnel.

"No," Kurshin shouted, and he laughed, this time the sound high-pitched, almost animal-like in its intensity.

"You have the skills, and I'm certain you have the money, to hide yourself somewhere. Mexico, maybe. Cuba. Somewhere in Russia, perhaps. Siberia. But then what, Arkasha?"

"It doesn't matter, I tell you. Once you are dead, nothing will matter."

"What then, Arkasha?" McGarvey called softly. "How long before you crack? Before you can no longer stand the lack of purpose? How long, Arkasha, before you put the barrel of your gun into your mouth and pull the trigger?"

Kurshin laughed.

"Why not do it now, Arkasha? Save us the trouble."

"Die!" Kurshin screamed.

McGarvey reached out into the tunnel and cocked the hammer of his pistol, the noise loud in the darkness. Kurshin could not have missed hearing it and understanding what it was.

Hans Meitner and Lötti Jodl hurried across the gravel courtyard of the castle, their guns drawn. Jodl was leaving a trail of blood from the gunshot wound in his side. Both men were professionals. Both had been lured away from positions with the BND, West Germany's secret intelligence service, to work for the generals, lured by a rate of pay three times what they had received for their government service.

Neither of them had met the elusive "generals," of course. As far as they knew, none of the foot soldiers had. They had been interviewed and hired by a law firm in Stuttgart. It was the law firm to which they made their monthly reports, and from which they received their assignments.

This outbreak was a bad one. The worst of all. The opposition had finally penetrated the silence the old fools had maintained for nearly thirteen years.

They should have been killed in the beginning. But as the man who had hired them said: "You will be ordered to kill only under the most extreme circumstances, gentlemen. Only at such time as our true aim is compromised or threatened."

It had happened, finally. The generals' worse fears had come true, and now it was up to Meitner and Jodl to contain the terrible secret once and for all.

They hurried around to the open door that led down into the crypts, hesitated a moment, then continued to the far side of the Moorish keep. There Jodl pried the cap off a six-inch-diameter clay pipe that jutted some two feet out of the ground.

Meitner opened the satchel he'd been carrying and took out the single stick of dynamite, the delay fuse, and a roll of black tape.

Their orders had come by telephone. Two words. No mistaking their meaning.

"Destroy it."

Kurshin fired three times in rapid succession, the bullets ricocheting off the stone walls and ceiling in long, ragged sparks. But the muzzle flashes marked his position.

McGarvey fired twice, adjusting his pattern right to left against the probability the man had moved the instant he fired.

Kurshin fired back, this time the bullet smacking into the stone wall barely an inch from McGarvey's face, stone chips nearly blinding him in one eye. He had to pull back.

The Russian was shooting an automatic. Probably a Makarov or even a TK by the sound of it. Nine shots, if he had started with a full clip and one round in the firing chamber. And if he hadn't brought extra ammunition with him.

"You won't get out of here alive, Arkasha," McGarvey called softly. He immediately dropped down on all fours and silently crawled out into the tunnel, flattening himself against the far wall.

Kurshin fired twice more, both shots high and to the left.

McGarvey jumped up, fired once to the left of where he'd seen the muzzle flashes, once to the right, and once directly at them, and then dropped back down.

Kurshin cried out and fired three more times, wildly. An instant later there was a distinctive click as the hammer slapped home on an empty firing chamber.

"Game over," McGarvey said, getting to his feet. He had three bullets left in his own gun. One would be enough.

He started forward, almost immediately stumbling into something lying on the floor. Even before bending down to feel with his hands, he knew *what* it was; but he wanted to find out *who* it was. He felt for the face and neck, fearing that it would be Maria. But it was the caretaker. He could feel the rough skin, and the much larger features. The back of the skull was wet and mushy.

"You son of a bitch," McGarvey muttered. He heard something metallic clatter to the floor a few feet ahead. For a split second he didn't know what it could be, but suddenly it came to him.

The empty clip from Kurshin's gun. The man was reloading.

McGarvey fired once from where he crouched, and a second time as he got to his feet. Then he charged blindly down the tunnel, slamming into the Russian within ten feet.

Both of them went crashing backward off the rock wall to the wet floor, blood spurting all over McGarvey's face from a wound just beneath Kurshin's left collarbone.

McGarvey's right shoulder smashed into the rock, his hand went numb for a moment, and his pistol slipped out of his grip. He held Kurshin's gun hand off with his left, and with his right he dug into the Russian's neck, trying with everything in his power to rip out the man's throat.

The beam of a flashlight suddenly filled the tunnel with light.

"Kirk!" Maria screamed from behind him.

McGarvey lifted Kurshin's head from the stone floor and smashed it back down. He pulled it up again, and smashed it against the unyielding floor. And again, and again, all the while Maria screaming something behind him.

As life faded from Kurshin's eyes the man's trigger finger jerked reflexively. His pistol fired, sending a long, jagged spark down the tunnel.

McGarvey was just pulling back when, from the darkness a long way down the tunnel, the spark suddenly blossomed and built into a huge fireball that raced along the wall below the gas line toward them.

* * *

Landau had pulled up behind a red Mercedes with diplomatic plates, and another car, one with a rental company sticker on the trunk lid, parked in front of the gatekeeper's house. A second Mercedes was parked just off the road in the woods, nose out, ready for a quick escape.

No one was around, but a small access gate was open in the tall fence.

"Inside," Potok said, leading the way.

They raced across the broad courtyard to the base of the stairs up to the main entry.

There they found the shotgun lying in the gravel.

Landau started up the stairs, but Liebowitz headed around toward the back.

"Here!" he called from a few yards away. He bent down and picked up two shotgun shells.

The three of them hurried the rest of the way to the Moorish keep, spotting the open door as soon as they rounded the corner.

There was a deep-throated rumble, and a sheet of flame roared out of the doorway.

Meitner stood directly over the clay pipe, holding the stick of dynamite just above the black opening as he set the delay fuse.

Jodl was directly behind him, looking over his shoulder.

They both heard the ominous rumble from below, and Meitner started to say something. A ball of flame raced up from below, roaring out of the clay pipe, blinding him at the same instant it ignited the dynamite in his hand. . . .

McGarvey had managed to scramble back to where Maria crouched by a gate to one of the crypts and cover her with his body as the tremendous ball of fire erupted through the tunnel.

The heat was so intense for a moment that it began to melt the back of his jacket, and scorched most of the hair off the back of his head.

An instant later there was a huge explosion from somewhere far above them, and the ceiling began to come down. Water was spraying everywhere.

Not like this, the single thought crystallized in McGarvey's head. After everything in his life, all the close calls, all the near misses, he was not going to die like this, buried in a tunnel.

There was one thing left for him to do. Something he'd been deciding now for several years. Something inevitable.

He rolled away from Maria and looked down the tunnel as he got up. Water was flowing in from a dozen different breaches along the walls and ceiling, but there was still light from as many gas flames.

"We've got to get out of here," he shouted, reaching back and dragging Maria to her feet.

She collapsed against him. "I can't," she cried breathlessly. "My leg."

Without hesitation McGarvey slung her over his shoulder, the effort nearly causing him to black out.

Water was rising steadily in the tunnel, up over his knees by the time he had slogged his way past where the gatekeeper's body was floating. The gas flames were dying out now, and within seconds the tunnel would be in absolute darkness again.

McGarvey didn't know if he could take much more of it. He could feel panic building up, ready to explode inside him, destroying his will to live.

Maria was crying something in his ear, but he couldn't make it out. There was nothing left for him but to continue. If he was going to die here, he would die. But he would be moving when the end came.

The last of the lights faded as the water came up to his chest. The tunnel ceiling was higher here, so he could stand up taller.

But it was too late. He could not go much farther.

He stumbled on something, falling forward into the water. For a moment he thought he might be seeing lights now. But that was impossible.

Maria was gone, suddenly, and there were hands on his arms. He was being dragged upward, his feet and legs bumping up the stairs.

"McGarvey! McGarvey!" Potok was shouting at him.

Then nothing.

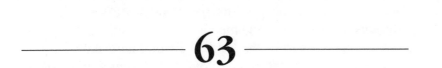

63

THE SUN WAS SHINING brightly through the windows of McGarvey's Lisbon hospital room ten days later when Lev Potok walked in, an oddly wistful smile on his craggy features. He closed the door before he came over to the bed.

"How are you doing, Kirk?" He was dressed in khakis and soft-soled desert boots. He looked very military, very competent.

"Better," McGarvey said. "I'll be out of here in a few days." The burns on his neck and scalp had been second and third degree, but the pain had finally begun to fade. He no longer had to take morphine.

"That's what I was told," Potok said. "Then what?"

"Back to the States, I think. For a while at least."

"Have you briefed your government yet?"

"About what?"

"What you found in the crypt."

"No," McGarvey said after a moment. "I don't know what I found, actually. Some gold the Nazis hid." He smiled wanly. "Besides, I wasn't on assignment."

"You found a part of the ledger," Potok said evenly.

McGarvey looked at him. "I don't know what you're talking about."

"The list you took from one of the coffins. I found it on you after I dragged you out of the tunnel."

McGarvey remembered it now. "I never got a chance to look at it."

"And Maria never explained it to . . ." Potok shook his head. "But then, she never knew."

"Explain what, Lev?" McGarvey asked. "What the hell was it all about? It was more than just Nazi treasure."

Potok nodded. "The Germans, in their fanatical need to keep meticulous records, went one step too far," he said. "There's gold there, a lot of it, that came from the property of Jews. From their bodies."

"I guessed that much."

"Each bar of gold is stamped with a serial number."

"Yes . . ." McGarvey said, and then he had it. The curse, Rhein-fälls had called it. And so had Maria's father.

Potok could see that he had figured it out, but he went on. "The sources of the gold that went to make up each bar were written down on a list. The ledger. Names and items. Isser Havrel: three gold teeth; one gold necklace, thirty centimeters; one gold fountain pen nib. And so on. The serial number on each gold bar corresponds to a list of victims and what was taken from them."

It was monstrous beyond anything McGarvey could have imagined. "The Portuguese will cooperate with Israel."

"No," Potok said sharply. "It's one of the reasons I've come here to talk to you. Kirk, we want to leave the gold buried here. Right where it is. We want to leave those memories untapped."

"But—?"

"Reliving that horror will do no one any good. Those people are dead, and so are most of their kin. Trying to distribute the gold fairly would be impossible. And the Germans themselves would not want to get involved."

"The generals?"

"Yes," Potok said. "Ex–Third Reich officers who were soldiers first, and Nazis only by force of circumstance. Men who were against the death camps, against the wholesale slaughter of an entire people. They managed all of these years to keep this business quiet. We agree."

It was an odd thing for an Israeli to say, but McGarvey nodded.

"We ask that you say nothing. Tell your people, if they ask, that you found nothing down there except for Arkady Kurshin, whom you killed."

McGarvey stiffened at the name. He half rose out of the bed.

"He's dead. His body floated up out of the tunnel. He's definitely dead this time."

"But I left him a thousand feet back . . . I killed him."

"No, he drowned, Kirk. Trying to get out."

McGarvey lay back and closed his eyes, imagining Kurshin's last minutes. It was horrible, yet fitting. He opened his eyes again and Potok was gone. Maria was standing there. He had no idea how much time had passed.

"I didn't know when you would wake up," she said.

So, he'd drifted off. "How are you?"

"Fine," she said. "I came to . . . thank you," she said.

"Do you know the entire story now?"

"Yes. Lev told me."

"Where will you go?"

"Back to Tel Aviv. That's where I got my training, and Buenos Aires is out now. Everyone else is gone, and Esformes is still looking."

McGarvey said nothing.

"We're leaving within the hour. I wanted to say good-bye. I'm sorry that we're not—"

"Don't," McGarvey said, reaching out and touching her hand.

She looked at him for a long time, tears filling her eyes. Finally she bent down, brushed a kiss on his lips, then turned and hurried out of the room.

He wished her well. If only half the things she'd told him had actually happened to her, she needed a life for herself now. Everyone did.

Washington was cold after Lisbon, but the sky was perfectly clear and the sun sparkled on a fresh coating of snow.

The house was an expensive two-story colonial in Chevy Chase, across from the country club. It sat back on what in summer was a half acre of perfectly manicured lawn.

He paid the cabbie who'd brought him out, and stood looking up at the house for a long time. It had been a few years since he'd been here last, and much longer than that since Kathleen had divorced him. That had happened on the same day he'd been fired from the CIA.

The memories, which had always been so painful for him, had finally faded into a dull regret at the back of his head. He'd always loved his wife, and by her own admission she'd always loved him. They had simply not been able to live with each other.

"It's no life for our daughter," Kathleen had cried. "Waiting, wondering if you would come home in one piece. Wondering what dirty little spying mission you were on. What political leader you were assassinating."

He'd wanted to explain about being a soldier, about defending what he believed in, but the words had never come. It had always been impossible for him with Kathleen. She had intimidated him.

And now their daughter was, how old? He had to count back. The last time they'd been together was for her eleventh birthday. Seven years ago. She was eighteen now, he realized with a start. No longer a little girl.

He went up the walk and rang the bell. Kathleen was expecting him. He had called from his hotel that morning. She had sounded cool but reasonably receptive when he asked whether he could come out to see her.

The door opened, and a beautiful woman was standing there, her eyes startlingly green, her complexion creamy, unmarked with even the slightest blemish.

She was Kathleen. But Kathleen of twenty-five years ago. Suddenly McGarvey realized that this woman was not his ex-wife. She was his daughter.

"Elizabeth?" McGarvey asked, his throat thick.

"Oh, God, Daddy, is it really you?" Elizabeth cried, and she came into his arms. "Are you back? Have you come back?"

Beyond her, in the hall, Kathleen had come out of the living room, and she stood there, tears coming to her eyes. She said nothing. She only looked at him, the expression on her face unfathomable.

But it wasn't a look of scorn, or of disapproval. Not that. Not like the old days.

Rather, it was a look of . . . expectation.